Under a
Storm-
swept Sky

D1506353

Under a Storm-swept Sky

BETH ANNE MILLER

This book is a work of fiction. Names, characters, places, and incidents are the product of the author's imagination or are used fictitiously. Any resemblance to actual events, locales, or persons, living or dead, is coincidental.

Copyright © 2018 by Beth Anne Miller. All rights reserved, including the right to reproduce, distribute, or transmit in any form or by any means. For information regarding subsidiary rights, please contact the Publisher.

Entangled Publishing, LLC
2614 South Timberline Road
Suite 105, PMB 159
Fort Collins, CO 80525
Visit our website at www.entangledpublishing.com.

Embrace is an imprint of Entangled Publishing, LLC.

Edited by Stacy Abrams and Alexa May
Cover design by Fiona Jayde
Cover art from iStock
Skye Trail Map from Harvey Maps
Skye Overview Map copyright Cicerone Press Limited,
and Helen and Paul Webster. Contains OS data © Crown
copyright and database right (2018)

Manufactured in the United States of America

First Edition April 2018

embrace

To Julie Young, for reading countless scenes and several full drafts of this book; for your enthusiasm, suggestions, and eagle eye; for all these years of friendship, and for being the bestest roomie ever.

To Nicole Pinto, for reading many drafts and scenes, for your advice and suggestions, and for being a sounding board and a dear friend. We may not have Grimm anymore, but at least we have Kiefer and Milo!

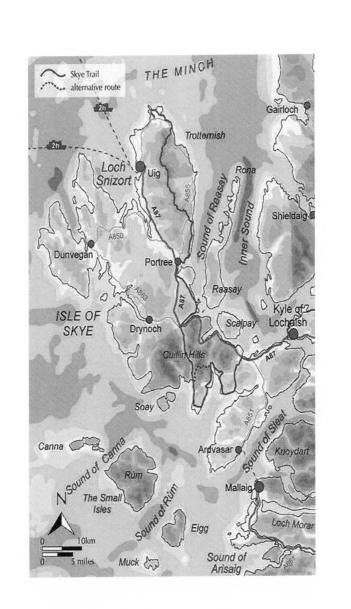

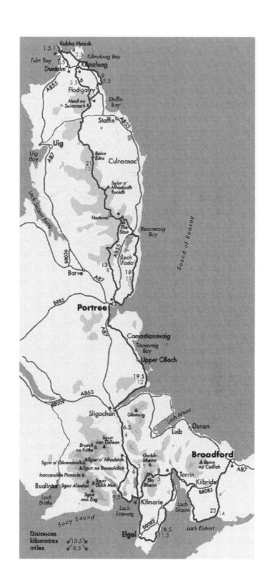

Prologue

All I'd known for the last few hours was pain. *Four small summits,* they'd said, like it was no big deal.

Lies. All lies.

I wanted to drop to the ground and refuse to go any farther. But there were so many reasons why that wasn't an option, not the least of which was tall, Scottish, and sexy. And had been the bane of my existence since the beginning.

He was keeping pace with me, looking over every few minutes to make sure I was still there. It was mortifying, but I took some sadistic pleasure in knowing that his long legs were probably aching from the effort to go slowly as much as mine were from trying to keep up with the group.

My thigh and calf muscles screamed on the ascents, and my knees screamed on the way down. My eyes burned from the wind, and my shoulders ached from my pack.

And we hadn't even made it to lunchtime yet.

What the hell was I doing here?

Chapter One

AMELIA

Two Days Earlier

"Welcome to the Isle of Skye!"

The enthusiastic shout startled me from the weird stupor I'd fallen into following my overnight transatlantic flight from New York to Glasgow, the four-hour train ride from Glasgow to Fort William in the West Highlands, and nearly three hours in a van, broken up by a few stops along the way to stretch our legs and take photos of the increasingly more spectacular scenery as we ventured deeper into the Highlands before crossing the bridge to Skye.

Where I'd spend the next week *walking* over eighty miles from the northernmost tip of Skye down along the eastern side of the island.

I had a vague impression of the other people in the van from our brief meeting in Fort William before we were picked up by the guys from Scotland By Foot, the trekking company

I'd be hiking with: a couple from Florida and two women from London, all around my parents' age, and two bearded brothers in their thirties from somewhere in New England. They had all looked super-fit and super-excited, and if their well-used gear was any indication, super-experienced, too.

Unlike me.

And they were all pairs. Couples, friends, brothers—and me. Traveling by myself, sitting in the front bench seat of the van with the two male guides. As if being a novice hiker doing a week-long trek on the Isle of Skye wasn't bad enough, I would be the only solo traveler in a group full of pairs.

Rather than dwell on that, I focused my attention on the jagged mountains in the distance, a blue-gray haze against the bright blue sky.

I sat up straight. Wait, were those mountains part of the Skye Trail? *Carrie, what the hell were you thinking? And what the hell was I thinking when I decided to do this?*

It was so wrong to be doing this trip without her. Carrie was the hiker, not me. We did everything else together, but not this. I was from flatter-than-flat Long Island, New York—how the hell would I be able to hike that mountainous trail?

Somehow, I would do it. I *had* to do it. For Carrie.

"How much longer?" asked one of the women in the back.

"About another half hour," said Tommy MacDonald, the guide who sat next to me on the bench seat, the one who'd just welcomed us to Skye.

"If we don't get stuck behind too many tourists," muttered Rory Sutherland, the other guide and driver of the van. If Tommy was the "friendly guide," as evidenced by the way he'd bounded up to us in Fort William with a blinding smile on his face, Rory appeared to be playing the role of "surly guide," barely saying a word on the three-hour drive except to swear at the drivers ahead of us.

Hopefully his grouchiness was due more to the long, slow drive on the narrow, one-lane-each-way roads—which I could relate to, coming from Long Island, where *every* hour was rush hour and every road was permanently under construction—and not an indication of how he'd be on the hike.

Otherwise, this would be a really long week.

God, the scenery was awesome. On one side of the road, jagged mountains stretched off into the distance as far as I could see; on the other side was the sea, sapphire blue in the afternoon sunlight. And all around were hilly, green fields dotted with fluffy, white sheep and frolicking lambs. Skye was remote, stunning, and intimidating.

But Carrie, did you really have to hike *it?*

I lowered the window so I could take a few photos. Then I looked at them to make sure they came out okay.

Rory said something under his breath.

"I'm sorry, were you talking to me?" He hadn't spoken to me at all other than a mumbled hello when Tommy introduced them both in Fort William.

"I said, 'there she goes again with her phone.'"

I stared at him. "Do you have some kind of problem with me?" I knew I sounded bitchy, but I so did not need this guy's attitude after eleven million hours in transit.

He glanced at me, then back at the road, his facial features obscured by dark sunglasses and a ball cap. "I just don't understand why people travel thousands of miles from home to see a new place, and then spend the entire time on their phones. You haven't put yours down for more than five minutes since you got in the van. Maybe you should try stepping away from Instagram, Twitter, and Facebook for a little while and experience Skye for yourself rather than for all your many friends and followers."

I opened my mouth to tell him to piss off, but Tommy cut

me off before I could speak. "Not this again," he said, looking at me apologetically. "Rory's like a broken record. He hates technology, would probably toss his phone and live off the grid if he could. Don't pay attention to him."

Tommy's diplomatic response derailed most of my angry retort. But I couldn't let Rory's condescension go unanswered. "You don't know anything about me, Rory," I hissed. "Not. One. Thing. So how about you don't make snap judgments, and I'll show you the same courtesy and not call you a jerk to your face."

"Burn," muttered Tommy.

"I shouldn't have said that," Rory acquiesced after a moment, looking over at me again.

I couldn't tell if he was sincere, but at least he'd sort of apologized. I nodded once and then focused my attention out the window again.

I was right. This was going to be a long week.

My room at the B&B in Portree was charming, with a large bed that was covered with a white duvet that looked like a cloud. I emailed my folks, gushing about the beautiful scenery.

Then I gave in to the lure of the white duvet and napped for an hour. That, plus a long, hot shower, went a long way to making me feel human again, as did the soothing routine of running my fingers through my long hair as I blow-dried it. I wasn't much for makeup, but with some concealer on the dark circles beneath my eyes and a touch of eyeliner, I looked less like a zombie.

I pulled on jeans and a black V-neck top and scrutinized myself in the mirror. Still pale, still tired-looking, but otherwise not bad. Besides, dinner in a pub I could handle easily enough.

It was hiking eighty-odd miles on the mountainous Isle of Skye over the next week, camping out nearly every night along the way, that might very well kill me.

Chapter Two

The "welcome" dinner was at a pub a short walk down the street from the B&B. A long table was set up for us in the middle, and I took a seat next to Lucy, the woman from Florida.

"How are you feeling, dear? You look more rested than you did before."

I smiled. "Don't underestimate the value of a hot shower and some makeup."

"Oh, I never do."

The table filled in with the rest of the group, including two women who hadn't been in the van, and Tommy, Rory, and another woman, all in polo shirts bearing the "Scotland by Foot" logo of a figure with a walking stick.

Rory had ditched his hat and shades, and I finally got a good look at him. The light in the pub was dim, but there was enough sunlight coming in through the curtains to see that his wavy, longish hair was a lovely dark red color and his eyes were light—I couldn't tell the color from where I sat. He was also younger than I thought, probably not much more than twenty-one, like me.

Unlike Tommy, whose default expression seemed to be a cheerful grin, I'd yet to see Rory smile, even a little. In spite of the attitude, he was hot, and I couldn't help but imagine what he would look like if he *did* smile.

We all ordered drinks, and then the woman from SBF stood. She was in her thirties and lean and pretty, with a blonde ponytail.

"Hi, everyone, I'm Scarlet. I've been in touch with all of you via email, and I'm thrilled to welcome you to Skye in person. As I'm sure you've noticed, Skye has an extremely varied landscape. It won't be an easy week, but I promise you that it will be amazing to experience Skye on foot. You will feel small in the shadow of the Cuillins and the Quiraing, and you will feel tall when you stand atop Beinn Edra on the Trotternish Ridge.

"Rory Sutherland and Tommy MacDonald will be your guides. They're both certified Mountain Leaders, trained in first aid and with extensive experience leading treks all over Scotland, so you're in excellent hands."

She paused while the waitress passed around our drinks. "A quick toast to the start of our trek. *Slàinte mhath!*"

I raised my glass of white wine and repeated the toast.

We ordered our dinner, and then everyone went around the table to introduce themselves. The new arrivals were sisters in their mid-twenties from Edinburgh, who'd driven up that morning. I was glad there were some girls my own age, though it made my chest ache to look at them. Their constant touches—a hand on the other's arm as a story was shared, a shoulder jostle when one of them razzed the other—was so reminiscent of how Carrie and I were together that it just made me miss her even more.

Each of the others mentioned some of the previous hikes they'd been on. I mumbled something about some of the day hikes I'd done with Carrie back home (when I was like fifteen, which I *didn't* mention), but reality was setting in fast.

I was so out of my league.

The group seemed nice, and dinner was fun. But before long, I could feel my body begin to crash.

"I can see that you're all tired, so we're going to wrap this up," said Scarlet. "Tomorrow morning, we'll meet at eight forty-five, at the market right across from your B&B so you can get your lunch for tomorrow and the day after. You'll also want to have at least two to three liters of water with you, as well as some bags for trash."

We settled the bill and exited the pub into the early evening. It was May, and although it was after eight p.m., the sun was only now beginning to set. The road we walked along was atop a hill, providing a view of the brightly colored buildings along the waterfront below.

"I'm going to take a walk by the water," I said to Pat, the fifty-something woman from London, who was traveling with her friend Linda while their husbands were golfing in St. Andrews. "I'll see you in the morning."

"You sure you can find your way back to the B&B?"

She sounded like a British version of my mother, and I had to smile. "Yes. I'll be fine."

"All right, then. Good night."

"'Night."

I snapped a few shots of the waterfront and then followed the road down and leaned against the railing. Small boats and dinghies were tied off to cleats, and sailboats sat quietly at anchor.

I glanced at the time. Just after three p.m. back home. I dialed the number.

"Amelia? Where are you?"

"Hey, Helen," I said to Carrie's mom. "I'm on Skye. We just had dinner, and we start the walk tomorrow. How is she?"

"No change. But that means she's not any worse," she added brightly.

Every day for three weeks now, it was the same. *No change.* And every day, it killed me a little more to hear that desperate brightness in Helen's voice. She was right; "no change" meant that she wasn't any worse. But would she ever get better?

"We just have to stay positive," I said, knowing I should take my own advice. "Can I say a quick hi to her?"

I gave Carrie a quick rundown of the scenic drive to Skye and briefly described the group, making sure I sounded as upbeat as possible.

After I ended the call, I gazed out at the harbor, willing the serenity of the scene before me to seep into my soul and relieve some of the ache that had been there for so long.

The two sisters from Edinburgh, Molly and Megan, walked on the shore below, their arms linked, laughing about something.

One blonde and one brunette, just like Carrie and me. They could *be* Carrie and me, the way their strides matched exactly, the way their long ponytails swung from side to side as they walked. The way they laughed so hard that they had to hold onto each other to keep from toppling over.

Tears filled my eyes, and a wave of pain washed over me, so intense that I had to clutch the rail. Would Carrie and I laugh like that again?

Yes, we will. I had to believe it. Anything less was unacceptable.

"You should get to bed. We have a long day tomorrow."

I wiped my eyes and turned to see Rory standing a few feet away. Something about his tone got my back up. "Scarlet didn't mention that we had a curfew."

He frowned, clearly not expecting my sarcasm. "You don't. But even though it's only about eight miles tomorrow, I don't want you holding up the group because you're tired and jet-lagged."

My whole body stiffened. "First I'm addicted to social media, now I'm holding up the group. Looks like I'm off to a good start. Thank you for your concern," I hissed. "It's time for me to go, anyway."

He looked down for a moment. "Amelia—"

I held up a hand. "You're right. I *am* tired, and it'll be a long day tomorrow. But you don't need to be a jerk about it. Again."

I stomped up the hill, all of my earlier serenity gone. Why was he such an ass to me?

It didn't matter. I didn't need him to like me. He just had to do his job and guide the trek.

Only eight miles tomorrow, he'd said. I'd done a few ten-mile walks back home over the last two weeks in an effort to prepare myself. But as I looked at the hills overlooking Portree and remembered the peaks that loomed in the distance on the way here, I didn't think that those flat, paved paths on Long Island were going to be any help at all.

I had bigger things to concern myself with than Rory not liking me.

Chapter Three

Way to go, jackass. I watched Amelia stalk up the hill, her curtain of shiny brown hair swinging against her back. Though I wasn't sure why my advice had caused a confrontation. *Well, accusing her of holding up the group before you've even started walking might have had something to do with it. After insulting her in the van.*

I shouldn't have said that. I was already on edge, which was why I'd walked down by the water. I'd hoped to clear my head, to find some zen in preparation for the week to come, and it hadn't worked. And suddenly she was there, gazing out over the quiet harbor, looking as though she'd found the peace I'd failed to achieve—except for her hands, which had clutched the railing like it was the only way she could keep upright.

Like she was terrified of what lay ahead.

That was what had set me off. If she was afraid, it meant she was likely inexperienced. Which was fine on an easy trail, but not on Skye. Inexperience led to mistakes. It put other people in jeopardy and led to injury—or worse. You just had to look at the reports from Mountain Rescue to see how true that was.

Maybe I was overreacting. Tommy, with all his psychology classes, would say I was projecting—transferring my own worries on to her. And maybe he would be right.

I trudged back to my B&B and entered the room I was sharing with Tommy. He looked up from his phone, his smile fading. "What's wrong?"

I sighed. Tommy knew me too well. "I just had a confrontation with Amelia."

His eyebrows went up. "Amelia from the group?"

I pulled my fleece over my head and stared at him. "Do you know another Amelia I'd be likely to encounter in Portree on this particular evening?"

He rolled his eyes. "No. I guess I'm just trying to figure out why you would have started another fight with a lass in the group who you barely know."

"What makes you think I started it?" Christ, I sounded like a twelve-year-old.

"Because she seems like a nice lass, because you already picked one fight with her, and because I've known you for a long time. You always get snappish when we do the Skye Trail."

"I don't—"

"You do. You could say no, you know, ask Scarlet to have one of the others do Skye. But you never do."

I sank down on the edge of the bed and scrubbed my hands over my face, then met his steady gaze. "No. I *have* to do it. You know I do."

He nodded. "Aye, I know. I just wish you'd stop torturing yourself."

The Skye Trail was challenging, but that wasn't what

either of us was talking about. I'd guided plenty of other treks, some much more difficult than the mountainous and unpredictable Skye Trail, and I'd "bagged" dozens of Munros—the nickname for Scotland's peaks that stood three thousand feet or higher.

There were other reasons why the Skye Trail was difficult for me—and why I would keep doing it, over and over again. I had to.

It was my penance.

Chapter Four

AMELIA

The next morning, after a forty-minute ride from Portree, our group gathered in a car park on the north end of Skye. Our guides were in cargo shorts and lightweight fleeces, while the rest of us were in long pants and heavier jackets against the chilly morning. Was it a macho thing, or were they really not cold?

"Welcome to the beginning of the Skye Trail," said Scarlet. "Tommy, you want to start the briefing?"

"Rory and I will alternate who leads and who brings up the rear. The Skye Trail isn't easy. Sometimes we'll be walking along the edge of a cliff, or out on an exposed ridge in the wind. There are sections where there's no trail at all, and sections where we'll be crossing a bog or a burn—that's a small river for the Yanks who don't know the lingo. And the weather is often unpredictable. If either of us gives you an order, we expect it to be followed, as it's for your safety and that of the group. There won't be any facilities along the way—pretty much ever—but feel free to duck off the trail when you need to.

"As you'll see this week, the trail does occasionally run close to a town or village, but sometimes it doesn't, which is why some nights we'll be in a B&B or hostel, and other nights we'll be camping."

Right. While most people our age chose to vacation near a beach, or perhaps someplace where you could do a hike in the afternoon, Carrie had chosen to walk across half the Isle of Skye. Not because that was the only way to get around— the map had clearly shown that there was at least one perimeter road that would get us almost to the same places— but because she wanted the challenge. And so I would do it. Because she couldn't.

Rory spoke up. "Today's walk will probably take about six hours, but remember, it's not a race. We are a group, and we will do this trek as a group. If you wander off ahead, you are no longer our problem, as we won't be leaving the others behind to go look for you."

I thought about that jagged, imposing mountain range that had been silhouetted against the sky, and a shiver ran through me. I pictured myself wandering around looking for the trail. Alone. Terrified. Hours passing, watching the sun beginning to set, knowing it would soon be dark and a wrong step could mean injury or death. I closed my eyes. *I can't do this. I'm so sorry, Carrie, but I can't.*

A hand came down on my shoulder. "We won't leave you behind, Amelia."

I opened my eyes to see Rory in front of me. His sunglasses were pushed to the top of his head, and his eyes were steady as he looked into mine. I hadn't noticed their lovely gray-green color the night before.

"Wh-what?"

"It's Tommy's and my job to make sure the group stays

together. We're not going to leave anyone behind, I promise. It's bad for business," he added with a slight quirk of his lips.

His attempt at levity worked, and I could feel myself calming down. "Good to know."

"It's why Scarlet keeps the groups small," quipped Tommy. "So the guides don't have to worry about counting too high."

"Yeah, once you guys run out of fingers, it gets dicey," she said.

Everyone laughed at that. I managed a small chuckle. "Okay?" murmured Rory.

"Yeah, sorry. I just had a moment. Thanks."

He nodded and returned to his pack, leaving me both surprised and relieved by his unexpected kindness after last night's jerkage. He squatted down, his cargo shorts riding up to reveal his muscled thighs—not that I noticed—and opened his backpack. "My first aid kit is at the top of my pack. Tommy's is in the same place. It's extremely unlikely that either or both of us will become incapacitated, but just in case."

Just in case?

"We both carry emergency blankets, extra torches— flashlights to you Yanks—and extra food and water," Rory continued. "You'll find that most mobile phones don't get consistent service out here, but we're both wearing transponders on our packs, which Scarlet will monitor. In the event of an emergency, we can activate an additional signal that she'll see. There is also a volunteer Mountain Rescue group, which you can reach by dialing the police first. But it could take them a while to get out here."

He said it so calmly, but my stomach was roiling again.

Calm down. These guys are professionals. They've done this many times before, and they know what they're doing. It's just a safety announcement, like the ones they do on airplanes.

I knew that. But still.

He zipped up his pack and slung it onto his back. It looked a lot heavier than mine, though he didn't seem bothered by it.

"Okay, guys," said Scarlet, "Tommy and Rory will update you on the terrain and conditions as you go, as well as tell you about the sights you'll see. Don't hesitate to ask them questions—challenge them a little," she added with a grin. "And if you have any issues, please let them know so they can help."

"Especially blisters," said Tommy. "Those will be your worst enemy on the trail, but if you start to feel one forming, we can hopefully prevent it from getting worse."

"Today should be sunny and mild, though as we've said, Skye is known for its unexpected weather changes. Make sure you use sun cream so you don't burn. Okay, have a great walk, and I'll see you later!"

I took a few quick shots of the group as we fell in line behind Tommy.

And we were off.

The path was easy enough to start with, and before long, we caught a glimpse of a ruin on a cliff that jutted into the sea.

"That's Duntulm Castle," said Rory. "It was once a MacDonald stronghold—though not Tommy's branch of the clan—and is, of course, rumored to be haunted."

It looked like a strong wind would send the rest of it tumbling off the edge. What kind of people had lived in this forbidding place, subject to the whims of the wind and the sea?

A short while later, we reached a fence with a gate. Tommy approached it first.

"This is called a kissing gate," he said. "You'll see why in a moment." He slipped off his backpack and unlatched the gate, pushing it open as far as it would go, which was just wide enough for him to step in and sidle around it. He would have to face us and push the gate closed in order to continue. "It's sometimes considered tradition for the person going through the gate to kiss the next person in line as they face each other when passing through. Who's next?" he asked with a waggle of his eyebrows.

"That'll be me," said Gordon, sauntering up as everyone laughed. Tommy planted a loud kiss on Gordon's cheek. "Sorry, Lucy," he said with a wink.

"Oh, that's okay. You can have him," she said, but happily accepted a real kiss from her husband as she passed through after him. Everyone seemed to be up for the "tradition," kissing cheeks or lips as they passed through the gate.

Mike from Maine gave me a friendly peck on the cheek as he passed through. But when I turned around, it was just Rory behind me. We stared at each other for an awkward moment, and then he suddenly knelt to re-tie his boot.

Whatever. I let the gate slam into place and joined the rest of the group.

"Well, that was a cop-out," said Megan.

I laughed at the disappointment on her face. "It's okay. He's not my type, anyway."

"Girl, that lad is *everybody's* type," said Molly.

"Ohhh, aye," said Pat, and we all laughed—even harder when Rory looked at us questioningly as he passed.

Maybe this wouldn't be as bad as I'd anticipated. The group seemed nice, and the walk was easy so far. I was starting to sweat under my layers, so clearly Rory and Tommy knew what they were doing with their lightweight clothes. We went up a hill and veered off onto a small path that continued to a summit. The wind was stronger there, and it felt good against my hot skin.

Rory slung his pack to the ground. "I'm sure some of you are overheated, so let's take five minutes to de-layer. While the mornings might be chilly, once you start moving, you'll warm up fast."

With that, he stripped off his fleece, the bottom of the shirt beneath riding up to reveal a tantalizing glimpse of his taut abs. I looked up just as his head emerged from his fleece, the sun catching the tousled waves and turning them burnished copper.

Okay, fine. He *was* my type.

My fingers itched to touch that gorgeous hair. *Down, girl. It's only a matter of time before he opens his mouth and ruins the moment, anyway.* He ran his own hands through his hair, then tied some kind of bandanna/headband thing around it to keep it out of his face in the increasing wind.

I dragged my eyes away, focusing on my own de-layering. I peeled off my fleece and shoved it into my pack. That done, I looked around. There was a small hut a few yards away.

Tommy led us to it. "This is a bothy," he said. "It used to be a coast guard lookout, but is now primarily used by walkers as a shelter. And like other bothies you'll find scattered around the Highlands and islands, anyone is welcome to use it."

The bothy had a long, low shelf to place a sleeping bag, as well as some chairs. Windows provided an incredible view out over the water. It would be amazing to spend the night there (even though there was no toilet or electricity). I took a bunch of pictures for Carrie.

"Amelia!"

At Rory's shout, I turned to see the rest of the group already descending the cliff path on the other side. Shit. The last thing I needed was for him to snipe at me again. I stuffed my phone into my pocket and hurried to catch up.

He was waiting for me, his sunglasses hiding the impatient look I was certain was there. "Sorry," I mumbled. He just gestured for me to precede him down the path.

We climbed over a few stiles—sections of fence where a short, ladder-like setup enabled us to swing our legs over—and then skirted around a huge boulder sitting terrifyingly close to the cliff edge.

From there, the path dropped down at an impossible angle. I froze, clutching my poles against a sudden wave of vertigo.

"It's not as bad as it looks," said Tommy, forging ahead without even pausing. I could hear Carrie's voice in my head. *Come on, Amelia. You can't quit two minutes into the first day.*

No, I couldn't. I cautiously started down the rocky steps, using my poles for balance. But Tommy was right, it wasn't quite as bad as it had appeared to be, and it wasn't too long before we scooted down over some tricky parts and emerged onto a grassy path at the bottom. Breathing a sigh of relief to have made it down in one piece, I turned to look at where we'd come from—and gasped.

The cliffs towered over us. We'd hiked all the way down *that*?

I turned back as Tommy spread his arms wide, encompassing the view of the sea behind him. "Welcome to Rubha Hunish, the most northerly point on Skye. We'll explore the headland for a few minutes; then it's back up the cliffs and south along the coast."

Wait, what? We'd come all that way down to poke around for a few minutes and then go back up? What the hell was the point? I looked at my fellow trekkers for commiseration, but they all seemed to take it in stride, eagerly—if carefully—following the path along the cliff.

Okay, it was a pretty awesome place; gulls cried out as they circled overhead, and larger white birds with black-tipped wings dove dramatically into the sea beyond.

"The big, white birds are gannets," said Rory. "You can sometimes see puffins here as well, but it's too early in the season for them. And if you look closely at the sea stacks," he continued, pointing at the tall columns of rock that jutted up from the foaming water, "you can see ropes hanging, left by climbers."

"People climb those?" said Linda. "Are they crazy?"

"It's like any other extreme sport," said Rory. "More challenging means more exciting."

We reached the end of the headland, where the sea churned menacingly. Farther out, it almost looked like—"Did I just see a blow out there?"

"You might have," said Tommy. "We get minke whales here in the summer, but sometimes they're here earlier in the season, too. Show me where." I pointed slightly to the right of the headland. After a moment, I saw another, followed by a brief glimpse of a dark back as a whale broke the surface. From the excited murmur of the group, everyone else saw it, too. I tried to take a photo, but it was just too far away.

Megan was also trying to get a photo, but she had a proper camera, not just her phone. "Can you get it?" I asked.

She snapped a few shots, then lowered the camera. "Maybe? I zoomed it in as far as I could, but I think it will probably just end up being a splotch on the water. I'll have to check when I can see it on my computer."

"That's what happened to me the first time or two I went whale watching," I said. "I could never time it right, and all I got were photos of splashes."

She looked at me with interest in her eyes. "You've seen whales before, then?"

"Yeah, off Massachusetts. My best friend and I go every summer."

"That sounds brilliant!" she exclaimed. "Will you go this

summer as well?"

"I'm not sure," I said. "We're starting new jobs out of town, and I don't think we'll have the—" I broke off suddenly. What the hell was I doing, rambling about the new jobs Carrie and I were supposed to start later in the summer, as if everything was normal? How could I have forgotten, even for a second, that things were anything *but* normal?

"Is everything okay, Amelia?"

I managed to smile. "I'm fine. Sorry. I, uh, hope your photos come out."

I turned away from the edge and started following the trail back around the headland, cursing myself.

The path back up the cliff was even steeper than I expected. I had to stop every few steps to rest my aching legs and catch my breath. I'd thought I was in pretty decent shape, but this climb was kicking my ass.

Everyone else passed me, which was a relief. Bad enough to be struggling, worse to hold up everyone who wasn't.

Two minutes later, I stumbled, catching myself on my pole. God, it wasn't even two hours into the first day. I had *seven* days of this—of ascents and descents and uneven ground and trying to keep up with a group of people whose hiking experience was clearly more extensive than walking all over New York City and one awful hike five years ago.

I hated hiking. I'd sworn I'd never do it again, no matter how many times Carrie had coaxed, cajoled, and begged me to go with her. And while it hadn't been bad when it was easy, now I remembered why I hated it—that feeling of being at the back of the group, with everyone always impatiently waiting, watching others making it look so easy.

I took a few quick photos of the intimidating cliffs above, hoping everyone would assume that was why I'd stopped.

"Amelia," Rory began, but when I glared at him, he paused. "Are you all right?" he asked, coming down to me.

"It's a bit steep," I muttered.

"It *is* steep, the first real steep section of the trail." *And not the last*, was what he didn't say. "Take your time, and don't look up. Just focus on what's right in front of your feet."

I fixed my gaze on the path and started forward. The damn pole came down on a rock and I stumbled. Again. "Dammit!"

Rory steadied me. "Give me your poles. It will be easier if you use your hands for balance on this section."

He didn't look like he was messing with me, so I reluctantly complied. He tucked them under his arm and bounded up the path, as nimble as a mountain goat, the showoff. He reached a point a few yards up and turned. "Come on, Amelia. You can do it."

Cursing him under my breath, I slowly made my way up the rocky steps, using my hands on the steepest sections. Without the poles getting in the way, it *was* easier—which only made me curse him more—and it wasn't long before I was edging around that boulder at the top of the path and making my way back to the bothy.

The others were sprawled out on the ground. I took off my pack and collapsed beside Linda, shivering as the breeze hit the sweaty patch on the back of my shirt.

Rory handed me back my poles. "These can be really helpful out here, but you don't want to become so dependent that you can't walk without them. Sometimes they aren't useful, and you need to be able to keep going anyway."

He went to sit by Tommy, leaving me feeling like I'd just been schooled. Again.

After five minutes, we were on our feet once more. I was still exhausted from the steep climb and found myself at the back of the group with Tommy. He smiled encouragingly. "We're crossing a small headland now. When we reach the end of this section, there'll be a good spot to have lunch."

Knowing that we would be stopping soon kept me going, and it wasn't too long before we slipped through a gap in an old stone wall and followed a soft, grassy track to a ruin.

"Lunchtime," announced Tommy. "It's about half twelve now, and we're past the midway point for today." My groupmates made an assortment of relieved sounds, clearly as eager for a real break as I was.

I flopped down in the grass and just sat there for a moment, taking in the scene around me. In contrast to the raucous cries of the seabirds and the crash of the waves out at Rubha Hunish, this was a peaceful spot, and my fellow hikers were quiet as they scarfed down their lunch.

As I ate my sandwich—slowly, as the sudden inactivity left me feeling a little nauseated—I gazed at the mountains in the distance. It *was* beautiful here, about as different from the suburban sprawl back home as I could get. I inhaled deeply, breathing in the fresh air, grateful for the soft grass that cushioned my aching body. When was the last time I'd sat in the grass? Years and years ago. Back home, the thought would never even cross my mind—there were ants and other biting insects. My pants would get stained or wet. But here, it just felt right.

Past the halfway point meant we'd done over four miles so far. *'And miles to go before I sleep,'* I thought, recalling the line from Robert Frost.

I packed away my trash and eased my left leg in front of me, bending the knee so I could reach the boot laces. I'd felt a spot beginning to rub on the bottom of my foot as we'd descended to Rubha Hunish, and recalled what Tommy had said about blisters when we'd started out.

A shadow fell over me. Rory.

"You shouldn't take off your boots when we stop for a break. Your feet might swell, which will be really uncomfortable for the rest of the day."

I refrained from rolling my eyes. "I think I may have the start of a blister, though, so I should take a look at that, right?"

"In that case, let's take a look." He squatted down beside me.

Feeling rushed under the weight of his gaze, I unlaced my boot and tugged it off, scrunching my toes in relief. I started to yank off my sock.

"Go slowly with the sock, in case it sticks to the blister."

Okay, so he wasn't rushing me. I carefully peeled off the sock, foolishly glad that I'd had a pedicure before I left New York ("Skye Blue," according to the label on the bottle).

I crossed my foot over my knee so that I could look. Sure enough, there was a blister forming right where the second toe met the ball of my foot. "Shit."

"Let me see." Rory took my foot in his hand, lightly tracing his finger over the blister. I couldn't help the shudder that ran through me at his touch. Ticklish feet. *Right.*

"Sorry," I muttered, but he didn't seem to notice.

He went to his backpack, returning with the first aid kit. Kneeling beside me once more, he applied a blister bandage, placing the wrapper in the pocket of his shorts. "It's a tricky spot for a blister because it's hard to keep a plaster in place," he said, wrapping first aid tape around the width of my foot, careful not to press too hard on the blister. His gentleness was surprising, given his earlier impatience with me and his overall gruffness. He smoothed the edge of the tape to seal it and sat back. "Hopefully that'll do the trick. Does it feel okay?"

His silvery-green eyes met mine, and for a moment, I couldn't form words.

"Amelia?"

"Um, yeah, it feels okay. Thanks."

"You should probably open it tonight."

"I thought you're not supposed to open a blister."

"Generally that's true, but tomorrow is going to be a

difficult day, and having a blister won't do you any favors."

"Okay. Thank you." I pulled on my sock and reached for the boot.

"Show me how you lace it up," he said.

Was this some kind of test? I laced up the boot and tied the bow.

He untied it again, then unwound the laces from the hooks. "A blister on the bottom of your foot means that it's sliding around too much. If you lace them like *this*, it will hold your foot in place better."

Starting from where the laces were going to go up the ankle, he crisscrossed them and brought the end through again as if he was about to tie a knot, then looped them around the hooks. He did that the whole way up, and then tied the bow. "How does that feel?"

I wiggled my foot. "A lot tighter, but in a good way. I didn't know to do that."

"When you buy boots, you should always go to a shop where the salespeople know what they're doing. They can make sure they fit properly and advise you on how best to tie them." He stood and picked up his pack. "Re-tie the other one, too. That should hopefully prevent more blisters."

"Thanks. I appreciate it." I tied my other boot the way he showed me.

He nodded once and then walked to the center of the group. "Anyone else think they have blisters? Now would be a good time to tend to them before we hit the trail again."

Rory was full of really great advice. I just wished he was less of an ass when he dispensed it.

Twenty minutes later, our lunch break was over. Backpacks were repacked; trash was stowed away. And thankfully, I wasn't the only one groaning as we got to our feet.

It was fairly easy going for a while until we once again climbed to the cliff tops.

"Guys, hold up here for a second," said Rory. While everyone gathered around, I took a few photos of the view out to sea and down the coastline. "The next bit—almost until we get to Flodigarry and our stopping point for today—is tricky. We'll be along the cliffs, where there is often no path. And though we haven't had much rain here lately, the ground may still be wet underfoot. Take your time, and *pay attention*," he said, looking at me.

I didn't roll my eyes. Much.

As promised, the next hour or so, as we picked our way along the edge of the cliffs, was harrowing. And it wasn't really wet at all, which made me wonder how much worse it would have been.

Coming from Long Island, where aside from some bluffs on the north shore and a few scattered hills, everything was dead flat, this scenery was just breathtaking. I'd been on the Pacific Coast Highway once, driving from San Francisco south to Los Angeles, and this reminded me of that. Only there were no guardrails here.

There were more of those weird, twisted sea stacks, like the ones we'd seen at Rubha Hunish. I stopped to look at them.

"Have you ever seen anything like that before?"

Molly stood beside me, her bouncy blonde ponytail so like Carrie's it hurt to look at her. I quickly turned back to the sea stacks. "No, we definitely don't have anything like that in New York. They seem—lonely somehow, like they're almost in reach of the shore they used to be part of, but will never again be able to touch it, the seabirds their only company until the sea reclaims them." The words tumbled out of me, and I cringed. "Sorry, that was really corny, wasn't it?"

"No, actually. I thought it was lovely. And quite sad, as well."

I was startled to see her wiping her eyes. She smiled and shook her head. "Oh, don't mind me. I cry at everything. Megan always teases me for it."

"I do, too," I replied. "And my best friend always teases *me* for it." *Carrie, I think you'd really like Molly and Megan. They're so much like you and me.*

There wasn't much chatting as we walked along the cliffs, with everyone intently focused on their feet. That, too, was a refreshing change of pace from the people back home who walked through the city glued to their phones, stepping off the curb into traffic without looking up. Even I had been guilty of that once or twice, but after watching a texting mom with a stroller nearly get creamed by a taxi, I never did it again.

We descended a steep, grassy section, also precariously close to the edge of the cliff, then finally reached the lower level. There was a collective sigh of relief.

"It's pretty easy from here," said Rory. "We just follow the coast until we reach the path that will lead us into Flodigarry. No more hills to speak of. You guys have done brilliantly today."

It *was* an easy walk around the coast. The sea was a glorious deep blue, which contrasted sharply with the green of the grass.

And then we reached the path that Rory had mentioned, which climbed up. "No more hills, eh, Rory?" said Gordon, voicing what I was sure we were all thinking.

"Aw, come on, Gordon, that's barely a wee bump."

"We have to work on the language gap," Gordon mumbled. "When you say 'no more hills,' we assume the rest of the way is flat."

"This is Skye. Nothing here is flat. Come on, now, you can practically smell your afternoon tea. Just over the wee bump and we're there. Almost."

Almost, but not quite. I sang some of my favorite songs in my head to distract myself as we ascended.

A little while later, we trudged into a tiny village. "Welcome to Flodigarry," said Tommy. "The hostel is just up this way."

We followed him up (!) another path to the hostel, where Scarlet greeted us with a wide smile. "Well done, guys—you got through your first day of the Skye Trail! Eight miles down."

It didn't sound like a lot. I'd walked more than that in less time on more than one occasion. But that had been on flat pavement, and this had been along the edge of cliffs and up and down steep paths. I hurt everywhere, but I couldn't help the smile that spread across my face. Carrie would be so proud.

"You made really good time today," she continued. "How do you feel?"

The response was a combination of enthusiastic chattering and pained groans. She laughed. "That's the same response I get from everyone at the end of the first day. No one can really sum up the energy for actual words."

She glanced at her watch. "It's just after four now, and I've booked you a table in the restaurant at the hotel next door at six, so you have some time to relax and put up your feet before dinner. Anything to add, lads?"

Rory stepped forward. "Great job today. Tomorrow will be challenging. It's over seventeen miles, with difficult, exposed terrain, and you'll be camping tomorrow night, so enjoy the bunks, showers, and bar food tonight. Tommy and I will meet you out front at nine a.m. Have a good night."

"You're not joining us for dinner?" asked Mike.

"Not tonight. Tommy, Scarlet, and I have some things to go over, so we'll have our dinner early. We may see you in the bar later. Speaking of which, even though you've earned yourself a beer or two, trust me when I say you don't want to walk tomorrow with a hangover, so take it easy."

It would be a relief to eat our dinner without the guides there. I was tired and aching and didn't want to feel obligated to pretend otherwise, especially in front of Rory.

The room I was sharing with the other ladies had several sets of bunk beds. I chose a lower bunk by the window and sat down, grateful to be off my feet. I switched my phone off "airplane mode," which I'd turned on so it wouldn't drain the battery while I was out in the middle of nowhere.

No messages from home. I tossed the phone to the bed.

"Well, we survived the first day, ladies," said Pat.

"Barely," I said. "I had to keep stopping when we went up the cliff. My only excuse is that I have no hills anywhere near me with which to train."

"You said you're from New York?" asked Linda. "The city?"

"Long Island, not too far from the city. It's very flat," I added, and we all laughed. I rummaged in my pack for my shower stuff and a change of clothes, eager to stand under the hot water.

"What made you come do this trek by yourself? That's so brave of you."

I froze. *Brave? If they only knew.* "I... My friend was supposed to do it, actually," I said, trying to keep my voice even. "But she...got hurt...and couldn't do it. So here I am."

"I'm sorry to hear that. But now I understand why you were taking so many pictures," said Pat.

I felt my cheeks get hot. "You noticed?"

"How could we not?" asked Molly. "Every time we stopped, there you were, snapping away. At one point, I thought Rory was going to have to drag you down the path."

"Personally, I wouldn't have minded that," said Linda.

Everyone laughed but me.

Chapter Five

RORY

"Well, first day's in the bag," said Tommy as he flopped down on his bed in our shared room and immediately started playing on his phone. "I think they did well, even the pretty Yankee lass."

I tugged my shirt over my head, tossing it on the floor with my socks. "You're kidding, right?"

He looked up. "You don't think she's pretty?"

Aye, she was pretty, with all that long, shiny hair and those expressive brown eyes. That wasn't what I was questioning.

"No, I mean you think she did well? She got a blister because she didn't tie her brand new, clearly-not-broken-in-properly boots the right way, and she barely made it up from Rubha Hunish. She stopped every thirty seconds to take another damn photo to post on Instagram or Twitter or whatever to impress her friends back home. She was so fixated on her phone at the bothy that she didn't even realize we'd all gone ahead already. How is that doing well?"

"You're being too hard on her, Ror. She wasn't the only one with a blister. The climb up from the Hunish *is* a tough one. And so what if she takes a million pictures? That's what they're here for."

"Whatever," I muttered, rummaging in my pack for clean clothes. Amelia's obsessive picture-taking wasn't my problem until she held up the group or put herself at risk. Then I'd have to say something.

"I'm not sure what your problem is with her, man, but you might want to lay off a little. At the end of the day, these folks are here to have a great time. They've *paid* to have a great time. If the guide's a dick, that puts a real damper on that, you know?"

Clothes in hand, I sat on the edge of the bed. "I know. I just think she's too much of a novice to do the Skye Trail. You saw how terrified she was when I gave the safety briefing this morning—she was practically shaking. She probably came out here on some whim, and has no clue what she's doing. She should be on an easier trek where she won't put herself in danger."

I pictured her velvet-brown eyes, shining with awe as she stared at the sea stacks, sparkling with mirth as she giggled with the other lasses earlier, narrowed in anger when I'd told her to go to bed last night. And then I imagined them wide with shock and fear as her inexperience drew her too near the crumbling edge...

I scrubbed my hands over my face to banish the vision. "Anyway, I need a shower."

Tommy stared at me for a long moment. He knew me too well to be fooled by my poor attempt to change the subject.

"I think you're wrong about her," he finally said, returning to his phone.

I rolled my eyes. "What, do you like her or something?"

He grinned without looking up. "And if I do?"

A flash of—something—went through me at the thought.

I just as quickly brushed it off. "Whatever. Just remember that tomorrow's a tough day and you need to stay focused. And so will she." I started for the bathroom.

"Rory."

I turned back. "What?"

His expression was serious. "Just give her a chance. She came here all by herself, to do this trek with strangers. If she wanted an easy holiday, she'd be sunbathing in Aruba or some shit, not getting blisters and strained muscles in this place, you know?"

I sighed. "I do know. And you're right. I'll be better tomorrow." I nodded at his phone, which had chimed no fewer than ten times in the past two minutes. "You'd better deal with whoever that is—the lass from Fort William? I'm gonna hit the shower."

After dinner, I took a long walk in the surf to clear my head, letting the sea air fill my lungs and the cold water soothe my feet.

The first day was always challenging, as we had to get a sense of the group's skills. Plus, we had to set a good example and give a good impression of Scotland By Foot. *You haven't done a brilliant job with Amelia, though, have you?* No, I hadn't. And that would have to change. Tommy was right. I needed to stop being so hard on her.

I walked for half an hour before turning back. Tommy never understood my need to walk in the evenings after walking all day, but he thrived on getting to know the different people that came into our lives, a week at a time.

I, on the other hand, found people to be exhausting. It wasn't that I didn't like them; I was just an introvert and always had been. I loved being out on the trail—the scenery, the ever-changing weather, the challenge. But I needed my quiet moments, when I didn't have to be "on"—answering questions, making conversation, or laughing at jokes. More importantly, I needed time each day when I didn't have to be watching everyone, worried that someone would get hurt or wander off. I needed time to just be in my own head.

Besides, a stroll along the beach was hardly the same as the walking we did during the day.

I scooped up a flat, round stone, running my finger across the smooth surface. It was perfect for skipping. I hadn't skipped stones in years, not since my brother Connor and I were lads. I rolled the stone in my hand, and then cocking my hand to the side, I chucked it at the water, watching as it skipped three, four, five times across the surface before sinking.

I hadn't forgotten how.

I made my way back along the shore. The sun was still warm, so I sat on one of the picnic tables outside the hostel, tipped my face back, and closed my eyes. *Heaven.*

"Hey there. So, I made it through the first day of the trek." The raised female voice startled me out of my almost-doze. Amelia sat on a boulder a few meters away, talking on the phone. *There goes my peace.*

I closed my eyes again, trying to tune out the next few minutes of what sounded like small talk.

"God, I should be there, not three thousand miles away doing this stupid hike. What was I thinking?"

I opened my eyes. She was off the phone, holding it in her hand as she stared out at the sea. Okay, she was clearly upset, but was she saying she didn't *want* to be on the trek? It was bad enough that she was inexperienced, but why would she choose to do the Skye Trail if she didn't want to? I got up from the table and headed inside.

Whatever that phone call was about, Amelia had better get her head on straight by tomorrow.

Chapter Six

One foot in front of the other.

I repeated the mantra over and over in my head as I trudged up the steady incline. My leg muscles, still sore from yesterday, were screaming, and we weren't even an hour into our seventeen-plus mile day.

A shadow fell over the path. I looked up—and gaped at the towering cliffs before me.

"This is the Quiraing," said Tommy. "It was created by landslides, as was most of the Trotternish Ridge."

We reached the top of the incline, and I just stared. To the right were tall rock formations, including one solo pinnacle that had to be over a hundred feet high, and to the left was a huge one that almost looked like a castle that had been hewn from the rock.

I pulled out my phone and shot a few pictures of the alien landscape.

A sudden, hard gust of wind from behind caused me to

slip on the loose gravel of the path, my foot nearly going out from under me. I caught my balance on my trekking pole, but my phone flew out of my hand.

"Shit!"

A large hand caught it before it hit the ground. Rory, of course.

"Oh my God, thank you," I said. If my phone had broken, I'd have no way to take pictures for Carrie, no way to be reached if anything changed.

"You need to watch yourself out here," he said. "The wind can knock you off your feet. Focus more on staying upright and less on taking pictures. I appreciate how much you enjoy the scenery, but maybe you can just look with your eyes instead, enjoy the view in the moment without the distraction of your phone."

I felt my face get hot. Why did he always have to talk down to me like I was a naughty child?

"Got it. Thanks," I said through clenched teeth. I held out my hand, and he hesitated for a moment before placing the phone into it.

He tugged his sunglasses down the bridge of his nose, forcing me to stare into those silvery-green eyes. "Today's walk requires your full attention." His tone was *almost* apologetic.

"The wind surprised me, that's all."

"It will be windy all day, so be careful, and keep your eyes on your footing." He pushed his sunglasses back into place and moved on.

"Everyone, watch out on the path here," he announced to the group as we started walking again. "The loose rock, or scree, is slippery." He strode to the head of the group. *Thanks for the tip, Rory. Better late than never.*

"He's just looking out for you," said Tommy from behind me. "His social skills are just a bit…lacking, sometimes."

"I would have said 'nonexistent,'" I replied. Shit, that was his colleague and friend. "I mean—"

He snorted with laughter. "Oh, I know exactly what you mean." He sobered. "You're okay, though? Do you need a break?"

"Nope, I'm fine." Even if I did need a break, I wouldn't admit it. Not after my scolding by Rory.

"Good. After you," he said, gesturing grandly.

The path dropped down to reveal an incredible landscape before us: grassy slopes dotted with sheep, blue lochs, mountains stretching as far as the eye could see. And a long, lonely, winding trail running through it all. Rory could give me the stink eye as much as he wanted, there was no way I wasn't taking pictures of that view for Carrie. Though I did brace myself this time.

The wind was unpredictable, sometimes dying down completely, other times blasting us when we came around a curve. Not unlike what you'd sometimes have in Manhattan, when you turned a corner into a wind tunnel.

But in Manhattan, you wouldn't be blown off a path to possibly tumble over a cliff.

Though you might end up in a slimy puddle or a pile of garbage, face-to-face with a giant rat.

Still, the path wasn't too bad as we left the bizarre formations of the Quiraing in our wake. There were other walkers out there, most of whom came from the other way, requiring us to step up on the rocks to our right (the side that didn't have the drop-off) to let them pass.

We descended to a road and a car park, where we took a short break. I scarfed down a granola bar and some water.

"Are we going that way?" asked Linda, her voice a little shaky as she gestured to the intimidating line of peaks before us.

"Aye," said Rory. "That's the Trotternish Ridge. To recap

what Tommy said in this morning's briefing, we've ten peaks to summit before we finish for the day, ranging from four hundred sixty-six meters to six hundred sixty-eight meters. And if you still have energy left at the end of the day, one of us can take you up to the top of The Storr, over seven hundred meters high."

I'd been preoccupied during the briefing, my head foggy after a sleepless night, and hadn't noted the specifics of today's walk. "Ten summits?" *Hell of a thing to miss.*

"Yep," said Tommy. "Some are steeper than others, but the descents between them aren't all bad. The first one is actually the worst."

"Goody," I muttered. *Carrie, I was wrong. You're not nuts—you're a goddamn masochist!*

He laughed at that. "Slow and steady, Amelia. You'll be fine."

Why couldn't Rory be like Tommy, friendly and...just easy to be around? I glanced ahead to where Rory walked with Pat, who was struggling a bit—close enough to help if she needed it, but letting her find her own way. Why was he so kind to everyone but me? *It doesn't matter. You're here for one reason only, and that's not to hook up with a guy.* But then the sun glinted off his hair, causing it to shine like a new penny, and my heart skipped a beat.

Clearly, nothing about this trek was going to be easy.

The first ascent wasn't too bad, leading up to the grassy top of Biodha Buidhe, which Tommy helpfully spelled for me when he saw me typing it into a memo.

"That's how you spell it? But it's pronounced Beeta Booyeh."

He shrugged. "I just work here; I didn't invent Gaelic."

We both cracked up at that. I turned to get a panoramic photo and saw a bank of dark clouds rolling in at an alarmingly fast rate. "Uh, guys?"

"Aye, weather's coming in," said Rory, as casually as if he were describing a tree. "Okay, everyone, you're about to have your first experience with Skye's unpredictable and rapidly changing weather. The good news is we're going to descend from Biodha Buidhe into the pass of Bealach Uige, where we'll be less exposed," he said, the Gaelic words rolling effortlessly (and not unappealingly) off his tongue. "The bad news is that the descent into Bealach Uige is steep. It's challenging in good weather, and difficult in bad weather."

"What does that mean?" asked Linda.

"It just means that if that rain gets here as fast as I think it will, we'll need to take it slowly and carefully as we descend. You should put on your rain gear now."

I opened my pack, withdrawing my purple rain pants, borrowed from Carrie, as was pretty much all my gear except my boots. I pulled them on over my trekking pants and shrugged into the matching jacket, tucking my phone into the pocket. I fastened the waterproof cover over my backpack just as a light rain started to fall.

"Okay, let's move out," said Tommy, pulling up the bright orange hood of his rain jacket. "And remember to take it slow. A little rain isn't going to kill you, especially now that you're all kitted out in your sexy rain gear. We just want to get out of the wind as much as we can."

We fell in behind him. It wasn't so bad at first, but then the rain started falling harder, not only blinding me, but turning the ground into a slick, muddy mess. I remembered another hike, in another place, where the weather had turned suddenly, a torrential storm making everything treacherous. It had been a nightmare. It was why I hated hiking. *I hope this isn't going to be a repeat of that.*

I slowed down, carefully planting my poles before taking a step, my feet uncertain. The others passed me, which was fine. There was less pressure at the back of the group, without worrying that anyone was champing at the bit to pass me like a New York tailgater.

A sharp gust of wind blew back my hood, and cold rain poured down the back of my neck. Shivering, I reached up to pull my hood back into place, tying the strings as tightly as I could without strangling myself.

"You'd love this, Carrie," I muttered under my breath. I hated being out in the rain, but bad weather didn't bother her—in fact, she thought it was an essential part to any outdoor adventure.

"Beautiful, sunny weather is for when I'm at the beach. When I'm in the mountains, I want dark, brooding clouds. I want to taste the rain and jump in the puddles."

"Okay, fine, I'm not going to jump in the puddles, but I can taste some Scottish rain for you."

I tipped my head back and stuck out my tongue to catch the rain—something I would never do back in New York. I took a quick selfie of my wet face under the purple hood and tucked my phone back in my pocket. Carrie loved taking selfies, and would probably get a bigger kick out of that photo than the damn scenery. I pictured her slightly crooked grin and how it would light up her face.

But a selfie wasn't the same if you didn't have your best friend in it with you. A wave of sadness swept over me, so strong I stopped short—and my foot immediately slipped in a patch of mud.

The rain had created a deep rut in the ground, leaving a steep step down to the next section. My pole stuck in the mud, and when I tried to tug it free, I completely over-balanced.

As if in slow-motion, I felt myself toppling over. *Shit.* I was going to go down hard, and it was going to hurt. All I could do was throw out my hands and hope I didn't hit a rock when I landed.

But the fall never happened. An arm came around my waist and my hands flattened against the hard wall of Rory's chest. His strong legs were planted firmly, easily keeping us both upright.

He stared down at me, his eyes the color of the rain, a strange look on his face. "Are you okay?"

"I…" God, I couldn't even *think* with those eyes on me. I looked down, focusing on his bright blue rain jacket. "Yeah. Thank you. I thought for sure I was going to fall. How did you"—*catch me like some kind of superhero*—"get to me so fast?"

"I was right behind you, and I saw your foot slip. Didn't you see the mud?"

"I was…distracted, and wasn't paying attention. Go ahead, yell at me. I deserve it this time."

"I'm not going to yell at you, Amelia. But you can't be distracted—not on this part of the trail. Okay?"

I dared to meet his gaze. "Okay," I whispered.

His heart throbbed against my palm once, twice, three times before he blinked. His cheeks reddened slightly, as if he suddenly realized he was still holding me against him like we were something more than haughty guide and hapless trekker.

He set me on my feet, holding my arm to steady me. "Are you hurt?"

"No." *Just my pride.*

"Take a few steps to make sure."

Under his close scrutiny, I walked in a small circle around him. "See, I'm fine."

"Good. Let's keep going."

The rest of the descent to Bealach Uige, over five hundred feet down, passed without incident. The rain had lightened to a drizzle, and the clouds seemed to be breaking up a bit.

Up ahead, Linda slipped in the mud and went down on her butt, thankfully on a relatively flat patch of ground. Rory hurried over to help her to her feet.

I caught up to her as he was walking on ahead. "Are you all right, Linda?"

"Oh, I'm fine," she said, brushing mud off her green rain pants. "I knew one day all this extra cushioning on my bum would come in handy." She narrowed her eyes at me. "But I want to hear about you, missy."

"What are you talking about?"

"She's talking about how we looked back earlier and saw you in young Rory's arms, like something out of a romance novel," said Pat. "We'd like to hear about that."

My face grew hot. "I stumbled, and he caught me. That's it."

"If you say so," said Linda. "I'm just saying that I wish he'd caught *me* like that." The two of them giggled like teenagers. *Would Carrie and I still giggle together in thirty years?*

"Linda, you're married!" I exclaimed, trying to distract myself from thoughts of Carrie.

"And happily so. But that doesn't mean I can't admire a fine-looking young man. And between him and Tommy, we have plenty to look at if the scenery gets dull. Though it doesn't seem likely that will happen. Look at that!"

I turned, figuring for sure that it was Rory, unknowingly striking some kind of sexy pose—and my jaw dropped open.

The dark gray clouds still hovered menacingly overhead, but they'd parted enough to allow a beam of sunlight to shine through, accompanied by a rainbow. I took a panoramic photo to capture it.

"Without rain, we wouldn't have rainbows," said Pat.

I closed my eyes for a moment. Carrie always used to say that when I bitched about rain messing up our plans. "That's definitely the caption for this photo," I finally said as we continued on.

It was a more gradual ascent this time to the top of Beinn Edra, over six hundred meters high. We stopped for a break at the top, from which the view was incredible. The sky was a weird steel-blue, and still looked threatening, but the sun had fought its way through the clouds, casting the landscape before me in a stunning light.

I moved as close to the edge as I dared to take pictures, then set my phone to record video and slowly moved the phone from left to right. "It looks like Middle-earth, Carrie. I wish you could see this, because the video won't do it justice."

Tears welled in my eyes, but I ignored them, needing both hands to hold the phone steady. I caught sight of something below the ridge. "There's some kind of huge bird down there," I said into the microphone. "Definitely a bird of prey—I can tell by the wingtips."

"It's a golden eagle."

I spun to the right. Rory stood a few feet away, his gaze trained on the bird circling below. I stopped recording. "Really? I heard golden eagles were pretty rare."

"They are, but there are a few mated pairs around here. This is one of the best places to spot them because they like to ride the air currents."

I zoomed the camera as much as it would go and snapped a photo of it.

"You probably won't get a great shot from here."

"I know, but I can hopefully adjust it on the computer when I get home."

He reached out and gently lowered my hands. I looked at him in surprise. "What are you doing?"

He put one finger to my chin and turned my head so I looked out over the edge and not at him. "Forget about taking pictures for one second, and just look. Watch the eagle soar.

Imagine what kind of view it sees. Feel the wind gliding over its feathers. You can take a hundred shots that will show a brown speck against the sky, and they will never capture this moment the way your eyes can."

I blinked at him for a moment, stunned by not only the amount of words he said in a row, but how passionate they were. Then I looked back at the eagle. He was right. We didn't have eagles where I lived, and seeing this one soar through the air was something I'd never forget.

We watched it in silence until it disappeared over the next ridge.

"Thank you for that," I said when it was gone.

"Everyone is so focused on their phones these days— even if it's taking photos and not texting—that they forget to appreciate the view they're trying so desperately to capture." He glanced at his watch. "Anyway, we're about to get moving, so finish up with your pictures." He turned from the edge and rejoined the group.

It was only then I realized I'd never wiped away my tears.

Chapter Seven

RORY

As I walked away from the edge of Beinn Edra, I glanced back over my shoulder to see Amelia brushing her fingers under her eyes. Why had she been crying? She'd insisted she was fine after her stumble—and if she wasn't, she should have told me—so what was it? Did it have something to do with that phone call I'd overheard part of last night? *And why do you care?*

It was my job to care. I had to guide these people safely through the Skye Trail, and to do that, I needed to monitor their emotional state, to make sure they weren't endangering themselves or anyone else. I'd seen her lose her balance, and I'd grabbed her before she'd fallen. Like any guide would have done.

I thought back to that moment. She'd been hunched into herself, clearly cold and miserable, and then she'd suddenly stopped in her tracks, tipped her face up, closed her eyes, and parted her lips as if she were about to be kissed.

A jolt of desire had gone through me. I'd frozen in place, staring at the long line of her throat, the raindrops on her eyelashes, the curve of her mouth as she'd smiled. She'd looked so damn *beautiful*.

And then her feet had gone out from under her, and I'd caught her against my chest, our bodies so close I could smell her scent. She smelled like springtime and sunshine, and I'd had to force myself not to press my face into her neck and inhale her.

I grinned to myself, imagining the look on her face if I'd actually done that. She probably would have whacked me in the head with one of her damned trekking poles. It would have been worth it.

We started off again. There were four quick peaks to go over before we'd break for lunch.

The group was moving at a good clip. I was walking with the two brothers from Maine, who were sharing stories of hiking in the mountains of New Hampshire. At one point, I glanced behind me to check on everyone. I didn't see Amelia's bright purple rain gear. Had she taken it off? It had stopped for now, but the sky was still threatening. She should probably put it back on.

"You guys go on ahead," I said to the lads, and then I turned on my heel and walked back the way we came. The ladies were all in a group, and Tommy was walking with Gordon. But there was no Amelia.

Shit, where was she? My heart pounding, I kept walking, and when I reached the top of a small hillock, I saw her, a purple shape against the green, moving slowly up the hill. I let out a breath I hadn't realized I was holding and strode down to her.

She looked up as I approached. Her cheeks were flushed and she looked—well, not very happy to see me. "Are you all right?"

"I'm fine. Just pacing myself."

I watched her walk for a minute, checking for signs of injury. She didn't seem to be limping, so maybe she was just tired. I fell into step with her, slowing my pace to match hers. When we reached the top of the hillock, she swore under her breath. I looked over to see her staring at the steep trail ahead of us.

"You okay?"

The glare she threw at me was cold enough to freeze the sea.

Chapter Eight

Four small summits, they'd said. They may have been *relatively* small summits, but they were in quick succession, and there was no real path to speak of. Gorgeous scenery all around, but no shelter from the relentless wind.

My thigh and calf muscles screamed on the ascents, and my knees screamed on the descents, sometimes so bad that I had to bite my lip to not cry out.

I'd fallen to the back of the group, which wasn't the bad part. The bad part was that Rory was at the back of the group with me. Because it wasn't embarrassing enough that I was slow and near tears on the hills, I also got to enjoy the added humiliation of this super-hot guy at my side.

"How are you doing?" he asked. For the third time. I couldn't take it anymore.

"I'm fine," I said, far less politely than I should have. "Look, you don't need to stay so close. I'll get there. Eventually." He looked at me for a long moment, and then finally nodded and moved off to the front of the group.

Without the pressure of his close scrutiny, I found my stride and caught up to Pat and Linda, who were also having a tough time. Tommy fell back to walk with the three of us. Somehow, I didn't mind his company as much. Maybe it was because he didn't keep asking how we were, just told funny stories that had us in hysterics and kept our attention away from the difficult path. *And maybe it's because you're not attracted to him.* No, that definitely *wasn't* it.

Rory stayed up front with the faster walkers, though he glanced back a few times when we were especially loud, probably annoyed by the sound of laughter and fun.

After the fourth peak, we descended into another wide *bealach*—or pass, as opposed to *beinn*, which meant mountain or peak. I'd made it a point to ask Tommy for the Gaelic words so I could tell Carrie.

We stopped for lunch, and I dropped to the ground, practically weeping with relief. The ground was wet, but I didn't care—I still had on my rain gear. The sun was shining through the clouds, its warmth lovely on my face. My squished PB&J was the best thing I'd ever tasted, and after I shoveled it in, I leaned against my pack and closed my eyes.

I lay on the sand, the sun warm on my skin, the scent of the sea filling my nostrils with every breath. It was one of those random summer-like days we'd sometimes get in early spring, and Carrie and I had headed for the beach, along with seemingly everyone else in Nassau County.

I trailed my fingers back and forth through the sand, feeling the grains sifting over my skin.

Carrie sat up, took a sip of her iced coffee, and lay back down. "Just think, Mee, in a few months we'll be in Miami, working at a fancy new hotel. Warm sunshine will be our life every day."

"It's going to be awesome, especially after this shitty

winter. No more shoveling snow and driving on black ice."

"I just wish you were doing the Skye Trail with me. It seems wrong for me to do it without you."

I sighed. "Carrie, we've talked about this."

"I know. I just keep hoping you'll change your mind."

"You'll have much more fun without me whining about how hard it is. And this way, if there's a hot guide, you can go for it without worrying that you're ditching me. And then you can tell me all about it when we're on our road trip."

"I'll drink to that," she said. We clinked iced coffees and drank, giggling at the silliness of us.

"Amelia?"

I slowly opened my eyes, blinking in confusion at the blonde woman standing over me, backlit by the sun. "Carrie?" I whispered.

"No, it's me." She stepped forward, into the light, and I could see it was Molly. *Of course it's not Carrie, you twit. Carrie is three thousand miles away from here.*

"Our lunch break is over, unfortunately." Molly knelt beside me as I shoved myself upright to sit. "Are you all right? You looked like you were out cold."

"I can't believe I fell into such a deep sleep so quickly," I said, pulling my bag close so I could drink from my CamelBak water pack. "I was dreaming of my friend Carrie."

"The one who got hurt and couldn't be here?"

"Yeah. I dreamed of one of the last times we hung out before she got hurt. We had this crazy hot day at the end of March, and we went to the beach."

"It sounds lovely."

"It was."

"Okay, everyone, let's get moving," said Rory. Molly hopped up and went to fetch her pack.

I tried to stand, but my muscles protested, and I literally groaned like an old lady as I pretended to rummage for something in my bag while I gathered my strength.

A hand appeared before me, and I looked up into Tommy's grinning face.

"Are you laughing at me?"

"Only a little."

Sighing, I grabbed his hand. "C'mon, up you go," he said, tugging me to my feet. "All right?"

"Yep. Thanks."

"No worries. Everyone's always a little stiff from sitting. The key is to groan silently. If no one hears it, it didn't happen."

I glanced over to see Rory helping Linda up. She looked at me and placed her hand over her heart as if in a swoon, and I busted out laughing.

"I'm not even gonna ask," said Tommy. He waited for me to heft my backpack onto my shoulders and handed me my poles.

In spite of my protesting muscles, the ascent to the next peak, about a hundred meters, wasn't too bad. When I reached the top, I followed the others out to the edge, which looked like the prow of some giant, grassy ship. It was unnerving to stand there, with the wind lashing my braid against my back, surrounded on three sides by air.

Holding my phone tightly against the wind, I recorded the stunning view, all the way to the sea. Then I stuffed the phone into my pocket. I'd spent every moment of every break today taking pictures of the views. Now I wanted to look for myself. The thought that Rory would approve entered my brain, but I shut it down. That wasn't why I was doing this.

I was exhausted beyond description and I hurt *everywhere*. But standing out on this strange promontory in the middle of this spectacular, alien scenery, I felt exhilarated. *I'd* done this. I, Amelia Benson, unrepentant beach girl, who didn't hike, had summitted seven peaks of the exposed and barren Trotternish Ridge.

Carrie would be so freaking jealous when I told her about it.

And just like that, my exhilaration disappeared, that warm feeling replaced by a chill so powerful, I shuddered.

How could I even think that? She wasn't here *because of me*.

My eyes filled with tears, turning the view into a green, brown, and blue smear.

"Are you all right?"

Great, this would be the second time today that Rory had seen me in tears. Wiping my eyes and plastering on a smile, I turned to face him. "I'm fine. I've just never seen a view like this before, and I guess I got a little emotional."

It wasn't the whole truth, but it was true enough. He nodded once and turned back to gaze out at the vista without saying anything.

I cleared my throat. "Which peak is this?"

"It's the Peak of the Red Fox," he replied. Then he said it in Gaelic, which sounded like "Skoor ah vatee ruay."

He spelled it for me as I typed it into my phone: *Sgùrr a'Mhadaidh Ruaidh*. "Are you fluent in Gaelic?"

"No. But I know the names of the sights we come across on the trail and how to pronounce them."

"Don't sell yourself short, Sutherland. You also do a damn fine job of cursing out slow drivers and asking where the loo is. Flawless accent," said Tommy.

Rory's fist shot out in a quick jab to Tommy's arm.

"Owwww!" Tommy cried, dramatically clutching his arm and staggering.

Then his eyes widened in horror as his heel slid off the edge.

Before I could even gasp, Rory's hand shot out once more, grabbing Tommy's arm and hauling him to safety.

Then he ripped him apart.

Chapter Nine

We stood on the top of the world, the view spectacular from every angle. This was what I lived for. I was thrilled to share it with my closest friend. A mock insult, which naturally had to be retaliated against with a mock punch. And then his eyes grew wide with terror, his arms pinwheeling uselessly—

"— Rory. Did you hear me? I'm all right, man. Rory!"

Fingers dug hard into my upper arms. I blinked, and Tommy's face came into focus. He hadn't... He wasn't...

"You can let go now, Rory. I'm okay," he said quietly. I was clutching his shoulders, and we were locked in some kind of weird embrace at the top of Sgùrr a'Mhadaidh Ruaidh. *What the—?*

And then I remembered.

"Are you fucking daft? What were you thinking, horsing around like that up here? You could have gone over the goddamn edge!"

My fingers ached, and I realized that they had tightened

on his shoulders and I was shaking him. He didn't try to break my grip, didn't say a word. He just stood there calmly as anger, fear, and guilt poured out of me in a crazy tirade.

Then his eyes flicked to my right, and he shook his head once. Who was he looking at?

The Skye Trail. We were guiding a group on the Skye Trail. And the entire group had just witnessed my meltdown, had just watched me tear into *another guide* like he was a foolish child. Because of *my* carelessness.

My face burning with mortification and shame, my stomach roiling, I let go of Tommy and turned away, sinking to the ground a few feet from the edge.

Voices faded away behind me. A shadow fell over the grass and Tommy dropped down to sit beside me.

"Tommy, I—"

He bumped me with his shoulder, cutting me off. "Don't even say it, man."

Taking a deep breath, I turned to face him. His eyes met mine, and there wasn't even the slightest hint of anger or judgment in them. "I just…I saw—"

"I know. I know what you saw. Just sit here for a minute." He held out a water bottle. "Have some water."

Wishing it was whisky instead, I took a sip, then capped the bottle and held it to my forehead. "The group?"

"They're taking a ten-minute break at the top of the path."

"Fuck, Tommy. How can I face them?"

"Honestly, none of them said a word. And why would they? They saw me do something stupid and saw you rightfully yell at me for it. Let me finish," he said when I started to interrupt. "They may wonder why you reacted as strongly as you did, but they're not judging you for it."

I shook my head. "I didn't *rightfully* yell at you, Tommy. I'm so sorry."

"If you say that one more time, I'm going to short-sheet your bed the next time you have one."

"How can you joke about this?"

He clapped his hand on my shoulder. "Rory, you seem to be forgetting that I'm your best mate. We've been through a lot together. And I will never—*could* never—be angry with you for reacting the way you did." He grinned. "But I bet you'll be super-nice to me for the rest of the day, right? And maybe even buy me a beer when we're in Portree?"

"I—" He narrowed his eyes at me, and I knew I had to agree with him, at least to his face. "Fine. Your next beer is on me."

"And?"

I sighed. "And I'll be really nice to you for the rest of the day."

"Good. Now let's get off this godforsaken peak."

He got up and held out his hand. I clasped his forearm, and he pulled me to my feet and then into a hard hug. I held on for a moment, grateful beyond words for his understanding, and then thumped him once on the back and let go. "Time to face the music."

"Go easy on yourself, Ror. They're fine."

Swallowing hard, I rejoined the group. They all looked at me with concern. No judgment, just concern. Exactly as Tommy had said.

"I'm...sorry. I...Tommy got a bit too close to the edge, and I overreacted. I shouldn't have yelled like that. I'll understand if you'd rather I step aside as your guide after today."

Tommy whipped around to stare at me, his eyes wide with surprise. But I had to make the offer. As he'd put it yesterday, the people in the group were here to have fun, not to worry that their guide was going to lose his shit. They'd be within their rights to complain to Scarlet.

"I don't know about the rest of you," said Gordon, "but

I'd rather have a guide who's overly concerned for everyone's safety than one who isn't. We all chose to do this trek with a guide, which means we all wanted to be led by someone who knows what he's doing and will make sure we get to the end in one piece. Even if that means yelling at us for putting ourselves at risk."

"I appreciate you saying so, Gordon, but—"

He held up his hand. "Son, I've owned a travel company back in the States for twenty years. One thing we do for our clients is book tours. I've spent many hours looking at what makes a good tour company, and one key thing is having guides that prioritize safety. You—both of you—" he said, gesturing to include Tommy, "impress the hell out of me, and I'd hire you in a second. So no, I don't want another guide."

The others all nodded or murmured their agreement. Amelia even smiled at me. And my heart felt a little bit lighter.

"Thanks, guys. I really appreciate it."

Tommy cleared his throat noisily. "Well, if we're done talking about our *feelings*, perhaps we can continue the trek?" I opened my mouth to retort, but he shook his finger at me. "Uh-uh, Sutherland. You promised to be nice to me for the rest of the day, remember?"

Everyone laughed. I managed a small smile, hoping it was enough to fool everyone into thinking I was okay. Even though I was anything but.

Chapter Ten

As we crossed yet another peak and began a steep descent down its rocky slope, I couldn't stop thinking about what had just happened.

I'd frozen as Tommy's foot started to go over the edge. There wouldn't have been a hope in hell of me doing anything to help him. But Rory's reflexes had been lightning-fast, almost as though he'd trained over and over for exactly that situation.

He'd been truly scary when he'd lit into Tommy. His eyes had turned silver, like the liquid mercury that had spilled on the bathroom floor years ago when I'd broken one of those old glass thermometers. And the look in them—at first I'd thought it was anger, but then I listened to his words, and I knew. Yes, there had been anger there, but the anger had come from fear.

There was more to Rory than the serious, surly, overly critical side I'd seen. His response had been visceral. And he'd gone to some other time and place. That had been evident when Gordon had taken a step toward him and Tommy had waved him off with a shake of his head, startling Rory into returning to *this* time and place.

Thank God he'd had Tommy, who knew what was really going on, who knew how to talk him down. If it had just been Rory guiding us, and one of the group had been in Tommy's place, I don't know what would have happened. I thought of how confident he'd been yesterday during the briefing, how he'd convinced me in two seconds that while he may not always be nice to me, he wasn't going to let anything happen to me. And now I wasn't so sure.

I was saved from any more thinking by the "path" before me, which was all rocks. Like yesterday, I hummed to myself and just concentrated on where I was putting my feet, forgetting about Rory and Tommy and everything else.

We reached the bottom, but there was no time for a breath of relief before there was a sharp climb, which eased out a bit before the next summit.

Finally, we reached the Storr, the last peak on the ridge. It was an optional summit, as the trail didn't go over it, but when Tommy asked if we wanted to go up to the top, none of us hesitated. There was no point in coming this far only to avoid this last, tallest peak. We posed for a group photo at the summit and then began the descent, which took us down another rocky slope and over a fence.

And then we were faced with the stunning Old Man of Storr, a solitary pinnacle of stone in front of the cliffs. Beyond the Old Man was a view out to a sparkling loch.

For the first time since the Quiraing, there were other people around. Lots of them, taking advantage of the now beautiful day. It was jarring after so many hours of relative silence to hear dozens of voices, to have to wait for the split second when no one was in front of me to snap a photo. I much preferred the quietness we'd had all day.

From there, it was a relatively easy descent to a car park.

"Just a little farther," said Rory when we reached it. "There's a great spot to camp on the beach at Bearreraig Bay, which is a shortish walk from here."

"When you say 'shortish walk,' what exactly do you mean?" asked Linda.

"Yeah, don't think we've forgotten your 'this is the last hill today' promise yesterday that turned out to be a lie," added Gordon.

"They've got you there, boyo," said Tommy.

Rory's lips quirked. "Shortish in that you could be sitting down, pretending you're drinking a cocktail, within half an hour. Or so. If we stop talking about it and start walking. And I don't lie," he said to Gordon. "It's just that our definitions of 'hill' are not the same."

"He lies," Gordon quipped.

"Okay, let's get moving," said Tommy. "We'll be on the road for a bit, so stay alert."

It was the main road up the coast from Portree, and I was glad that we weren't on it for more than a few minutes before we turned onto a path. From there, we crossed a dam and then veered away from the path to a viewpoint overlooking the bay.

Rory stopped us there. "Okay, guys, the path down is pretty steep, so take it easy. I know everyone's knackered, and I don't want you twisting your ankles—or worse—because you're too tired to watch where you're walking."

Rory had, in fact, lied, despite what he'd said earlier. The path wasn't *pretty* steep, it was *very* steep. My knees, already shaky from hours and hours of steep ascents and descents, were screaming. *One foot in front of the other.* I tuned out everything and everyone, and just took one step at a time, clenching my teeth so I wouldn't cry out in pain. The path zagged to the right, and I stopped for a moment, leaning heavily on my poles.

"Let me take your pack." I looked up to see Rory, hand extended. I shook my head. "Amelia, give me your pack. It will be easier for you."

"I just need a minute." I didn't want it to be easy. Nothing about this trek was supposed to be easy.

He nodded once and stayed where he was, not saying another word. After a minute (okay, maybe more like two), I adjusted the straps of my pack and started down the path once more. Rory walked in front of me, glancing over his shoulder every few steps to check on me.

He didn't ask how I was or offer to help again, for which I was grateful. Finally—*finally*—we reached the bottom of the path, emerging onto a pebbled beach. The others were already setting up their tents as far back from the shore as they could.

Rory gestured to a flattish spot with only a few pebbles. "You can set up here. Give a shout if you need anything."

I set down my pack and rolled my shoulders, grateful to have the weight off me for the rest of the day. I undid the straps holding my tent and withdrew it from its sack, setting everything out in front of me.

I'd set up the tent before I left home. I'd watched YouTube videos on it, read the directions. I had this.

I reached into the tent bag for the directions. But they weren't there. "What the hell?" I turned the bag inside out. Nothing. I rummaged through my pack, messing up my meticulous packing job. But they weren't there. I must have left them at home.

Okay, I could do this. It wasn't rocket science. I unrolled the tent and spread it out flat, then picked up a pole and began working it through the narrow sleeve. So far, so good.

But when I got all the tent poles inserted and tried to

stand it up, it caved in.

"Dammit! What am I doing wrong?"

"What *are* you doing wrong?" said Rory, looming over me with a frown on his face, like a teacher disappointed with his student. "Let me see."

I couldn't deal with him schooling me again. "No, it's fine. I've got it."

"Don't be daft. Let me help you, or you'll be sitting here all night trying to figure it out."

"Then I guess it's a good thing that I brought a flashlight with me, isn't it?" I retorted. I knew I was being unreasonable—okay, bitchy—but it had been so mortifying to have him watch me struggle all day, and I didn't want him to think I couldn't do anything right.

He opened his mouth as if to shout at me, and then snapped it shut and closed his eyes for a moment.

I knew what he was doing—I'd done it myself often enough. "Are you counting to ten?" I hissed.

He opened his eyes, which were that same silvery color they'd been earlier when he'd yelled at Tommy. "Aye, I am," he said, his accent rising to the surface. "Because I don't know what the hell you're tryin' to prove. It's been a long day, and you must be knackered. Why can't you just let me help? You clearly don't know what you're doing."

I stomped over to him. "Stop talking to me like I'm a child!"

His eyes flashed with anger. "Then stop goddamn acting like one and let me help you!"

"No!"

I could hear Carrie cackling, imagined her with a sack of popcorn, her head turning to one of us, then the other, as if she were watching a tennis match. But I couldn't give in. Not now. "For the last time, I don't want your help. I'll set up my own damn tent."

"Not tonight, you won't."

We spun to see Tommy standing beside my fully set-up tent, staring at us like we were *both* children. The others were very carefully *not* staring at us, but I could only imagine what they were thinking.

All the wind went out of my sails. Now I just felt... ridiculous. "Tommy, I—"

He held up his hand. "It's been a long, hard day, and we're all tired and hungry and cranky. You two can fight about the tent—and whatever else—later, okay?"

"I... Thank you," I said, my shoulders slumping.

"You're welcome." He headed for his tent.

Rory stalked to his own tent and ducked inside.

How had this turned into such a mess? *Because* you *turned it into a mess. He was just trying to help.*

By the time I unrolled my self-inflating sleeping mat and my sleeping bag and set them both inside the tent, I'd calmed down enough to face everyone. I grabbed a spoon and a packet of some sort of freeze-dried meal from my pack, pulled on a fleece, and joined the others, who congregated at a cluster of boulders.

"I'm sorry, guys," I said. "I don't know what the hell came over me."

Jack, one of the brothers from Maine, waved away my apology. "You're just over-tired. Makes for a short fuse."

"We're all tired. No one else acted like an angry toddler. Just me."

"Don't be so hard on yourself, honey," said Lucy, laying her hand on my arm. "You'll sleep well tonight and can start fresh tomorrow."

I wasn't so convinced.

We gathered around the camp stoves that Rory and Tommy had carried in their packs. The stoves were essentially small fuel tanks with a water canister attached to the top. You lit the flame, boiled some water, and then poured it right into the food packets, stirred it up, and voila, dinner. I dug into my "Chicken Pad Thai," expecting it to taste awful, but it was actually pretty good.

Everyone was quiet as we ate, as if we all had enough energy for eating or for speaking, but not for both. Tommy told us that the beach was a good place to look for fossils, so after we packed the empty food packets and utensils into plastic bags and tucked them inside our packs to be disposed of in Portree the next day, the others set off to see what they could find.

I looked around for Rory—now, while everyone else was occupied elsewhere, was a good time for me to apologize to him, something that I needed to do before we started out tomorrow. I *had* been acting like a stubborn toddler, and I should have just accepted his help.

I looked up and down the beach, but didn't spot his distinctive red hair. His tent was a few yards away from mine, and I cautiously approached. "Rory?" I rattled the zipper. "Rory, it's Amelia. Are you in there?"

No answer, so he was either ignoring me, or more likely—because he was our guide and probably wasn't allowed to ignore me—he was just using the "loo," the out-of-the-way spot beyond the camp they'd designated for us to take care of business, with precise instructions on what to do—and what not to do.

Whatever, I'd find him later. I took out my phone to call Helen. But I had only two bars of battery power, and no way to charge the phone until tomorrow night. I could make a quick call, but then I wouldn't be able to take any pictures tomorrow, because I couldn't let the battery run completely down and be unreachable.

It was a no-brainer, really. I needed to document every moment of this trip for Carrie, and she would understand if I didn't call. "I'm sorry, Ree," I muttered.

The sea was deep blue in the evening sunlight. It would probably feel good on my sore feet. I tucked the phone in my pocket, rolled up my pants legs, and pulled off my boots and socks, wincing as the small pebbles dug into my tender soles.

The water lapped gently against the shore. So inviting. I dipped my toes in—and shrieked. It was *frigid*. I was used to cold water—the ocean off Long Island's south shore never got above the mid-seventies, and that was in August or September, after it had been baking in the sun all summer. But this was like an ice bath.

Gritting my teeth, I forced myself to step all the way in. The cold water did feel good on my aching feet—or maybe my feet had just gone numb and that was why they didn't hurt anymore.

I turned back to the beach just as Rory, clad only in a pair of blue gym shorts, strode into the sea and started swimming parallel to the shore with long, powerful strokes, as if this was the Caribbean and not a freezing Scottish bay.

Is he insane? How could he swim in that water without a wetsuit? I watched his figure get smaller and smaller before he turned around and started heading back.

"He does this a lot," said Tommy, joining me at the water's edge.

"Is he a masochist? Or one of those exercise fanatics?"

"He doesn't do it for the exercise. He does it to clear his head."

Oh. With the stress of that climb down, and the stupid argument with Rory, I'd forgotten about the earlier incident between him and Tommy.

"Isn't there—I don't know—a less cold way for him to

clear his head? Isn't he worried about hypothermia?"

"Nah, he's been swimming in these waters his whole life. We both have. When he has a lot on his mind—which is more often than not—he goes for a swim or a walk in the evening to tire him out so he can sleep."

He turned to me, no trace of humor in his eyes. "I know you two have butted heads, and that you probably think he's a dick. He really isn't, he's just…complicated. It doesn't excuse the way he's treated you, and I swear I've never seen him act that way before—he's usually just quiet and broody. So try not to take it personally, and I'll talk to him."

"No, that's okay."

"He can't act that way to a paying client."

I laid my hand on his arm. "Please don't. It was totally my fault. He was trying to help, and I was frustrated and being stubborn. I lost my temper, and he reacted in kind. Just let it go. Please?"

He studied me for a long moment, and then nodded, looking relieved. "All right. But if you change your mind…"

"I know where to find you."

Smiling, he squeezed my hand. "You're a nice lass, Amelia."

Rory emerged from the sea, raising both hands to slick the water from his hair. His upper body was incredible. Tommy hadn't been exaggerating when he said Rory swam a lot. I couldn't keep from checking him out, my eyes dropping from his broad shoulders to his sculpted chest and abdomen, stopping for a long moment on his deliciously cut obliques, and continuing down to where his wet shorts clung to thighs muscled from what must be thousands of miles of walking.

His skin was golden and lovely and only slightly darker on his forearms, so either he used really good sunblock or went bare-chested often, which really wouldn't be fair to— well, any other men.

I realized I was staring at him, and snapped my eyes back up, feeling my face grow hot. But I needn't have worried. His gaze was focused on my hand, still resting on Tommy's forearm, and Tommy's hand covering mine. I started to pull my hand away—why, I didn't really know; it wasn't like I was doing anything wrong—but Tommy tightened his grip and leaned in close.

"You'll let me know if you change your mind about me talking to him?"

"I will." It would never happen, but it was kind of him to offer.

He let go of my hand and stepped back. "Okay. Catch ya later." His grin seemed broader than the moment warranted, but whatever.

I turned back to talk to Rory, but there was only a trail of wet footprints on the rocks leading toward his tent.

Just as well. There was no way I could look him in the eye right now, anyway, let alone have a serious conversation.

I was weary to my very bones, but it was still light out, and I knew I wouldn't be able to fall asleep yet. Maybe a (slow) walk would clear my head. I wandered down the beach in the opposite direction from the rest of the group, needing the time to myself. I stopped by a large pile of rocks and absently poked through them, but my mind was on my confrontation with Rory.

Why did he get under my skin so much? That was easy. Because he kept tapping into the questions I'd been asking myself: What was I doing here, on this difficult trail, when I had practically no hiking experience? What made me think that being in decent shape and doing a few long walks on a flat path came even remotely close to preparing me for a trail that ascended and descended mountains and skirted cliff edges, where a moment's lapse in concentration could mean injury…or worse?

The answer to those questions was simple: I was doing this for Carrie. Because she couldn't. And so, I would do it for her, every single step, no matter how painful. Until the very end. And I wouldn't let Rory, no matter how surly or critical—*or hot*—distract me from that.

But why was I *letting* him get to me? With that last argument, we'd practically devolved into "I know you are, but what am I?" I certainly had enough on my mind without wasting the energy and breath picking fights as if we were in junior high school.

Maybe that's why *you're doing it.* I froze, my hand buried wrist-deep in the loose rocks. No, that couldn't be it. *Couldn't it, though? When you were arguing with Rory, were you thinking about Carrie?*

I thought back to the confrontations we'd had. Each time I'd mouthed off to him, each time I'd let him get to me, my mind had been focused on him. Each time, I'd walked away angry, grumbling under my breath or in my head about what a jerk he was. And each time, I hadn't thought about Carrie— why I was here and she wasn't. I hadn't felt guilty for enjoying a fantastic view or for being exhilarated from a quick climb up to a peak.

I'd subconsciously been fighting with Rory to make myself feel better. But this wasn't about making myself feel better. Not when Carrie was…not okay. And it wasn't fair to Rory. I needed to stop picking fights with him.

The sun was dropping behind the Trotternish Ridge. I needed to return to camp. Yes, I'd snidely told Rory that I had a flashlight with me, but right now it was in my pack, which was in my tent. The last thing I needed was to get stuck out here in the dark—or worse, have him come looking for me with an "I told you so."

I braced my hand on a rock and pushed myself to my feet, knocking over a pile of smaller rocks in the process. One of them landed faceup, displaying the embedded spiral of some kind of fossil.

"Oh, cool," I breathed. Yes, this beach was supposed to be excellent for finding fossils, but I didn't think I'd actually stumble upon one. I stuck it in the pocket of my fleece and returned to camp.

"Tommy, I found one!"

Grinning, he took it from me and examined it. "It's an ammonite, a prehistoric mollusk. Pretty neat, right?"

"It's awesome. What did everyone else find?"

It turned out I was the only one who'd been successful. Maybe it was a sign. Of what, I didn't know. That Carrie would be okay? That she wasn't mad that I might have subconsciously sought to distract myself from worrying about her to argue with a cute guy?

Exhaustion swept over me. I needed to get to bed before I collapsed.

While it was still light enough to see, I hurried out of sight of the camp to pee, then brushed my teeth.

I returned to my tent and zipped it nearly all the way up, leaving a small opening for the last bit of daylight to come in. I changed into my pajamas and slithered into my sleeping bag.

I turned the gray rock over in my hand, tracing the delicate grooves and ridges with my fingertip. Because of my exasperation with Rory, which had led me to wander down the beach, I'd found a perfect souvenir for Carrie. Maybe it was a sign.

• • •

Sometime later, I was pulled out of a deep, dreamless sleep. I opened my eyes, disoriented at first by the utter darkness, and then remembered where I was. What woke me? Then I heard a voice.

I sat up, opening the zipper enough so I could peer out. Nothing. I must have imagined it. But then I heard it again. I kicked free from the sleeping bag and held my breath, listening closely. The New York girl in me, who locked her doors every night even in the suburbs, came to attention. Was someone out there, someone not from our group? For the first time, it occurred to me how isolated we were out here.

There it was again. It was a sound of distress, the words indistinct but the tone clear. Someone needed help. Grabbing my flashlight, I left the tent—and froze. The sound was coming from Rory's tent.

Shit. What was I supposed to do? The last words I'd said to him were petty and childish, and even if they hadn't been, it wasn't like we were friends. But he sounded so anguished— how could I do nothing?

I called his name, softly. There was no response. I unzipped his tent and peered in, shining the light to the side.

In the dim glow of the flashlight, I could see that he lay on his back, his sleeping bag tangled around him, his T-shirt twisted. He was clearly in the throes of a nightmare. I knelt beside him and reached out, then drew back my hand. Were you supposed to touch someone who was having a nightmare? But then he made that sound again, and I knew I had no choice.

I laid my hand on his shoulder and gently shook him. "Rory? Rory, wake up!"

His eyes remained tightly closed. "I can't see," he said brokenly, over and over again.

His anguish was heartbreaking. This had to be related to what had happened earlier with Tommy. I smoothed his damp, tangled hair off his face, then stroked my thumb over his cheek, leaning close to murmur in his ear.

"Shh, it's okay. It's only a dream. You're safe now. Just

open your eyes, and you'll be able to see." God, what was it that haunted him? "Rory, wake up."

He thrashed again. I lost my balance and sprawled across him, my face just inches from his. I started to lever myself up.

And then he opened his eyes and stared at me.

"It's okay, Rory, you were just—"

His arms closed around me, and he kissed me.

Wait, what? said my brain.

Who cares? said my body as I kissed him back. His stern mouth wasn't so stern anymore as he kissed me desperately, his arms holding me so tightly, as if I were a lifeline pulling him out of the dark. And I kissed him just as desperately, my body coming alive for the first time in so long.

His tongue stroked mine, and I heard a whimper escape me as I shifted so that I lay fully on top of him, my legs straddling his hips. His hand slid down to my butt, bringing me closer still. I felt him hard against me, felt the answering rush of desire run through me—

—and then like a bucket of ice water dumped over my head, my brain finally kicked back in. *What are you* doing?

I froze. What *was* I doing? We didn't like each other. Ninety percent of the words we'd exchanged had been in anger. And now I was two seconds away from tearing off my clothes and riding him like he was a Thoroughbred? Was he even *awake*?

I tore my mouth from his—God, even now my body protested the sudden withdrawal—and looked down at him.

His eyes were wide and glittering in the blue light cast by my flashlight, which had fallen to the ground at some point.

He ran his thumb over my swollen lower lip. "Amelia?"

Well, at least he knew who he'd been kissing. "Good, you're awake. I, uh, have to go."

But his other arm was still around me, lightly holding my hips to his—*God*—and I needed to get away before my traitorous body made me do something we'd both regret come sunrise. "Rory."

His eyes narrowed for a moment in confusion, then widened comically. His arm immediately dropped from around me—*dammit*—and I clumsily rolled off him and scuttled back, breathing deeply in a vain attempt to calm my raging hormones.

He pushed himself up to sit. "Amelia, I'm sorry. God, I didn't mean...I didn't know—"

"It's fine," I interrupted, lurching to my feet. I grabbed my flashlight, aiming the beam toward the ground. "I'll see you in the morning." Without waiting for a response, I hurried out of his tent into the blessed chill of the night air.

When I turned back to zip up the tent, he was sitting with his knees drawn in and his head hanging low, like the weight of the world was on his shoulders.

I fled back to my own tent before I did something stupid, like go back to him and let our bodies take the comfort we both so clearly needed.

Chapter Eleven

RORY

I watched Amelia run from my tent as if she were being chased. *What the hell did I just do?*

I remembered the dream—of course I did. It was always the same one. I was on top of a mountain. The fog had rolled in so quickly that I'd lost my bearings. I was utterly blind, frozen because I didn't know where the edge was. A voice came from somewhere nearby—I couldn't tell where—telling me to stay put, that he was coming for me.

But I panicked. The mist was so thick, so pervasive, that I couldn't breathe. I *had* to get out of there. And he kept telling me not to move, that he would find me, his disembodied voice calling out to me, over and over.

Always the same dream, and it always ended the same way.

Except this time, when the dream changed, when the voice calling to me changed. I knew that voice; it had been shouting at me earlier. Then it was pleading with me. A hand was on my face, and warmth surrounded me, driving away the chill.

I'd opened my eyes, and Amelia's beautiful face was so close to mine; her body was so soft against me, like a living blanket.

I'd kissed her, my body coming awake as if from an endless sleep, *feeling* for the first time in so long. I'd held her close, my body burning for her, wanting more, *needing* more. As if I was still caught up in a dream—of a completely different kind.

But it hadn't been a dream. I'd really been holding her, kissing her, feeling her body move against mine.

And then she ran out of the tent.

I needed to see her, to apologize.

I peered outside. Her tent was all zipped up. The last thing I wanted to do if she was asleep was wake her and make her revisit the whole thing. What I needed to say could wait till morning.

But there was no way I could stay inside that tent. Not now.

I gathered up my sleeping bag and the mat underneath and stepped outside, shivering slightly as the cool breeze touched my sweaty skin. I placed the mat on a relatively pebble-free spot, then laid the sleeping bag on top of it.

Returning to my tent, I felt around for the flask I'd set aside earlier. I ducked back outside and slid into my sleeping bag, zipping it up to my waist. I didn't know what time it was—late enough for it to be truly dark, the sky flickering with stars.

Just a few yards away, the waves lapped softly against the shore. I opened the flask and took a sip. The whisky slid down my throat, warming my chilled body. But I didn't feel as warm as I had when I'd kissed Amelia. *Don't go there.*

I took another sip and stared at the sea. Though my

earlier swim had cleared my head a little bit, it hadn't purged the memories that haunted me. Nothing truly could, but sometimes they were a little further out of reach.

But not after today, and likely not for the rest of this week. And if Amelia hadn't heard me, hadn't brought me out of that nightmare, it would have been even worse.

I pictured the way she'd looked just a few hours ago, her brown eyes flashing, her face flushed, her chest heaving as she got closer and closer to me in her rage. She was so beautiful, and even though she was shouting at me—we were shouting at each other—all I could think of was how badly I'd wanted to kiss her, to see those eyes flashing with desire instead of anger, to see her cheeks flushed from passion, to see her chest heaving because I was taking her breath away with my kisses.

And now I *had* kissed her, but it hadn't exactly gone the way I'd imagined it might. Not only that, she'd run from me.

I'd fucked everything up.

She was a hiker in my group for a week, and then she'd be on her way home. I'd just needed to get along with her. And now that would never happen.

I took another sip of whisky, then lay back, zipping the sleeping bag up to my chest. I stared at the stars and breathed in the cool sea air, longing for a few hours of dreamless sleep.

Chapter Twelve

AMELIA

I tossed and turned in my sleeping bag, unable to shake the memory of Rory's mouth pressed to mine, the taste of his tongue, the feel of his body against me.

He'd stared at me like I was his salvation—until he remembered where he was and who *I* was. The way he'd looked as I left the tent...

He'd been mortified—maybe even horrified.

Maybe he'd forget it all by morning. That would be ideal. I could pretend it never happened and forget about it, too.

Liar! shouted the voice inside me, like the old crone in *The Princess Bride*. I sighed, rolling over again. Yeah, it would be better if he didn't remember it, or thought it was just part of his dream going from nightmare to...not a nightmare.

But that kiss, that explosion of desire I felt even in that strange moment—it was a hundred times more than I'd felt with either of my college boyfriends. If Rory had been aware that it was me he was kissing, had felt even a fraction of that passion for me, then no, I didn't want him to forget it. Even if it made the rest of the week awkward as hell.

In the darkness of my tent, I pressed my fingers to my lips. He'd tasted like whisky and the sea.

In the darkness of my tent, I couldn't help but wonder who he'd thought he was kissing—who he'd *wished* he was kissing—because he'd definitely been surprised when he realized it was me.

And in the darkness of my tent, I could admit that I was just a little jealous of whoever that was.

. . .

The remainder of my night was long and mostly sleepless. When I did doze off, I had a disturbing dream of Rory, lost and wandering in the dark, and though I could hear him, he could never hear me.

I had another dream, too, one in which Rory and I were entwined together in a sleeping bag. He'd known who I was this time, had murmured my name more than once—and I'd murmured his. And there hadn't been any apologies.

I wasn't sure which dream bothered me the most.

When the sky was gray with the approaching dawn, I gave up on trying to sleep. I got dressed and braided my hair, then grabbed my phone and stepped outside. Bearreraig Bay faced east—maybe I could get some sunrise photos.

I shivered in the cold morning, glad I'd put on my fleece. I glanced at Rory's tent, hoping the rest of his night had been more restful than mine.

As I passed by, something moved. I did an actual double take when I realized what it was. Rory was in his sleeping bag, *outside* his tent. He was curled on his side, his head pillowed on his arm, apparently oblivious to the layer of silvery frost that clung to him, including his hair.

My sleep had been restless, my dreams disturbing, but how bad must *his* nightmare have been if sleeping in the cold air—*with frost*—was preferable to the warm confines of his tent?

The sleeping bag had slipped down, exposing his arm. He had to be freezing. Carefully, so as not to wake him, I tugged up the sleeping bag so it covered his shoulder.

I continued down to the shore and settled on a boulder to await the sunrise, wincing as the cold from the rock seeped through my pants. I snapped a few photos of the pink and lavender clouds that splashed across the horizon and then started recording as the sun began to emerge from the sea.

"Morning, Ree," I said quietly, not wanting to detract from the serenity of the moment. "Just wanted to share this glorious sunrise with you. Can't wait to see you and tell you everything. Love you."

I ended the recording after the sun exploded from the horizon, then turned to go back to my tent. Rory stood a few feet away. He had dark circles under his eyes and strain lines around his mouth.

He looked like hell.

"Hey," he murmured, his eyes not meeting mine. "I, uh… I'm sorry about last night." He made a disgusted sound and scrubbed his hands through his already-crazy hair. "God, it sounds like I'm apologizing for finishing your whisky without asking, not for… How can I even apologize for what I did?"

I stared at him. What was he talking about? And then it hit me. I laid my hand on his arm. He looked at my hand and then at me, his eyes troubled.

"Rory, you didn't do anything you need to apologize for."

He laughed humorlessly. "Amelia, I'm one hundred percent sure you didn't come into my tent to be kissed, much less anything else."

My whole body grew hot as I recalled that moment, my

memory of which was apparently vastly different than his.

"Look, Rory. It's true that you kissed me as you were coming out of your nightmare, but then we both got caught up in the moment, and I…wasn't an unwilling participant," I said, my face flaming. "Okay? It happened, and it's over. You don't need to apologize." The look in his eyes went from despondent and self-deprecating to hopeful. "You really don't remember what happened?"

Now *his* face turned red. "The dream—it's not the first time I've had it, and each time I wake up from it, I'm usually pretty wrecked. I…didn't trust that what I remembered was what actually happened."

"It was. And I think we should just forget about it, okay?"

His eyes searched mine for a moment, and then he nodded. "Okay. Then I'll just say thank you."

"For what?"

"For being there." He looked away again. "It was a… rough night."

It couldn't be easy for him, especially as the guide for our group, to have been so vulnerable in front of a stranger.

"I'm glad I could help." I turned toward my tent, then paused. "Rory? Wasn't it cold, sleeping outside?"

He shrugged. "Aye, a little, but it's always better than being inside." He turned on his heel and made for Tommy's tent.

It's always better than being inside…

I watched him go, wondering just how many times he'd awakened in a panic, alone in the dark, and had chosen to sleep outside with no walls or roof to close him in.

It took almost as long to break down my tent and get it to go back into its sack than it had to fail at setting it up, but I finally got everything packed away by the time we sat down to breakfast.

"How was everyone's night?" asked Tommy, who looked annoyingly bright-eyed and well rested. The others chimed in, while I just concentrated on my porridge. A quick glance at Rory showed that he was also focused very intently on his breakfast.

"And you, Amelia? Sleep well after the long day?" asked Tommy.

I looked up, meeting Rory's stare across the circle. In spite of the inscrutable look on his face, I knew what he was thinking, and for a crazy moment, I almost wanted to tell the truth. *Well, Tommy, since you asked, my night wasn't too bad until your buddy woke me up with his weird nightmare and kissed me in the dark. And that part wasn't exactly bad, either...*

Rory sat up straighter, as if he was reading my mind. His eyes burned into me, pleading with me not to say anything, and at the same time it almost seemed like he was daring me to.

Tommy cocked his head, looking from me to Rory and back to me. Shit, those blue eyes were more perceptive than he let on.

"Fine. It was fine," I said. "Looking forward to today's walk. It's like nine miles or so, right?"

Tommy narrowed his eyes at me, as if to say *I see what you did there*, but then nodded. "Aye, a lot easier than yesterday, and then you guys get to sleep in a B&B and eat real food tonight. More importantly, there will be beer..."

Rory finished his breakfast and got to his feet, heading for his backpack. I turned back to Tommy, who was chattering away, even as his gaze tracked his friend across the pebbled beach.

Next time, I'd need to be more careful about what I *didn't* say, as well as what I *did*.

Wait, what? There isn't going to be a next time! Ignoring the tingle in my lips, I crumpled my empty porridge package and stuffed it into my pack.

There was *not* going to be a next time.

Chapter Thirteen

Amelia

Tommy had said that today would be easier than yesterday, but you wouldn't know it from the first few miles. We started out by climbing back up the zig-zagging path we'd descended the night before. I'd thought my legs were used to steep ascents after yesterday's epic day, but it turned out that they weren't.

I trudged up the path, gritting my teeth to avoid whimpering at the soreness in my thighs and calves, mentally cursing the weight of my pack, the long, restless night on a thin mat, and Rory, who'd tried to apologize again. I mean, I appreciated that he was sorry for kissing me without getting my consent, but I'd told him it was fine. The fact that he kept apologizing hammered home that I'd been into it and he hadn't, and that just made me feel worse about the whole thing.

I really wished I could talk to Carrie about it. She always seemed to know the right thing to say.

We reached the top and stopped for a quick breather. I

took a swig of water and wiped the sweat from my brow.

"The next three kilometers or so—that's almost two miles to the Yanks—will be crossing a bog," said Rory, addressing the group for the first time that morning. "Stay to the high ground as much as possible, but you won't be able to completely avoid getting your feet wet. It's a good idea to put on your gaiters to keep your boot tops and pant legs dry, and avoid using your trekking poles through here—they'll only get stuck."

When everyone was situated, we moved out, shortly coming upon the bog, which was basically puddles of water and muck, sometimes hidden by long grass that made it look deceptively safe to step on but was actually a trap for innocent hiking boots.

If I occasionally looked up from my feet and happened to notice how Rory's tall, lean figure filled out his long-sleeved Under Armour shirt and cargo shorts, that was just so I could take mental notes for Carrie when she asked about the "hot guides." Not so I could remember how that strong body had felt beneath mine last night.

Our progress through the bog was slow. Rory stopped us when we reached one particular section, waiting for the group to catch up. As far as I could see, the ground was one big puddle, interspersed occasionally by a patch of grass or a heather shrub. How the hell did we cross that without getting soaked?

"The key to this is to keep moving," said Rory. "Step on the clumps of grass and heather. Just hop from one to the next, without letting your weight settle for more than a second or two." He led the way, his long legs carrying him easily through the bog as he hopped from one sturdy patch to the next without stopping.

He made it look so simple. I plotted out my path as best as I could, my attention focused on spotting those "safe" bits.

"So, what's up with you and Rory?" asked Tommy.

I froze with one foot on a patch of heather, the other in

midair, and would have toppled right into the muck if Tommy hadn't grabbed my arm to steady me. "Sorry," he muttered. "I'll wait until we're out of the bog to ask."

"Don't bother. There's nothing to tell," I said, trying to gracefully hop to the next clump of long grass. I felt his eyes on me and risked a quick glance. "Seriously. Nothing is 'up' with Rory and me. Why are you even asking?"

"I felt…something…during breakfast when I looked at the two of you."

"Aw, Tommy, I'm flattered, but I'm not into that sort of thing," I quipped.

He let out a surprised laugh at that. "It's always the quiet ones who say the dirtiest things. But you're deflecting…again. There was definitely some tension there this morning."

Crap. "Tommy, there's been tension between Rory and me since the first minute of the first day. You know that."

"This was different." At my glare, he held up his hands in surrender. "Look, if you're sure everything is okay, I'll stop bugging you about it."

I looked him in the eye and smiled. "Everything is okay. I promise."

"Okay. You seem to be doing great—as long as I'm not distracting you—so I'm going to go check on Pat and Linda." He caught up to them, and I breathed a sigh of relief.

"So, wait. *Did* something happen with you and Rory?"

Startled, I turned to see Molly and Megan blinking at me like ponytailed owls. Shit, I thought they were up ahead with the brothers and Rory. "What? No."

"I think she's lying," said Megan.

"She is *so* lying," said Molly. "Come on, you can tell us. You know you want to."

I forced myself to look them in the eyes, one after the other. "Guys, I swear, nothing happened with me and Rory. I don't even like him."

"Since when did liking someone have anything to do with it?" said Megan. "That lad is fi-i-ine, with that glorious hair and those sad eyes. I wouldn't need to like him to make out with him."

"Me, neither," said Molly, and the two bumped fists like kids on a playground.

"You guys," I said, smiling in spite of myself.

They linked arms with me, one on each side, and before I could say a word in protest, they dragged me the rest of the way through the bog, their quick, agile steps getting me over the tricky ground a lot faster than I would have done by myself.

By the time we reached the other side, we were all giggling. It felt so good to have someone to be silly with, even though I'd lied to them. I couldn't tell them what had happened without telling them why, and Rory's story wasn't mine to tell.

But it would have been nice to confide in someone.

Once we got through the bog and ascended to the grassy turf at the top of the cliffs, the rest of the day's walk was mostly uneventful. Beautiful views, of course—it was Skye, and everywhere had a beautiful view—but compared to yesterday's dramatic almost-eighteen-mile hike along the Trotternish Ridge, with its seemingly endless succession of high, windblown peaks, today's less-than-nine-mile walk to Portree was almost a letdown.

I stopped short. Had I really just thought that a day *without* ten summits, in bright sunny weather, was a letdown? That was a change from the first day, when I thought I would croak after eight miles. Carrie would be proud of me. *I* was proud of me.

Scarlet met us on the road leading into Portree and

walked the rest of the way in with us. "Three days down, four to go," she said with a big smile.

It was weird to think that in three days of walking, we'd only come the distance we'd driven in under an hour that first day. And a bit of a bummer to be back in the same place we'd started, but we were only passing through, and from tomorrow on, it would be all new territory again.

But knowing we were minutes away from a hot shower and a comfy bed gave us all an adrenaline boost, much like horses who speed up near the end of a trail, and we all walked a little faster to the B&B.

"Your rooms are ready. I didn't make any dinner reservations for you because I thought you might like to do your own thing tonight," Scarlet said. "I'll be at the bar in the restaurant we ate in that first night from six to seven or so this evening if anyone needs to talk to me about anything—any concerns about the rest of the trek, any issues you're having, whatever. And feel free to come say hi even if you're not having any issues. I'm much better company than these two numpties," she added with a grin, gesturing at Tommy and Rory.

I watched her walk off with Rory. She laid her hand on his shoulder, and he angled his head to talk to her, their bodies falling into step as if they were completely in tune with each other. I felt a sudden, sharp pang of jealousy. Was there something between them? Was Scarlet the one he'd thought he was kissing?

An image came into my mind of the two of them in an embrace, his hands sliding into her blonde hair as he kissed her. I shook my head to clear it. She didn't seem the type to shack up with her employees. I needed to get a grip. And I needed a shower.

But first, I needed to call Carrie.

Finally, I'd be able to tell someone about Rory.

Chapter Fourteen

Less than an hour later, after a debrief with Scarlet, Tommy and I sat in the dark corner of a pub, pint glasses of beer in front of us.

"Start talking," he said.

Tommy's perpetually cheerful demeanor led most people to think he was just a simple, happy-go-lucky lad who liked walking in the hills, but he had a psychology degree and had always been one for talking things out. He listened to every word, even if he didn't appear to be paying attention. He offered advice when he had some, but more often just acted as a sounding board. It made him a fantastic guide. Everyone responded to him, and by the end of the week, he knew their life stories—their hopes and dreams, their biggest regrets, whatever shit they'd be facing when they got home. And everyone always felt better after talking to him.

It was how we'd become friends in the first place. But that meant it was a pain in the ass to be around him if there was stuff I *didn't* want to discuss.

"What do you want to talk about?" I asked, being deliberately obtuse.

He rolled his eyes. "Come on, man. We've been mates for what, seven years? We've been through a lot of shit—shit that we've always been able to talk about. Why are you being so cagey now? Something's going on with you, and it involves a lass from the group we're guiding. You need to talk to me."

I took a long pull on my beer, wishing it was whisky. "I... had a rough night."

He nodded, unsurprised. "Nightmare?"

"Yeah."

"But that's not all, is it?"

I sighed. He wasn't going to stop until I told him everything, and he knew me too well for me to lie. I drained my glass and stood. "You ready for another yet?"

He raised his eyebrows. I wasn't usually a beer drinker, let alone a multiple-beer drinker. "Don't worry, Mum, I'm only having one more. I know we're working tomorrow."

"In that case, I'll be finished with this by the time you're back with my fresh one." I got us two more beers and sat back down, sliding one across to him. He accepted it with a nod of thanks. "Okay, now talk."

"I was having the nightmare—the unabridged version, complete with suffocating mist. I couldn't see, couldn't move, couldn't breathe."

He closed his eyes for a moment. When he opened them again, they were full of sympathy, and his mouth was tight with regret. "Shit, Rory, I should have crashed in your tent. I almost asked if you wanted me to. But you didn't look like you would have welcomed the company. I'm so sorry."

I shook my head, waving off his apology. "I would have said no. After that stupid fight with Amelia, I was in a shit mood."

He nodded. "Okay, so you had the nightmare. Then what happened?"

"I guess I was thrashing around, calling out, whatever," I muttered, feeling my face get hot. I cringed just imagining it, a twenty-two-year-old man crying out in his sleep like a wee lad—like the lad my father had loathed. "And Amelia heard and came in to check on me."

His eyes widened. "Shit—you *hit* her?"

I nearly spat beer at him. "What? Why the hell would you think that?"

"You said you were thrashing around in your sleep. I assumed you were going to say you flailed around and hit her."

I sighed. "No. I kissed her."

Now it was Tommy's turn to choke on his beer. "You did *what*?"

"You heard me."

"Aye, I heard you say you kissed her. I want to know how."

I felt my face get even hotter. "Fuck's sake, do I need to draw you a picture?"

He just stared at me. I leaned in so I could talk quietly. "I heard her calling me in my dream. I opened my eyes, and she was right there—I guess she'd been leaning over me, shaking my shoulder or something. I was still out of it, and she was like two inches away, and it just happened." He didn't need to know about the rest of it. "I'm sorry, man."

His brow furrowed. "Why are you apologizing?"

"I know you like her, and—"

He held up his hand. "Stop right there. I do like her, but just as a friend."

I crossed my arms over my chest, hoping my relief wasn't too obvious. "Really," I said skeptically.

"Aye, really."

"Then why is it that every time I look over, you're laughing with her or she has her hand on your arm, or vice versa?"

"Och, that's just a bit of flirting. You know I do it with everyone. Why, did it annoy you?" he asked slyly.

Yes. "No, why would I care?"

"Why, indeed."

"Stop psychoanalyzing me."

"Nope. Anyway, this would have been just a few hours after that ridiculous argument you two had, aye? So, did she slap you?"

She probably should have. "No, she was actually pretty understanding about it. But I've apologized a few times now, and she got mad at me for that."

"Interesting."

"What the hell does that mean?"

"I'm just saying that if she's mad at you for apologizing"— he made air quotes—"a few times now, then maybe there's more to it than you think."

"Oh, aye? Please, don't stop there, Doctor MacDonald," I said, rolling my eyes.

"Maybe she doesn't want you to be sorry you kissed her." He took a long swig of beer, then made a show of setting it down. He sat back with a smug look on his face. "What do you think about that?"

"I think you're a fucking numpty." There was no way she wasn't angry that I kissed her.

"Aye, that's not exactly breaking news," he said cheerfully. "But what if I'm right?"

"You're not." *But what if he was?*

"Are you sure? How did she respond when you kissed her?"

Even now, my body grew hot when I thought about it. "I... guess she might have been into it after the shock wore off." More than into it, if I believed what she'd said that morning. But I couldn't say more to Tommy without it feeling like I was betraying her trust.

"I dunno, man. It just sounds like there's more going on here than her being mad that you kissed her. There were definitely some...undercurrents...at breakfast, and when I asked her what was going on, she hedged as much as you did. Maybe she's not as immune to you as you think."

"Don't be daft."

"Just think about it."

"No, Tommy. I'm not going to go there. I *can't* go there. First of all, she keeps recording videos for someone back home, and she ends them by saying "I love you," so more than likely, she has a boyfriend. Second, we have half a week left on the trek, and then she's gone. Oh, and third, she hates me. And even if she didn't hate me, you know what happened with Emma. I'm not going through that again."

"First," he said, holding up his index finger, "you're totally speculating about the possible boyfriend back home. She was totally checking you out last night when you came out of the water all wet and muscley—even if she thought you were mental for going in the water in the first place. And that wasn't the first time, or the last. Second, I'm not saying you need to propose to the lass. Who's to say she wouldn't be up for a no-strings fling on the trek? Third, I don't think she hates you, and even if she did, it doesn't necessarily preclude her having a fling with you. And four, are you really going to compare her to Emma? I know that whole situation messed you up, but this could be just what you need to get over that."

"I'm pretty certain that Amelia is not one for a quick shag in a tent with a virtual stranger."

"Maybe you should find out."

A series of images popped into my head like a staticky film reel: Amelia in my arms, her lips parting for my kiss, her bare skin glistening with sweat as our bodies came together. I shook my head to clear it, shifting uncomfortably on the chair. "Enough, Tommy. I just have to get through the next four days of the trek without any more fucking nightmares or fights with Amelia, and I'll be happy."

"If you say so."

But as I finished my beer, I couldn't help but wonder if there was any truth to what he'd said.

Chapter Fifteen

AMELIA

The evening in Portree was nice. I had a glorious, hot shower to wash off the grime from two days on the trail, and then dinner (and drinks) at a pub. I talked to Gordon about the tourism company he owned in Fort Lauderdale, Florida. When I mentioned that I was going to be moving to Miami to work in a hotel, he gave me his card and invited me to reach out to him when I got there. I also had a beer with Scarlet, during which she told me about how she got into being a guide and starting her own company, and I told her about my upcoming job at the hotel.

But my burger and fries, while decent enough, didn't taste nearly as good as last night's Chicken Pad Thai, eaten with a spork out of a packet after being reconstituted with hot water.

And the bed, while infinitely more comfortable than a sleeping mat atop a bed of pebbles, felt almost like cheating.

"It sounds like you're enjoying the hike," my mom had

said on the phone when I called after dinner. *"I'm so glad."* But how could I let myself enjoy it? I couldn't forget why I was doing this—for Carrie, who should be the one hiking this trail. And I shouldn't be thinking about Rory, but it seemed like every time there was a quiet moment, my thoughts went right to him.

Things had been strained between us all day, after his umpteenth apology. Not that they'd ever been great, but now it was worse.

There'd been one awkward moment when we'd stopped for a break, and I'd happened to look over at him as he was wiping his face with the bottom of his shirt. When I finally tore my gaze away from his abs, I made eye contact with Tommy, whose huge grin indicated that he'd totally busted me checking out his friend. My face had grown hot, and I'd quickly busied myself with adjusting my pack, wishing I was bold enough to have just owned it. Looking away with my face bright red only made things worse.

But in spite of my embarrassment, as we'd continued the afternoon's walk, I couldn't stop my mind from wandering. And it kept goddamn going to the way Rory's lips had felt on mine.

My traitorous mind continued to torture me all through the night, showing me images of him chugging from his water bottle, the movement of his Adam's apple as he swallowed far more mesmerizing than it should have been. It showed me images of him running his long fingers through his windblown hair, and it showed me images of him striding from the water, droplets streaming down his chest.

It wasn't entirely the fault of the too-comfy bed that I didn't sleep well.

After a hearty breakfast at the B&B with Scarlet and a restocking stop at the market, we had a pre-walk briefing with Rory.

"Today's walk is about twelve miles. The terrain is pretty straightforward until we get to the last section along Loch Sligachan, where the path is rough and requires several river crossings, which can be a challenge if the water's high. But there's a great restaurant at the hotel in Sligachan, and you'll be sleeping in the bunkhouse there, so you'll be amply rewarded for getting through the day."

"Okay, everyone, have a good day, and I'll see you at the Slig for dinner," said Scarlet, reminding us that even though we'd be walking all day, she'd get to Sligachan in roughly twenty minutes on the road.

With the exception of about a mile of salt marsh, which required us to carefully navigate so we didn't get our feet wet, the first few miles were on paved road. Which I discovered was utter hell while wearing hiking boots, which were not made for pavement.

I know you're not bitching about your feet being sore, said Carrie's voice in my head. *Just remember why you're doing this. If it was easy, everyone would do it. Without some pain and hardship, it wouldn't be worth doing.*

I knew she was right—or at least, her voice in my head was—but that didn't make my feet feel better.

"Hey guys, let's take a break here," said Tommy. *Wait, a break?* I snapped out of my thoughts and looked around. We'd reached a crossroads, with a sign pointing to the left that read "Camustianavaig."

"How's everyone feeling?" Tommy asked. The response was a cacophony of complaints about sore feet from the paved road. "Right, so I have good news and bad news. Bad news first: there's another four or so miles of paved road before we get to the loch."

"And the good news?" asked Gordon.

"The good news is that we can take a detour to climb Ben Tianavaig, which will get us off the road for a couple hours. There's a fantastic view from the top, but it's about fifteen hundred feet up—and down again—so if you're already feeling knackered, you may want to skip it. If some of you don't want to go, I'll take you ahead to Sligachan and you'll get a head start on the beer while Rory takes the rest of you up. What say you all?"

The thought of doing that climb, with my feet already sore from walking on the road, was really unappealing. And it might be a good idea for me to have Rory out of my sight for a few hours, anyway.

"I think I'll sit this one out, if that's cool," I said.

"No problem," said Tommy. "Anyone else?"

"Oh, come on, Amelia!" said Linda. "If Pat and I can do it, you certainly can."

That wouldn't have been enough to make me agree to do the climb, but then I thought of Carrie. *She* would totally do it. And she'd be bummed if I didn't, though she wouldn't have insisted.

"It'll be fun!" said Megan. "You don't want to miss out, do you?"

When it came down to it, no, I didn't—and I didn't want Carrie to, either. Plus, it was nice to know that they all genuinely wanted me with them. "Okay, you convinced me. I'll go."

We took a short break, everyone taking off their packs and sitting on the ground for a snack and some water.

"You shouldn't go up if you don't want to."

A little shiver of pleasure ran through me at the sound of Rory's voice. I looked up to see him looming over me. "Why not? Everyone else is." I cringed as I said it. I could hear my mother's voice. *Just because everyone else is doing it doesn't mean you should.*

He squatted down beside me. "*That's* why you want to go up Ben Tianavaig, because everyone else is?"

"Why? Do you want me to stay behind?"

He tipped down his sunglasses. "No, I don't want you to stay behind," he said quietly, gazing at me with those eyes, clear green like sea glass. "I just don't think you should let anyone force you into climbing a fifteen-hundred-foot hill you don't want to climb."

I couldn't think when he stared at me like that. I looked at his unsmiling mouth, remembering how those lips had felt against mine. I wished he would smile. I wished he would kiss me again…

"Amelia?"

I dragged my eyes back to his. His expression was unreadable, but his cheeks were slightly pink, and I wondered if he'd been remembering our kiss, too, and wishing it would happen again. Then I remembered what we were talking about.

"No one's forcing me. I didn't come all this way just to sit out."

"There's no shame in admitting you need a break."

And we were back to the condescension I hadn't heard in two days. The pleasure I'd felt that he was talking to me, the desire for him to kiss me, winked out like a light.

"What I *need* is to go up goddamn Ben Tianavaig, see this amazing view I keep hearing about, and take some pictures. If you don't want me around, why don't you just come out and say it?" I knew I sounded petulant and ridiculous—I *knew* it—and yet I couldn't seem to stop myself. The more he tried to talk me out of it, the more I was determined to go—determined to prove to him that I could do it.

Thwack! He slammed his palm down on his knee, so hard I jumped. "Damn it, Amelia, stop putting words in my mouth! Why are you being so goddamn stubborn?"

My face hot, I glanced around, but no one else seemed to have heard. "Why do *you* have to be such a jerk about everything? It's bad enough that you've had some kind of issue with me from the first moment we met, but I thought maybe after the way you had your tongue in my mouth the other night, we'd be past that. I guess not." As I said the words, his eyes widened and the color drained from his face, and I wished I could take them back.

But it was too late. I laid my hand on his arm, and he flinched as if I'd burned him. *Shit.* I needed to say something, to explain *why...* "Rory, I—"

He got to his feet, the movement lacking his usual grace. "You want to go up Ben Tianavaig, fine. I'm done arguing with you. God knows you *need* more fucking pictures."

He stalked off without a backward glance.

I closed my eyes and dropped my head into my hands. Why did I keep doing this? I could picture Carrie slowly shaking her head, her mouth tight with disappointment. *Babe, that was pretty harsh. It's one thing to stand up for yourself, but this went beyond that. You need to apologize this time, no excuses.*

If he'd even listen to me.

I chatted with Molly and Megan for part of the way up Ben Tianavaig, trying to keep my mind off the argument with Rory. But after a while, I intentionally fell back a bit under the guise of taking a photo and told them to go on ahead. I needed some solitude.

I had been truly horrible to Rory. Part of that was an instinctive response to being told not to do something—it just made me want to do it even more, like a rebellious teenager.

And the other part? I didn't want to admit that maybe he was right that I could use a break from yet another ascent and descent. But that didn't give me the right to be a heinous bitch to him—to bring up the kiss he was obviously still conflicted about. After the fight about the tent, I'd vowed to stop picking fights with him, but I couldn't seem to help myself.

I reached the top of Ben Tianavaig, and my argument with Rory faded into the background. We'd summited a number of peaks so far—of varying heights and difficulties. But that feeling of taking that last step up to the top never got old. And this was no different.

The view was amazing. I could see Portree harbor and all the way back to the Storr and Trotternish Ridge.

I snapped a few photos—knowing Rory was probably watching me do it and rolling his eyes in disgust—and then I remembered what he'd said when we watched the eagle. I lowered the phone and just *looked*. I looked at the harbor, remembering the peace I'd felt gazing out at the anchored boats on that first night. I looked at the Trotternish Ridge, stretching into the hazy distance like the spine of a stegosaurus. I looked at the Old Man of Storr, the solitary pinnacle that was such a Skye icon.

Skye was utterly stunning. Everywhere. Each time I thought *this is the best view yet*, we'd get to the top of another peak or ridge and *that* view was the best one.

The others had all sat down for a break, but I stayed where I was. I looked to the north, back the way we'd come, and opened the voice recorder on my phone. "I'm sorry I told you I wouldn't do this hike with you. It's the hardest thing I've ever done, but it's so worth it, and I promise to come back and hike it again with you when you're better." I shuddered, remembering how she'd looked the last time I'd seen her. "You need to get better."

My voice broke, and I sniffed back tears. "Oh, Carrie,"

I murmured, "I keep acting so awful to Rory, when what I really want is for him to kiss me again. I wish you were here to tell me what to do. You always know the right things to say." I swallowed hard. "I...I've become someone I don't think you'd like very much. Anyway, I'm sorry...so sorry, for everything. I'm going to apologize to Rory and I'm going to do better from now on. I love you, and I miss you."

I ended the recording and turned away from the edge. And stopped short. Rory stood barely two feet away. His sunglasses were in place, but I could feel his gaze on me.

Well, I'd wanted to apologize, and now was as good a time as any. I took a deep breath. "Rory, I'm—"

"It's time to go," he said. He stepped back so I could go in front of him, clearly not interested in anything I had to say. And really, why would he be?

I started down the trail, thinking of Carrie and how it was my fault she wasn't here; of Rory, who would probably never speak to me again. *I'm such a fuckup.* I used to think I was a nice person—a *good* person—but now? I didn't know who I was anymore.

My vision blurred, turning the steep, rocky path before me into a gray smear. I stepped down—

—and my foot jammed hard into the rock below, which was farther than it had looked through my veil of tears.

My knee buckled. It felt like a hot knife ripped through it as I went down, crying out in pain.

Chapter Sixteen

I slid a few feet down the slope. A wave of nausea rolled over me, and I clenched my teeth so hard I could hear them grinding together as I tried not to puke.

Footsteps slid to a halt beside me. "Amelia, are you all right?"

Rory's face swam before me. I blinked hard, shaking loose the tears, and he came into focus. "It hurts, Rory," I gasped. "My knee…"

"Take her pack, Tommy." Hands brushed impersonally down my front, unclipping the straps. My pack was tugged from my shoulders, and then Tommy sat beside me, his arm around my back.

Rory took my hand. "Deep breaths—in through your nose, out through your mouth." His voice was calm, soothing, and I instinctively obeyed. "Good. And again, slowly—that's it. Look at me."

I stared into his eyes, soft gray-green, like the sea during a rainstorm. There was no sign of his earlier anger. "I'm going to examine your knee. It will hurt, but I have to do it, okay?"

I nodded, bracing myself for even more pain.

"Here, hold my hand," said Tommy. I let go of Rory and clutched Tommy's hand.

Rory knelt in front of me and rolled up both my pant legs to above the knee. *At least I shaved my legs last night*, I thought, stifling the more-than-slightly-hysterical giggle that threatened to break free at the absurd thought.

He thoroughly examined my knee, moving it back and forth, up and down, side to side, then did the same actions on my other knee for comparison.

All through those excruciating minutes, he kept telling me to breathe. *In through your nose, out through your mouth. That's it. You're doing great.*

My hand hurt from crushing Tommy's fingers. "I'm sorry," I gasped, after one particularly hard squeeze.

"Don't worry, love, squeeze as hard as you need to."

Something cool and metallic pressed against my lips. "Take a sip, lass—just a small one," said Rory. Liquid filled my mouth, and I reflexively swallowed. It burned slightly going down, leaving behind a smoky, not-unpleasant taste. Whisky. "One more sip."

I felt warm all over, and the pain receded a bit. I opened my eyes. Rory knelt beside me, a silver flask in his hand, his eyes worried. *That can't be good.* "What happened?"

I licked my lips, brushed away the tears. "I...misjudged the distance as I stepped down, and my foot jammed into the rock. My knee gave out. And it felt like a hot knife was being stabbed into it."

He nodded, unsurprised. "I'm pretty sure you sprained one of the ligaments in your knee. Without an MRI, it's hard to be sure." He pulled out the first aid kit from his pack. "I'm going to wrap it." His hands fast and efficient, he wrapped an

ACE bandage around my knee and secured it, then rolled down my pants legs. "Take these." He dropped three pills into my hand.

"What are they?"

"Just ibuprofen. Here." He handed me a half-full bottle of water. "Sorry—this is mine, but it'll be easier than using the tube from your CamelBak."

I swallowed the pills with a swig of water and handed the bottle back to him. "Thanks."

"Let's see if you can stand." He nodded to Tommy, and with the two of them supporting me, they got me upright, with my weight on my left foot.

"Can you put any pressure on your right foot?"

Steeling myself, I slowly placed my right foot down and shifted some of my weight to it.

Pain shot through my knee, and I staggered. Rory caught me. "Here, lean on your poles and try again." He handed me the left, which I planted in the grass. "Now the right. It's okay, I'll hold on to you." His left arm came around my shoulders.

Slowly letting go of him, I took the right pole and dug it into the ground. "Now see if you can stand on both feet."

I leaned forward slightly, supporting myself on the poles, and put my right foot down. My knee hurt—a lot—but I stayed upright.

"Good. Try taking a few steps, using your poles for support."

I shook my head. "I can't." What if I fell again?

"I promise I won't let you fall. Go on now, nice and easy."

His strength gave me confidence, and I hesitantly took a step with my left foot, and then my right. More pain, but I did it. And then another step. Left, then right.

"Good!" he exclaimed. I flicked my gaze to him.

He was *smiling.* Okay, it wasn't a real smile—not even a grin, just a curve of his lips. But still. Figured that it took me fucking up my knee to make that happen. *And I'd do it again if he'd smile for real.* I shifted slightly, and my knee screamed. *Okay, maybe not.*

His hand tightened on my arm. "All right?"

I nodded. "Let me try by myself." He let go, and I took a few more steps, leaning heavily on the poles. My knee hurt, but the leg held.

"You're doing great, Amelia. Can you carry your pack?"

"I think so?"

He helped me slip it on. I tightened the straps across my chest and waist and took a few more steps. The weight of the pack made it more difficult, but I stayed upright.

He shrugged on his own pack. "Okay, let's get you down this hill."

The ground was relatively level at first, and the going was slow, but steady. Then we reached a downward slope. I took a tentative step, and my knee buckled. "Shit!" I said as Rory caught my arm and kept me upright. I tried another step, but it was too much.

"Tommy!" he called. Tommy was up ahead, catching up to the group. He trotted back to us. "Can you take her pack and poles?"

"Of course."

I unclipped the chest and waist straps and Tommy eased the pack from my shoulders and set it on the ground. He secured my poles to the pack, scooped it up, and strode off as if it weighed nothing.

Before I could blink, I was swept off my feet. Rory's right arm was around my back, his left arm under my knees. I gaped at him. "What are you doing?"

"Your knee isn't stable enough for the descent."

"You're...going to carry me down the hill?"

"Yep," he said, matter-of-factly.

"With your pack on your back?" Mine had to weigh

thirty pounds or more—and he had more stuff than I did.

"Yep." He started walking, and I tightened my arms around him, hanging on for dear life. If he stumbled...

He stopped. "Amelia," he said, his breath soft against my ear. I turned my head to look at him. "You're strangling me. Relax."

"If you lose your balance—"

"I'm not going to fall," he said, interrupting me, "and I'm not going to drop you. Trust me."

I looked into his eyes. They were calm and steady, confident. I loosened my death grip around his neck and let my weight settle against his chest.

"That's it. Just relax."

He started forward again. The rhythmic left-step-right-step motion of his body was strangely lulling, and I leaned my head on his shoulder and closed my eyes. If I didn't see what he was doing, maybe it wouldn't freak me out.

With my eyes closed, my other senses were amplified. I heard a cuckoo calling, somewhere to my right, and the swish-swish of Rory's pack as he moved. I felt his strong arms around my back and under my knees, his even breaths against my face. I smelled the citrusy scent of his soap, the coffee he'd had with breakfast, the not-unpleasant scent of his sweat.

Then my body started to tip. I gasped, tightening my arms around his neck, my eyes shooting open. "It's okay. We're at the bottom, and I'm just setting you down."

We were at the bottom already? I blinked, then looked around. We were on flat ground. Rory led me to a boulder and helped me sit. Tommy gave me my poles and set my pack at my feet.

The others gathered around, looking worried, asking if I was all right.

"Rory thinks I sprained one of the ligaments in my knee." He stood a few feet away, conferring with Tommy, their voices too low for me to hear.

"Oh, you poor thing," Pat whispered, taking my hand. "That's your trek ended."

My trek, ended? I'd been so focused—first on the pain, and then on praying that Rory didn't drop me—that I hadn't even thought about what the injury meant.

No. It can't be.

"Hey guys, go have your lunch while we get Amelia sorted," said Rory. When they scattered, he knelt beside me. "I'm going to call Scarlet to come get you."

"No!" I clutched his arm, hard enough that his eyes widened in surprise. I heard the hysteria in my voice but couldn't help it. I *couldn't* stop now. "Please don't call Scarlet. I can't quit now."

"What are you talking about? You need to get to a doctor and have your knee looked after. I'm sorry, but—"

"I need to finish the trek!"

His eyes were sad as he shook his head. "I'm sorry, Amelia, but you can't."

No! All the sorrow and guilt and self-loathing I'd stuffed down inside me for the last three weeks welled up, and I started sobbing.

Rory gently squeezed my shoulder. "I know it hurts, but it will start to feel better once you get some ice and rest it."

"You don't understand! I have to finish the trek. I have to!" I shoved him back and lurched to my feet, needing to prove to him I could walk—but as if to spite me, my knee buckled again, and I went down.

Chapter Seventeen

Rory

The sound that Amelia made as she hit the ground was indescribable. It was agony and anger and sorrow and I didn't know what else, and it tore through me like a knife in my guts. It was even worse than watching her fall and being unable to stop it.

I wanted to wrap my arms around her and make her pain go away.

Where the hell did that thought come from?

I helped her to sit with her back against the rock and her leg resting on her rucksack. I activated an instant cold pack and wrapped it in a bandanna before setting it gently on her knee. "Keep this on for as long as you can stand it."

She held it in place, then looked up at me, her eyes red-rimmed and bright with tears. "Rory, *please*. I have to finish the trek."

"Amelia, you can't. There's no way—"

"Please, you don't understand!" Now there was

desperation in her eyes in addition to everything else. She grabbed my hand. "I need to do it, for Carrie! *She's* the one who should have been out here, not me, and it's my fault that she's... I have to do this for her, because she wanted to hike Skye more than anything, and maybe if she knows that I did, she'll..."

She trailed off, shaking her head. Her words were almost like a stream of consciousness and nearly incoherent, but I knew that desperate helplessness. I squeezed her hand, and she looked up, startled, as if she'd forgotten I was there. "Tell me."

"Carrie's my best friend, the sister I never had. She's the hiker, I'm the beach girl. This was supposed to be her dream trip—her college graduation gift from her parents—and I was supposed to meet her after for a week of sightseeing in Scotland. She'd talked about nothing else for months. And then...we were in my car, fighting about something so stupid, and I was yelling at her, which I *never* do, and I looked away from the road for one minute. Just one minute," she whispered, her voice breaking. She lowered her head, a lock of hair falling into her face.

Dread settled in the pit of my stomach like a rock. As if of its own accord, my hand reached out and lifted her chin. Tears streamed down her face, and she looked so damn lost. I tucked the lock of hair behind her ear.

"What happened, Amelia?"

Her lip quivered. "I didn't see the stop sign. And the truck—he didn't have a stop sign, and he couldn't swerve in time. He slammed right into her side of the car."

Oh no. "Is she...?"

"Broken femur, broken ribs, broken arm," she recited. "And she's in a c-coma. They don't know... It was my fault, and I walked away without a scratch. And she might..."

Die. She didn't need to finish the sentence.

Suddenly it all made sense—the endless photographs and videos in which she'd said "I love you and I miss you" into the microphone. That call where she'd said she should have been there, not thousands of miles from home. Her lack of preparation for the hike. And her need to go up Ben Tianavaig today.

She'd taken it upon herself to do the hike for her friend, even though she'd never done something like this before. And I'd made that comment about her taking pictures. I should have known there was more to it than that.

I knew what she was feeling—guilt, sorrow, worry, fear, self-loathing—I knew all of it. And my heart broke for her.

"I thought if I took her place on the trek and experienced it *for* her—took a million photos and described everything in detail, I could somehow get her to wake up. I call her mom when I can, and she holds the phone to Carrie's ear. But it hasn't worked. I mean, rationally I know I can't make her wake up, but still..." Her breath hitched in her throat. "And now, because of my stupid knee, I can't finish the hike, can't go home and tell Carrie—"

"I'll help you finish." The words were out of my mouth before I thought them through. But I didn't regret them.

Her mouth dropped open. "What?" she whispered. Her eyes shot up to mine, and the light of hope that suddenly appeared in them sent a feeling of warmth—of rightness—through me that I hadn't felt in a long time. Maybe not ever.

"I'll help you finish the trek," I repeated. "If you trust me to."

Her brow crinkled. "Why wouldn't I?"

"I haven't exactly been at my best this week," I muttered, my face growing warm. Freaking out on Tommy, the nightmare, the kiss. The way I couldn't keep from shouting at her. "I could tell you until hell freezes over that you're safe with me, that I'm damn good at what I do and that I'll get you to the end of the trail no matter how long it takes, but—"

Her fingers wrapped around mine, and I looked into her velvet-brown eyes. "I trust you. Please don't take back your offer. It would mean everything to me if you could help me finish the trek."

I searched her face for any sign of uncertainty. If she didn't trust me, this would never work. But her eyes were clear, her gaze steady on mine.

"I'm not going to take it back. But you have to follow my directions without question. If I say we need to stop so you can rest your knee, then we stop. If I say that we can't go on due to the conditions, or because your injury is too severe, you have to accept that. Can you handle doing what I tell you to do, without argument?"

She blushed, her lips curving in a sheepish smile. "I mean, I can't promise not to argue a little bit. But I trust that you're the expert, and I will follow your directions."

"Good enough." Even after witnessing my meltdown and then the weird aftermath of my nightmare, she trusted me. Maybe it was because she was desperate, but she was a smart woman. If she was afraid that I would somehow endanger her, she wouldn't have agreed.

And I couldn't deny that there was a small part of me that looked forward to arguing with her. I wasn't sure what that said about me.

"Rory, can I speak to you for a minute?" Tommy sounded…un-Tommy-like. He turned and walked a few feet away, but not before I saw the look on his face. It was one I hadn't seen in a very long time.

"I'll be right back. You should eat something in the meantime."

"I will."

I pushed to my feet and joined Tommy. "Are you mental?" he asked without preamble. "She can barely walk. We can't ask the rest of the paying clients to go at a snail's pace."

"I wasn't planning to."

"Then what...?"

"You're going to take the group on ahead, and I'll stay behind with Amelia and help her do the rest of the trek."

His mouth dropped open, and then he snapped it shut. "You know Scarlet's rules. Two guides for the Skye Trail."

"I know. Which is why I'm going to call her and ask her to take my place."

"And if she says no?"

"Then I'll quit, and she'll have to come anyway."

He stared at me. "What the hell is the matter with you? This morning you could barely look at the lass, and now you're risking your fucking job to help her on a whim?"

"It's not a whim. Her best friend—practically her *sister*, who was supposed to do the trek, is in a coma, because of an accident that Amelia blames herself for." Tommy closed his eyes briefly, then reopened them, his expression sad—and understanding. "She's been taking the damn pictures for her friend, while all this time I thought she was just another social media addict obsessed with how many likes she got on Instagram. Now do you get why she has to finish—and why I have to be the one to help her?"

He nodded. "I do get it. But..." He broke off and looked down, then back up again, his eyes troubled. "Will you be all right? I know it's been...a tough few days."

Anger rose up inside me, but just as quickly dissipated. I could never be mad at Tommy for speaking his mind. We'd been through too much together.

"Aye, it has been a tough few days. But she trusts me to get her to the end, Tommy. I need to do this, just as much as Amelia does—maybe even more. Do you understand?"

"I do," he said solemnly. "You'll be careful out there?"

"Always."

And just like that, the argument was over.

I grabbed my phone and walked away from the group, not wanting anyone to overhear my certain-to-be-ugly call with Scarlet. At least, being near the village, I could get decent reception on my mobile.

She answered on the first ring. "Rory, what's wrong? Where are you?"

"Camustianavaig. Amelia's hurt. It's her knee."

"What happened?"

"She jammed her foot on the descent from Ben Tianavaig. I'm pretty sure she sprained something."

"Shit. Okay, I'm getting in the van now, and I'll be there in—"

"Wait, Scarlet. I have to ask you a favor."

"You can ask me while I'm driving. I don't want to delay the group any more than they already are."

"I need you to listen to me first."

"Make it quick," she said. I knew her brusque tone wasn't directed at me—*yet*; it was because she prided herself on an excellent track record, with a 95 percent success rate of her trekkers finishing without incident.

"I need you to take my place as guide." Silence. I hurried to continue. "Amelia needs to finish the trek, and I'm going to help her."

"Are you kidding me?"

"No. Listen, there are reasons—"

"Sutherland, I couldn't care less about her reasons. And frankly, I'm stunned that you would even suggest this after everything that happened with Emma."

I was glad she couldn't see my face flush. "I'm not—that's not why."

"Then why the hell are you even wasting my time with this?"

"Because I know exactly what she's going through!" I

told her what Amelia had shared with me about Carrie. "The helplessness, the guilt—I know what it's doing to her, and I have to help her, Scar." Scarlet knew about my past. I couldn't in good conscience let her hire me without telling her about it. She'd put me through a pretty strict trial period, observing me on the Skye Trail and other trails more than once over a period of several months before she officially hired me. And it had never come up since the day I told her.

More silence. Then, "And if I say no?"

"Then I'll quit, and you'll have no choice. But I don't want it to come to that. You owe me one, Scarlet. I've given my life to SBF for the last three years, rushed to fill in on more than one trek at the drop of a hat without a moment's hesitation. And I've never asked you for anything in return. I'm asking now."

"You're putting me in a terrible position, Rory. You know I'm already struggling to keep up with coordinating the treks and managing the bookings these past few months. It's not easy for me to drop everything to go out on the trail."

"I know, and I'm sorry."

She sighed. "I need an hour or so to get my gear together and take care of a few things. I'll drive to Broadford and leave the van at the end of the trail, and I'll ring Eddie to drive me back up the road to Sligachan. I'll meet the group along the way as soon as I can. But Rory, how are you going to manage?"

"We'll take it as slowly as we have to, and make camp when she can't go any farther. We'll stop near Camustianavaig tonight so she can rest her knee, and set out in the morning."

"They're expecting rain for tomorrow, so take care on the crossings before Sligachan, okay?"

"I will."

"And don't be any more foolish than you're already being. If you need help, call me."

"I will, I promise."

"Oh, and Rory?"

"Yeah?"

"If this goes badly, you'll be putting SBF and my career at risk. I'm agreeing to this against my better judgment because I trust *your* judgment. Don't make me regret trusting you, and don't ask me to do something like this again. Next time, I'll let you quit." She disconnected the call before I could reply.

I started back to the group, feeling like I'd just been called before the headmaster. Tommy met me halfway. "So, do you still have a job?" His tone was casual, but his eyes were worried.

"For now. Scarlet wasn't happy, but she agreed to take my place."

Tommy grinned, his relief evident. "How'd you manage that? She would have sacked my ass for even suggesting it."

"Oh, I'm on the shit list, trust me. Listen, she wants you to get back on the trail with the group. She'll leave the van in Broadford and meet you on the way to Sligachan."

We walked over to the group to tell them the news. I knew they were surprised that we were even considering letting Amelia continue, even more so that I was going to help her do it, but no one said anything...at least not to me.

I returned to Amelia. "Are you positive that you want to continue? There's still time for you to change your mind. I can call Scarlet back and have her come get you."

"I'm sure—if you're sure."

"Let's do this, then."

Tommy handed me two fuel canisters for the camp stove. "Take these, in case you end up wild camping more than you anticipate. Scarlet will have extras."

"Thanks." I placed them on the ground beside my pack.

"You have food, chlorine tablets for water?" I nodded.

"And you have your map, right?"

I rolled my eyes. "Of course I do. But you know I know the way, right? I *have* done this before. We'll be fine."

"I know you will. Just…don't be a hero, okay? If the weather looks dodgy, be smart about it. After the Sligachan Hotel, there's no shelter till the bothy at Camasunary. If it rains, the burns might flood, and crossing them will be difficult for Amelia. And if it rains hard, there'll be erosion on the cliff trail to Elgol. You'll have to—"

"Tommy, I *know*. Believe me, I'm not going to put her in danger. If it gets that bad, I'll suggest we quit." Though she likely wouldn't listen to that advice.

"Don't put yourself in danger, either."

"Tommy."

"I know, I'm being a worried mother hen. I'm sure you'll be fine. You'll get the lass safely and triumphantly to the end of the infamous Skye Trail, and win her heart in the process," he added with a grin.

What? "Where the hell did that come from?"

"Just keep an open mind, that's all I'm saying."

An image came into my head of Amelia and me, our bodies entwined, our hands all over each other, her crying out my name as she… No, I couldn't go there.

"Get outta here, you numpty," I said, my face hot.

We returned to the others, who were saying goodbye to Amelia. She hugged everyone, leaning heavily on one pole, her mouth tight with pain. Then she turned to Tommy.

"Thank you for everything," she said. He wrapped his arms around her and then whispered something in her ear that made her eyes go wide and her face turn red. *What was that about?* Then he kissed her cheek and stepped back. "Look after this guy, okay?"

"I'm pretty sure it'll be the other way around." She glanced at me. "As you've seen, I'm pretty helpless."

"Don't say that, lass. You're not helpless, you just got hurt. It can happen to anyone."

He turned to me next, pulling me into a bear hug, then scruffed up my hair like we were kids again, grinning when I smoothed it back into place. "You need anything, you call, okay? And be careful out there."

"I will. Don't worry."

His eyes searched my face. "I *do* worry about you, Rory." He clasped my shoulder and then looked at Amelia. "Be nice to each other, okay? Catch ya on the flip side."

He shouldered his pack and trudged off with the others, stopping at the road to wave. We watched in silence as they disappeared from sight.

And then I was alone with Amelia. Who I'd argued with since the first day. Who I'd kissed while coming out of a nightmare and had wanted to kiss every moment since then. Who had sprained her knee and insisted on completing the Skye Trail anyway.

It was likely I was about to make the second biggest mistake of my life.

Chapter Eighteen

AMELIA

I watched the group vanish from view, wiping away a few (more) tears. I'd gotten pretty choked up when I'd said goodbye to them, particularly to Molly, Megan, Pat, and Linda, whom I'd become strangely close to in the few short days I'd known them. Would I ever see them again? Probably not—they all lived in the UK, and though we'd all promised to email each other, it wasn't the same. Though Megan's parting words had been "Have fun alone on the trail with Rory. Do us all proud," which had made me laugh in spite of my tears.

I sank onto the boulder, grateful to get off my feet, dreading the rest of the day.

I could barely walk, yet I somehow thought I could complete this trail.

Not to mention that Rory was clearly dealing with some kind of PTSD that caused him to freak out on his best friend and have terrible nightmares.

Was I insane to even think about being alone on the trail

with Rory, who may or may not be unstable?

No. He wasn't unstable. If he was, he wouldn't be working for Scotland By Foot. Scarlet seemed too on the ball to have a guide who might be a danger to the clients. And Tommy wouldn't have let him stay behind with me. If I knew one thing about Rory, it was that Tommy loved him like a brother and trusted him with his life. That was obvious enough, even though I'd only known them a few days.

Why had he offered to help me, when we could barely spend two civil minutes together? It obviously had to do with what I told him about Carrie. Or was it something else entirely?

Tommy thought I was into Rory—and that he was into me. *"If there's an opportunity for you to kiss him this time, you should take it. While you're both awake,"* he'd whispered in my ear when he'd hugged me goodbye. I should have expected that Rory would tell Tommy what happened the other night, but I hadn't thought Tommy had picked up on my conflicted feelings about it, or that he thought it was a good idea.

Which it wasn't. At all. And likely not even on the table anyway, after the things I'd said to him.

"Think you can walk for a bit?" Rory asked. "Just to the other side of the village. We'll take the afternoon off for you to rest your knee and then head out in the morning."

I was relieved, but surprised. He was going to give up hours of walking time? "Are you sure? I mean, it's only midday…"

He rolled his eyes. "The smell of Tommy's socks hasn't even faded from the air, and you're already arguing with me?"

I snorted with laughter—and was rewarded with a grin in return. His eyes sparkled, and there was a deep crease in his right cheek that I hadn't seen before—because he hadn't smiled like that before.

It was like a ray of sunlight shining through a dark cloud, and my heart skipped a beat.

It was so worth the wait.

"You should smile more often," I blurted out. Then immediately wished I'd kept my damn mouth shut, because the smile immediately dropped from his face like a switch had been flicked.

"I leave the smiling to Tommy," he quipped, but the moment was over. He picked up my pack. "Let's head over to the bay so we can get situated. We'll take it slow."

Clearly, our conversation was over. Because I didn't know when *not* to speak. I carefully pushed upright and balanced my weight on my left foot. I turned so he could slide the pack onto my shoulders, then grabbed my poles. "I'm ready when you are." Big words, considering I couldn't stand without help.

He shrugged into his own pack. "Okay, let's go." He moved to my right side and took my arm. I opened my mouth to protest, but the look in his eyes stopped me.

It was going to be a long few days.

• • •

The walk to the village was a slow one. I ended up being grateful for Rory's support, because my knee was throbbing and shaky, and only his quick reflexes and the strength in his forearm kept me from falling on more than one occasion. And that was on a paved road—what the hell was I going to do once we were on the trail?

Thankfully, he didn't say anything when I failed to hide the tears of pain and frustration, though at one point he handed me a napkin from his pocket so I could wipe my eyes. In fact, we didn't speak at all, except for him telling me to watch my step or asking if I was all right after the zillionth time I nearly fell.

Why did I have to make that comment about him smiling? We'd actually been getting along for five minutes, and now, this tense silence.

God, this was a terrible idea. And then I pictured Carrie, so pale and small in her hospital bed, her leg in traction, her right arm in a cast, her head bandaged, hooked up to so many machines you could barely tell there was a human under there.

Because of me.

And suddenly, it didn't matter whether Rory and I passed the rest of this trek in complete silence and without eye contact. I was there for one reason, and that wasn't to make friends or engage in small talk with my taciturn guide.

It was to finish this trek so that Carrie would wake up. I had to believe it was possible, because the alternative was unthinkable.

The village was tiny, and I didn't see any B&Bs or hostels, or even more than a small convenience store. "Where are we staying tonight?"

"We're going to camp on the beach."

"Oh." I didn't want to protest or start another fight, but camping on the beach? With my knee?

He looked at me sympathetically. "There aren't any B&Bs or hostels in Camustianavaig, and it's too far to the next village. You need to get off that leg as soon as possible. It'll be fine, I promise."

"Okay." I would have to trust him on this, like I was trusting him on everything else. But there was no way this wasn't going to suck.

We passed through the village and came out onto a rock-strewn beach, not unlike the one from the other night. We walked a short distance down, so we'd be out of sight and out of the way. Every wobble of my foot on the small rocks was agonizing. But I kept my mouth shut, forcing myself not to ask when we'd be able to stop. I needed to be strong—if I couldn't handle this, he'd never let me do the rest of the trail.

We stopped in a not-too-pebbly spot where we'd be mostly sheltered from the wind. Rory helped me to a large rock. I gingerly lowered myself to sit and slung my pack to the ground. He unclipped my tent and began to set it up.

"Can I help with that?" I winced as I said the words, remembering what happened the last time I tried to set up my own tent.

He glanced over, his eyes lit with—was that *humor*? "I've got it."

"Right. I'll just sit here and supervise," I said. His lips quirked at that. Okay, maybe things weren't going to be awful.

I watched as he quickly and easily threaded the tent poles through the nylon sleeves and anchored it in place. He set up my sleeping mat and sleeping bag, too.

"Why don't you go in and lie down for a while, get that leg up."

"Okay," I said.

He raised his eyebrows. "You're not going to argue with me?"

"Nope. I'm tired and sore, and lying down sounds amazing right now."

He looked almost disappointed, like he'd been *hoping* for an argument. But he just took my arm and ushered me into the tent, and then helped me lower myself to the ground. He brought my pack inside and set it at my feet, then removed my boots and socks. I stripped off my outer shirt and folded it up for a pillow, straightened my T-shirt, and lay back. Rory helped me elevate my leg on top of the pack. "Do you need anything else right now?"

"No, thanks." He nodded and slipped out, partially zipping the tent door. I closed my eyes, grateful for the chance to rest.

• • •

The air inside the car was full of tension. "I can't believe this," said Carrie. "I've asked you to come hiking with me for years and you've always said no. You've never wanted to share that part of my life. And I was disappointed, but I sucked it up because you're my best friend and I love you and we don't have to have all the same interests. And suddenly, you're going to do it for a guy? That's shitty, Amelia. Really shitty." She sank back against the seat and crossed her arms over her chest, her expression hurt.

Guilt swept through me, but I forced it back. Chris was the first guy to catch my interest in a long time, and while I truly didn't want to go hiking, he'd asked me to come with him and I wasn't about to say no.

"You know what, Carrie? You need to stop acting like a goddamn baby about this. It isn't always about you!"

She muttered something under her breath that sounded an awful lot like—

I turned to stare at her. "Did you just call me a bitch?*"*

Her eyes widened, and she threw her hands toward the dashboard. "Stop sign!"

What? I whipped around and slammed both feet down on the brake, but I knew that I wouldn't be able to stop.

There was a loud horn and a flash of something to the right and Carrie screaming—

—and then impact, glass shattering, metal crunching, the car tumbling.

And Carrie wasn't screaming anymore.

Gasping for breath, I opened my eyes and stared up at the arch of the tent, willing my heartbeat to slow down. It wasn't the first time I'd dreamed about the accident, and it never got any easier to deal with. I took a shuddering breath and wiped the tears from my face.

I thought about Rory's nightmare—and how he'd awakened from it—and I couldn't help but wish he'd been there for me when I'd awakened from mine.

As the nightmare faded and my breathing slowed, I became aware of my knee, which had swelled up and felt like it was being squeezed by a giant hand. The trekking pants weren't helping.

I sat up, intending to grab a pair of shorts, but I couldn't lift my leg off the top of the pack. I had to use my hands to move it, clenching my teeth so I wouldn't cry out.

Breathing shallowly, I dug in my pack, finally pulling shorts from the bottom. I unsnapped my pants and started to ease them down. But when I tried to lift myself up to slide them over my butt, I jostled my knee and a cry of pain tore from me.

Seconds later, there was the *hiss* of a zipper, and Rory was inside my tent. "Amelia, are you—?" He broke off mid-sentence, his eyes wide. He was wearing gym shorts and a T-shirt with the sleeves ripped off, and he looked really hot, and it took me a moment to realize why he was staring at me like that.

Crap. My pants were half off my butt, and the T-shirt wasn't long enough to hide my underwear. Frantically (and irrationally) trying to remember which underwear I'd put on that morning, I reached for my discarded shirt to try to cover myself, but that jostled my knee again. "Shit!"

Rory dropped to his knees and covered my hand with his. "Amelia, let me help you."

Help me take off my pants?

"Aye, I'll help you take off your pants," he said, his voice tight. My face burned, and I closed my eyes. I hadn't realized I'd spoken out loud. "Amelia." I opened my eyes. "I can control myself around an injured woman in her underwear, if that's what you're worried about."

I was more worried about *my* reaction to his hands on me, to be honest, but I just nodded.

He slung one arm around my waist, the other around my thighs, and lifted me up. I slid my pants over my butt, and he lowered me back down. He knelt at my feet, hooked his fingers over the waistband, and started to slide the pants down my thighs, raising his gaze to mine.

The look in his eyes—which were green and intense and burning into me like lasers—made my body go hotter than if he'd just stared at my crotch. My breath came faster, and I could feel my heart pounding. It was possibly the most erotic moment of my life.

Oh, this was not good. *I don't see a problem with it,* said Carrie's voice in my head. *Not helping!*

"Christ," he muttered, finally looking away. He swore again when my knee was revealed—as did I. It was really swollen.

In a split second, he became all business, stripping off my pants and whipping the gym shorts up my legs and over my hips.

He unwound the ACE bandage and set it aside, then scooped me up and ducked out of the tent. The sun was still high in the sky, so I hadn't been asleep for too long.

I assumed he was going to set me down on a rock and tend to my knee, but he kept walking.

"Um, where are we going?"

"We need to bring down the swelling. I don't have another instant ice pack."

Bring down the swelling? How was he going to—?

Hoping I was wrong, I turned to look over my shoulder. Nope, I wasn't wrong; we were heading right for the water. The *ice-cold* water.

I turned back to look at him, digging my fingers into his shoulder. "Rory, that water is freezing!"

"Aye, I know. That's why it will help with the swelling."

I knew he was right, but still. "Fine, put me down, and I'll walk the rest of the way."

"Not with your knee like that."

"Rory—"

"Remember that time when you agreed to follow my directions?"

"Remember how I said I couldn't promise not to argue?" I retorted. I started to struggle, but his arms were like a steel band.

"Calm down! It's just water." A gleam came into his eyes, and I knew what he was going to do.

"Don't you dare, you—"

I was cut off mid-rant as he bent at the waist and dunked me in the frigid Scottish water.

Cold. It was so cold, I was gasping like a landed fish. I tightened my arms around Rory's neck and tried to climb him.

"What are you doing, you...you...?" I sputtered, unable to think of a good enough insult.

"You needed to cool off."

"What?" I shrieked. "*I* needed to cool off? What about you? I saw that look in your eyes when you took off my pants, you—"

His arms tightened around me, my only warning before he dunked us both up to our necks.

"I can't believe you just did that," I said when I could speak again.

"I needed to cool off, too."

Startled by his admission, I looked up. He held my gaze for a long moment, and then he looked away. He began walking parallel to the shore, his strides slow and steady. In spite of myself, I began to relax, leaning my head against the crook of his neck.

"You can put me down," I grumbled. "Now that I'm completely soaked."

"I don't want you on that leg, and I don't want to have to rescue you if you go under."

"I *can* swim. I'm actually pretty good at it."

"Amelia, just shut up and enjoy the water."

I lifted my head. "Enjoy it? Are you nuts?"

He glanced down at me, his eyes a strange bluish-grayish-greenish from the reflection of the sea and sky. I couldn't seem to tear my gaze away from them. "Probably. But can you honestly tell me that this water doesn't make you feel alive?"

I wasn't sure about the water, but I'd never felt more alive than I did right now with his strong arms holding me close, his beautiful, expressive eyes staring into mine. Even the other night couldn't compare to this, as passionate as that had been.

If there's an opportunity for you *to kiss* him *this time, you should take it,* Tommy had said. This would definitely be that opportunity; I could almost hear Tommy's voice in my ear, telling me to go for it.

I parted my lips—to speak or to "go for it," I didn't know—but then he looked away, and the moment was gone.

Just as well. It would only make things awkward when we inevitably got into an argument an hour from now—or sooner. I relaxed against him once more as he walked back and forth through the water like I was a cranky baby he was trying to get to go to sleep.

I looked at the mountains, silhouetted against the sky,

then at the sparkling water around us. "You're so lucky," I said.

He glanced down at me. "Why do you say that?"

"Look around. You get paid to be in the middle of this beautiful scenery in all kinds of weather, to see it over and over again through the eyes of so many different people. You must love it so much."

He didn't answer, just stared at me with his bright, sea-glass eyes. He was so stoic sometimes, but in his eyes I saw all the emotion he tried to hide; so much that it was impossible to parse any of it, to tell what he was thinking.

As if in a dream, I watched my hand reach up and touch his cheek, watched something flare in those eyes. "Rory?" I whispered. "Don't you...love it here?" I felt so tired suddenly, the words struggling to come out.

"Sometimes more so than others," he finally said.

What? "What does that mean?"

He didn't answer; just tightened his arms around me and headed for shore. Clearly, he was not going to elaborate. As my body emerged from the water, I began to shiver.

"Why are we heading back in?" I said. *And why does my voice sound so slurred?*

"Because your lips were turning blue. I wanted to bring down the swelling in your knee, not give you hypothermia." He walked faster, his long legs cutting through the water. When we reached the shore, he strode to our campsite, walking over the rocks in his bare feet like they weren't even there.

He set me down on a rock and then pulled a small pouch from his pack. He opened it and shook it out. It was one of those tiny emergency blankets. He draped it around me, and I snuggled into it, my teeth clattering together. Then he ducked inside my tent and emerged with my pack.

"Take out dry clothes. Something warm."

My whole body shaking with cold, I dug in my pack with clumsy hands and pulled out underwear and clothes.

"N-now what?"

"Now I hold that blanket in place while you get out of your wet clothes."

I raised my eyebrows. "S-seriously? Why can't I just g-go in my tent?"

"Because you're shivering too hard. You need help."

Damn it, he was right—I couldn't even make my fingers cooperate. "Are you going to help me with my underwear, too?" I snapped, unable to help myself.

To my surprise, he grinned. *Oh, I could really get used to that grin.* "Only if you ask nicely."

I'd definitely walked into that one. But two could play at this game.

I looked down the neck of my shirt. I was wearing my navy sports bra, which covered more of me than most of my bathing suits did. I dropped the blanket and whipped the T-shirt over my head.

His eyes grew comically wide. "What are you doing?"

Now it was my turn to grin. I could almost feel Carrie's smile of approval—and surprise—at my boldness. "Calm down, Rory. I wear less than this at the beach. I'm trying to minimize the amount of time you need to hold up the blanket as I awkwardly get changed under it."

I hooked my still-clumsy fingers in the elastic waistband of my shorts and shimmied on the rock so I could carefully slide them over my butt and down my legs.

I looked up—and sucked in a breath. There was that look in his eyes again, hot enough to melt steel.

"Are you ready?" he asked, then swore under his breath.

I'm getting there, I nearly said aloud. I wished I had the *nerve* to say it out loud. But I just nodded. He held the blanket loosely at my neck and waist, keeping his eyes averted as I wriggled out of my wet sports bra. Shit, the dry one was out of reach. I cleared my throat. "Um, can you reach my bra? It's on top of my pack."

He muttered something that sounded like "give me strength," grabbed the bra, and handed it to me under the blanket.

"This was your idea, you know," I mumbled as I slid my arms through the straps and quickly did up the hooks, then adjusted the front. "I probably could have managed in my tent."

"Next time," he said, handing me my shirt.

I checked that everything was where it should be and slipped the shirt over my head, tugging it down to my hips.

Now for the fun part. I picked up my clean panties so that I wouldn't have to ask him to hand them to me.

No longer needing to cover my chest, he lowered the blanket a few inches. "Okay, go for it."

"Don't let go of the blanket."

"I won't. But if you could be quick, that would be brilliant."

He kept his gaze fixed on something—or nothing—over my shoulder as I peeled off my wet panties, shimmying as I had with the shorts to get them off my butt without jostling my knee too much.

"Okay, I'm going to stand up. Just, like, stay close." I held the blanket around my hips as he pulled me up. I shifted most of my weight to my left foot and anchored the blanket around my waist as if it was a towel. "Can you hold my arm?" I asked.

He nodded and took my upper arm, steadying me as I eased my right foot into the leg of my panties, and then I leaned on him and slipped my left foot through. "Okay, if you could take my arm again, and just look over at the sea for a second?" He obediently shifted his eyes and I yanked the panties up, maneuvering awkwardly under the blanket.

"God, that was an effort."

"Tell me about it," he muttered. "Have a seat before you put on your pants, and let me see your knee."

I re-tucked the blanket around my hips and sat on the rock once more. He carefully prodded my knee, which looked less swollen than it had before. He glanced at his watch. "It's too soon for more ibuprofen, but you can take some before you go to bed." He retrieved the ACE bandage and wrapped my knee, then handed me my sweatpants. "Can you manage these yourself?"

I nodded, and while I pulled them on, he picked up my wet clothes and began laying them out on some large, flat rocks to dry. Including my underwear. "Hey, I can do that," I protested.

He looked up at me, his eyes wide and incredulous, my panties clutched in his hand. "Seriously?" he drawled, his accent thicker than usual, "you had no problem with me seein' you wearin' them, and no problem strippin' them off six inches from my face, but you don't want me spreadin' them on a rock to dry?"

"It's different," I muttered, feeling foolish. "You weren't touching them."

"Aye, well, holding your wet underwear is not as titillating as you seem to think it is," he said. He wrung them out, slapped them on the rock with the rest of my wet things, and went into my tent, returning with my fleece. "Put this on, and sit here in the sun to warm up."

He handed me the fleece, and then stripped off his shirt, wrung it out, and spread it on a rock, then strode back into the water without a backward glance, wading out until he was waist-deep. He turned to the right and began swimming, as if a leviathan were chasing him.

Unfortunately, I didn't have a similar outlet at the moment. All I could do was sit on my rock.

Chapter Nineteen

RORY

I swam until I could barely move my arms. And all the while, I couldn't clear my head of the images that flashed by like some dirty slideshow.

No, not dirty, not Amelia. Beautiful, feisty, stubborn, *sexy as hell.* When I'd knelt before her in the tent to help her with her pants—I didn't think I'd ever been so turned on. It had taken every ounce of strength in me not to kiss her. Judging by the look in her eyes, she might even have kissed me back.

And then that ridiculous scene after we got out of the water—why the hell hadn't I just let her get changed in her tent? I was some kind of masochist. I pictured her in my mind, stripping off her wet shirt and shorts and sitting before me in her navy bra and underwear like a goddess. *Are you ready?* I'd asked her, not realizing what I'd said until the words fell out of my mouth. Her lips had parted, her cheeks had turned pink, and I had held my breath, hoping—afraid—she would say *yes*.

When she'd protested me wringing out her wet underwear—as I'd known she would—I'd nearly said that while handling them wasn't sexy, seeing her in them had nearly killed me.

I needed to get her out of my head. She'd put her trust in me to help get her through this trek. Taking advantage of her—even if she might not slap the shit out of me for doing so—was not part of the deal.

And I still haven't cooled off, I thought as I emerged from the water a few hundred yards down from where we were camped and trudged down the beach.

What the hell had I been thinking, to agree to this? And how the hell were we going to get through the next few days, just the two of us?

When I reached the camp, Amelia was sitting right where I'd left her. I pulled my towel from my pack and dried off, uncomfortably aware that she was watching me.

"You swam for a long time."

"Yeah, well, I didn't get in my usual amount of exercise today," I replied, knowing it was a dick thing to say, but spoiling for an argument. To my surprise, she didn't answer, and I looked up.

Her face had gone pale, and she didn't meet my gaze. When she spoke, her voice was small. "You must regret offering to help me. I've messed up your whole routine—and saddled you with a helpless girl who can't even manage to undress herself."

Damn it. A wave of shame swept over me. I knelt before her. "I'm sorry, Amelia. I shouldn't have said that about the exercise. It's not even why I swim. And I don't regret offering to help you." She did look at me then, one eyebrow raised. "I don't. It's just…different…from the way I usually do things, and it'll take some getting used to."

"If you say so," she said.

"I do." I pushed myself to my feet. "Give me a minute to change, and then we can get dinner going. It will be good for both of us to turn in early tonight. Oh, and Amelia?" She looked up, that lost expression still on her face. I needed to make that go away. "I think you did a pretty damn good job of undressing yourself. But maybe practice will make perfect?"

The light came back into her eyes, and her lips curved in a smile. "I'll keep that in mind."

A few minutes later, I poured boiling water into Amelia's beef stew pouch and my chicken stir-fry. We sat on two boulders side by side to eat.

"So why the Skye Trail?" I asked after a few minutes.

"I'm sorry?"

"I'm just wondering why an American lass who'd never been to Scotland would choose to do the Skye Trail." Amelia looked down, absently swirling her spork in the stew without actually eating any of it. I laid my hand on her arm, and she raised her eyes to meet mine. She looked…hollow, and I immediately regretted bringing it up. "I'm sorry. We can talk about something else."

She smiled slightly and shook her head. "No, it's okay. Sometime last year, Carrie did one of those at-home DNA kits and found out she was 30 percent Scottish, which she hadn't known."

I gaped at her. "How can you not know you've that much Scottish blood?"

She let out a surprised laugh, her eyes sparkling with humor. It lit up her whole face, and made me…want things I had no business wanting. "What's so funny?" I mumbled.

"The horror in your voice. Like, you can't imagine anything worse than someone not knowing she's Scottish."

"Och, no, I cannae think of anything worse. We Scots have oor pride, ye ken," I replied, purposely exaggerating my accent, since she'd seemed to like it when I'd done so before. She blinked, her cheeks going slightly pink. I cleared my throat. "Anyway, go on."

"Um, right. She didn't know she was Scottish because it was on her maternal grandfather's side, and he died when her mom was very young, so it never came up. She wanted to know more, so that led her to do her family tree, and found that her family lived on Skye in the early nineteenth century before emigrating to New York.

"And that's what led to her wanting to see Skye. I suggested we do a trip to Scotland for our college graduation. We could see castles and men in kilts—what?"

"So you fancy a man in a kilt, do you?"

"I mean, is there anyone who doesn't? Do *you* have one?" she asked, her eyes lighting with interest.

"Aye, of course I do. The Sutherland tartan is a forest green and navy blue with red, black, and white."

"Do you ever wear it?"

"I've worn it to a few weddings, but it's really just for special occasions. I don't have it with me, if that's what you're wondering. It's not exactly practical for the trail."

"I guess not, but it doesn't cover much less of you than the shorts you're wearing, does it?"

"If I'm just standing around, no. But if I were to trip on a tree root and fall arse over teakettle while wearing it, you'd see quite a lot more of me than if I was wearing shorts, if you know what I mean."

Her gaze immediately dropped to my lap, and I realized I'd made a tactical error with my flirting, because her stare was so intense it felt like I was naked, and my body was reacting accordingly. I needed to get this conversation back on track. "What else were you planning to see in Scotland?"

Her eyes snapped up, and her face was even redder than before. "What?"

"Castles, kilts—what else?"

"Oh, right. We wanted to see the scenery, drink whisky, stuff like that. Carrie was all for it, but there was this weird gleam in her eyes as she'd paged through the guidebook I'd bought. A few days after we'd started planning, she came to me with this 'great idea.'"

"Let me guess. She wanted to hike the Skye Trail."

Amelia nodded. "Yeah. It was totally out of left field. I told her I thought we were planning to do a road trip. She suggested we come for two weeks and spend one of them hiking. She had all the info on Scotland By Foot printed out for me to see. God, she was so excited about it, raving about how awesome it would be to hike Skye," she said, her voice almost a whisper. "I totally shot her down. I'm not a hiker. There was no way I could do something as mountainous as this trail. And definitely not for a week. She insisted we had plenty of time to train, but she wasn't getting it. It wasn't just that I didn't think I could do it...I didn't *want* to. I hated hiking."

"Did you tell her that?"

"Yes. And I felt awful about it. But a few days later, she had a new plan. She'd go to Scotland a week before me and do the trail. Then I'd meet her after, and we'd do our road trip. I was so happy, because it meant she didn't have to give up the hike she was now dying to do, and I didn't have to hike eighty-whatever miles across the Isle of Skye. It was the perfect solution." She looked up at me, her eyes brimming with tears. "Until I nearly got her killed."

That despondent look in her eyes was one I'd seen in the mirror far too many times. I got up and gestured to her rock. "Scoot over," I said to her.

She looked at me questioningly, but shifted over.

Taking a chance, I sat down and slung my arm around her shoulder. She stiffened at first, then melted against me with a shuddering sigh.

I held her to me, breathing in the scent of the shampoo she'd used that morning. "I'm sorry for asking you to talk about Carrie."

"Don't be. I just miss her." She raised her head from my shoulder and looked out at the sea.

"For what it's worth, you may not have started this trail as a hiker, but you became one pretty damn fast."

She turned to me, her eyes wide with surprise. "How can you say that? I went—how did you say it?—*arse over teakettle* just a few hours ago."

"Yeah, but injuries happen to all of us. I've had at least one hairline fracture in my ankle—possibly two. Plus countless sprains and muscle strains. It's just the nature of constantly being out on the trail. Before you took that tumble, you kicked Old Ben Tianavaig's ass."

"You really think so?"

"Aye, I really do."

"Thank you for saying that," she whispered.

We passed the rest of the meal in silence. Amelia started to get to her feet. "What are you doing?"

Her face turned pink. "I, uh, need to pee."

"Let me help you," I said. Her face turned *more* pink. "I mean, let me walk you over there."

"I can do it," she said. I just raised an eyebrow, reminding her of her promise to follow directions. "Fine," she huffed.

I handed her the trekking poles and helped her to her feet. I walked her to the "pee spot," not holding on to her, but staying right by her side in case she lost her balance.

When we got there, she turned to me, her eyes narrowed. "You're not going to hold on to me while I pee, are you?"

"No, unless you need me to."

"I'll be fine."

Her tone clearly said that she wouldn't ask for my help under any circumstances, so I held up my hands and backed away. "I'll be just over there. Shout when you're ready to walk back."

I wandered far enough to give her privacy but stayed within earshot. A few minutes later, she said she was ready.

The walk back was slow. She stumbled at one point, and though I caught her before she fell, I could tell that she was just done. I picked her up, poles and all, and carried her back to the campsite. Her complete lack of protest was the truest indication of how exhausted she was.

I helped her lie down on her pallet with her leg elevated, gave her more ibuprofen to swallow, then zipped up her sleeping bag.

"Try to get some sleep, and if you need anything—especially an escort to the loo—just yell. Don't try to wander around in the dark by yourself, even if you feel better. I'll wake you around eight." I started to push to my feet, but she caught my hand. I looked into her pain-filled, troubled, exhausted eyes. "What's wrong?"

"How am I going to do this?"

"What do you mean?"

"This!" She waved with her other hand, encompassing the tent and the world as a whole. "I needed you to carry me because I couldn't walk fifty feet." She closed her eyes in defeat. "How am I going to do the rest of this trek? There's no way," she said, her voice small.

I tightened my fingers around hers. "Hey, look at me." I waited until she complied. "You and I will do this, together. No matter how long it takes. For Carrie."

Tears welled in her eyes, and she nodded. "For Carrie. Thank you," she whispered. Her voice was shaky, but her lips curved in a small smile. She squeezed my hand and then let go, burrowing deeper into her sleeping bag. "Goodnight, Rory."

"Goodnight, Amelia."

I ducked out of her tent and zipped it almost all the way up, leaving a small opening so I would hear her if she called out.

I checked the campsite, making sure everything was secure for the night, then looked in on Amelia one last time. She seemed to be asleep, her sleeping bag pulled up to her neck, one hand tucked under her chin.

She might loathe me at times, might want me at others, but none of that mattered now. She trusted me to get her through the Skye Trail, and that's what I would do, even if it killed me.

Which it just might.

Chapter Twenty

AMELIA

I didn't sleep well, since even the slightest shift of my leg resulted in shooting pain that jarred me awake. And by six a.m., my bladder made it abundantly clear that if I didn't get up *now*, things would be bad.

I rolled to my left side and pivoted so I was on my good left knee and both hands. I reached for a trekking pole and planted it, then gritting my teeth so hard I was afraid I'd break one, I got my good foot under me and dragged myself upright.

I paused for a moment to catch my balance, then limped outside. The sky was gray and heavy, which didn't bode well for the day.

I hobbled the few feet to Rory's tent. It was zipped only partway, as mine had been. I peered inside. He lay on his back, his sleeping bag shoved down to his waist. He was asleep, his jaw relaxed and grazed with dark stubble that I knew would look coppery in the sunlight.

One muscled arm was under his head and his other hand rested on his bare chest, and because that wasn't goddamn sexy enough, he'd also fallen asleep reading. There was a book on his chest under his hand. The pages looked soft and a bit dog-eared. It was clearly an old favorite. His hand was blocking most of the cover, but I could see part of it, and I knew it well.

It was *The Fellowship of the Ring.* I literally thought I might swoon. The *Lord of the Rings* trilogy was in my top five movies of all time, and I loved the books as well, had written several papers on them in college.

Rory loved that book enough to carry it around with him to read in his spare moments of downtime? It made me want to crawl in there and snuggle against him like a cat. *Go on, I dare you,* said Carrie's voice in my head.

Don't tempt me.

The insistent pressure in my bladder reminded me why I was there gawking at him. He'd said to wake him if I needed to pee, and he'd also said not to walk in the dark. But he looked so peaceful, and since it wasn't dark outside, I would manage on my own. I'd have to walk several miles that day; if I couldn't make it fifty feet by myself, I might as well pack it in now.

It was slow going, but I made it to the trees and back with the help of my poles. I returned to the campsite and gingerly lowered myself to "my rock" to wait for him to wake up.

It was silent, as if the ominous clouds were muffling the rest of the world. Then, as I watched, the sun broke through the bottom of a cloud, golden rays of light hitting the water below. If someone had asked for my interpretation of "God," I would have shown them the scene before me.

I wasn't particularly religious, generally just going with my folks to synagogue on the High Holy Days and celebrating the holidays, but sitting on this quiet beach in the early morning, with those perfect beams of light shining through the cloud, it was easy to believe in *something*.

I closed my eyes and raised my face to the sky. *Please let Carrie be okay. Please don't punish her for my mistake. Please let me be strong enough to get through this trek. And please let Rory find some peace from whatever haunts him.*

When I opened my eyes, the beams of sunlight had vanished, and the sea was a uniform gray once more. Was that a good sign or a bad sign?

There was a rustling sound, followed by the hiss of a zipper, and then Rory emerged from his tent.

He was clad only in a pair of black gym shorts, and his hair was tousled. I stared at his beautiful body, lean and strong from endless miles of walking and swimming. I remembered our brief conversation about kilts and indulged myself by imagining him wearing one...and nothing else. Then he stretched his arms up over his head, the motion causing his shorts to ride low on his hips, displaying the yummy indentations of his obliques and a line of paler skin, and my mouth went completely dry.

Suddenly, his arms dropped to his sides. "Amelia? What are you doing up?"

"What?" I murmured absently. He started toward me, the graceful motion of his body as he walked utterly mesmerizing.

"Amelia," he said sharply.

I blinked. And felt my face burn as I realized he'd totally caught me staring at him. *Oh, good grief.* I closed my eyes for a moment, then looked up, mortified. His face was a bit pink, too, as if my gaze had burned him. The image that accompanied that thought was absurdly funny, and a giggle burst from me before I could stop it.

"Are you okay?" he asked, obviously concluding that I'd lost my mind, which only made me laugh harder.

"I'm sorry," I gasped, wiping the tears from my eyes, "I just...maybe you could go back inside your tent and come out again, so we can start this whole scene over?"

He smiled—just a small curve of his lips, but it still counted. "I don't know what just happened, but it's nice to hear you laugh. How's your knee this morning? And why are you up and around?" he asked, the smile dropping from his face. "I told you not to try to walk without help."

I stiffened, bracing for confrontation. "I had to pee, and you were sleeping."

He flicked his gaze to the sky, as if calling on the same higher power I'd just spoken to, then looked back at me, his eyes stern. "You should have woken me up."

"I didn't want to."

His eyes turned silvery with anger. "Because you're stubborn and prideful and would rather fall down than ask for help!"

"Yeah, that's exactly it. You have me figured out. You know, when you offered to help me finish, and I gratefully accepted, neither of us seemed to consider that most of the time, we don't actually get along."

He stared at me for a moment, and then his shoulders sagged as the fight just fell out of him.

"Damn it," he muttered. He sat beside me, tunneling his hands into his hair and tugging, as if he needed the pain to center him. He looked at me once more, his eyes now a troubled grayish-green.

"Look, I get that you don't want to be dependent on me to escort you to the loo. But *I* don't want you to fall and risk further injury, especially if I'm asleep in my tent and have no idea that you're out there. Can you understand that?"

I sighed. "I do understand, and I'm sorry. It's just that you—" *No, better not to say it.*

He cocked his head. "I what?"

He pinned me with those eyes, and I couldn't *not* tell him. "You looked peaceful, for the first time since I met you." He looked totally taken aback, and I hurried to continue. "I know you don't sleep well, and I just couldn't bear to disturb you if I didn't have to."

He didn't say anything. I closed my eyes, wishing I could crawl into a hole. I should have just apologized and left it at that.

His hand suddenly covered mine, and I opened my eyes. He was looking at me with the strangest expression on his face. "Thank you. That was…I'm sorry for yelling at you."

God, those eyes! First, they were silver and angry, like molten steel; then they were gray-green and turbulent, like a stormy sea. Now they were bright green and luminous, like a piece of sea glass shimmering in the sun, and I couldn't look away from the vulnerability they revealed.

As if in a trance, I watched my hand brush a lock of hair off his face and then touch his cheek. Watched his eyes widen in surprise, his whole body going rigid. And then he leaned into my touch.

It wasn't more than a few seconds that we stayed like that before I drew back, knowing if I didn't, things were going to get awkward. I cleared my throat and met his eyes, which were back to the calm gray-green of a rainy day.

"I'm sorry for doing what you told me not to do. It was light out, and I felt stable enough with the trekking poles. But you're right—if I'd fallen, that would have been bad."

He nodded—slowly, as if he was still processing what just happened. Then he patted my thigh and stood. "Okay, I think that's settled."

"I think so."

"Sit tight for a moment, and then I'll check your knee." He put on his flip-flops and then strode down the path to the trees. I watched him go, wondering for the thousandth time why either of us had agreed to this.

He returned a few minutes later and ducked into his tent. When he came back out, he was wearing a T-shirt. *Damn it.*

"Let's have a look at that knee." He was all business now, that earlier moment of vulnerability gone as if it had never happened. He knelt at my feet and started to push up the leg of my sweatpants, but the elastic around the ankle wouldn't stretch over my swollen knee. He peered up at me, his eyebrows raised.

I carefully stood, placing my hands on his shoulders. "Do it."

His eyes widened, and then comprehension set in. Averting his eyes, he reached under my T-shirt, snagged the waistband of my pants, and started to pull them down.

"Could you go slower with that?" I muttered, squirming as his touch ignited little fires inside me.

He looked up at me from under his dark copper brows. "If you insist," he said, his lips curving into a wicked smile. I sucked in a breath as his thumbs *slowly* grazed my thighs, those little fires exploding into conflagrations as every cell in my body responded to his touch. My heart pounding, my legs wobbly for reasons having nothing to do with my knee, I clutched his shoulders. *If he leaned a little closer, his mouth would be—*

His hands tightened around my thighs, his eyes bright green and scorching in their intensity, and I knew he was thinking the same thing.

"Rory..." I whispered, not sure if I was asking him to stop or keep going.

He blinked, and the spell was broken.

He whisked the pants down my legs and off. I let go of his shoulders and sat down, trying not to feel disappointed that he could turn it off that quickly, while I still felt the imprint of each of his fingers searing into my skin.

He unwrapped the bandage and hissed in a breath through his teeth. My knee was still swollen. "You know what this means?"

"No, wha—" I followed his gaze to the peacefully rippling sea a few yards away. "Oh, come on. Can't I just take, like, extra ibuprofen or something?"

"You already are. The cold water will help more." He went into his tent and returned with the shorts I'd worn into the sea the day before. "I brought in your things last night before I went to bed. You were already sleeping, so I didn't want to disturb you."

"Thanks." I slipped on the shorts, which were mostly dry. Not that it was going to matter. He lifted me in his arms and waded into the water until my knee was submerged. "Aren't you getting tired of schlepping me around?" I asked, whimpering at the cold.

"Not yet," he said as he started walking. "So what's the deal with you and hiking?" he asked. I flicked my eyes to his, surprised at the topic. "You said you hated hiking. Seemed extreme."

If we weren't going to talk about that heated moment we just shared, it was as good a topic as any. "It was the spring of our junior year of high school. Carrie and I had joined the Environmental Club, because it would 'look good on our college applications.' It was a lot more fun than I expected, with various field trips and cleanup days at the beach. Until the hike, at some mountain in upstate New York. Unlike with you guys, there was no organization to it—and no guide. We were told to meet back at the van after we finished, and then we were left to our own devices."

He looked horrified. "They left a bunch of teenagers to fend for themselves on a mountain?"

"Yep."

"That's not okay. Tommy and I do a lot of work with

teens, taking them out on the trail to teach them orienteering and survival skills. Eventually, they do go out on their own, but not before they've had days of training. And even then, we aren't far."

"Well, I wish we'd had leaders like you and Tommy. Our group separated almost immediately, with the more experienced hikers charging off ahead. Soon it was just Carrie and me. I started to get blisters and had to go slowly. Carrie said we should turn back, but she'd been so stoked about the hike, and I didn't want to ruin it for her, so I said I was okay, and we kept going.

"And then it started to pour. We turned back, but by then the trail was a slippery mess, and we got completely lost. We were out there for hours trying to find our way back. By then it had gotten dark, and we were both chilled to the bone.

"It was terrifying, Rory. I thought we were going to be out there all night, freezing to death or getting attacked by a fucking bear. A park ranger finally found us."

"I'm sorry that happened. That was a shitty introduction to hiking, and I hope someone got sacked over it?"

"The teacher that ran the Environmental Club got in trouble for not employing proper safety procedures. I couldn't get warm for days, and had nightmares for weeks after that. Carrie got super into hiking, and *I* swore I'd never go hiking again." I looked into his sympathetic eyes. "And yet, here I am."

"Has your opinion of hiking changed at all these past few days? Other than the sprained knee?"

I thought of how I felt when I reached the top of Ben Tianavaig, before everything went to hell, the sense of accomplishment, of pride—the exhaustion and soreness replaced by the adrenaline rush of standing atop a mountain with the wind rushing around me, the fresh air filling my lungs.

"I might not hate it so much now."

"It's a start," he said with a smile.

God, I would never get used to his smiles. They were like a rare gift—that was maybe not so rare anymore. *And that wicked grin from a few minutes ago—I want to see that again.*

"Anyway, we need to get ready to head out. Thank you for telling me that story. Just so you know, I'm going to do my best to get you to love hiking before we reach the end of the trail."

"Well, you can try," I said, though in all honesty, he was off to a decent start.

"Fair enough."

A moment later, he was carrying me out of the water and setting me down on the rock.

And all I could think of was how much I missed being in his arms, icy water or no.

Chapter Twenty-One

AMELIA

After our dip, he re-wrapped my knee. "Do you, uh, need me to help you get dressed?" he asked.

"No, I can do it." Even if it took me an hour. I couldn't handle his hands on me like they were before, not if it wasn't going to go anywhere.

It didn't take an hour, but it did take a while. I limped out of the tent, carrying my boots and socks—there was no way I could put them on without help. As I was getting dressed, the reality crashed down. Getting back on the trail today was going to suck.

Rory helped me with my boots, and then we ate quickly.

"You ready to head out?"

I just nodded, knowing that if I said yes, he'd be able to hear in my voice that I was afraid I was nowhere near ready.

I stood, and he helped me into my pack, waiting while I adjusted to the heavy burden. He handed me my poles and then shrugged into his own pack. "Okay, we're aiming to get to Sligachan today, where you'll have a non-reconstituted meal and an adult beverage at the hotel restaurant before you sleep in an actual bunk—after you shower. How's that for motivation?"

"Sounds amazing."

"Aye, it does. But you're going to let me know if you need to rest, right?"

"I will."

"And if we can't make it to Sligachan today, then we won't, all right? I would rather we go at a steady pace, even if it's slow, and sleep out another night, than completely wear you out so you can't move tomorrow."

His face flushed slightly at his double entendre. "That didn't come out right," he muttered. Maybe it wasn't what he meant to say, but it conjured all kinds of naughty images in my mind, and I wondered if he was seeing similar ones in his.

"Trust me, if you wear me out so much that I can't move tomorrow, you'll know it," I said with a grin.

He stared at me for a moment, his eyes wide. Then he looked away, muttering something under his breath that was either a prayer or a curse, which made me laugh. It was fun to see him flustered, and it momentarily distracted me from worrying about how I would get through the day. He glanced back at my laugh, then rolled his eyes and grinned. "Come on, let's go."

The first few miles were on the road. While I had complained the day before about how uncomfortable it was to walk in hiking boots on pavement, today I was grateful for the stable ground.

It was still slow-going, and although my knee seemed to be doing okay, Rory insisted on holding my upper arm "just in case." But I could feel the tension running through him, and I knew this pace was nearly impossible for him to maintain, with his long, uninjured legs.

After about a mile, I couldn't take it anymore. "Rory, stop for a second."

"What's wrong? Do you need a break?"

"No, I'm fine. And I think I can manage okay without you holding my arm."

It was fascinating to watch the series of emotions that ran across his face. First relief, then guilt, then doubt. He shook his head. "What if you fall?"

"Then you'll help me up, say 'I told you so,' and then I'll let you hold my arm for a while."

His lips quirked at that. "All right. But let me know if I start walking too fast, okay?"

"I will."

It was much easier to walk without him holding my arm, though I missed his touch. I was also able to move faster, and although it wasn't anywhere close to his usual pace, it was obviously easier on him, too.

But the silence was starting to grate on my nerves. "Tell me about Tommy," I blurted out after we'd been walking for a while.

He looked over at me, clearly surprised. "Why?"

"It's your turn to share. I told you about the Hike from Hell."

He visibly relaxed. "What do you want to know?"

Why you're being weird about it. "How long have you guys known each other?"

"I've known him since I was a lad, but we didn't really become friends until years later. He's actually the one who got me into the outdoors and hiking, which, like you, I used to hate."

"*You* hated it?" I knew why I had hated it, but he'd had this incredible scenery as his playground. "Why?"

"It's...complicated," he said after a moment. "I was small for my age and not great at anything athletic, and I couldn't keep up with my... I just had a tough time."

Okay, then. Obviously not a favorite subject. "How did Tommy get you into it?"

He didn't answer, and the silence became uncomfortable. He walked as if on autopilot, his thoughts clearly far away.

Suddenly, my knee buckled. Rory grabbed my arm and wrenched me upright before I hit the pavement. "Let's take a break."

"I'm okay, I just didn't see a rut in the road."

"I know. We're just about to the point where we leave the road for a path. We'll rest for a bit and then carry on."

There was no sense in arguing with him. Besides, my knee was aching and my other leg was tired from doing extra work to keep me upright. I needed the break.

I took off my pack and sat on a rock overlooking the sea. Rory sat a few feet away on another rock.

"I was a pretty messed-up kid," he said suddenly. Startled by his out-of-the-blue admission, I looked over at him. His gaze was firmly fixed on the sea. "I was flunking my classes, running with a bad crowd, picking fights at school, getting suspended. And it didn't make a difference," he whispered, almost as an afterthought.

"Only one person seemed to care," he continued, "my literature teacher at school, Mrs. MacDougall." He paused for a moment, a smile that looked almost sad curving his lips. "I'd always liked to write but had never shown my work to anyone. My dad...thought writing was for girls." He put that part in air quotes, his lip curling with disgust. "So I'd always been embarrassed to show it to anyone. But Mrs. Mac was amazing. She cared, you know? And she was the first one to encourage my writing. She knew me before...everything. And when...it all went to shit, and I stopped doing anything much at school other than causing trouble, I always did my work for her class, because I didn't want to disappoint her."

I pictured young Rory, putting on a tough facade, lashing out at everyone and everything except this one teacher. What could have sent him down that path?

"One day, after my latest round of mischief, I was expelled. I didn't even care anymore. But Mrs. Mac found out and got them to give me one more chance, saying she'd vouch for me. She told me I was at a crossroads, and I could either keep going as I was and end up amounting to nothing—or worse, wind up dead in an alley—or I could take the hand that was being offered to me and let her help me turn my life around. I was fifteen."

This was the most he'd ever said about himself. There was so much more he *wasn't* saying, but I didn't dare interrupt him.

"For so long, I hadn't cared about anything, not even whether I lived or died. No, that's not true—I *did* want to die," he whispered. He clenched his fists on his thighs, as if to force down the emotion that threatened to burst forth—that he couldn't let burst forth.

Blinking back tears, I hesitantly reached out and covered his hand, waiting for him to yank it away.

But he didn't. He opened his fist and clutched my hand instead.

"I wanted to die," he repeated without looking at me, "but like with everything else, I was too scared to make it happen. Which is ironic, given that the Sutherland clan motto is *Sans Peur*, 'No Fear.' No wonder my father fucking hated me."

My heart broke for that lost boy. "Rory, that doesn't mean you were too scared; it means that deep down inside, you *didn't* want to die, not really. You wanted to live; you just needed someone to help you see that."

His lips curved slightly. "Maybe. Anyway, Mrs. Mac thought Tommy was the one who could get through to me, and she was right. Tommy's two years older than me, but he knew—" He broke off for a moment, and then said, "He knew what I was going through." From the way he'd hesitated, I knew that wasn't what he'd started to say.

He pulled his hand from mine and stood. "Long story short, he made me join this group of kids he took out hiking nearly every weekend. I resisted at first—it was like opening up a wound, and I couldn't bear it. But then I started to actually like it, no matter how hard I tried not to. It was a program that encouraged kids from all over the UK to go outside and get involved with nature, with the community, and so on. I stuck with it, earned my awards and certifications, and got myself back on the right track at school."

"And now you work with those kids."

"Aye, I wanted to give something back. I owe everything to Tommy and Mrs. Mac. If not for them, I don't know what I would have become. They saved my life." He cleared his throat. "Anyway, I graduated secondary school and eventually got my Mountain Leader certification. And Tommy and I have been best friends ever since."

I had no doubt it was more involved than that, but I knew he wasn't going to say more. Not now, anyway. That he'd confided so much was a surprise—and a hell of a lot more than I'd bargained for with my simple "so tell me about Tommy" comment. I wondered what had driven him into such darkness—darkness that still clung to him today. It wasn't fair for him to have had so much heartache in his life.

"I'm glad you have Tommy, and I'm glad you had Mrs. Mac. Sometimes just one person can truly make a difference in someone's life. Do you still write?"

"I don't have the time to do it during the busy season, but in the off-season, when the nights are long, yeah. Short stories, mostly, but I have some other things I've been playing around with. I jot ideas in my phone so I don't forget them.

Anyway, we need to get going. I don't like the look of the sky."

Indeed, it had gotten darker while he'd been talking, and now the sky was an angry charcoal gray, the clouds heavy and full, as if they were about to burst.

Which they probably were.

Chapter Twenty-Two

RORY

The sky looked truly ominous, more so than it had when we were on the Ridge a few days ago. "Before we go, put on your rain gear and cover your pack," I said to Amelia, then got busy doing the same for myself. It was a necessary precaution as well as a distraction. That conversation had taken an unexpected turn.

What the hell was she doing to me? First, with her comment this morning about why she didn't want to wake me, and now... What was it about her that made me want to tell her everything? Every goddamn dark thing from my past, things no one knew but Tommy—things even *he* didn't know?

Tell me about Tommy, she'd said. I'd immediately felt a crushing jealousy that had stopped me in my tracks. After this morning, when she'd devoured me with her eyes, when she'd touched my face, when I was helping her take off her pants and both of us had nearly combusted... She was going to ask about *Tommy*?

But then she said she'd asked so we'd have something to talk about, and it was like the goddamn floodgates had opened. I'd actually told her I'd wanted to die—something I'd never told Tommy, though he probably suspected it.

I couldn't let my guard down like that again. I needed to get her to the end of the trail so she could go back to her life and I could go back to mine.

The minute we stepped off the paved road and onto the path along Loch Sligachan, the skies opened up, torrential rain pouring down. *Shit.* This was already a difficult path, with frequent burns to cross, all of which would become flooded in this rain, especially after the downpour a few days ago.

We couldn't go much faster, or I'd be putting Amelia at risk. There was nothing to do but push forward and try to get to Sligachan as soon as possible.

We reached the first of the burns. It was a small, shallow one, with stones that made it easy to cross—unless it was pouring and you had a bum knee. I stepped on the first stone, then turned back. "You're going to step exactly where I step, okay? The rocks are going to be a little slippery, but I've got you."

"Okay," she said quietly, staring at the stream.

"Hand me your poles."

Her eyes shot up to mine. "What?"

"They're not going to help you across, and they'll likely make things worse. You're going to hold my arm, and I'm going to hold yours."

I prepared my response to her argument, but she wordlessly handed them over. I secured them to my pack and took her arm, just above the elbow. "Okay, now hold onto me." She clutched my forearm as if it were a lifeline.

I stepped to the next stone, testing it to make sure it wasn't going to move. "Okay, step to the one I was just on. Lead with your left foot. Go ahead, I've got you."

She stepped with her left foot, then brought her right foot forward, wobbling only a little. "Good! Now the next. Always lead with your left foot." Within moments we were on the other side. Amelia closed her eyes in obvious relief. "I hate to burst your bubble, but that was just the first of many burns we have to cross today."

She nodded, her lips curving in a slight smile. "I know, but the first one's always the hardest, right? Now I'll know what to expect."

That was just a wee stream, and the worst was definitely yet to come. But I wasn't about to shatter her confidence. This morning, when she'd come out of her tent with her boots in hand, she'd looked terrified, but she'd gamely soldiered on without complaint.

"I'm so proud of you, Amelia."

Her eyebrows went up, and a pink flush stained her cheeks. "What? Why?"

"Because you're doing brilliantly and have an amazing attitude, even though I know your knee hurts like hell and the trail is complete shite right now."

"What choice do I have?" she whispered.

I tipped up her chin so I could look her in the eyes. "You had the choice to quit, and you didn't, when anyone else would have."

She scoffed. "Most people would say that I'm stupid for doing this."

"Well, *I'm* saying that you're brave and determined. Are you going to believe me or 'most people'?"

She grinned. "Well, when you put it *that* way..."

"Exactly."

I kept hold of her arm as we continued on our way. After

two more burns, each one worse than the one before, she began to falter. "Your turn," I said.

"My turn for what?" she asked through gritted teeth.

"To tell me a story. I need a distraction," I added, tossing back the words she'd used earlier. "Tell me one of your favorite Carrie stories. I want to know more about the lass I didn't get to meet this time around, but hope to next time."

She blinked rapidly, and I caught a brief glimpse of tears before she managed a tremulous smile. "I think I told you that she and I have known each other since we were children, right?"

"Aye."

"She's always been the adventurous one, trying to get me to go along with her crazy ideas."

"And did you?"

She grinned. "Almost every single time. She has this look. It's hard to describe, but it's kind of like this…"

She lowered her head and stuck out her lower lip in a small pout, then looked up at me from under her eyelashes and blinked slowly.

I pictured her peering up at me just like that, begging me to… I tore my eyes from her and turned my attention back to the path. "I, uh, can see how that would make her impossible to resist."

"It worked really well on the guys she dated."

I cleared my throat. "Aye, I can see that, too. Anyway, you were going to tell me one of your stories…?"

"Right." She chattered away, animatedly sharing some anecdote about a crazy road trip they'd gone on to see some band play in three different cities down the east coast of the U.S. I couldn't tell you who the band was, or what the cities were, or anything else about it.

All I could think about was how goddamn much I wanted her.

· · ·

The rest of the afternoon passed in a wet, gray blur. The rain was relentless, and the burn crossings became harder and harder, which was just what I needed to clear my head and get my attention back on the trail where it belonged.

The wind had picked up as well, churning the surface of the loch into a sea of whitecaps. The Cuillins—the mountain range just south of Sligachan—were shrouded in clouds and barely visible. And the rain wasn't letting up.

There were two rivers we'd need to cross before reaching Sligachan, and I was dreading what we'd find when we got to them.

"How are you holding up?" I asked as we slogged through the mud. She didn't answer. "Amelia?"

'F-fine. I'm…fine."

She didn't sound fine. At all. "Stop for a minute."

"W-we have to k-keep…m-moving," she stammered.

I dug in my heels and tightened my grip on her arm, forcing her to stop. I turned her to face me. Her face was dead white, her lips blue with cold.

"Dammit, why didn't you tell me you needed a break?"

"B-because there's nowhere to stop until we get to S-sligachan. There's no shelter!"

"Amelia, I'm *carrying* shelter on my back! We both are."

I looked around. There was a boulder a few yards off the path, with a relatively flat bit of ground a few yards from that. I led her to the rock and gently shoved her down to sit, then slung my pack off my shoulders.

"W-what are you d-doing?"

"I'm going to pitch the tent and we're gonna take a wee break."

"Here?"

"Aye. You can't go any farther until you warm up."

"B-but—"

"No arguing. Not about this."

Within minutes, I'd pitched my tent. I'd done it countless times, in bright daylight and the dark of night, in every kind of weather—rain, sleet, snow, wind—and it took no time at all. So little time, in fact, that I mentally kicked myself for not thinking of it sooner, like before she'd nearly frozen to death.

I set up both of our sleeping mats so we'd have someplace to sit. Then I carried Amelia into the tent. That she didn't resist at all really worried me.

After setting her down on the pallet, I brought in our packs. I took off our boots, setting them in the little "mudroom" area just inside the door to the tent. I removed her rain gear from her still-unresisting body and draped it over the top of her pack, then did the same with mine.

I unpacked my sleeping bag and tucked her inside. She curled on her left side, and I slipped in behind her and zipped it up. It was a tight fit, but that would only help. I pulled her back against me and chafed my hands down her arms. But she continued to shiver.

She wasn't getting warm. I knew what I had to do next, even though I'd hoped it wouldn't come to that. I pulled my fleece and T-shirt over my head. That was the easy part. "Amelia, honey, I need to take off your shirt."

She nodded. "C-cold, Rory."

"I know, love. I'm going to get you warm."

"...b-being so nice to me."

"I can be nice sometimes. Just don't tell anyone."

"'Kay."

I lifted her body across my lap and pulled off her fleece and T-shirt, leaving her in her bra. It was a sports bra just like the one from yesterday, but purple this time. Just like the other one, it covered more of her than the most modest of bikini tops. And just like the other one, modest though it may have been, it was the sexiest thing I'd ever seen, making every cell in my body stand at attention.

She's freezing to death while you ogle her, jackass. I pulled her back against me once more, making sure we didn't touch below the waist. She didn't need to deal with *that* on top of everything else. She grabbed my wrist to pull my arm more fully around her, mumbling "thank you."

"You're welcome. Now just relax."

This time, skin against skin, it made a difference, and little by little, she stopped shivering.

I listened to the rain pound against the tent. Hopefully, it would let up soon. We could stay in the tent for an hour, maybe, but no more. We still had to get the rest of the way to Sligachan, and those river crossings would be a bitch.

A little while later, Amelia stirred, snuggling her body more fully into mine. "Warm," she murmured.

Aye, among other things, dammit. I needed to change it up, or she was going to be furious with me in about two seconds. I couldn't roll her over—she needed to be on her left side so she didn't put pressure on her bad knee. Trying not to jostle her, I moved to her other side so we were chest-to-chest and wrapped my arms around her once more.

Amelia opened her hand so that her palm lay over my heart and buried her face in the hollow of my throat. I closed my eyes and breathed in the scent of her.

She mumbled something against my chest. I touched her cheek—warm, thank God—and lifted her chin a bit. "What did you say, lass?"

"You're always taking off my clothes," she murmured. "Next time I need to take off *yours*," she added in a husky voice that logically I knew was not her trying to be seductive, but damn if it didn't sound that way. She was obviously delirious. *Shit.*

"Amelia, honey, can you hear me?" I asked, shaking her

shoulder.

"Of course I can hear you. You're practically shouting at me," she said irritably.

I exhaled in relief. She sounded like her usual self—maybe she *wasn't* delirious? "Do you know where you are?" No response. "Amelia?"

She sighed. "*We're* in your tent, somewhere on the way to Sligachan, taking a break so that I could warm up. And you're talking at me very loudly."

O-kay, so she definitely wasn't delirious. "Your skin doesn't feel as chilled as it did before. Are you warm now?"

She opened her eyes and peered up at me from under her lashes, just as she had earlier when she was talking about Carrie.

"Oh, I'm definitely warm," she said.

Just before she pulled my head down and pressed her lips to mine.

Chapter Twenty-Three

I kissed him.

There, in our warm cocoon, skin to skin, with the chill finally gone from my bones, with the rain drowning out the world around us. I needed to know what it would feel like when he was fully awake and we both knew what was going on.

He went still for a heartbeat. Then his arms tightened around me and he kissed me back—as if he'd been dying to his whole life.

The world outside faded away but for the sound of our breath, the touch of lips and tongues, our soft moans as we kissed and kissed. I shivered, but not from the cold this time.

I delved my fingers into his lovely hair, damp from the rain but still so soft. He shifted so I was lying partially beneath him, his hand skimming down my side and up to caress my breast through my bra. I arched against him, wanting more.

He tore his mouth from mine, breathing hard. I opened my eyes, confused. Why was he stopping? "Rory—?"

"We have to go. Now, while the rain has stopped."

Sure enough, it was quiet outside. How had he even noticed? I certainly hadn't, while we were kissing like there was no tomorrow.

He handed me my T-shirt, then averted his eyes while I pulled it on, as if he hadn't stripped it off me barely half an hour ago, as if he hadn't had his hands all over my body barely *two minutes* ago. We put on our rain gear, and he helped me with my boots. He got to his feet and helped me to mine, and we ducked out of the tent.

The rain had tapered off to a light mist. I sat on the rock while Rory quickly and efficiently—as always—repacked our gear. A few minutes later, we were slogging our way down the path.

Without one word spoken. As if our interlude in the tent had been nothing more than a dream.

The heavy rain had turned the path into a muddy mess, and I was grateful for Rory's supportive hand on my arm as we silently trudged along. I kept replaying the tent scene in my head as if it were a movie (more like a short film). I imagined the press of his lips, the wet slide of his tongue, the rough pads of his fingers tracing over my bare skin, the eager hardness of his body pressed against mine.

I wondered if he was imagining the same thing.

A few minutes later, I heard a roaring sound up ahead. "Uh, Rory, what's that?"

He looked over at me, his face grim. "The river."

"One we have to cross?" I asked, even though I knew the answer.

"Aye."

We reached the bank, and my heart began to pound.

The earlier streams had been bad enough—and progressively worse as the rain had continued—but this was more than a stream. "How are we going to get across?"

"The old-fashioned way. We're gonna walk."

"We're gonna *what*?"

"Don't worry, it's not so deep that you can't stand. We're just going to get wet. The good news is, it's just about a mile from here to Sligachan."

"And the bad news?" Because there was *always* bad news.

"There's another river after this one."

I studied the rushing water for a moment. "Well, at least we'll already be wet."

His lips quirked. "Exactly. Stay here for a second while I check it out."

He took off his pack and stepped into the river with only the slightest hesitation. He slowly waded across, occasionally altering his course a fraction. At its deepest point, the water came no higher than the middle of his thighs. But it was moving pretty rapidly, and he stumbled once.

He reached the opposite bank and climbed out, then began to make a pile of stones, one atop the other. What was he doing? He finished the pile when it was maybe six inches high and waded back over.

"What are the stones for?"

"It's called a cairn. It'll give us something to aim for as we cross. With the exception of that one spot, about ten steps in, the water came no higher than mid-thigh on me. I'll take our packs over and then come back for you."

"Okay," I said, glad to defer to his expertise and confidence.

He took his pack across without incident, then returned for mine, attaching the poles to it first. And then it was my turn.

He took my upper arm, and I held his forearm, the way

we had earlier. "Slowly, now. The worst that will happen is you'll get soaked. I can carry you, if you want."

I wasn't opposed to being swept up in his arms and held close to his chest, but… "No, thanks. I appreciate the offer, but I can do this. Like you said, the worst that'll happen is that I'll get wet—wetter."

"All right. Let's go."

Rory was considerably taller than me, so while the water had only come up to his thighs, it came up nearly to my waist. It made for slow going, but we got across without any extra excitement.

On the other side, the path all but vanished, requiring us to move slowly and carefully.

We crossed the second river as we had the first one, going as far to the left as we could to where it was the shallowest.

A little farther, and we crossed through a campsite, then came out onto the road. And then the Sligachan Hotel loomed before us, as glorious and welcoming as any fairy-tale castle.

Heat. Shower. Real food. Bed.

Heaven.

Chapter Twenty-Four

When we arrived at the bunkhouse, the proprietress, Mrs. Anderson, told us there was no availability. A large group of trekkers, who'd planned to camp out that night, decided to treat themselves to four walls, a roof, and real beds after the soaking they got on the trail that day. We could pay to use the showers, but there were no beds.

Amelia made a small sound, and when I looked over at her, she looked like she was about to sob. The whole day, she'd been so strong, bravely pushing through the pain and the cold and the wet with determination and a sense of humor, and now, when we finally reached the end of this day, she was going to be undone because of this?

Not if I could help it. "Mrs. Anderson, can you call over to the hotel and see if they have a vacancy?" The rooms there were expensive, but it would be worth it.

"Aye, of course, lovey," she said. She knew me well after all this time.

She dialed a number and spoke for a moment, then covered the mouthpiece and looked up at us. "There's one double room available." She quoted a price that was high, but not as high as if it were a Saturday night. It didn't matter—I'd pay anything for Amelia to have a bed.

"We'll take it," I said without hesitation. "Cheers, thanks."

The look of relief in Amelia's eyes was worth every pound I'd spend on the room. "I'll shower at the bunkhouse and meet you for dinner at the hotel," I said.

Her brow crinkled. "Shower at the bunkhouse? What are you talking about?"

"You can pay a few pounds to shower there even if you're camping."

"No, I mean, I know that—I read the sign. Why would you camp? We have a room."

"No, *you* have a room."

"You're not going to share it with me?"

"Amelia, a double room means one double bed, not two beds."

"I *know* what it means. And I'm not going to spend a nice cozy night in a real bed while you shiver in your tent on the hard ground!"

"I've camped in far worse conditions—and my sleeping bag is warm." All true.

"Why are you being so difficult about this?"

"Excuse us a moment," I said to Mrs. Anderson, who was watching us avidly, and led Amelia to the corner of the room. "I can't share a bed with you. You're a paying client, and it's not appropriate." Also true.

She scoffed at that. "First of all, who would even know? Second of all, barely an hour ago, you had your hands all over me, or have you forgotten? I think we left behind 'appropriate' two miles and a few rivers back."

How could I forget? I could still taste her lips, still feel the shape of her breast against my hand, remember the way my body had fit against hers. But as much as I'd wanted to give in to the chemistry between us and make love to her in that cozy tent, I couldn't. Amelia had been half-frozen, practically delirious. And though she had initiated the kiss, and seemed more than willing to take it wherever it might have gone, I couldn't be sure she was truly of sound mind in that moment. It had taken every ounce of strength I had to tear myself away from her, and it had taken being submerged waist-deep in a river to finally quench the heat in my body.

"That won't happen again," I muttered. My focus had to be on getting her the rest of the way without further injury, not getting entangled with a lass who would be gone in a few days.

Her cheeks turned pink. "Whether or not *that* happens again also has nothing to do with you sharing the room with me," she said.

"Amelia, I'm sorry, but we just can't—"

Her eyes flashed with anger. "Rory, for God's sake. I'm not going to force myself on you! I can take a hint, okay? Since you don't want anything to do with me, it should make it easy for you to share the damn bed. But if you can't handle it, then by all means, sleep in your goddamn tent."

She turned and stalk-limped back to the desk. I stepped outside and walked a few feet away. I stared at the mountains and concentrated on my breathing, trying to calm my inner turmoil.

She thought I didn't want her, but it was the complete opposite. I wanted her so much that I needed to keep my distance. She made me feel more than I'd felt in so long— whether we were fighting or trading stories, whether I was holding her against me in the icy water or curled around her in a sleeping bag, kissing her till the world outside faded away.

She had made my heart beat again, and she had the power to destroy it.

The door slammed behind me, and Amelia headed for the hotel, her back straight, her head held high, like the brave, feisty woman she was.

And though I knew I should stick with my original plan and camp outside, I couldn't help but follow her.

Chapter Twenty-Five

When we got to the room, I immediately plugged in my phone to charge. Rory hadn't said a word since the lobby, but he had followed me to the room, so I guessed the lure of a warm bed outweighed his fear that I would throw myself at him again.

I had never felt so humiliated in my life, and it was my own fault. What was I thinking, starting an argument like that in a public place? When Rory had left the bunkhouse and I'd returned to the counter to retrieve my pack, the other people milling around in the lobby had blatantly stared. I'd thrown them my best New York glare and hefted my backpack, slinging my arms through the straps.

Mrs. Anderson had looked at me sympathetically. When I'd thanked her for her help, she'd smiled kindly. "Of course, dearie. Just go to the front desk at the hotel. They're expecting you." She'd hesitated for a moment, then added in a low voice, "For what it's worth, I think you're wrong about young Rory."

I was pretty sure she was right. Rory's response to me in the tent had been pretty damn real. The question was, why was he fighting it? I needed to think—but first I needed to get clean.

I turned to him. He looked disturbed, miserable. Well, that made two of us. "Do you mind if I shower first?"

He shook his head. "Of course not. I'll go to the bar and give you your privacy. But we need to talk about something."

"Don't worry, I won't assault you in your sleep."

He sighed. "That's not what I was going to say. Look, today was really hard for you, and it's likely to be worse as we go on, especially if the rain continues. I think you should consider stopping here in Sligachan. It'll be easy enough for us to get a ride from here."

I was shaking my head before he even finished the sentence. "No. I'm not quitting."

"Amelia, please. If you keep pushing your knee, you could do permanent damage to it. If you quit now and take care of yourself, you can come back another time and do the trail."

He was right—I *knew* he was right. But I couldn't quit now. "I can't. I need to do it now. I know you must think I'm ridiculous, but I just…I'm so afraid that if I don't finish the hike, Carrie will never wake up."

I sank down on the edge of the chair, utterly drained from the fight in the lobby and now this.

Rory knelt before me. "I don't think you're ridiculous. Determined, brave, and stubborn as hell, but not ridiculous. Never that."

I forced myself to look away from those eyes, like bottomless pools of seawater after the rain. He spoke so sincerely, but all the pretty words in the world didn't matter if he was refusing to help me. I *had* to finish. If he backed out on me now, I'd have to find someone else to guide me. It wouldn't be the same, but I couldn't let him derail me. Maybe

Mrs. Anderson would know of someone that I could hire.

He laid his hand on top of mine. "Look, I promised I'd help you, and I won't go back on my word."

I snapped my gaze back to his, hope rising within me. "Really?"

His lips curved. "Especially since you'll just do it anyway." I felt my face grow warm. Was I *that* transparent? "At least this way I won't have to worry about you hiring some feckless jackass to help you finish. But I had to ask."

I nodded. "I appreciate you looking out for me." Even if he was the most frustrating man on the entire island, and likely the entire country.

He got to his feet. "Do you need help with anything before I go?"

I wondered what he'd say if I asked him to help me get undressed. He'd probably do it out of obligation, but I didn't want that. If he undressed me again, I wanted it to be because we were about to give in to the attraction between us. "No. I've got it. Thanks."

"Look, I'm sorry about before—"

"I really need that hot shower, Rory," I said, not wanting his apologies. If he couldn't admit to himself that he wanted me, then there was nothing to say.

He just nodded and left the room.

Chapter Twenty-Six

RORY

I left Amelia to her shower and headed for the bar. I didn't think she'd agree to turn back, but I'd had to ask. It was the responsible thing to do. *Yeah, because you've been so responsible up until now.*

I lowered my weary body to the barstool and waited for Gavin to notice me. When he did, a big grin broke out on his face. "Sutherland!" He came around the bar, clasping my hand and pulling me into a hard hug.

"Good to see you, man," I said, hugging him back. Gav was Tommy's age and had been tending bar here for as long as I'd been guiding on Skye. He'd even come with us for some day treks a time or two.

"I was hoping you'd show up. Tommy said you'd stayed behind to help a lass who got injured? That was surprising to hear—until he mentioned she was pretty."

"Pretty" was too ordinary a word to describe Amelia. I pictured the sleepy look in her eyes before she kissed me, the curve of her lips, the rosy flush on her cheeks, the rise of her breasts above the navy fabric of her bra. No, *pretty* was too mundane a word for her.

"Rory?"

Gav was looking at me questioningly, and I realized I needed to answer him. I rolled my eyes and pretended a nonchalance I didn't feel. "She had an important reason to finish, and I told her I'd help her. The fact that she's pretty has nothing to do with it."

"If you say so." He dodged the fist I aimed at his arm and went back around the bar. "So, where is this bonnie lass? I'd like to meet her."

"She's showering in our room—" *Shit. Why the hell had I said that?* As soon as the words left my mouth, I regretted them—especially when Gav's face lit up.

"*Our* room, eh? Well done, you!"

"It's not like that." *But it could be if you would only get out of your own way.*

"So you're not interested in her, then? Tommy seemed to think otherwise."

"Tommy needs to get a hobby that doesn't include me," I muttered.

"Aye, he does, but we're talking about you, not him. What's the big deal, anyway? You're both adults."

"You know why I stay away from the lasses in the groups I'm guiding."

"Rory, not every woman is going to be like Emma," Gav said quietly.

Gav had met Emma a few times. He'd advised me to stay away from her, saying there was something off about her, which I'd ignored. And after all the shit went down with her—after she'd nearly cost me my job—he'd kept my glass topped off and just listened to me talk, then let me crash on his sofa. He was a good friend, never saying "I told you so" when that relationship had gone to hell.

"Sorry, Ror," he continued. "I didn't mean to butt in or to bring up Emma. I just know she did a number on you and that you haven't really let anyone get close to you since then."

"I haven't been completely alone since Emma, you know." I might not be like Tommy, with a lass in half the towns we passed through on our treks, but I wasn't a total monk, either.

He nodded. "Aye, I know. You've been with a few lasses here and there. But you haven't let anyone get close to *you*. As in the man, and not just the warm body," he added with a waggle of his eyebrows.

I lunged for him, but he jumped back out of reach. "Seriously, man," he said, all traces of humor gone. "You haven't."

I sighed. "Amelia has already gotten closer to me—the man—than anyone else has in...ever. She was also close to me—the warm body—when she nearly froze to death on the trail today." *And after.* "But she's not the kind of lass you walk away from after a few days. And I can't have anything more than that, not with Amelia. She and I are just sharing a room for the night, and that's it."

And how in the hell is that *going to go, exactly?*

Gav pulled down two short glasses and poured a splash of Talisker Storm into each. "On me," he said, sliding one my way and picking up the other.

"*Slàinte,*" I said, holding up the glass. He repeated the toast and we drank. The peaty whisky was like an old friend, its comforting warmth spreading through me.

The bar started to get busy, as it always did in the evenings. I ordered a Magner's cider and nursed it, chatting with Gav every now and then when he had a quiet moment, but otherwise keeping to myself.

I texted Scarlet to let her know where we were and that Amelia was holding up okay. Then I texted Tommy.

*At Sligachan. Amelia's doing okay. BTW, Gav thinks
I stayed behind "because of a pretty lass," so thx for
that. You know he'll never drop it.*

Tommy's response came a few minutes later.

*Hey man, I just said you'd stayed behind to help a
lass who got injured. He asked if she was pretty—was
I supposed to lie?*

Whatever. All good with the group?

*At Elgol now—about to meet for dinner. The cliffs
were really shitty after that rain today, so be careful
when you get there.*

Thx. Will take it slow.

You staying at the bunkhouse?

Shit. I could lie and say yes, but there was no way Tommy
wouldn't find out from Gav.

*The bunkhouse was booked. Got the last avail room
at hotel.*

You're sharing with Amelia? Dude.

I told her I'd camp, but she insisted. We can handle it.

If we didn't kill each other first.

Can't wait to hear ALL about it.

Bugger off.

:) Take it easy, and maybe even try to have fun?

Bye, Tommy.

I set aside my phone and stared into my glass, my thoughts drifting back to Amelia. How could she think I wasn't interested in her? How could she not know that I wanted her more than I wanted my next breath?

Tommy—and Gav, too—would tell me to stop overthinking, to just enjoy a short hookup with Amelia if she was up for it, and then say goodbye when the trek was over.

But honestly, I didn't want that. Not with her. I'd already let her get closer to me than anyone had in a long time, and if we took it further, I'd be that much more wrecked when she left. And I couldn't go through that again.

I glanced at my phone. It had been nearly an hour since I'd left Amelia in the room. I drained my cider and bumped fists with Gav. "See you in a few." Even if Amelia was still mad at me, I didn't think she'd pass on a hot meal that didn't come out of a bag.

I reached the room and tapped lightly on the door. "Amelia, can I come in?"

"Yeah," came her muffled voice.

I inserted my key in the slot and pushed open the door. Amelia sat on the edge of the bed in the jeans and black top she'd worn that first night. Her hair fell around her shoulders in loose waves, and she looked—utterly defeated, her phone dangling limply from her hand. *Oh no.* I closed the door behind me and strode to the bed. "Is it Carrie?"

She shook her head. "No." *Thank God.* "But I thought—"

I hesitated a moment, then dropped down beside her and took her hand. "What did you think, love?"

The endearment just slipped out, but she either didn't notice or didn't care, because I didn't get a glare. Then she looked up at me, her chocolate-brown eyes shining with unshed tears, and all I could think was that I *wished* she'd glared at me, because her anger was better than the sadness that was there now.

"I guess I just hoped that when I turned on my phone after two days, there'd be a message that Carrie had woken up, or at the very least, there'd be some good news about her condition. But there's nothing—no missed calls, no messages, nothing. It's stupid, I know. But I just *hoped*—"

Her voice broke, and I reached for her. I expected her to resist after our earlier argument, but she turned in to my arms. I ran my hand down the smooth length of her hair, offering the only comfort I could, knowing it wasn't enough. She let out a few shuddering breaths but was otherwise quiet.

After a few minutes, she pulled back and sat up. Her eyes were a little red, a little damp. But she was still so damn beautiful. More than ever, I wished things could be different between us.

"While we're on the trail, it's easy enough to focus on putting one foot in front of the other and clearing my mind of everything else, you know?" She looked down at her hands. "But then at the end of the day, I have time to think and it just…"

Her voice trailed off, but I knew. "It crushes down on you like a lead weight."

Her eyes met mine. "Yes."

"Listen, you can't give up hope. Remember, no news is good news. Maybe Carrie hasn't taken a turn for the better, but at least she hasn't taken a turn for the worse."

"I know. And I haven't given up. I just had a moment, you know?"

"I do know. Believe me."

She didn't say anything more, didn't ask me how I knew what she meant. Telling her wouldn't make her feel better, anyway.

I got to my feet. "I think it's almost time for a drink, don't you?"

"God, yes."

"I'm going to grab a quick shower, and then I'll be ready

to go."

She smiled. "I might even have left you some hot water." It was a small smile, and it didn't quite reach her eyes, but after her tears, it was like seeing the sun.

I grabbed a change of clothes from my pack and headed for the bathroom door.

"Rory?"

I turned back. "Yeah?"

"Thanks for listening."

"I'll always listen, Amelia. No matter what's going on between us, I will always listen when you need me. Okay?"

She smiled for real this time, and I smiled back. "I won't be long in the shower, and then we can go to the bar and get dinner."

"You had me at *bar*. Take your time. I'll be here when you get out."

I did take my time, as it turned out. The hot water felt amazing after the cold misery of the day's walk, and I just stood there for a few minutes, my head bowed under the spray, enjoying the feel of the water cascading down my tired body.

It felt weirdly intimate to use the shower after Amelia. The bathroom was still steamy when I'd stepped inside. It smelled like her shampoo and some kind of lotion. I washed my hair, then lathered up my hands and started to scrub away the grime of the day. I tried not to picture Amelia doing the same thing just a few minutes earlier, tried not to imagine her hands sliding all over her wet body. Tried not to imagine *my* hands sliding all over her wet body.

No. Stop. What kind of a creep was I for lusting after her when she'd just been crying over Carrie? Amelia needed a friend, and I would be that friend—if she wanted me to.

And that was all.

Sighing, I turned the water to cold—as far as it could go. So much for the relaxing shower.

Chapter Twenty-Seven

AMELIA

While Rory was in the shower, I picked up my phone and dialed Carrie's mom. She answered on the first ring. "Amelia, are you all right? I was worried when I didn't hear from you yesterday."

"Hi Helen. I'm okay. We just had no service."

"I know you told me it would be spotty, but you know I can't keep from worrying about my girls," she said, her voice breaking.

My eyes immediately filled with tears. "I know," I managed. "How is she? I'd hoped that when I had signal again, there'd be a message or something…"

She sighed. "No change, sweetie. She's still lying there, not moving. But she's alive, and she's stable," she said brightly. "And that's all that matters. We washed her hair today, and they let me braid it. She looks so pretty. The cuts on her face are almost gone, which means her body is healing itself. She's going to wake up soon. I know it. We just have to believe."

"I do believe. Can I talk to her for a sec?" Just then, Rory came out of the bathroom, wearing khakis and a polo shirt. He pointed to himself and then the door, and raised his eyebrows. *Do you want me to go outside?* I shook my head. *No.*

There was a muffled sound. "Okay, I'm putting the phone to her ear," said Helen.

"Hey Ree. I'm calling from the Sligachan Hotel. Today was pretty rough—it poured like cats and dogs for most of the afternoon, and we had to cross a bunch of streams and rivers that were pretty high. I've never been so cold, even on that awful hike we did with the Environmental Club. But I had the most wonderful hot shower a few minutes ago, and I'll get to sleep in a warm bed tonight, so it's all good. Hang in there, Ree. I love you, and I miss you, and I'll see you soon."

I took a deep, shuddering breath, then spoke louder. "Hey, Helen, I have to go."

There was another muffled sound, and I knew she was putting the phone back to her own ear. "All right, sweetie. Be safe."

"I will. I'll try to call tomorrow, but if I can't, don't worry about me, okay?"

"I'll try not to. And don't forget to check in with your mom."

"I did." I'd emailed her before Rory returned to the room, leaving out the knee injury.

We said goodbye and ended the call. I went into the bathroom, locked the door, sank down on the toilet lid, and sobbed. It killed me to hear Helen's forced cheer, to talk at Carrie, who couldn't respond—and maybe never would.

Finally, I wiped my eyes and stood in front of the mirror to repair my makeup from the kit I'd left on the counter.

Taking a deep breath, I left the bathroom. Rory's eyes were filled with concern, but he didn't say anything. He didn't need to. Maybe one day he'd share his story and I could reciprocate the kindness he'd shown me tonight.

I mustered up a smile that probably looked like something out of a nightmare. "Are you ready to go? I really need that drink."

When we got down to the bar, the cute, dark-haired bartender came over, a big smile on his face, his blue eyes friendly. "You must be Amelia," he said. He turned to Rory. "She's just as bonnie as Tommy said she was."

"Um, thank you?" I said, my face flaming.

Rory rolled his eyes. "Amelia, this is my friend Gavin. Great guy, but unrepentant flirt, so watch out for him. Gav, this is Amelia. Behave yourself."

"Don't listen to him," Gavin said. "He just doesn't know how to have fun."

Gavin was charming and friendly and reminded me of Tommy. He ragged on Rory for a bit longer, then handed us menus. We took them to a booth along the wall and sat down.

"What are you thinking of getting? Everything here is really good."

"I'm getting the cream of vegetable soup and the shepherd's pie," I said. "I want all the hot things after today."

"Sounds good. I'll go up and order. What do you want to drink?"

"What are you getting?"

"Whisky, most likely."

"Do they have the one you had in your flask—was that yesterday?"

"Talisker Storm? Aye, I had some earlier. You liked it?"

"I did." It was smoky and strong, and I liked the way it warmed me from within. I also remembered how it tasted on Rory's lips when he'd kissed me after his nightmare. *No, don't go there.*

"Okay." He got to his feet. "I'll be right back."

"Wait, I'm paying." I rummaged in my purse for my credit card.

"We'll split it."

"No. You're helping drag my gimpy ass all over this island, and you're paying for the room. The least I can do is buy you dinner." He started to protest, but I laid my hand on his. "Rory, please let me do this."

He studied me for a moment, then nodded. "All right, thank you." He stuck the card in his pocket and went up to the bar.

Dinner ended up being much better than I'd feared after our earlier argument. The food was amazing, and so was the whisky.

He kept the conversation light, telling me about more colorful guiding experiences he'd had. Some of them were so outrageous, he had to be embellishing them, but he did it so smoothly, I couldn't tell what was true and what wasn't.

After a second round of drinks—and a shared dessert of sticky toffee pudding, which was heaven in a bowl—I was suddenly hit with a wave of exhaustion.

Rory stood and held out his hand. "Come on, let's get you to bed."

My whole body ran hot at his words, even though I knew he didn't mean them the way they'd sounded. I stared at his outstretched hand and then looked up at his face. He looked pained.

"You can't have it both ways, you know," I said.

"I'm not trying to. I only meant that you look like you're going to fall over if you don't lie down really soon. And I'm one step behind you."

I took his hand and let him pull me to my feet. He handed

me the trekking pole he'd insisted I use as a cane, though I felt more than a little stupid using it inside.

We stopped by the bar to say goodbye to Gavin, who pulled me into a hug as if we'd been friends for a year instead of meeting for the first time an hour earlier.

Then Gavin and Rory did the hug-backslap thing guys do. "Great seeing you again, Ror," said Gavin. "And about before? I get it, but you should think about what I said."

"Gav," Rory growled. *What was that about?*

Gavin held up his hands, palms out, and took a step back. "I'm just saying you should think about it."

"I'm not getting into this again with you," Rory said. "You're just like Tommy."

"Och, and is that so bad? That lad knows you better than anyone—probably including yourself. And there's no better friend a man could ask for."

Rory sighed. "Aye, I know that. Look, we need to go. It's been a long day, and we're in for a longer one tomorrow, if the weather continues as it has. Can you spare a bag of ice?"

"Of course." Gavin filled a bag and handed it over.

"Cheers, Gav," said Rory. "Catch you next time." They man-hugged again, and Rory headed for the door.

"Hope your knee feels better soon, Amelia," Gavin said. "And don't worry, you're in great hands with this guy."

I knew that all too well, but he probably didn't mean it the way I did. I just smiled at him and thanked him for the ice. "Hope to see you again sometime," I said.

He glanced at Rory and then winked at me. "Maybe you will," he said with a cheeky grin. What did *that* mean?

We left the bar and walked toward the entrance of the hotel. "Thank you, Rory."

He looked surprised. "For what?"

"For keeping my mind off...everything...with your stories. I really appreciate it."

"I'm glad I could be there." He hesitated a moment. "I can't imagine how difficult it must be to talk to Carrie's mom."

"She doesn't hate me," I whispered. "Neither does Carrie's dad, and I don't understand why. I ran a fucking stop sign, and now their daughter might die. How can they *not* hate me?"

"Because they've known you all your life, and they know how much you love Carrie and would never intentionally hurt her. Because accidents happen, and they've *chosen* not to blame you for it. You're lucky to have them—and they're lucky to have you."

From the sudden bitterness in his voice, I suspected that he'd had an experience that was just the opposite.

I wondered if he'd ever tell me about it.

A few minutes later, I sat on the bed in shorts and my sleep shirt, icing my knee, which was elevated on some throw pillows.

"How does it feel?" asked Rory, who sat in a chair by the window, doing something on his phone. He'd changed out of his khakis and polo into a T-shirt and the shorts he slept in, and I was trying my best not to stare at him.

"Sore. The ice feels good, though. Thanks for getting it from Gavin—I hadn't thought to ask."

"That's because you've gotten used to a dip in the sea instead."

"Ha, maybe."

He grinned. "Admit it, you wish we were having a swim right now instead of this."

My smile faded as I pictured him cradling me in his arms, walking through icy water to bring down the swelling in my knee; pictured him kissing me in the tent—and then pulling back and going about his business like it meant nothing. "Actually, what I wish is for you to stop flirting with me if you don't want me."

I grabbed the bag of ice and staggered to my feet. "I'm going to get—" I began, but my words were cut off as he strode across the room, cupped my face in his hands, and kissed the breath out of me.

The bag of ice dropped to the floor as I flung my arms around his neck and kissed him back, every cell in my body jumping for joy. *He* does *want me!* Without breaking the kiss, he scooped me up, holding me to him with one arm across my back. He flung the throw pillows to the floor and laid me on the bed, his body coming down on top of mine. *Yes!*

He shoved up the hem of my shirt and tore his mouth from mine to yank it over my head and toss it aside.

He stared down at me, his eyes hot and hungry as they roved over me, taking in my low-cut black lace bra, definitely *not* like the sports bras I wore on the trail. "So beautiful," he breathed.

I drew him to me, my head falling back as he dragged his open mouth down my throat and into the valley between my breasts. He cupped them, caressing me through the lacy fabric. His fingers and lips and tongue danced over my skin, sending a rush of desire racing through me, and I arched into his touch, wanting, needing…

And then I cried out in pain as he shifted his weight and bumped my bad knee.

It was like a bucket of ice water had been dumped over us. His lovely, warm weight left me as he pulled back with a curse and stood. "I'm sorry! Are you all right?"

I took a deep breath and let it out slowly as the pain subsided. "I'm fine," I said, reaching for him once more.

But he just shook his head and tossed me my shirt before

crossing to the other side of the room, as far away from me as he could get.

"I can't. I should never have..." He turned away and dragged his hands through his hair.

I pulled on my shirt. "You can turn around now," I said flatly. I thought we were finally moving past this hot-and-cold bullshit, but it seemed I was wrong.

He turned around. His hair was wild from his fingers, his lips were swollen from our kisses, and his chest was heaving as if he'd just run up a hill—except he never got out of breath when he ran up a hill. "I'll sleep in my tent," he said, and took a step toward his pack.

"Don't be an idiot," I hissed. "Just get in the goddamn bed. I promise to keep my hands off of you."

"Amelia—"

I slapped the switch to turn off the lamp and turned on my side, scooting over as far as I could without falling off the edge (which wasn't very far), my body still burning for his touch.

I felt the bed dip as he climbed in on the other side. I lay there for several long minutes, waiting for my temper to subside, then rolled to my back. "Why?" I asked, not caring if I woke him. "I'm pretty sure you want me as much as I want you."

He laughed humorlessly, clearly as awake as I was. "How can you even question that after what just happened?"

"Well, it was pretty easy for you to stop."

"Because I hurt you!"

"For a second."

"Long enough to remind me where we were and who *you* are. And it made me come to my senses."

"Well, that's just what I wanted to hear," I snapped, blinking back tears. "I'm glad we clarified things."

"I said that wrong," he said quietly. "Amelia, we can't be

together. You'll be finished with the trail in a few days, and then you'll be returning home to your life." His hand found mine in the dark. "No matter how much we both want it, it can't happen."

I took a deep breath and plunged. "Look, we have what, three more days of the trek, maybe four? It's just the two of us, with no one else around to judge or criticize. We're adults. Why can't we just…be together? Until we finish the trek? I mean, I live in New York, and I'm starting a job in Miami in a few months. It's not like I can stick around anyway."

The silence between us was palpable. My face burning, I started to pull my hand from his, but he tightened his grip. "Forget I said anything, Rory. I get it. It's fine."

"You *don't* get it."

"Then explain it to me!"

"It wouldn't be enough!"

"What?" I whispered.

"Three or four days with you wouldn't be enough, Amelia. I've only known you for a short time, but it's enough to know that you would never be happy with a quick fling and a goodbye handshake at the end."

"That's not true."

"You know it is."

I closed my eyes in defeat. He was right. A quick fling had never been my style with the guys I'd dated back home, and I wanted Rory far more than I'd wanted them. There was nothing more to say, then. I started to roll to my side once more, but he stopped me with his hand on my shoulder, turning me to face him in the dark.

"And neither would I," he added. "Be happy with it."

I froze. What was he saying?

He sighed. "I had a girlfriend. Emma. She was a lass in my group on the West Highland Way last year. She was up from London with friends, and they were doing the trek for their twenty-first birthdays. Emma flirted with me from the minute we met at the welcome dinner. She was pretty and funny, and I was into it. On the third night, when everyone else went to bed early after two strenuous days in a row, she knocked on the door of my room at the B&B. I should have said good night and closed the door, because I was the guide, and she was a client. But I didn't."

Oh no. Had something happened to her? I tightened my hand around his in sympathy. To my surprise, he made a sound that was almost like a laugh.

"This is not a tragic story, Amelia. I'm sorry if I worried you."

"It's not?"

"Emma isn't the reason for my nightmares. Just hear me out, okay?"

"Okay."

"Anyway, after the trek ended, I had a week off, and I went to see her. We had a great time. She was smart and funny, and when I was with her, I didn't think about...things."

I knew he meant the things that haunted him in his sleep.

"For the first month or so, we saw each other a few times, and it was great. But that was at the beginning of the season. Once things really got busy, I barely had any time off. And she couldn't handle it. She called me incessantly while I was working, and if I didn't answer in the evenings—which was usually because I was out for dinner with the group or asleep—she got paranoid. She accused me of messing around with the girls in my group. Which I never, ever did."

No, he wouldn't. "I believe you," I said.

He scoffed. "I wish *she* had. She assumed that there was always a lass in my group that was hitting on me, and since I'd said yes to *her*, that obviously meant I said yes to everyone.

"I should have just ended it, but I hated that she thought of me that way. I hated that she thought of me that way, and

I didn't want to lose her, so I took a week off and went to see her, which seemed to reassure her. But then my holiday was over, and it went right back to the way it had been before, with her accusing me of being unfaithful. Tommy and Gav couldn't understand why I didn't break it off with her. I should have, but I didn't want her to think it was an admission of guilt.

"I was miserable—all the time. It was affecting my work and my friendship with Tommy because I was angry with him for saying what I didn't want to hear."

Tommy must have been so frustrated, watching Rory spiraling because of this girl and not being able to help.

"Then she showed up on a West Highland Way trek I was guiding in late September, near the end of the season. It was on the third day, and we'd stopped for lunch at this hotel along Loch Lomond, like we always did. I was chatting with one of the women—whose boyfriend was in the loo at the time—and suddenly there was Emma, shrieking at me about how she knew I'd been cheating on her and now she had proof. And then the boyfriend came out and heard Emma's ranting."

"Oh crap." I could just picture how that went down.

He laughed harshly. "Aye, you could say that. He immediately believed Emma—which says something about his relationship with his girlfriend—and threw a punch at me."

"Seriously?"

"Yep. I ducked it, and he later apologized, but the damage had been done. In one minute, Emma had undermined my authority over the group. I told her we were done. Then I called Tommy, who was off that week, and asked him to cover the rest of the trek for me. He agreed immediately, even though I'd said some nasty things the last time I'd seen him. I waited for him to get there, introduced him to the group, and then left, so furious I couldn't see straight."

I squeezed his hand. "I'm so sorry, Rory. I want to punch

Emma in the face. I mean, you can't, but I can, right?"

He laughed, for real this time. "I'm picturing you striding up to her, your cheeks flushed with anger, your eyes shooting daggers. I don't even need to picture you actually punching her; the righteous indignation is good enough."

"Your experience with Emma was truly shitty," I said quietly, "but I'm not sure I get how it's related to us."

"Her actions—and my *in*action—could have put SBF in jeopardy. People don't pay good money to hike with a group where the guides have drama, and SBF is still a fairly new company that relies on word of mouth. We were lucky that the folks in the group were decent people who didn't leave shitty reviews or badmouth SBF online. But Scarlet was worried for a few weeks after that group finished. And she wasn't happy with me. And that wasn't even the worst part, really."

There was more?

"Even though Emma turned out to be a disaster, even though she nearly cost me my job and my friends, for a while I had someone to come home to. Someone who missed me when I was gone. Someone I was looking forward to lying around with on a winter day, watching movies. For those months, I wasn't alone. And then suddenly, I *was* alone, and it fucking sucked."

It explained so much.

"Amelia, I'm always on the road, guiding a trek almost every week during busy season, or doing weekend hikes with clients or kids in the off season. I live with Tommy and a bunch of other guys in a shitty flat in Fort William. My life isn't conducive to a real relationship. There are a couple of girls I hook up with from time to time, but they don't want more, and neither do I—not with them. But it's different with you. I've already told you things that I've never told anyone, not even Tommy. I would want more with you, but I—we— can't have that. And to go down that road, even for just the few days we have together, only to then be alone again once you're gone—I can't do it."

His words were both thrilling and devastating. "So, what? We just ignore this?" I whispered. I practically burned every time he touched me. How could we not act on it?

"We have to," he said sadly. "We'll finish the trek, and then we'll say goodbye, and you'll go back to your life. Maybe we'll email once in a while. And maybe you'll come back to Scotland one day, and we'll meet for a drink. That's all it can be."

I could picture it going down exactly as he'd just described. And it hurt, so badly, to think that after all this, we'd be reduced to an occasional email when he wasn't busy with a trek.

"I'm sorry, Amelia," he murmured.

"Me, too. I kind of wish we could go back to hating each other."

"I never hated you, though I admit to being a condescending dick on several occasions."

"Why'd you act like that, then, if you didn't hate me?"

"I thought you were too obsessed with taking photos to post on social media, defeating the purpose of being out in nature and leaving technology behind for a week. I also thought you were too inexperienced, and I was afraid you'd get hurt. I may have also liked the way you looked when you shouted at me," he admitted, sending a little thrill through me. "Why'd you hate me?"

"I didn't hate you."

"Then why'd you keep picking fights?"

"Because when I fought with you, I wasn't thinking of Carrie. And I felt alive again, for the first time since the crash."

"The two of us are a fuckin' mess," he said.

"We really are."

"I can be a condescending dick again, if you want."

"And I could pick fights with you."

"Pretty sure that'll happen anyway."

I laughed at that. "You're probably right. Maybe we could just try to get along and enjoy the occasional fight?"

"Deal." He shook my hand, lingering for a moment before letting go, then rolled to his side, away from me. "Good night, Amelia. Sleep well."

"'Night." I curled up, making myself as small as possible so I wouldn't brush against him. *Sleep well,* he'd said. As if I would sleep at all with him lying six inches away from me.

An hour later, he was asleep, if his even breathing was any indication, and I was still wide awake, my mind unable to rest. I'd offered myself to him in a way I never had before with any other guy I'd known for so short a time, and he'd turned me down in so gentlemanly a way that I couldn't even be mad about it, damn him.

The bed shifted, and I was suddenly pressed up against a wall of heat. I peered over my shoulder. In his sleep, Rory had rolled to his back, his arm coming to rest against me. I tried to ease away from him, but there was no room.

This was going to be the longest night, ever.

I should have just let him sleep in his tent.

Chapter Twenty-Eight

Rain poured down, the sound a violent drumbeat against the nylon walls of the tent. But inside, it was another world entirely: dry and warm and smelling of spring and sunshine.

She leaned over me, her long hair tumbling over my bare skin with an erotic tickle. I sucked in a breath as the motion brought her hips flush against mine, only a few layers of fabric keeping me from her.

Her tongue stroked along mine as she kissed me. Then she broke the kiss and sat up, her lips curving into a smile as she gazed down at me. She reached back and unhooked her bra, then slowly dragged it down her arms and tossed it to the side. Wordlessly, she took my hands and brought them to her breasts, her lips parting on a gasp as I cupped their weight in my palms and traced them with the pads of my thumbs.

Then it was my turn to gasp as her hands slid down my abdomen. My hips rose to meet hers, and I lifted my gaze in time to see her lips curve in a slow, seductive smile. She leaned over me once more, her hair falling around me as her hand dipped lower...

I came awake as the dream faded. Unlike my other dreams lately, it didn't leave me wracked with horror and grief. But it did leave me with my body painfully aroused from the most vivid erotic dream I'd had in a long time.

There was a soft sigh, and a warm body snuggled into mine. My eyes snapped open. *What?* And then I remembered.

I was in a too-small bed in the Sligachan Hotel, curled around Amelia with my face buried in her hair. My right arm was wrapped around her waist, my hand nearly touching her breast. Her hand lay over mine, as if she'd pulled my arm around her and hadn't let go.

We couldn't have been any closer to each other unless we were naked.

I needed to move away from her, even though that was the very last thing I wanted to do. But I couldn't stay wrapped around her like this. Not after turning her down the way I had.

I carefully disentangled myself from her and eased out of the bed. It was early yet—the light coming in through the window was the pale gray of dawn—but I couldn't go back to sleep. Not with my body hungering for hers.

There was an indentation on the bed from where I'd lain so close to her, and I wondered what it would be like to wake up with her in my arms for real, to make love to her as night gave way to dawn.

I'd taken things too far last night. But she'd been going on about how I didn't want her, and I'd had to show her how wrong she was. How much I *did* want her. I'd intended just to kiss her, but then she'd pressed her body to mine and kissed me back, and I'd just given in.

I thought of how she'd felt under me, how her body had responded to my touch, how she'd arched against my hand.

If I hadn't jostled her damn knee, I was certain the evening would have ended differently, with our bodies sated and entwined for real, without this misery hanging over us. But what I'd said to Amelia was true. I couldn't bear the thought of being with her and then letting her go. She was an amazing woman who would do anything for those she loved, even at her own peril.

The kind of woman I could love. The kind of woman I'd be devastated to lose.

But she was here to finish the trek and return home to her life in the States. It was no use dwelling on those thoughts.

I sank into the armchair under the window and stared out at the mountains. Our walk today would take us past Bla Bheinn, the mountain that had irrevocably changed my life. The source of my nightmares. And the reason I continued to guide the Skye Trail, month after month, year after year. I could never let myself forget, even for a second.

I needed to get through today, get past Bla Bheinn without incident. Then we'd be in the homestretch, and with any luck, we'd complete the Skye Trail in three days and my life could get back to normal.

Amelia made some small sound in her sleep, and I dragged my thoughts away from the mountain to just look at her for a moment. Her dark hair was spread across the white pillowcase, her lovely face was relaxed in slumber, her lips were parted slightly.

The next three days were going to be torture.

Chapter Twenty-Nine

I opened my eyes, suddenly cold, as if my blanket had been yanked off. But no, it was still there. I rolled to my back, my body dipping into an indentation in the mattress that was still warm, as if…well, as if Rory had been snuggled up behind me and had just gotten up.

The room was bathed in the silvery light of morning, and Rory sat in the armchair by the window, his hands tunneling into his unruly hair.

"Are you all right?"

He jolted, then slowly took his head from his hands and turned to look at me, his features indistinct in the shadowy room. "Yeah, just couldn't sleep any longer." He scrubbed his hands over his face and stood. "I was going to wake you in a few minutes, but since you're up, let's have a look at your knee."

He sat down on the edge of the bed and eased my leg onto his lap. His hands on my skin were an uncomfortable reminder of last night, even though his touch was far less intimate. He unwrapped the bandage and gently prodded my knee. "The swelling's gone down a bit. How does it feel?"

I carefully flexed it a few times, then got to my feet and walked around the room. "It doesn't hurt as much as it did. I mean, it's not great, but it's definitely better than it was."

"Good." He slid from the bed, retrieving his phone from his nightstand and poking at it. "It's almost seven. Let me re-wrap your leg, and then we should get moving. It's nearly twelve miles to Elgol. That's going to take us all day. And there's more rain expected later, so we want to get to it."

"Super. I can't wait to be wet and cold and miserable again. Okay if I grab the bathroom first? I won't be long."

"Go ahead. Might as well put on your rain gear, too."

A little while later, we were on our way. We went over a lovely old stone bridge that offered a stunning view of the glen cutting between the mountains. I stopped on the bridge to take some photos, the first since before we traversed all the streams and rivers yesterday, when I was afraid I'd drop my phone in the water.

"This is a very famous view," said Rory. "It's actually more famous if you take the photo with the bridge in it. Let's compromise, for Carrie. Give me your phone and go stand over there." He gestured to the right side of the bridge. When I was in position, I turned. "Say 'Sligachan.'"

Grinning, I said it, and he snapped a few pictures before handing back the phone. "I took a close-up of you and then a zoomed-out one so you can see the background. Glen Sligachan separates the Black Cuillins to the right—so called because they're comprised of black igneous rock—from the Red Cuillins to the left, so called because they're mostly granite and look reddish when the light hits them. There's your geology lesson for the day."

"Take a selfie with me," I blurted out. I didn't have many

pictures of him (and those I did have may or may not have been ones I stealth-snapped earlier in the trip under the guise of taking scenery shots) and wanted at least one good one.

"Sure. I'll take it; my arm is longer than yours." He sat beside me on the stone wall and leaned in close. "I think we got some of the view as well," he said after he snapped a few shots.

"Thanks, Rory."

"No worries. Ready to go?" He handed me my poles, and we started off.

"Would you like me to take a picture of the two of you?" We turned to see two middle-aged women behind us on the bridge.

"Aye, that would be brilliant, thanks," said Rory. "Can I bother you to take one with mine as well?" My heart gave a happy little kick at the thought that he wanted to remember me after the trek was over.

They took pictures of us, and then we returned the favor before crossing the bridge and going through a gate to pick up the path.

The sky over the glen was dark and brooding, and the tops of the mountains on either side were cloaked in mist. It had been amazing when we were up on the Trotternish Ridge and we could see the mountains stretched out on either side, but walking at ground level between Marsco on the left and Sgùrr nan Gillean on the right, looking nearly straight up at their imposing faces and cloud-enshrouded peaks? It was *awesome*.

I took a few pictures and then just stared. No photograph could begin to do justice to this place.

"Are you all right?" asked Rory, after I'd stopped for maybe the tenth time in as many minutes to gape at the mountains. "Is it your knee?"

"No. I just never imagined a place like this. Not ever."

"Glen Sligachan is pretty damned impressive."

I shook my head. "Not just the glen. All of Skye. I mean, I've seen *The Lord of the Rings* and *Game of Thrones*, where they film in exotic, scenic places. Of course I know that those places exist in the world. And I knew that Scotland had some pretty amazing scenery, too. But I just never—" I broke off, not even sure how to put my thoughts into words.

"Never what?"

"Never imagined the way it would make me feel to be here, to be standing among all this beauty. I know it's been spectacular all along, but I think in the first few days, I was so focused on putting one foot in front of the other and taking all the photos I could, and trying to remember every detail for Carrie, that I just forgot to take it all in for myself. And now that I am, it's going to be hard to go back to flat Long Island and even flatter Miami."

I could stay here. The thought came to me, sudden and unbidden. I shook my head to clear it. No, of course I couldn't. My life was back in the States, where an iced coffee was never more than ten minutes away, where my family and Carrie were. Where my new job was. I pictured the wide beaches of Miami, the avenues lined with palm trees, the beautiful weather. Then I thought of the traffic. And the crowds, and the noise. And the oppressive heat and humidity in the summer.

It was almost painful to think about.

"Those places have their own beauty."

I shrugged. "They do. But it's not the same."

"No, it's not, but I'm biased," he said with a smile, which I tried and failed to return.

It was a few minutes before he spoke again. "You never mentioned what you'll be doing in Miami."

"I...it's hard to think about it, you know? Carrie and I are supposed to be going together, to start these new jobs at a hotel that's opening there. And if she doesn't wake up, then how can I still go?"

"You'd go because it's what she'd want you to do, Amelia. She'd want you to go on living."

"But then I'd always wonder if I was following her dream instead of mine," I whispered. And that was it, the thing I hadn't admitted to anyone, not even myself.

He stopped walking. "Hey, look at me."

I did, meeting those incredible eyes.

"Carrie would want you to be happy."

"How can you know that?"

"Because you've been showing her to me this whole time. I feel like I know her, and I know this to be true. Okay?"

I nodded. "Okay." I could almost believe anything he told me when he looked at me like that.

"So, tell me about the job."

"It's at a new hotel that's opening up in South Beach, which is the happening place in Miami. It'll mostly be working reception at the beginning, but there's plenty of room to advance. I eventually want to get more into the tourism side of things, like arranging excursions and activities for the guests—sailing, parasailing, scuba diving, trips to the Keys and the Everglades. I'm hoping it'll be a stepping-stone to working not just for the hotel but booking tours for anyone visiting the Miami area."

"It sounds like you're enthusiastic about it. I don't think you have to worry that it's just Carrie's dream. Gordon from your group mentioned he works in that field. Did you talk to him at all?"

"I did. He gave me his card and said he'd be happy to meet with me when I get to Florida, which was nice of him."

"Yeah, he was a nice guy."

We stopped for a quick break and a snack at a spot overlooking two lochans ("wee inland lochs," according to

Rory), but he didn't let us linger there. "We've still got about eight miles to Elgol," he said, staring at the forbidding clouds overhead, which had not dissipated throughout the morning, as they'd sometimes done.

Another mountain soon came into view on the left, its summit lost in the clouds. "What's that one?"

Without looking at it, he muttered something that sounded like *bla-ven*, then quickened his pace. I thought about hustling to catch up to him, but the path was flat enough that I could manage without his help.

I wondered at his sudden mood change. I didn't think it was anything I'd said. At one point, he looked back and did a slight double-take when he saw that I was like twenty feet behind him.

He strode back to me. "Can you go any faster? It's gonna start pouring any second."

Indeed, the air felt heavy, electrified, the way it often did in July or August back home, when it was ninety-five degrees with 100 percent humidity, and a thunderstorm was imminent.

I picked up the pace, though only a little, because while my knee was holding up, I didn't want to push it.

Bla Bheinn continued to tower over us on the left, but Rory didn't even look at it as we passed. He was focused on the path before us, the sky over our heads, or on me. We hurried across no fewer than five streams as we passed a biggish loch on the right.

And then with a mighty crash of thunder, the skies opened up and rain poured down as if some great dam in the sky had been breached.

"We have to move faster," he said. He took a firm hold of my arm and practically dragged me down the path. We hurried along, trudging through yet another stream and slogging through another bog, the mud sucking at our boots as if it wanted to keep us there for eternity.

And all the while, the rain continued to pour down as the sky rumbled. Finally, the path emerged at a bay. The sea was roiling, the whitecaps churning angrily.

"Almost there," yelled Rory.

Almost *where*? There was no way we'd come twelve miles.

Then I saw a small hut a short way down the beach. "Please say we're going there!"

"Yes, that's the bothy at Camasunary Bay. We'll take shelter there and see if the storm passes. We're still about four miles from Elgol."

When we reached the bothy, Rory opened the door and quickly ushered me inside the stone structure.

I stood there for a moment, so relieved to be indoors that I could have cried.

Rory touched my shoulder. "Are you all right?"

I smiled. "Just happy to be out of the rain."

He smiled back. "Yeah, it was pretty rough out there. Let me help you with your boots."

We stripped off all our wet gear and hung it in the entryway. I entered the main room, chafing my hands up and down my arms, trying to warm up. "It's left unlocked? I mean, I'm obviously not complaining, I'm just surprised."

"Aye, that's the point. It's maintained by the Mountain Bothy Association for exactly this purpose—for walkers to have a place to shelter."

The front room had a picture window that offered a gorgeous view of the stormy bay. Below that was a counter that held a coffee can, a box of teabags, a few decks of cards, and some other random things. Along the opposite wall were two tables with benches. The back room had platform bunk beds along the right wall, each one roughly the width of a double bed, and additional single-layer platforms along the back and left walls. A decent number of people could stay in that room.

"Look what I found," said Rory. I turned to see him holding a small bottle of whisky. "It's still sealed, and this note was under the bottle." He held out a scrap of paper.

To the next folks who use this bothy—this should help keep you warm. Slàinte!

"I wouldn't say no to a sip or two of that," I said.

"Neither would I. But first, let's have some coffee and those sandwiches, and see if this weather clears."

Rory began fiddling with the camp stove, and I pulled out the sandwiches he'd charmed the cook at the Sligachan Hotel into making for us. As we drank our coffee and ate our late lunch, I stared out the window. "It doesn't look like it's going to stop anytime soon."

He sighed. "No, it doesn't." He glanced at his watch. "We'll see how it looks in an hour. If it hasn't let up by then, we'll have to stay here tonight and set out for Elgol in the morning. I don't want to be on the path in the dark."

We played a few hands of gin with the deck of cards. After I beat him in a best-of-five, he put on his boots, grabbed his raincoat, and went outside. He returned five minutes later, shaking his head.

"It's still pouring, and a text just came through from Tommy from a few hours ago—the signal is dodgy out here. They're in Torrin, and he says the storm is expected to last all night, but clear out by morning, and there's supposed to be good weather tomorrow. Might as well make yourself comfortable."

Fine with me. The eight miles we'd done today had pushed the limits of my endurance. I was content to call it a day and watch the rain through the windows.

I slipped my feet into my boots and pulled on my jacket for a quick trip around back (the bothy had no bathroom), then changed into my sweatpants, T-shirt, and fleece, along with a pair of thick socks. There was no electricity or heat in the bothy, and neither was there a fireplace. But there were four walls and a roof, and that's what mattered.

He gestured to the bottle of whisky. "No reason to wait any longer to drink this."

"I was hoping you'd say that."

"It'll keep us warm, anyway." He dug a cup out of his pack, poured a healthy amount of whisky into it, and handed it to me. "Ladies first." I raised it in salute and took a sip, then passed it to him. He finished it and poured more.

We sat at the table with the deck of cards. I dealt a round of War, which would keep us occupied for a while. I took another swig. I could get used to sipping whisky while listening to the rain pour down outside. All that was missing was a fire.

"So, *The Lord of the Rings*: books or movies?" I figured it was time to get to the important stuff.

"Och, that's a tough one." He took the cup from me and spun it between his long fingers. "I think I have to say the movies," he said after a moment. "I love the books, especially *Fellowship,* but the movies are brilliant. You?"

"I love the books, too, but they're my favorite movies of all time. Extended editions, obviously."

"Obviously. What made you ask?"

"I saw that you have *Fellowship* with you."

His brow crinkled. "When did you see that?"

"The other morning, when I went to the loo by myself while you were sleeping. When I looked in your tent, you'd fallen asleep with it in your hand. You must love it a lot to carry it around with you."

"I do," he said. He drained the whisky, then refilled the cup again.

I could tell he didn't want to talk about it anymore.

I snagged the cup from him and took a sip. "What kind of music do you like?"

"Classic rock, all the way. I don't listen to the radio enough to hear what's current, anyway. You? Wait, let me guess."

I sat back, crossing my arms smugly across my chest. No way would he get it.

"Eighties hair bands?"

I gaped at him. "How could you possibly have guessed that?"

He grinned. "You sing or hum sometimes while we're walking. I think I've heard Guns N' Roses, Def Leppard, maybe even some Poison? Definitely Bon Jovi."

"Wait, you've heard me sing? I thought it was mostly in my head."

"Not always, as I'm still trying to master my mind-reading skills. So, leather pants and long hair, eh? That's what does it for you?" He ran his hand through his own longish hair and raised his eyebrows suggestively.

Under Armour and cargo shorts did it for me, too, but he probably already knew that. "Don't forget the guyliner."

He'd just taken a sip of whisky, and he sputtered slightly, clapping his hand over his mouth. "Who could forget that? I have some in my pack, but I don't like to wear it on the trail, because it gets in my eyes when I sweat."

I grinned. "Trust me, I know all about that."

We continued playing cards and making small talk as the rain came down. Dinner was beef stew and chicken stir-fry again, but this time we just passed them back and forth, neither of us caring about double-dipping our sporks.

Rory didn't say much during dinner, and in spite of our earlier light conversation (and my repeated kicking of his ass in cards), he was growing more and more tense as the evening wore on. Wordlessly, I poured him some more whisky and slid the cup across the table. He practically chugged it, not bothering to savor it in his mouth like he usually did.

"Rory, what's wrong?"

He glanced up at me and smiled, but it didn't reach his eyes. "Nothing. I'm fine."

"Is there something I should know about spending the night here?" If he was nervous about staying in this place, I wanted to know.

His brows drew together, and he cocked his head to the side. "No. The bothy was just built last year, and it's well insulated. Why do you ask?"

"Because you seem tense."

"I'm fine," he repeated.

But the long sip of whisky that followed belied his statement.

Chapter Thirty

I'm fine, I'd said to Amelia. Twice in the last two minutes.

I wasn't fine. The cards and small talk had kept the demons at bay for a while, but as the sky grew darker outside, it all began to press down on me.

It was always this way for me on the Elgol leg of the trek—too many bad memories. It never got any easier. And I didn't want it to.

I wished we could have pushed on to Elgol, rather than lingering here, but there was just no way. If it had only been me, I would have kept going, storm or no storm. But Amelia had been struggling for the last few hours. *And you charging on ahead didn't help, jackass.* No, it definitely hadn't, but even if I hadn't done that, there was no way she could have slogged on for another four miles, especially with the cliffs up ahead.

I wanted to down the rest of that bottle of whisky and forget about everything, but it wouldn't help. I couldn't forget, no matter how much alcohol swam through my veins. I'd tried that before—more than once.

It was nearly dark. I retrieved our sleeping bags and mats from our packs and went into the back room.

I laid out Amelia's bedding on the bottom bunk and set up mine on the top. I couldn't handle having her close to me again, waking up with my body wrapped around hers, breathing the scent of her, my need for her impossible to hide.

I returned to the front room and her too-perceptive stare. "You should step outside again before it gets dark." She nodded and got to her feet. She was walking a little better than she had been earlier, but I could tell from the set of her mouth that her knee was bothering her.

She slipped into her boots and coat and ventured out into the rain. Then I took my own turn outside. The rain hadn't let up at all, which was going to make the trail muddy and difficult tomorrow, even if it cleared like it was supposed to.

Amelia was at the table when I returned. "Do you think anyone else will show up here tonight?" she asked.

"No. It's nearly dark, and it's been pouring for hours. Anyone else on this leg of the trail would have turned back to Sligachan when that storm hit, or else they'd have been here by now. I'm going to turn in. I'm pretty beat, and there's not much we can do once it's dark in here. I'd rather not use our torches if we don't have to."

"Okay, I'll be in soon, too."

"If you do need the loo during the night, take a torch with you, and be careful. If you're even the slightest bit worried about it, wake me up, okay?"

"I will."

"Good night."

"'Night."

I went into the back room and changed into the shorts I slept in, then climbed up the ladder and crawled into my sleeping bag. I heard the slap of cards on wood and knew Amelia was playing solitaire, obviously making the most of the last dregs of daylight.

I listened to the wind rattling the windows, the rain falling in sheets outside. It was bad out there. I muttered a *thank-you* to the Mountain Bothy folks for our shelter. It would have been a rough afternoon and evening without it.

Amelia came into the room a little later, partially covering her torch with her hand so that she wouldn't wake me. I could have told her not to bother, but I just pretended to be asleep. There was a slight *unf* as she settled in to the bunk. Then a *click*, and the room was completely dark.

I heard the rustle as she moved around in her sleeping bag, heard her soft sigh as she finally got comfortable. I pictured her hand curled under her chin, her long hair sliding around her shoulders, her long, dark lashes like wee fans grazing the tops of her cheekbones.

I wanted so badly to climb back down that ladder and join her. I wanted to feel that hand on me, to tangle my fingers in that curtain of hair, to press my lips to those delicate lashes. I wanted to wrap my body around hers and let her feel how much I wanted her—and have her want me back just as much.

I didn't do any of those things.

"Good night, Rory," she whispered.

I didn't answer.

. . .

I finally stumbled on to the summit, after over an hour of scrambling and fighting the wind and ignoring their calls from behind me—one taunting, the other pleading. But I had barely a moment to look around in triumph before I was completely surrounded by a thick mist.

I froze. Where was the edge?

I had made it all the way to the summit, only to be completely helpless. I couldn't see, couldn't move. I was so afraid I'd plummet to my death.

"Rory, where are you?"

I closed my eyes in relief. He'd found me. "Here! I'm at the top!"

"You made it to the top! I knew you could!" I could hear the smile in his voice, and my chest swelled with pride. "Hang on, I'm almost there."

"Be careful. It's really socked in. I can't see anything."

"No worries. We'll wait until it clears and go down together. Just stay where you are. Do you hear me? You just stay where you are, and I'll come to you."

"Okay," I said, my voice barely a whisper.

I was completely blind. My breath came faster and faster; my heart pounded so fast it hurt. If I could only just see *him, I'd be okay. But the mist was too thick.*

"Rory, talk to me."

"I'm scared," I gasped, cringing at how weak I sounded. If he *had heard me, he would have mocked me for that, too.*

"I know. Just breathe. In through your nose—hold it— out through your mouth—hold it. And again. Can you do that? I'm almost there, I promise. Just stay where you are and breathe."

I breathed, just as he told me to. In through my nose, out through my mouth, holding it for a moment in between each inhale and exhale. I found a boulder and clung to it.

The mist suddenly dissipated, and I saw his face. He smiled and took a step closer, his gaze holding mine. "There you are." Another step. And then...

"Shh, Rory. It's okay." A cool hand touched my cheek, then a soft weight settled against me. I reached for it—for *her*—and held on. "It's okay. Just breathe."

I took a deep, shuddering breath. "Amelia?"

"Yeah, it's me. You were dreaming."

Something wasn't right—something other than my nightmare. "I'm in the top bunk."

"I know."

"You climbed up here?" I said stupidly.

"I did. It was really, really far. And I didn't even get a kiss this time," she joked, reminding me of that other time she'd awakened me from a nightmare and I'd kissed her. *Like I could forget.*

Amelia ran her fingers through my hair, over and over. I closed my eyes and just let her soothe me. It was so exhausting to keep trying to resist my need for her touch. "Rory?"

"Mmm?"

"Will you tell me what happened, what it is that haunts you?"

My heart seemed to stop, and then started to pound. I opened my eyes and stared at the ceiling. "I...I don't know if I can." I hadn't told anyone since I told Scarlet when I joined SBF, and even then, it was only what she needed to know.

"Maybe it will help you to talk about it, here in the dark. Just say the words. Pretend I'm not here."

As if I could do that, with her body pressed close to mine, her scent all around me, her hand in my hair.

"I...don't want you to think badly of me," I whispered.

Her hand left my hair to touch my cheek again. She turned my face to hers, and I could feel her eyes on me. "Rory, listen to me. My best friend is in a coma because of my carelessness. I'm the last person who will think badly of you. Tell me."

Tell her. You've kept it bottled up inside for so long. Just tell her.

I took her hand from my cheek and held it like a lifeline. And then I told her.

Chapter Thirty-One

AMELIA

"I told you about my father," Rory began.

"Yes. You said he bullied you because you were a reader and a writer, and not into the outdoors." *Which makes me so mad…*

"Yeah. He thought I was some kind of freak. He didn't understand why I wasn't like Connor, who was always out walking in the hills or climbing something. And he tormented me for it. I still don't really know why. I tried asking my mum once, but she just told me to be respectful of him. I still resent her for that, for not defending me. The only one who did defend me was my literature teacher, Mrs. MacDougall."

"She was the one who believed in your writing and wanted you to turn your life around?"

"I'm impressed you remembered all that."

"I remember everything you've said," I replied. Then cringed as I realized how that sounded. "I mean, I—"

"I remember everything you've said, too, Amelia," he

interrupted, his breath warm against my cheek. "From the very first day."

A thrill ran through me at his words, said without hesitation, without embarrassment. "Anyway, you were saying?"

"When I was fifteen, before...everything, Mrs. Mac entered my short story in a school-wide contest, and I won. My father was furious with her for encouraging my writing, and they had words at my brother Connor's secondary school graduation ceremony. Her husband, Captain MacDougall—a man I *wished* was my father, stood up to my father, and then told me I was welcome at their house anytime. Well, Dad took particular offense to that—like he had to prove himself, now that others knew he was a bastard. So, the weekend after Connor's graduation, he took the two of us to Skye to hike."

That sounded like a recipe for disaster, but I kept my mouth shut and let him talk.

"The weather had been dodgy all weekend, with rainstorms that came out of nowhere—like you've experienced this week. It made the paths muddy and the hills treacherous. But Dad didn't care. We did the Quiraing, which was miserable in the wind and rain, as you might imagine."

"That was where I nearly got blown off my feet on the second day?" Yeah, that place was no joke, even without a storm.

"Aye, where you almost dropped your phone. The next day we hiked up Glen Sligachan, as you and I did earlier today. And he was just relentless, taunting me for being too slow on a hill, or being hesitant about crossing a stream or bog. Connor kept telling him to stop, but Dad didn't listen. He never did.

"We were on the path through the glen, and were just passing Bla Bheinn, the mountain we saw yesterday. The sun was out, and the mountain was right there, and I thought, fuck it, I'm going to climb it. And once I've shown him I *can* do it, even though I don't *want* to, he won't have any reason to bully me anymore, and I won't have to go out hiking with him again."

He couldn't even *look* at Bla Bheinn yesterday, so what did that mean?

"So, when Dad and Connor left the trail for a pee, I started up Bla Bheinn. I could hear Dad yelling at me to come back, that I was an idiot for going off by myself—and then he said it didn't matter—I'd chicken out anyway. And I heard Connor shouting for me to wait for him. But if Connor helped me, it would just prove Dad's point that I wasn't 'man enough' to do it myself, so I kept going.

"It was harder than I expected. There's a false summit, and then you have to scramble down the rocks and then up again to reach the real summit. I finally made it to the top, and I was so proud of myself. And it had been more fun than I'd expected it to be. But then, the mist came up out of nowhere, and within seconds I couldn't see anything. It was like being smothered with a blanket. I couldn't see the edge, so I was afraid to move, afraid I'd fall. I started to panic."

Rory's breathing quickened, as if he was back there, atop the mountain in the fog. I squeezed his hand tighter, dread creeping up inside me.

"Then I heard Connor, calling for me. I shouted back that I was at the summit, and he told me he knew I could do it, that he was so proud of me. It was the most amazing feeling. I knew I'd never hear it from Dad, but I worshiped Connor, you know? He was my hero, my defender. My brother."

I closed my eyes, as if I could block out his words. But I knew. Oh God, I knew.

"I told him I couldn't see anything, and he told me to stay where I was, he was coming for me. I was freaking out, panicking, and he told me to breathe. 'In through your nose—

hold it—out through your mouth—hold it. And again.' Over and over, he said it, trying to keep me calm until he could get there."

That was what Rory had told me to do when I hurt my knee and couldn't breathe from the pain.

"I found a boulder and just clung to it, terrified. And then the mist cleared for a moment, and there he was, so close. He smiled at me, kept his eyes on mine as he climbed. And then—"

He broke off, and I could feel him shaking. *Oh God. Please don't say any more.*

"And he took another step, onto a rock. But…it was loose, and his foot slipped. He looked so surprised—he'd been so worried about me, he wasn't watching his footing. I flung out my hand. His fingers grazed mine, but I wasn't close enough, and my arms weren't long enough, and…"

No, no, no…

"…and he fell," Rory whispered, and my heart shattered. "God, he fell, and I was right there, and I couldn't stop it, couldn't reach him. And I just screamed and screamed and screamed…and my father finally got there, and I had no voice left. I could only point to a ledge about five meters down, where he lay there bleeding. And then my father screamed."

Rory took a shuddering breath. I clutched his hand and waited for the rest of it.

"Connor never screamed. He just quietly tumbled down the hill and hit his head on a rock. And he…died. It wasn't a fall that should have killed him. But that stupid fucking rock… We had to wait hours for Mountain Rescue to get there, and then I watched them go down to my brother and retrieve his body."

My eyes filled with tears at the utter despair that radiated from him. What a senseless, horrific tragedy, all because a kid wanted to prove himself to a father who would never love him the way he loved his brother.

I raised up on my elbow and cupped the back of his head, bringing his face close to mine. "I'm so sorry." There were tear tracks glistening on his cheeks, and I pressed my lips to them, tasting the salt of his grief and his guilt.

He took my shoulders in his hands, and I was sure he was going to set me away from him—

—but he crushed me to him and kissed me as though my lips held his redemption, his salvation.

I kissed him back. If I could be his salvation, I would be. I could be so much more, if he would only let me.

But for now, maybe I could take away some of his grief. His tongue traced the seam of my lips, and I opened for him, deepening the kiss. He dragged his mouth from mine to kiss my throat.

"Rory," I murmured, my body coming alive at the touch of his lips on my heated skin. He froze, and then pulled away. "Rory?" I said again, this time a question.

"I…we can't. Not like this."

I cupped his face in my hands and looked into his eyes, wishing I could see them in the dark, knowing they'd be green with desire. His desire for me. "Yes, we can. *Exactly* like this."

He took my hands in his. "Amelia, we can't. I don't want to take advantage of you, and that's what this feels like."

"Then let me make it feel like something else. I want you. Here and now. Let me take away some of your pain, just for a little while. And you can take away some of mine. It's not taking advantage—we've both wanted this almost from the beginning. Whatever the reasons for *not* giving in to it don't matter anymore."

He made a sound of despair. "It feels so wrong after everything I just told you. But I…can't fight it anymore. Make me forget, Amelia. Just for a little while."

"I can do that," I whispered, and pressed my mouth to his once more.

He kissed me back, his tongue sliding over mine, and I felt a tug in the pit of my belly—and lower.

He rolled me to my back and ran his hands down my sides, snagging the hems of my fleece and T-shirt and dragging them both over my head in one motion. I shivered as the cool air hit my skin, but then he covered me with his body, his warmth seeping into me as his lips trailed down my chest, and I wasn't cold anymore.

His hands came up to caress my breasts through the fabric of my bra. "Which one is it?" he asked.

"What?"

"Which bra? The navy or the purple? It's too dark to tell."

At another time, it might have struck me as strange that he remembered my bra colors. But that time was not now. "Purple," I gasped as his thumbs strummed over me.

He pressed his lips to the top of my right breast, then the left. "I'm picturing the way you looked in it, like a goddess," he said in a low voice. "Now I'm picturing you without it." His hands ran down my ribs and around my back to undo the clasp.

I delved my fingers into his hair and arched into him. The motion brought my lower body flush against his, and I sucked in a breath as I felt how much he wanted me.

He froze. "Did I hurt you? Your knee?"

"It's fine." It was sore, but I didn't care. "Please don't stop. Not this time."

"No, not this time." He dragged the straps of my bra down my arms and off. I dimly heard it hit the floor somewhere below. "I wish I could see you in the dark. I'll have to look at you like a blind man would."

He traced my breasts with his fingertips, slowly caressing every curve, until I shivered—and not from the cold. And then he did it again with his tongue.

My body was on fire. I needed to touch him, skin on skin.

"I need these off," I hissed, shoving at my sweatpants. He took over, hooking his fingers in the waistband and slowly easing them down. He paused, realizing at the same moment I did that he'd snagged my panties as well. *No more hesitation.* I covered his hands with mine, and together we peeled my sweatpants and underwear down my legs. He tossed them somewhere, then ran his hands down the sides of my body as he had earlier, seeing with his fingers what he couldn't see with his eyes.

He slipped his hands beneath my butt and lifted my lower body off the bunk so that my legs fell to either side of him, then began to slowly kiss his way down my belly.

And lower. Oh God, was he going to—? *Yes.* His tongue touched me, caressed me, over and over, until I was writhing in his hands, my body humming with anticipation and need.

"Rory!" All I could do was hold his head to me. It wasn't enough. I wanted to touch him—*needed* to touch him. I tugged at his hair until he kissed his way back up my body— *so goddamn slowly*—to my mouth.

His hand skimmed up the inside of my thigh. His fingers dipped inside me, continuing where his mouth had left off. I kissed him desperately as I arched into his hand—seeking, wanting, needing—*there.*

Chapter Thirty-Two

I heard her soft cries of pleasure, felt the ripples of her body as she shattered around my fingers—and wished I could see her face, look into her eyes. My body ached to join her.

"My turn," she whispered. She pushed me onto my back and kissed me as her fingers skipped down my chest and then slowly inched down my abdomen. She trailed her hand up and down my belly, barely dipping under my waistband before withdrawing. Driving me crazy.

And then, suddenly, her hand was on me, cool fingers cupping hot flesh.

My whole body jerked as I tore my mouth from hers. "Amelia," I gasped—*begged*.

"Shh," she murmured, biting my lower lip and then running her tongue over it as she stroked me. I thrust helplessly into her hand. "Amelia, please. Wait."

Her hand stilled. "You want me to stop?"

"God, no. Just...just wait a second."

I extracted her hand from my shorts, shifted her off me, and vaulted from the bunk, not even bothering to use the ladder. I barely noticed the cold floor as I went to my pack and groped for the Ziploc bag of condoms I knew was in there somewhere. Finding it, I ripped it open, grabbed a few, and then hurried back up the ladder.

"I'm disappointed," she said dryly. "I thought you were going to just jump back up."

I laughed as I kicked off my shorts. "Aye, well, I thought about it, but I was afraid I'd jump too high and bump my head on the ceiling."

Snorting at that, she rolled me onto my back again and crawled partway over me. "Now, where was I?" Her fingers tiptoed down my stomach. "Oh, that's right. *Here.*"

My breath caught as she picked up right where she'd left off. Slow, then fast, then slow again, the touch of her hand a sweet torture. But I could play, too. I ran my hand down her back, smiling at her sharp gasp when I touched her.

We tormented each other, fingers dipping and teasing and caressing. But before long, slow and teasing turned into fast and urgent. Panting, I tugged her hand from me. I fumbled for a condom and rolled it on, hissing as my fingers grazed my sensitized skin.

I rolled Amelia to her back and carefully brought her right leg around my hip, bringing me flush against her. "Is this okay?" I murmured against her lips. "Does it hurt your knee?"

"No." She wrapped her arm around my shoulder, pulling me closer. Her other hand closed around me.

I felt my flesh jump and pulse against her hand. "Amelia..."

"I know." Her leg fell to the side, and she guided me inside her, both of us gasping as I sank into her heat. *Finally.* I wanted to take it slow, but this had been building between us for far too long to go slowly now. Our breath came in gasps as our bodies came together, over and over. So close now. I dipped my hand between our bodies to touch her. She moaned, her head falling back.

"Look at me, Amelia. I want to see you."

Her eyes opened, and I held her gaze as I dragged my thumb over her. Once, twice, her hips meeting mine with each stroke. Then she cried out, her body clenching around me. I threw my head back and shouted her name as my body shuddered through its own release.

I opened my eyes and stared down at Amelia, both of us panting. I raised up on my elbows so I wouldn't crush her and cupped her face in my hands, kissing her lips, her forehead, and her cheeks, then returned to her mouth. I withdrew from her body and dealt with the condom, tucking it into a rubbish bag before returning to the bunk.

We crawled into my sleeping bag. I pulled her close and ran my fingers through her hair, combing out the tangles. Her fingertip traced idle circles on my chest.

"That was… Thank you," I said, then swore inwardly at my own lameness. *Thank you? Who the hell says 'thank you' after the best sex of his life?* "I mean…thank you for listening to me. And for making me feel alive again." *Just stop talking.*

"It was pretty good from this side, too," she murmured.

I grinned. "Tommy will be happy."

She lifted her head. "Why's that?"

"He told me to keep an open mind about the idea of you and me." She giggled, a sound I hadn't really heard from her before, but hoped I'd hear again. "What?"

"When we said goodbye, he said that if there was an opportunity for me to kiss you for real, I should take it. I guess he's playing Cupid. I'm glad he approves of me."

"Do you think Carrie would approve as well?"

"Oh, heck yes. I could practically hear her voice in my head just now, saying 'you go, girl!' She'd be so proud of me."

"Why? I mean, other than the obvious."

"And what would that be?"

"That you got together with such a fine, braw lad, of course," I teased.

"Oh, right. Obviously," she scoffed, flicking me with her fingernail.

Then she was quiet for a moment, her finger once more drawing circles on my chest. "I'm just...she's the outgoing one, not me. She's the one who would have gone to your room like Emma did that night, while I would have stayed put and imagined what it would be like to go knock on your door, but would never have done it.

"But this whole thing with Carrie has shown me that life can change in an instant, and I don't want to be the one who sits back and watches. I want to have the experiences. I want to be bold and go after what I want, not wait and worry and wonder."

"You were bold when you insisted on continuing the trek after you got hurt."

"That was the first time."

"That you were bold? I disagree."

She lifted her head and stared at me. "What do you mean?"

"I think it was pretty damn bold of you to come on the Skye Trail with barely any hiking experience, and on short notice."

"Liar. You thought I was a spoiled twit who didn't belong out here."

"At the beginning, yes. But that was before I knew why."

"I did it for Carrie."

"I know. And that makes you even more bold. You stepped outside your comfort zone to do an eighty-mile trek over mountains and along cliffs, in wind and rain and cold, for someone else."

"Is that why you offered to help me finish the trek? Because you thought I was brave? Or was it because of..."

Her voice trailed off, but I knew what she didn't say. "Because of Connor?"

"Yeah."

"It was both. You'd said that Carrie was like your sister, and my brother...he was everything to me. I would do anything—*anything*—to have him back. And yes, because you were so brave, and I admired that. I *still* admire that about you."

"Thank you. It means a lot to hear you say that."

I kissed her forehead and lay back, twining a lock of her hair around my finger. It was so nice, being with her like this, just holding her in my arms. It had been so long since I had someone to hold.

"Rory?"

"Hmm?"

"Can I be bold again?"

And she was.

Chapter Thirty-Three

AMELIA

I lay in Rory's arms, my head resting on his chest after we'd made love a second time. "Can I ask you a question?"

"Of course."

"Why do you keep guiding this trail? I mean, surely Scarlet wouldn't force you to."

"I force myself to. Or at least I did at first."

"What, like punishment?"

"Kind of, yeah. The first few times were…difficult. But I had to do it. I needed the pain and the guilt. It kept me going, when nothing else did."

It wasn't unlike my reasoning for doing the Skye Trail in Carrie's place and for refusing any assistance early on. But now? I wanted to—*needed to*—finish it for her. But I also wanted to finish it for *me*, to look back at my pictures of the intimidating peaks and glens and the scary cliffs and say "I did that. I walked all that way."

And I would do it, with Rory's help.

"Has it gotten any easier?"

"It has. But I still have the nightmares, and then sometimes something will trigger a flashback."

"Like Tommy almost slipping off the edge the other day."

"Exactly. And I haven't been over Bla Bheinn since then. I can't even look at it, as you probably noticed. But one day," he whispered, as if to himself, "one day soon, I will go back up there. I have to. For Connor—and for me."

"Will you tell me a little about him?" I asked hesitantly. "If it's not too painful."

He played with a lock of my hair. "You know, it's funny. I've spoken more about Connor these past few days than I have in years. Tommy was his best mate—"

"He was? Is that why Mrs. Mac brought you two together?"

"Yeah. She felt he would understand me in a way no one else could."

They really had been through a lot together, and I was so glad they had each other. What would Rory have become otherwise?

"Tommy and I talk about Connor every now and then if we've had a few pints and are feeling nostalgic. But otherwise? There's no one for me to really tell about him. The only constants in my life are Tommy and Scarlet, and Gav when I'm on Skye. And now you. And I've already told you the very worst things, so it can't get any more painful. What do you want to know?"

God, he was so alone. And he was so casual about it, like he had no right to expect anything different. My heart just kept breaking for him, over and over again. "Tell me your favorite story about him."

He didn't even have to think about it. "I remember when Connor taught me how to skip stones, at the loch where we'd grown up, before we'd moved to Glasgow. I was seven years old, and he was nine. I pestered him to teach me, until he finally gave in and sent me off to find the perfect stone. Each one I showed him got rejected: too bumpy, too thick, and so on. Then he found one, a flat rock the size of my hand. It was a purply-gray color with a silver vein running through it—the prettiest, smoothest stone I'd ever seen.

"Being a nine-year-old boy, and a few inches taller than me, he held it over my head so I couldn't reach it, and when I tried to get it, he ran off. He kept evading me, and I got so mad I started crying. He finally gave it to me, but then my father came outside. He'd been taking a nap and we woke him."

"Oh no," I murmured.

"Aye. He asked if I was hurt. I said no. 'So why the hell are you crying?' he asked. 'How many times do I have to tell you that boys don't cry?' When I didn't reply, he said, 'I asked you a question! What the hell are you crying about?' Connor stepped in front of me. 'It's my fault,' he said. 'I wouldn't give him his rock.'

"My father reached around Connor and grabbed me by the arm. 'You're crying like a wee lassie over a goddamned rock?' he asked. Of course, I started crying harder. He pried the rock out of my hand and tossed it in the loch. '*Now* you have something to cry about,' he said."

"Your father is a real piece of work." I said, my heart going out to that little boy. "I'm curious as to how this is your *favorite* Connor story, though."

"I'm getting there," Rory said. "I ran to the house, where my mother stood in the doorway. 'That's it, run crying to your mum like the little girl you are,' my father called.

"Mum tried to hug me, but I shoved past her and ran into the room that Connor and I shared, knowing if I let her comfort me like I was a bairn, it would only make my father hate me more. A little while later, I heard my father shouting at Connor, and ran out of my room. He *never* yelled at Connor, only me.

"Connor was soaking wet and shivering. My father screamed at him to go to our room and not come out till morning. "Why are you wet?" I asked him. He just reached into his shorts and handed me something."

Rory cleared his throat. "It was a perfect, purply-gray stone with a shiny vein of silver running through it."

"Connor went into the loch after your stone?" I bit my lip so I wouldn't cry. Rory and his brother had been everything to each other, and it was just so unfair that Connor was gone.

"Aye. I remember looking at him in shock, asking him why he'd done that. The loch wasn't too deep over there—it was just where the sandy bottom started to drop away—but still. 'That rock was yours. He shouldn't have taken it away from you because I was being a jerk,' he said with a shrug, as if diving repeatedly beneath the surface of a freezing loch to find a stupid rock was no big deal.

"I can still smell the loch water as it dripped from his clothes and the clean scent of the blanket that he wrapped around both of us as he hugged me. The two of us, standing together against a father who loved him more than anything, but thought I was a weak, scared runt who wasn't worth spitting on. So yeah, that's my favorite memory of my brother."

I pressed my lips to his chest. "Okay, that turned into a lovely story, in spite of your father. Tell me more—what was Connor like when he was older?"

"He couldn't bear to be still. I could sit for hours in the same position with a book—and still do—but he would get fidgety after five minutes. The only real exception was *The Lord of the Rings.* We loved the movies, and I coerced him into reading the books after Mrs. Mac got me into them. He loved *The Fellowship of the Ring* the best."

That was why he carried it around with him, and that was

why he was so quick to change the subject when I'd brought it up earlier.

I'd thought it was sexy as hell that he liked to read that book, but knowing it was Connor's favorite changed everything. Rory read it to remember his brother, to stay close to him in any way he could. My heart just kept breaking for him.

"Connor was really smart, but not book smart," Rory continued. "He would remember anything you told him, even when it didn't seem like he was listening, which drove his teachers mad." He chuckled. "He would tell me—very proudly—that he would be horsing around in class, and the teacher would ask him to repeat what she just said to try and embarrass him, but he always knew exactly what they'd been talking about, and he always did pretty well."

I smiled, picturing Connor looking like a slightly younger Rory, without the grief that Rory wore like an old jacket, but with the same irreverent grin I'd seen a few times now and a devilish gleam in his eyes. His teachers had probably loved the hell out of him, no matter how exasperating he was.

"I wish I could have met him," I said.

"Me, too. He would have liked you."

He was quiet for a moment, and then continued, "He obviously loved to be outside. It didn't matter what time of year it was, or how bad the weather. He would bundle up if it was cold, or put on rain gear if it was wet, and he'd be off walking the hills, trail running, ice climbing, you name it. He'd just begun working on his Mountain Leader certification."

"Is that why you do this, because he was going to?" I asked.

He went still, and I immediately wished I could take it back. It was too personal a question. *Girl, you're lying naked with him after just having two rounds of amazing sex. It doesn't get much more personal than that.*

"No, I do it because...because I got into it after Connor died, and I just..." He trailed off uncertainly.

"I'm sorry, I shouldn't have asked."

"It's okay. It's just...no one's ever asked me that question before, and I'm suddenly not sure." And now he was worried that he'd chosen this life, this career, out of guilt. *Way to go, Amelia.*

"Close your eyes," I said.

"Okay."

"Now picture your three favorite things about the Skye Trail, and tell me what they are."

"I see myself standing beneath the rock formations of the Quiraing, on top of the Trotternish Ridge with the sun on my face and the wind whipping my hair into my eyes, and at the end of the world at Rubha Hunish, surrounded by blue sea and diving whales."

I laid my hand on his lips. "I can feel the smile on your face as you picture those things. And having seen them myself, I know they're pretty freaking great."

He caught my hand and kissed my fingertips, one by one. My breath started to quicken as my body came alive once again. "Um, okay," I said, trying not to squirm against him, "now tell me three not-so-great things about the Skye Trail."

"Having to abort the Trotternish Ridge in the middle due to gale force winds, crossing the rivers when they're raging from the rain, dealing with a difficult group that questions me at every turn."

I pictured Rory confidently leading a group of wet, cold, nervous trekkers safely down the Ridge without batting an eye. "And even with the challenging parts, could you imagine yourself doing anything else?"

"No," he said without hesitation, but with a lot of relief. "I *need* to be out on the trail. I definitely feel closer to Connor out there. I can see him standing on the Ridge, with the rain soaking him and a big fuckin' grin on his face, or running up Glamaig in the Red Cuillins.

"But *I* love it, too. And when I think of how my life might have been, if Connor hadn't…if he was still alive? I was into reading and writing. That would have probably meant a desk job somewhere. Sometimes I imagine myself in an office, with the walls and ceiling pressing in around me, breathing recycled air, listening to the buzz of fluorescent lights, staring at a computer screen all day… Amelia, I think that would kill me."

It absolutely would—he was meant for open spaces and fresh air, with eagles soaring overhead, not the stifling confines of a cubicle.

"This is the life that I want, as lonely as it might sometimes be." He tenderly cupped my cheek, his thumb stroking over my lips. "Thank you for making me think of it that way. And for asking about Connor. I used to get this clench in my gut when I thought of him, but now? I feel sad, but not that crushing, crippling grief that used to almost bring me to my knees. I *wanted* to tell you about him, and that means a lot to me."

Maybe he was finally beginning to heal. And if I was able to help him with that, then this whole trip was worth it. "Do you…ever see your parents?"

"No. When I think of them, there's this…emptiness, as if they're these faceless people I knew once, long ago, in another time and place. I haven't seen them in years. After Connor…my father…" His voice trailed off, as if he couldn't make the words come out.

I laid my fingers over his lips. "You don't have to say it. I'll just imagine it from what you've told me about him and then multiply that by a factor of ten. Did he hurt you?"

"Not physically. I almost wish he had, because at least there would have been something, some kind of emotional response. But there was nothing, and that was so much worse. I told you before that I started to get in a lot of trouble at school. I just wanted them to remember I existed, you know? But they didn't. No matter what I did. It was as if someone took away their memories of their other son. Like in the final Harry Potter book, when Hermione 'obliviates' her parents so they'll forget about her and be safe."

"Oh, Rory." I didn't even know what else to say.

"I needed them, you know? At least my mum. Connor was my brother, and it was my fault he was dead, and I was shattered. But my mum just retreated into her own grief and that was it. And my father—I was dead to him, as dead as Connor was. He just looked through me as if I wasn't there. It was almost better when he was mocking and belittling me. I had to completely fend for myself."

I wanted to meet his parents, so I could tell them what I thought of them, so I could shake them until their teeth rattled. I already knew his father was a bully and an asshole, but his mom? How could she let go of her child—her only surviving child? And how could he blame himself for Connor's death?

"Rory, what happened to Connor wasn't your fault. How can you say that?"

"Because it's true. He climbed up Bla Bheinn in awful conditions because I went up there on a whim, because I couldn't just ignore my father's taunts and be the bigger person. If I'd just stayed with them, he'd still be alive."

I had to make him see that it wasn't his fault. "But it wasn't foggy when you started climbing, was it?"

"No, it was clear."

"So how could you have known? And how could you be expected to ignore your father's bullying? You were a kid, and he was your dad. He should have been the bigger person. If it's anyone's fault that Connor is dead, it's his. *He* drove you to go up there—even when he was calling after you to come back, he was goading you. And if they'd gone on that trip to Skye without you, who's to say the outcome would have been different?"

"They wouldn't have—"

"They wouldn't have climbed Bla Bheinn?"

"Oh, they would have climbed it. It's a Munro, a mountain over three thousand feet high. My father had a running checklist of all the Munros he'd 'bagged.'"

"So they would have gone up there anyway, since the weather was good. And the fog would have rolled in, and the same thing might have happened. You can't blame yourself, Rory."

His eyes widened in surprise, as if he'd never even thought of it that way. He took a shuddering breath. I touched his cheek, brushing away the wetness there. He caught my hand and pressed it to his lips.

"Thank you," he whispered, as if I'd given him a precious gift.

My heart broke for him all over again.

Chapter Thirty-Four

RORY

Tommy had been telling me for years that Connor's death wasn't my fault. I never believed him. Yet somehow, after knowing me for less than a week, Amelia had me thinking that maybe, just maybe, it was true. Another weight seemed to lift from my shoulders. I held her hand to my lips, unable to say more than "thank you" for fear I'd just lose it completely.

"Did you go to live with Tommy?" she asked after a moment.

"Not right away. A few months later, after Mrs. Mac stood up for me at school, I went to live with the MacDougalls. It wasn't really anything official, it just kind of happened. The captain showed up at my doorstep one day and told me to pack a bag."

I smiled, recalling that first bright moment in an endless cycle of darkness. "I remember every detail of that day: the rain pouring down outside, the deafening silence inside the house. I remember his confident knock on the door, the way he strode inside like he owned the place, his long coat flapping around him. He was like an avenging angel, rescuing me from hell. He wrote his phone number and address on a piece of paper and left it on the kitchen table, and he told my parents they could come get me when they were ready to be parents again. They never did."

Amelia gasped. "Oh my God, Rory, how can you be so matter-of-fact about this?"

I shrugged. "I've had almost seven years to come to terms with it. I stayed with the MacDougalls for almost six months, and then I went to live with Tommy when I was sixteen or so. He was eighteen, and by then I was working as an apprentice guide on weekends, earning money doing that and working in a bookstore after school. The place was a dump, and we didn't eat the healthiest food, but Tommy looked out for me."

"He still does," said Amelia.

"Aye. I love him like a brother. It feels...disloyal to Connor to say that, but it's true."

She shook her head. "Connor wouldn't think it was disloyal, Rory. He'd be so glad that his best friend was looking out for his little brother."

"Maybe. Anyway, when I was eighteen, I saw my parents once, in the market. They looked at me, and their eyes widened as if they'd seen a ghost. I guess I look like Connor. It's strange to think that I'm older now than he'll ever be."

"Did they say anything?"

"No, they just stared at me. My mum—for a moment, she looked like she wanted to say something. I took a step toward her, but then my father led her away. She glanced back once, and then that was it." And that still fucking hurt.

"I'm so very sorry," Amelia whispered. "Sorry that you lost your brother, but even sorrier that your parents threw you away. Their sweet, smart boy." She wrapped her arms around me, her breath hitching, and I felt the dampness of her tears.

I reached up to wipe them away. "No one's ever cried for me before," I said, swallowing the lump in my own throat.

"Well, someone should have! I can't—"

I kissed her, long and deep, cutting off her angry rant. "Thank you," I said when we came up for air. And then I pulled her on top of me, and we didn't speak again for a while.

• • •

I awakened to a pinkish gold sunrise—a welcome sight after two days of rain—and a soft, warm body in my arms.

Last night had been...indescribable. If Amelia wasn't lying in my arms right now, if my body didn't feel so sated and relaxed, I would think I'd dreamed it all. To have gone from the terror of my nightmare and the shame of telling Amelia about Connor to her warm embrace, first comforting, and then...

Hot. Sexy. The opposite of comforting.

The way she'd responded to me, the way her body had felt in my hands, over me, under me, around me. The way she'd touched me, with her hands and her lips. The way she'd made me *feel*, again and again—not just with her body, but with her compassion, with her understanding, with her tears.

The pain of Connor's death was still there—would always be there—but it had felt good to talk about him, to laugh at some of those memories.

I looked down at Amelia, sprawled across me, her hand tucked up against my chest. The dark shadows that had been under her eyes—from exhaustion, fear, worry, pain—had faded.

She murmured in her sleep and cuddled closer, her breath tickling my chest. A lock of hair slid across her face, and I reached up to tuck it back, winding the soft strands between my fingers.

Even though I'd known her for just a few days, I cared for her in a way that was more than just lusting after a pretty face and a sexy body. I *liked* her. I liked talking to her about books. I liked arguing with her about...everything. She was the first person since Tommy that I was able to tell my story to, and she didn't judge me, didn't do anything but understand me and want to take away my pain.

In all the time I was with Emma, I'd never felt compelled to tell her about Connor. She'd been a good companion—for a while—and I'd liked spending time with her, liked *the idea* of her. But she'd never known the real me. And in these few short days, Amelia *did* know the real me—knew more about me than Emma had ever learned after half a year of being together.

The few lasses I'd been with before and after Emma had been casual, girls I knew around town, or a friend of some girl Tommy was seeing. I'd made sure they were looking for the same thing as me: a brief hookup with no strings attached. No deep conversation, no sharing of hopes and dreams. Fun for a night or two, a kiss goodbye at the end, and that was it.

But this was different. Amelia was different. I'd tried to stay away, but it turned out that I had no willpower when it came to her. If she wanted to be together for the duration of the trek, then we would be—as together as two people could be, for as long as I could stretch it out. And then I'd say goodbye. It would kill me.

But it would be worth it.

Chapter Thirty-Five

AMELIA

I woke from the best sleep I'd had all week to bright sunshine streaming in through the window, turning Rory's hair to brilliant flame. To the sight of his bare chest and abdomen, strong and beautiful in the morning light. And to gray-green eyes, as luminous as a rainy morning, gazing down at me.

It had been exciting and mysterious to be with him in the dark, but it was glorious to see him in the light.

He kissed me—a sweet, tender kiss, so different from the passionate ones we exchanged just hours before. When I would have taken it further, he drew back.

"We need to talk, Amelia," he said, his eyes serious.

My heart sank. No *good* conversation in history ever began that way.

"Last night was...a gift. You made me feel alive, when I've been empty for so long."

I sat up, wincing at the ache in my knee. "I'm sensing a 'but.'"

He sat up, too, and took my hand. "In a few days, we'll finish the hike in Broadford, and you'll be on a plane back to New York."

"I know." *Only too well.*

"I know what I said the other night about how I couldn't be with you for just a few days and then say goodbye. *But*, I'd rather have that than nothing. If you agree."

I looked into his eyes, seeing a maelstrom of emotions swirling around in their silvery-green depths. Hope, doubt, dread, uncertainty. And something else, something more. And that was what I focused on.

"Rory, life is short. It's a phrase that's so widely flung around that it barely means anything. I know I'd never even given it a moment's thought, and I bet fifteen-year-old you never did, either. But seven years ago, that phrase took on a whole new meaning for you. A few weeks ago, it took on a whole new meaning for me. Life *is* short, and in a careless second, it can be irrevocably altered or yanked away completely. And we need to live it while we can. I don't want to go home and regret that I didn't make the most of my time with you." I grinned. "Not to mention that Carrie would kill me."

He smiled. "Then I guess I have my answer."

"I guess you do."

After our breakfast of porridge and coffee, we packed up. "We have a lot of ground to cover today," said Rory. "It's four miles or so to Elgol, and part of that is along eroded cliffs, so we'll have to take it very slowly. And then it's another ten-ish miles to Torrin. I'd like to get at least halfway from Elgol to Torrin before we stop for the night."

So, roughly nine miles today. My knee was feeling a little

better, but after yesterday's epic rain, I knew it wouldn't be easy.

"We can get some supplies at Elgol and then camp out on the beach near Kilmarie tonight," he continued. "How's your water supply?"

I pulled the CamelBak out of my pack. "About two liters." I'd filled it in Sligachan yesterday morning, and hadn't had much of it before the storm distracted us. Which wasn't good, I knew, but it was hard to concentrate on walking and remember to drink even if I wasn't thirsty.

"I have about the same amount. We can restock in Elgol. We'll have our lunch there, too—there's a nice café. You should be able to get good signal there to get online or call to check in on Carrie."

"Thanks, that would be great. Maybe there'll be some good news."

"I hope so," he said softly, his thumb grazing my cheek. "Ready to go?"

I took one last look at the plain bunk bed where we'd had such an unforgettable night, full of so much sadness—and so much passion. I pulled out my phone and took a quick photo of it, and then of Rory when I saw him gazing at it just as wistfully as I had.

We headed south along the shore on a path that was very boggy and slow-going due to all the rain the day before. But now when Rory occasionally took my hand to help me through a tough spot, he held onto it, his thumb stroking mine. And when I occasionally took his arm for balance, I leaned into him, breathing in his scent, loving the feel of his strong forearm under my hand.

For the most part, my knee behaved, but I picked the wrong patch of grass to step on at one point, and just barely managed to catch myself on my pole. After that, he held onto me for the rest of the way through the bog.

And I didn't mind at all. Nor did I mind the way he'd smile at me every so often. We didn't talk too much, needing to pay close attention to the path. It was warm in the sunshine, and I peeled off my fleece, then turned to say something to Rory.

And I just stared. He had taken off his fleece, too, and had raised the hem of his shirt to wipe his face. His shorts rode a little low, and I could see the indentations of his hips and the line of pale skin beneath his belly button. I remembered tracing that line with my tongue just a few hours ago—and everything that had followed.

"Eyes up here, Benson." Startled from my stupor, I snapped my gaze back to his to see him grinning at me.

"What?"

"The ground's a little boggy here, but I'm up for it if you are."

He was clearly joking, his words light and flirty. But I had the feeling that if I said *okay*, gave any indication I was on board, he would ravish me right there in the heather.

And I would let him.

"I mean, the idea is not totally unappealing," I said, "but you're the one who said we have a long day ahead of us."

"Aye, I did," he said, sounding regretful. "It can be our reward for making it to Kilmarie by tea time."

"You're on."

We continued through the boggy muck, finally reaching drier ground as we headed up a grassy slope. Then the cliff path—if it could even be called that—came into view ahead.

It looked terrifying.

"Um, Rory? Pardon my language, but are you fucking kidding me?"

"Don't worry, we'll take it slow. Just pay attention to your feet, and let me know if you need to stop. And maybe don't look down," he added.

"Great, thanks for the tip." I snapped a few shots for

Carrie—there was no way I was going to stop for pictures while we were on the cliff. And there was no way she'd believe that I willingly went on that "path."

"I'll go first. Watch where I step."

"Okay."

I followed in his footsteps, slowly and carefully picking my way over loose rock and crumbly bits with his helping hand, doing my best not to look at the sheer drop to the frothy sea below.

I paused to watch Rory traverse the next section. Keeping his weight on his left foot, he took a tentative step with his right, slowly bringing more of his weight forward—just as the earth dissolved under his foot and he tumbled from view.

"Rory!" I screamed, lunging forward to try to grab him somehow. *OhGodOhGod...*

"Stay back—I'm all right!" He'd grabbed the edge and was pulling himself up, his powerful forearms straining against the weight of his body and his heavy pack. I'd run my hands up and down those forearms last night, finding the ripple of tendon and muscle to be so hot, loving how he'd easily lifted me all those times on the trek, the way he'd held me as we'd made love.

Last night, his arms were sexy, now they were saving his life.

I inched forward, testing the ground as I went, until I could reach out and snag the loop at the top of his pack.

Rory hauled himself up, and together we scooted back from the unstable edge. A sob escaped me, and I threw my arms around him, nearly knocking him on his back.

Those strong arms crushed me to his chest. "Shh, I'm all right."

Then he winced, hissing through his teeth, and I pulled back. "You're hurt!"

He shook his head and rotated his shoulder a few times.

"I just wrenched my shoulder a little bit. I'll be fine."

"I thought…" *I thought I'd lost you, just when I'd found you.* I couldn't even say the words out loud, so I took his face in my hands and kissed him, channeling all my fear and relief into that kiss.

He kissed me back, then rested his forehead against mine.

"We can't go that way, Rory," I said. *Not. A. Chance.*

"No, we can't. It must have gotten hit hard with the wind and rain yesterday—it's eroded worse than I've ever seen."

"Is there another way to Elgol?"

"Not from here." He looked off into the distance behind me and then nodded once, as if to himself. He turned back to me. "But there is another way to get to Torrin, bypassing Elgol. We can go over Bla Bheinn."

I gaped at him. Bla Bheinn. The mountain that killed Connor, tore apart Rory's family, and nearly destroyed him.

I stood, leaning on my poles. "No. Absolutely not. We can just go back to Sligachan and…"

"And what?" he said, getting to his feet, too. "Abort the trek? No, we're not doing that. I promised I'd help you finish."

"It's not worth it! It's just a stupid trek that I decided to do on a stupid whim! I can't ask you to do this. Please don't make me ask you to do this." I couldn't bear the burden of making him face that particular demon because of me.

"You're not," he said, taking both my hands in his. "You're not asking me to do it, Amelia. I want to do it. You need to finish the trek, not because of a whim, but for Carrie, and I…" He broke off, swallowing hard, "I *need* to go over Bla Bheinn. For my brother. For fifteen-year-old me, who died up there with him and then drifted aimlessly until I came back to life. I said last night that I needed to face it, and can't think of anyone I'd rather face it with."

His eyes were bright green, boring into me like lasers, pleading with me to agree. How could I argue with that?

Maybe he *did* need to face that demon, in order to finally be free of it. In order to finally be at peace with himself.

I turned to look at the imposing peak. "But it's over three thousand feet high—will I even be able to do it with my knee?"

"Och, it's just a wee bump," he said, his attempt at humor not quite hitting the mark for either of us. "We'll take it slow. It's steep, and will be worse on the way down. And if we need to abort, we will, but I think you can do it." He shook his head. "No, I *know* you can do it. Look how far you've come since that first day, when you had blisters from your boots and could barely manage the climb up from Rubha Hunish. You made it over the Trotternish Ridge, you made it across all the rivers. This is just one more thing to conquer."

His words, spoken so sincerely, had me swelling with pride. I literally felt myself stand up straighter, as if he'd pulled a string at the top of my spine.

But then he looked down. "Unless you don't think *I* can do it. I wouldn't blame you…after I told you what happened, after my nightmares—"

I lifted his chin so I could look him in the eyes. "I told you I trusted you when you said you'd help me finish the trail, and that hasn't changed. Not even a little."

I put my arms around him, and he leaned into me with a sigh. "Thank you for saying that."

I pulled back and smoothed his hair out of his eyes. "Do you know the way, after all these years?"

He nodded. "Aye, I know the way. I see it every time I dream."

Chapter Thirty-Six

RORY

We have to go over Bla Bheinn… I want to do it…

Somehow, I'd said all those words, and somehow, I'd said them without my voice shaking and without puking. Last night, I'd said that I would climb it one day soon—and I'd meant it—but I figured it would be with Tommy, after days of psyching myself up for it.

Could I really do it *now*? With Amelia, no less, without freaking the fuck out? Did I have any right to subject her to that? She would understand if I changed my mind.

I stared up at Bla Bheinn, outlined perfectly against the cloudless blue sky just about two miles away. Then I looked down into Amelia's warm brown eyes, full of so much emotion: trust, worry—*for me?*—and something that I couldn't so easily identify, but it made my heart jump to see it.

It was the same look I'd seen in her eyes this morning when she woke up.

If that expression meant she felt for me even a fraction

of what I felt for her, then I could do this. I *would* do this. I'd get us over that fucking mountain and down the other side, and maybe I'd finally be able to stop dwelling on the past and start looking toward my future.

"We have to backtrack to Camasunary," I said. "Carefully, now." I did not need a repeat of that moment when the cliff had crumbled beneath my foot. In the split second between when my foot slipped and when I caught the edge and knew I'd be able to get back up, all I could think about was that if I fell, Amelia would be out there, alone. And while not helpless, she'd be at a dangerous disadvantage, since the emergency phone was in my pack. No, hiking over Bla Bheinn was preferable to worrying that one of us might go over that cliff.

We slowly made our way back along the cliff and up the shore. Where the path turned left toward the bothy, we turned right. The path curved left, and we had to ford a few streams, but we were able to cross on stones and stay dry.

And then ahead of us loomed the steep climb up the south face of Bla Bheinn. "Let's take a quick break before we start. Do you have any granola bars left?"

"I think so," Amelia said. She rummaged into her pack and pulled out one that looked a little squished, but still edible.

"Good—eat that, and have some water. And I want you to remember to drink as we ascend."

"I will." She looked nervous—though not nearly as nervous as I felt. But the sky was clear all around, and the path itself was actually pretty straightforward until you got near the top.

"Is it all right if I look in your pack?" I asked.

She cocked her head to the side. "Um, sure. Go for it."

I rummaged through her pack, pulling out her toiletry bag, a well-read book, which I turned over with interest.

"*Outlander*? Och, were you hopin' ye'd find braw Jamie Fraser out here, lass?" I asked, purposely exaggerating my Scots, loving the way she sighed as I did so.

Her eyebrows shot up. "You've read it?"

"Aye. After the umpteenth woman on one of my treks asked where the 'standing stones from *Outlander*' were, with a hopeful look in her eyes, I finally read it to see what the fuss was about."

She tipped down her sunglasses, her eyes slowly roving over me. It might as well have been her hands for the way my whole body came to attention. Her lips parted slightly, and a hot bolt of lust ran through me. Christ, what the hell was she thinking about?

"Amelia?" I said through clenched teeth.

She jolted, her eyes snapping up to mine. A pink flush stained her cheeks. "Um, I'm sorry, did you say something?"

I stared at her, trying to get my body under control. "No, but I'd give nearly anything to know what was in your head just then."

She smiled. "Maybe I'll tell you later. Did you like it?"

Hell yes. "The look in your eyes, as if I was lying naked before you and your hands were sliding over my body? Yeah, I liked it."

"I meant the book! Did you like *Outlander*?"

We were still talking about the damn book? "I liked it well enough. I got up to the third one, and haven't had a chance to get back to them. So, were you? Hoping to find Jamie Fraser?"

"Maybe. But I found something else instead."

"Oh, what's that?"

"A real-life braw and handsome red-haired Scotsman."

"And how does he compare to Mr. Fraser?"

"It's hard to say…"

There was no more talking for a few minutes as I showed

her some of the advantages of a real-life Scotsman. "I'll ask again," I said when I drew back, "how does your real-life Scot compare to Jamie?"

"Pretty well," she said breathlessly. "But I think I'd need to see him in a kilt to be certain."

"I'll see what I can do."

I continued my inventory of her pack, removing a small stack of tightly folded clothes and some other stuff, and jamming it all into my pack with the book and her toiletry bag.

"What are you doing?"

"Transferring some of your things to my pack to lighten yours."

"I can handle it, Rory—I've been handling it all week."

"Aye, I know you can. But I don't want you to, not for this climb. So don't argue," I added with a smile that probably looked like a grimace. She didn't argue, which meant she was worried. I squeezed her thigh. "It'll be okay. Like I said, let's see how it goes for the first part of the climb. If you're in pain, we'll scrap it and go back to Sligachan and figure out something else. No heroics, okay?"

"Okay."

Five minutes later, after I checked the bandage around her knee, we were on our way. The trail was steep, covering over four hundred meters of ascent in the first mile. We went slowly, with Amelia leaning on her trekking poles and me scouting ahead for obstacles and then doubling back to walk at her side.

"Let's take a break here," I said after the first fifty meters or so. She sank onto a boulder and took a drink of water. "How are you holding up?"

"I'm okay, actually," she said. "It's strenuous, and I know I'm moving slowly, but my knee is doing okay so far."

"Are you good to keep going?"

"I am if you are." She peered at me over her sunglasses. "How are *you* doing?"

"I'm okay." And I was. It was a beautiful day, and the ascent was going okay. Maybe this would be all right.

When I did this all those years ago, I was so focused on getting up to the top and proving to my father that I could do it, that I didn't even look up. I was just focused on the ground beneath my feet.

Now, wandering ahead to check out the trail and then going slowly with Amelia, I was able to actually see the beauty of the scenery around me: the craggy rocks, the green grass, the view behind us to the blue waters of Loch Scavaig.

We gained the ridge that would take us most of the way to the top, and we continued to stop every fifty meters or so for a short break and a sip of water. Neither of us spoke much, other than me asking Amelia if she was okay, and Amelia asking if I was okay.

The trail got steeper, and I knew we were within about two hundred meters of the false summit. That was where things would get difficult, because we'd have to scramble down a rocky path before ascending again to the true summit.

Clouds had started to roll in from the west, and the wind had increased. We needed to pick up the pace. No more breaks. I backtracked a few meters and took Amelia by the arm.

"What are you doing? I'm fine!"

"I know you are, and you're doing great. But we need to pick up the pace." I tried to keep my tone calm, but I guess I did a shit job of it, because she glanced to the west. Her eyes grew wide and she let me support her as we hurried up the ridge.

"We're almost at the top!" Amelia exclaimed a few tough minutes later. "Look—we just have to get over that last bit!"

"That's not the true summit."

"What? Ohhh, I remember you saying that there was a false summit."

"Yeah. We're at 926 meters now. The actual summit is 928 meters—a little over three thousand feet—and there's a smallish gully between them. Let me have your poles. It'll be easier for you to scramble down without them."

She handed them over, and I flipped open the locks so I could compress them to their shortest length, then attached them to the back of her pack. "Okay, you're going to go down this section on your butt. Just sit on the rock, reach down with your left foot, and scoot down to the next rock, and so on. But always lead with your left foot."

I focused all my attention on helping Amelia negotiate the scramble down the gully. We reached the bottom without incident. And then I looked up at the path to the true summit. The way was clear, but the wisps of mist we'd seen below us earlier were now all around us.

My heart was pounding and my breath came in gasps. Even though we really had no time to waste, I was grateful that Amelia had stopped to take a quick photo. I needed a minute.

I closed my eyes and focused on my breathing. *I can do this. I'm a Mountain Leader with years of experience. I've done the Skye Trail countless times, in all kinds of conditions. I've climbed Munros all over Scotland. This is just one more. I know what I'm doing.*

Hands came down on my shoulders. I opened my eyes to see Amelia's lovely face before me, her eyes like twin pools of melted chocolate. There was no concern there, no fear that I'd fuck up.

"You can do this, Rory. 'No fear,' right? That's your clan motto?"

"*Sans Peur.* You remembered."

"I told you, I remember everything you say. By the way,

and this may not be the right time to say this, but while I like hearing you speak French, the Gaelic is really what does it for me."

I smiled. "When we get through this, I'll speak Gaelic to you all night, though it'll mostly be the names of mountains and a few curse words."

"Maybe tomorrow. I don't intend for there to be much talking tonight," she said, looking at me from under her eyelashes, her voice full of promise.

My smile got bigger. "Well, we'd best get to it, then," I said.

She took my hand. "Together. For Connor. And for you."

A few minutes later, hand in hand, we stepped on to the summit of Bla Bheinn.

I'd done it—I'd gotten us to the top without incident.

All of the emotion I'd been suppressing for the last seven years crashed over me. My vision blurred, and I sank to my knees, my legs as shaky as a wee lamb's. I covered my face with my hands, my breath coming in harsh gasps.

Amelia's arms came around me, her lips grazing my forehead. "You did it, Rory," she said.

I did it. I pulled her close and kissed her until she melted against me and my body was no longer trembling from relief, but something else entirely.

I kissed her one last time and then gently pulled back. "Go take your photos for Carrie." There was something I needed to do.

"On it," she said with a grin, and carefully stood, peeled off her pack, and pulled out her phone. Wiping my eyes, I got to my feet and shed my own pack, then searched the ground, picking up a few stones.

"Oh my God, Rory, it's incredible!" She gaped at the spectacular views of the Cuillins and Loch Scavaig, clearly visible even with the thickening clouds. She slowly circled in place, taking a video of the view all around.

No, *she* was incredible. I set the stones on the ground and took out my phone. "Amelia," I called.

She turned, a huge smile on her face. I snapped a photo, then moved to her side. I put my arm around her, tipped my head to hers, and snapped a selfie, then took one with her phone. I wanted to be able to look back on this moment.

I scooped up the stones, then knelt beside a boulder that sat right near the edge where we'd just come up.

"Just hang in there." The mist suddenly dissipated, and I saw his face. He smiled and took a step, his gaze holding mine. "There you are." Another step. And then…

I touched the weathered surface of the boulder, which had probably sat there for tens of thousands of years, which a terrified fifteen-year-old lad had desperately clung to, watching in horror as his brother had died. I closed my eyes, picturing Connor's peaceful face that could almost have been asleep except for the small trickle of blood and the gray pallor to his skin, and a shudder ran through me. Then the vision changed to his last smile, and all the irreverent grins before it. *That's* how I wanted to remember him—how I *chose* to remember him.

"I miss you, Connor. So fucking much."

I piled the few stones I'd gathered into a small stack on the flattish top of the boulder. Then I reached into the zipper pocket of my cargo shorts.

Amelia came to stand beside me. "Is that…Rory, is that the stone Connor pulled from the loch when you were kids? Your skipping stone?" She stared at the flat, round stone I'd taken from my pocket.

"It is."

"You've carried it around with you all this time?"

"It…it's kept him close to me, you know? Like he was watching over me. But now I want to give it back to him."

I touched my lips to the purply-gray stone and carefully set it on top of the pile. "I'm so sorry, Connor. Sorry that I came up here by myself that day, and that you had to come up after me because I was an idiot. And I'm sorry that I haven't been back to see you in all this time. I've tried to honor you by doing what you loved—what *I* now love." I swallowed the lump in my throat. "It's been really hard without you."

I glanced at Amelia through a veil of tears, reaching out my hand. She took it, blinking back tears of her own. I looked back at the cairn. "But...I think I'll be okay now. And I'll be back to see you again soon, I promise."

The silvery vein in the stone suddenly began to glow with a strange light. A chill ran down my spine, and I heard Amelia gasp. *What the—?*

I looked up. A beam of sunlight had filtered down through the slate-blue clouds, hitting the vein in just the perfect place for the stone to shine. Almost as if Connor was there. And maybe he was. "I love you, too, brother," I whispered. "Goodbye."

Just then the light in the stone winked out. It took me a moment to realize that it wasn't Connor saying goodbye.

It was the mist, closing in around us.

I couldn't see anything but Amelia, who clutched my hand in a death grip. I couldn't see the path we'd taken up to the summit, or the path we needed to take down the other side.

And I couldn't see the edge.

Oh God, it's happening again.

It was exactly like my nightmare, that feeling of being smothered by the mist, completely disoriented and unable to move, for fear of tumbling off the side.

"Rory?" whispered Amelia, her voice shaky, "what are we going to do?"

"I don't—" I started to say *I don't know*, but then I heard

Connor's voice in my head, as clearly as if he was standing in front of me.

You don't know? You're not that inexperienced, scared, bullied lad anymore. You're a goddamn Mountain Leader. You've guided groups through worse weather than this many times, and you didn't suddenly forget what the fuck you're doing just because this is Bla Bheinn. You know what to do.

"Rory?"

Your lass is counting on you to help her finish this trek. Now do what you need to do to get you both the hell off that rock!

Chapter Thirty-Seven

AMELIA

One minute, I was staring through tears at a shining rock that I could swear was Connor's spirit saying goodbye to Rory, and the next I was staring at a thick mist that had come from nowhere. "Rory?" His hand went rigid and clammy in mine, and he didn't answer.

Oh no. Not now. Not here, on top of this mountain that took away everything from him. Not after that heartbreaking, beautiful eulogy.

I knew—I *knew*—that we were on level ground, that although we faced the edge, there was plenty of space right behind us. But not being able to see that edge—it was like being underwater in the dark, where you have no sense of which way is up. Suddenly, I *didn't* know for certain that we faced the edge. Maybe we'd gotten turned around when we looked to see where that beam of light had come from. Maybe the edge was to the right, or maybe it was behind us.

I couldn't see anything, Rory had said when he told

me about Bla Bheinn. *It was…like being smothered with a blanket. I couldn't see the edge, so I was afraid to move.*

That was exactly how I felt.

"Rory? Are you okay?"

His hand remained locked around mine, and his eyes had gone vacant.

"Rory?" Nothing. Shit, was he having another flashback? "Please tell me you're okay, because this mist is really freaking me out."

Then he turned to me…and smiled. "It's okay, love, I know what to do."

His smile was so unexpected that it took me a moment to realize he'd spoken. He knew what to do? *Of course he does. This is his job, what he's trained for. Surely he's been surrounded by mist before while on a mountain. It's fucking Scotland.*

"We're just going to sit down, right here," he said.

"What?"

He knelt beside me. "Hold on to me, and just sit down."

"Are you sure it's okay to sit here?"

"Aye, we're fine here. Just sit."

I braced my hands on his shoulders and lowered myself to the ground, wincing at the ache in my knee. "Okay, now what?"

"We're going to wait until the mist dissipates."

"For how long? I mean…does it generally disappear as fast as it came?"

"Hard to say—sometimes yes, sometimes no. But the clouds have been fast-moving, so hopefully it'll clear enough for us to descend."

"And if it doesn't?"

"It will." He said it so confidently that I believed him. Also, I had no choice.

"I saw fog like this once before," I said. "Back home, with

Carrie." I'd forgotten about it until just now.

"Tell me," he said.

"It was a few years ago. I live on Long Island, which may not be much for hills and terrain, but it does have beautiful beaches. The ones on the south shore face the Atlantic Ocean, and Lido Beach is Carrie's and my favorite. We went down there one day in early spring to walk on the beach. It was a mild afternoon, but overcast, and there was no one else out there. And between one minute and the next, we were completely surrounded by fog. You couldn't see anything— not the sand, not the ocean, nothing.

"We were weirdly frightened. I mean, it wasn't like being on a mountain top, where if you can't see, you could…"

"You could fall off the edge," Rory said, squeezing my hand. "It's okay, you can say the words."

I leaned against his shoulder. "Right. We were just on the beach. The worst that would happen is we'd stumble into some cold water and get our feet wet. But we just froze in place and clutched each other's hands like scared children. We were afraid to head back the way we came, because we didn't think we'd find the path between the dunes. We stayed there for maybe half an hour, damp and shivering, until the fog cleared enough for us to find our way back." I smiled up at him. "It seems silly to compare that to this, I guess."

"No, not silly at all. We fear the unknown, and suddenly being unable to see is a huge unknown. I'm glad you and Carrie were there together."

"Me, too. And Rory? I'm glad I was with you today, even though it's my fault you had to come this way."

"What are you talking about? How is it your fault?"

"If I hadn't insisted on continuing the trek after hurting my knee, you wouldn't have been two days behind the group. You would have taken the path along the cliffs with no problem and avoided Bla Bheinn."

He shook his head. "Amelia, I knew I'd have to go over Bla Bheinn eventually. I guide the Skye Trail often enough that it's shocking that it hasn't happened before now." He laughed. "I always figured Tommy and Gav would get me pissed on cheap beer and convince me to do it, then drag my ass up here before I sobered up enough to refuse."

His smile faded, and he gazed at me with eyes the soft green of sea glass. He reached up and tucked a strand of hair behind my ear, then traced my cheek with his thumb.

"There's no one I would have rather had here with me than you. Because of you, I can think of my brother—and talk about him—without being crushed by grief and guilt. I don't think I can ever repay you for that."

"You don't have to." I laid my hand on his thigh, blinking away a sudden rush of tears. "But if you insist, I might be able to come up with a few ways."

This time, his grin was wicked. "Oh, I definitely insist."

. . .

We spent the next hour talking. He shared some more stories about Connor, and asked me more about Miami.

"It's beautiful there. You can go to the beach year-round. There's no real hiking, but Carrie's already started looking into other outdoor things we can do, like scuba diving."

"My mate Tristan, Mrs. Mac's son, is a scuba diver. From everything he's said about it, I think you'd love it."

I probably would, though thinking about Miami was making me sad. No jagged mountain ranges outlined against the sky, no otherworldly-looking rock formations jutting up from the sea, no towering peaks half-collapsed by some ancient landslide. No misty glens, no sapphire-blue lochs. No terrain at all.

And no Rory.

"Though it sounds a little dull to me, having the weather be the same all year 'round," he continued. "Won't you miss the snow?"

That was an easy one. "Ugh, snow in New York is miserable. It's pretty when it's falling and just after, but then it gets filthy and the roads are treacherous. No, I won't miss that."

"You should see Skye in the winter, with the Cuillins covered in a blanket of snow, sparkling in the sunlight. All around you is blue sky and white snow, and you breathe in that cold, clean air, and you just…feel alive."

I closed my eyes and pictured it.

Rory, in his winter gear, carrying an ice axe and wearing crampons on his boots, reaches the top of the Munro. The snow is pristine and unbroken all around because he's the first person up there since the last snowfall. His cheeks and the tip of his nose are rosy from the cold. He turns, his grin stretching from ear to ear, and holds out a gloved hand—

To me.

Wait, what? No. I wouldn't be climbing Munros in Scotland in the winter. I'd be in Miami, out on the beach with Carrie, checking out the guys playing beach volleyball, or maybe paddle-boarding, laughing at our friends back home who were shivering in the cold.

I was here for Carrie, and I couldn't forget that. I couldn't forget that in a few days, I'd be heading back home to her, to begin the life that was waiting for me there.

I looked down at my hands, sadness overwhelming me. "Carrie and I are supposed to go to Miami in a few weeks to look for an apartment." I swallowed hard. "If she wakes up."

He tipped my chin up so our eyes met. "She will," he said fiercely. "You're going to have such an adventure to tell her about when you get home that she won't have any choice *but* to wake up so she can hear all the details."

"I hope you're right," I whispered.

He pulled me close, and we stayed like that, arms around each other, each lost in our own thoughts, until the mist dissipated.

We retrieved our packs, and I stood a few feet back while Rory said one last goodbye to Connor, touching his heart and then touching his fingers to the stone. "*Soraidh leat, mo bhràthar.* Farewell, brother," he murmured.

I had a feeling that he would be back here again soon.

The descent was challenging—one of the most difficult parts of the entire trail. There were sheer vertical cliffs on our left side, and the way down was over rocky ground, with no real path. After the first few minutes of trying to step down like a normal person would, I gave up and just scooted down on my butt until we reached a clear path that eventually led to a road and the car park for Bla Bheinn.

I never was so happy to see pavement in my life.

"It's another two miles along this road to Torrin," said Rory. "There's a café there, as well as a few B&Bs. I know it's only mid-afternoon, but I think I've had it for today, if that's okay with you. We can have an early dinner—the café closes at five—and then…"

And then… "Say no more. I'm in."

True to his word, less than an hour later, we reached the small village. As it was a weeknight, there was a vacancy at the B&B, a lovely en-suite room on the second floor with spectacular views of Bla Bheinn, nearby Loch Slapin, and the Red Cuillins.

And a king-sized bed.

Chapter Thirty-Eight

RORY

"Well, I don't think we have to worry that one of us will fall out of *this* bed, unlike the one in Sligachan," said Amelia.

"No, I think we'll be all right," I agreed. The bed was illuminated by the sunlight coming in from the above skylight like it was on display.

As if I needed a reason to imagine all the things Amelia and I could do on that bed. As if I wasn't instantly ready and dying to do all those things right now.

I cleared my throat and looked away, taking her things out of my pack. "Uh, why don't you have the first go at the shower? I want to check in with Scarlet and Tommy." Or I might tumble her onto that bed and forget about getting food at the café or checking in—or anything else.

She grinned. "Thanks. I feel so grungy," she said, seemingly unaware of my inner turmoil. She plugged in her phone, grabbed her toiletry bag and clean clothes, and disappeared into the bathroom, exclaiming over the plush towels as the door closed behind her.

I sank into the chair in the corner and pulled out my phone. There were texts from both Scarlet and Tommy, letting me know they'd finished the trek and asking where we were.

I plugged my phone into the charger and dialed Scarlet. She answered on the second ring. "Rory! Where are you? How's Amelia?"

"Hey Scarlet. We're in Torrin, and staying here tonight. Amelia's doing okay. "She's been"—*brave, strong, amazing, incredible, everything*—"a real trouper."

"How long until you finish?"

"I think two more days. We'll probably camp out at Boreraig tomorrow night, and make Broadford the day after. I don't think she's up for a twelve-mile day tomorrow." *And I'm not ready to say goodbye to her.*

"Okay. It sounds like you have everything under control."

"As much control as you can have with the weather on Skye," I said dryly. "Speaking of which, the cliffs between Camasunary and Elgol are impassable. The storm the other night caused a huge amount of erosion."

"Thanks for letting me know. I'll spread the word and let the Mountain Rescue folks know as well. So...does that mean you went over Bla Bheinn?" she asked hesitantly. Scarlet knew about my brother, had respected my wishes never to go up there.

"We did."

"Are you all right?"

"I am, actually. It wasn't easy, but I'm glad I finally did it." I didn't tell her we were delayed by the mist—she'd only worry, even though it had already happened, and we'd made it through okay. "We're both pretty knackered."

"I can imagine. Amelia did okay with the climb?"

"She did. We took it slow."

"Good. She does sound like a trouper. And you are, too,

Rory. I'm really proud of you. Go get some rest, and let me know when you reach Broadford."

"Will do."

I dialed Tommy next. He answered before it even rang on my end. "Rory! Where the hell are you?"

"Hi to you, too. We're in Torrin." I heard the clink of glass in the background. "Are you back in Sligachan?" Realistically, Tommy could have been in a pub in Broadford, but he hated to be alone, so I figured he was with Gav.

"Aye, Gav and I are having a few pints and gossiping about you." *Wonderful.* "You said you're in Torrin?"

"Yeah, we got in a little while ago."

"We were just chatting with some trekkers who said the path from Camasunary to Elgol was impassable after the storm the other night. They backtracked to Sligachan."

"I know it is. I just called Scarlet to check in and told her the same thing so she can spread the word. I nearly went over the fucking cliff."

"Christ, Rory. You okay?"

"I'm fine. Wrenched my shoulder a bit, and have a few scrapes, but I'm otherwise okay."

"How the hell did you get to Torrin, then? Did you just say fuck it all and hitch a ride from the Slig?"

"No."

"Wait, are you saying…"

"We went over Bla Bheinn."

Silence. Then, "Are you all right?" Same question Scarlet had asked, but I wouldn't be able to bluff my way through it with Tommy.

"I am now. It was…hard, but when I got up there, it was like…"

"Like what?"

"Like he was there with me, and it was okay, you know?" That didn't even begin to touch on what that moment on the summit had felt like, but I knew Tommy would get it.

"Aye, I know," he whispered.

"I needed to do it, Tommy."

"After all this time, I just never thought…"

"Don't be mad."

"What? Why the fuck would I be mad?"

"I know you wanted to go up there with me, and I know I told you no every time you asked. And the last time…"

Even though Tommy hadn't witnessed what happened to Connor, it wasn't easy for him to go over Bla Bheinn, and he'd only done it a few times. He'd wanted us to go together to pay our respects, and I'd never been able to. The last time he asked, I'd angrily told him I'd let him know when I was ready and he needed to lay off.

"I'm not mad, Rory," he said quietly. "I wanted you to go up there because I always knew you needed to face it before you could truly move on. And I didn't want you to do it alone. I'm just glad you did it, and that you had someone you loved with you when you did."

"What?" *Did he just say…?*

"You heard me. And don't try to deny it. That mountain has been your nightmare—the monster looming over you in the dark—for years. There's no way you'd suddenly decide to face it unless it was for someone you love."

A series of images flashed through my mind like a slideshow. They were all of Amelia: the flush of irritation on her cheeks when I'd scolded her on the first days of the trek, the awe in her eyes when she'd stood on the ridge and watched the eagle soaring below, tears streaking her face when she'd told me what happened to Carrie. Her eyes burning with anger when I'd talked about my father, the way she'd cried for me when I'd told her about Connor. Her brave smile when she'd hurt her knee, the trust she'd given me when I'd said we'd be okay in the fog, her body soft and languid with pleasure after we'd made love. How she would look in that shower right now, with water cascading down her naked body.

We'd shared so much in our short time together: arguments, fear, physical hardship, grief, triumph, passion, friendship.

And I wanted to share so much more with her.

I wanted to climb Ben Nevis with her, hear her shrieking with laughter as I dunked her in a cold loch on a warm summer day, watch the sun come up over the Red Cuillins with her after a night of making love in our tent, share a flask of whisky under a blanket in front of a crackling fire on a long winter night.

I wanted to wake up with her in my arms every day.

"Rory, you still there?"

"Yeah."

"You're not denying it?"

I sighed. "No." There was no point in denying what was true.

I was in love with Amelia.

It didn't seem possible, but somehow, it was. That Tommy didn't hassle me about it was an even stronger indication that it was real.

"What are you going to do about it?" he asked.

"About what?"

"Don't be dense. You know what I mean."

I knew. "Nothing. She has a great job waiting for her back in the States with her best friend."

"So that's it? You get to Broadford and then you shake hands and say it was nice to meet her, and then you hand her off to Scarlet to take her back to Fort William—after, of course, you send her a friend request on Facebook?"

The thought of doing that was like a knife to my chest—a literal pain that made it hard to breathe. "What am I supposed to do, Tommy? I told you, she has a—"

"'Great job lined up.' Yeah, I heard you the first time."

"So why are you even asking?"

"Because you've been alone for far too long."

"I haven't been alone—I have you." I knew I was being obtuse, but I wasn't prepared to have this conversation right now.

"Don't be a dick, Rory. You know what I mean. And I'm not going to sleep with you, even if you ask nicely."

"I *do* know what you mean, Tommy. Believe me, I know exactly how alone I've been and for exactly how long."

"So if you're in love with her, and if you have the slightest inkling that she might feel the same way, you don't just let that go without even trying, or you'll regret it forever."

"I can't think about this right now."

"That's fine. You're in Torrin, so you have a whole day to think about it," he said sarcastically.

"Two," I muttered.

"What's that?"

"Two days." *Only two days.* "We're in Torrin tonight at a B&B, and then we'll camp out tomorrow, and then reach Broadford the next day. I don't want her to do twelve miles on that knee in one day."

"A B&B, huh? Are you sharing a room?"

I rolled my eyes. "Aye, we're sharing a room. Are you happy?"

"Yes. And so is Gav. He tried to bet me that you were, but I didn't take that bet. He's giving you a thumbs-up, by the way."

"The two of you are numpties," I said mildly.

"Yeah, we are. Where is she now?"

"In the shower."

He scoffed, and I could almost hear his eyes roll. "What the fuck are you still doing on the phone with me, then? Tell her I said hi, and I'll see you in Broadford in two days."

"All right. See you then."

"And Rory?"

"Yeah?"

"Go get wet."

"Dammit, Tommy," I muttered, my whole body jumping to attention as I imagined doing just that.

He was still laughing when I disconnected the call. I glanced at the bathroom door. I could still hear the shower running as Amelia scrubbed away two days' worth of mud, sweat, and trail grime.

Go get wet, Tommy had said.

Aye, it was time to get wet.

Chapter Thirty-Nine

AMELIA

I stood under the spray, letting the hot water work its magic on me. It seemed like every muscle in my body was sore. Thank God Rory had called an early end to the day; I couldn't have gone much farther.

There was a knock at the door. Shit, I hadn't even washed myself or my hair yet. "Be out in a few," I called, reaching for the shampoo. The bathroom door opened. "Sorry, Rory, I know I'm taking forever. I'll be quick now."

I didn't hear him leave, so I put down the shampoo and peered around the curtain. And froze.

He stood on the tile floor, wearing only his boxer briefs.

Wordlessly, slowly, deliberately, I drew back the curtain, surprising myself a little with my boldness.

His eyes smoldered as they raked over my naked body from head to toe, leaving me hot and aching for him.

"I think you're a bit overdressed," I said.

His lips curving in a slow smile, he hooked his thumbs in

his waistband and drew his boxers down and off. And then it was my turn to ogle him as he stood before me—from the top of his lovely hair, down his lean, strong body to his feet, and then slowly back up. It was thrilling to see how much he wanted me; the evidence was right there before me, proud and unmistakable.

His eyes flared, and I realized I was unconsciously licking my lips. He stepped into the tub and backed me into the wall, his hands cupping my face, his lips taking mine in a kiss so hot, so hungry, it staggered me.

Now *he* was the bold one.

His hands dropped to caress my breasts, and then he tore his mouth from mine to follow the path his hands had taken. I held the back of his head, his wet curls twining around my fingers as he set me on fire with his touch.

His fingers skipped down my ribs to my waist, and then he lifted me off my feet. My legs instinctively wrapped around his hips as he pressed me into the wall, the tiles cool against my heated skin, his body throbbing against my center. He lifted his head to kiss me again, but this time slowly, as if he had all the time in the world.

But *I* didn't.

I skimmed my hands down his body, smiling as he sucked in a breath. "You started it," I said as I stroked him.

"So I did," he replied, and then it was his turn to smile and my turn to gasp as his fingers found me. He caressed me until I was writhing against the wall.

"Rory, please," I hissed. "I need you."

"Not yet." His fingers continued to torment me until I came apart, my hands clutching helplessly at his shoulders.

I felt his fingers leave me, and I watched as he reached around the curtain for a condom he'd left on the edge of the sink. I took it from his hand and put it on him, *slowly,* savoring the feel of him pulsing in my hands, smiling at the knowledge that I was driving him as crazy as he'd driven me.

And then he was inside me, both of us gasping as our bodies slid together until we were fully joined. I tightened my legs around his waist, ignoring the ache in my knee. He cradled the back of my head with one hand while the other supported my back.

"Open your eyes, Amelia," he said. I met his gaze—so green, so intense, I couldn't look away. And I didn't want to. I drew him deeper, my fingers trailing up and down his spine as he moved within me, his slow, languid pace belying his earlier urgency.

Time seemed to stand still as he made love to me, the water cascading over us. I arched against him, my body desperate for more. "Rory, please," I gasped. I was so close…

Finally, he gave in and began to move faster. I cupped his face, keeping my eyes locked to his, crying out his name as I tumbled over the edge. He rocked against me once more, then buried his face in my shoulder as he followed me into oblivion.

I ran my fingers through his wet hair, unable to do much else. My mind was spinning. "Rory, that was…" I didn't even know what to say.

He raised his head and looked at me, his eyes back to their usual gray-green. "Amazing? Fantastic? Brilliant?"

There was a vulnerability in his eyes that belied his light tone. And while it had been amazing, fantastic, and brilliant, those weren't the words that had come to mind. Nor were they the words he wanted to hear.

I smoothed his hair back from his face and stared into those luminous eyes. "Transcendent. The most intense experience I've ever had."

His beautiful smile told me that I'd said the right thing.

"It's been a hell of an intense day," he said.

"And after all that, I haven't actually gotten clean yet."

"Well, we'd better remedy that before the water runs cold." He pulled back, holding onto me as my legs fell away from his hips and waiting until I was steady on my feet. While he cleaned up, I reached for the shampoo.

"Let me," he murmured, taking the bottle from me. He squeezed some onto his hand, and I turned so he could reach. He massaged the shampoo into my scalp, making my sated body come alive once more. He turned me around so that I was under the spray, and I reached for him, but he stepped back, shaking his head. "None of that, or we'll never get out of here."

"I can think of far worse things."

"The café closes at five. It was after three thirty when I came in here," he said. "I mean, if you want another freeze-dried dinner...?"

"Okay, fair point," I said as he gently worked conditioner through my long hair. I was starving, and definitely didn't want to miss our chance at real food.

He rinsed my hair, and then I reached for the shampoo. "Your turn."

He was considerably taller than me, so I had him face me and lower his head so I could reach him. This unfortunately—or fortunately, depending on your point of view—put his face right at my chest. He pressed his lips to my wet skin. "None of that, or we'll never get out of here," I teased. He was clearly going to ignore me, but the moment my lathered hands sank into his thick hair, he just closed his eyes and practically purred with bliss.

While he rinsed his hair, I quickly soaped up with the body wash and then traded places with him so I could wash off and he could soap up. I put on a sleeveless top and jeans and did a quick blow-dry of my hair while he got dressed.

I checked my phone. No messages. "I'll call Carrie's mom

after we eat."

"Are you sure? We have some time."

"Yeah. I want to actually sit and enjoy my food."

We headed to the small, blue-shingled café, where we both ordered big bowls of thick vegetable soup with homemade crusty bread. The simple meal was delicious, but Rory was quiet, pensive, his eyes gray-green and turbulent.

Which, given the way he'd stalked into the shower and taken me against the wall less than an hour earlier, seemed strange.

"Are you all right?" I finally asked.

He looked up from his soup and smiled, though it didn't quite reach his eyes. "Yeah. I guess I'm just tired. It's been a...long day."

I wished I could read his mind at that moment. Was he thinking about Connor? Did he regret what he and I had done—that we'd gotten together? Was it something else entirely? Or was he really just tired?

I couldn't stand the silence. "Did you speak to Tommy before? Did they finish?"

I wondered how the rest of the group fared. I'd just gotten to know Molly and Megan and Pat and Linda when we'd parted ways, and it sucked that we couldn't have finished as a group.

This time, his grin was real, crinkling his eyes at the corners and making my heart leap. "Oh, aye. They finished the trek, and he's bumming around with Gav in Sligachan. He said to tell you hi."

"Aww, that's sweet," I said, dunking a piece of bread in my soup.

"Sweet? Ha. Gav tried to bet Tommy that you and I would hook up."

"Those two need a hobby. And what do you mean, 'tried to'?"

"Tommy refused to bet against it."

Which, given what he'd said to both of us a few days—*a lifetime*—ago, wasn't surprising. "I feel like Tommy's been pretty invested in the two of us getting together."

He took a sip of his beer. "He likes you. Has from the very beginning—even before I did."

I licked my lips. "And now?"

"Now what?" he asked, dipping his spoon into his soup.

"Do you like me?" It sounded very junior high school, and a stupid question given what we'd been doing a short while ago, but suddenly I had to know.

His spoon froze midway to his mouth. He set it back in the bowl and took my hand. "Aye, I like you," he said, his gaze steady on mine. "So much, I don't know how I'm going to say goodbye to you in two days," he added, his voice so low I could barely hear him.

"Me, either," I whispered back.

He brought my hand to his lips and kissed my fingers, then turned it so that my palm lay against his cheek. I ran my thumb over his bristly jaw and stared into his eyes.

"You never did tell me what had you staring at me like you wanted to devour me when I was going through your pack earlier," he said suddenly.

I felt my face grow hot. "Oh, that."

"Aye, that. I think you'd better tell me."

"You were saying you'd read *Outlander*. And I got this image in my head of you lying in your tent, your head propped on your pack, the sleeping bag bunched around your bare waist. You were holding the book in one hand while your other rested on your belly."

His brow crinkled. "I don't understand why imagining me reading got you all hot and bothered."

I rolled my eyes. "You reading *Outlander* got me all hot and bothered. I'd been ready to crawl into your sleeping bag with you when I saw that you'd fallen asleep reading

Fellowship. Outlander is like a million times sexier than *Fellowship.*"

A shadow fell over the table. "Sorry to interrupt, but did you need anything else before we close in a few minutes?" asked the owner, a plump, pretty woman in her fifties.

"Should we get some sandwiches for later?" asked Rory. "We can take them to the beach and watch the sunset."

"Oh, that's a lovely idea!" said the woman. "It should be a nice one this evening, now that the sky over Bla Bheinn has cleared."

"That sounds great," I said, and we gave her our order.

A few minutes later, she returned, a big paper bag in her hands. "One tuna mayo on multigrain, one turkey and avocado on ciabatta. I threw in a few apples and two bags of crisps as well. You can have a proper picnic on the beach overlooking Loch Slapin."

She walked away to ring us up. "Or we can just go back to the room, and I can take off all my clothes and read *Outlander* while you stare at me if you'd prefer," he said in a low voice.

"If you read it aloud and let me video it, you have a deal. It would go viral."

"Done."

I grinned. Rory had a great sense of humor, once he let it show.

We grabbed coffees to go and headed back to the B&B. Rory went up to the room, while I wandered to a nearby bench and called Helen.

"Hey, how is she today?" I asked when Helen picked up.

"No change, honey," she replied, sounding utterly exhausted. "Her injuries continue to heal, but she's still in the coma. How are you? Please, tell me something good. How's the trek going? You have to be almost done by now, right?"

"Yeah, we're almost to the end. We should finish in two days." Though I didn't consider that to be a good thing. I wanted to tell her about Rory, but that story couldn't have a happy ending. In a few short days, we'd go our separate ways. "It's been an amazing experience, Helen." At least that part was true. "The scenery here is just breathtaking. The weather's been up and down—we've had some pretty serious rain and wind, which has made for a few interesting moments—but I wouldn't trade any of it."

As I said the words, I realized how true they were. I wouldn't trade one minute of this experience—even the knee injury. *Especially* the knee injury, because if I hadn't gotten hurt, I never would have had this time with Rory, would never have hooked up with him.

"That's wonderful, sweetie. I know you don't have long—let me put the phone to Carrie's ear for a second."

"Okay, thanks."

A moment later I heard her muffled voice say, "Okay, you're on."

"Hey Ree," I said, speaking quietly so Helen wouldn't hear. "I was just telling your mom that we're almost done with the trek. I can fill you in on all that when I get home, but I wanted to tell you that I, um, met a guy. His name is Rory, and he's actually one of the guides for the trek, and we kinda hooked up."

Carrie loved romance—other people's almost more so than hers—and she'd been disappointed over the years by my lackluster boyfriends, even more so than I was. Maybe telling her about Rory would get her to wake up.

"He's so serious, and I didn't like him much at the beginning, but he's had a shitty life, with so much heartbreak. Other guys would have let that turn them into angry, bitter people, or let it destroy them completely, but he hasn't. He's kind, and strong, and brave, and so beautiful, with these amazing eyes that change color depending on his mood."

Usually calm gray-green like the sea; more intensely so

*when he's concerned or troubled. Silver when he's angry.
Bright green when he looks at me like I'm the most beautiful
thing he's ever seen, when he touches me like he'll die without
the feel of my skin under his fingertips, when he kisses me like
only I can provide the air he needs to breathe.*

"And I...I think I love him. No—I *know* I love him. I know what you're thinking—how can I love him when I've only known him for a few days? But it's been a pretty intense few days, and we've spent every minute together, and I just know. I wish I knew how he felt. I mean, I'm pretty sure he cares about me—you can't fake that look he had in his eyes when we were—"

Making love in the shower and he stared at me like he could see my soul.

I paced back and forth, too agitated to sit still. "Anyway, I suggested that we hook up for the duration of the trek. No promises, no plans for after. We'd both go back to our lives. He tried to tell me it wasn't a good idea, but I wanted him so much, and I knew he wanted me, and life can change in a second, and I didn't want to come home and regret that I missed out on the chance to be with him, even if it was just for a few days.

"But a short fling isn't me. I knew that. And I didn't care. I thought it would be enough. But now..." My eyes filled with tears. "What am I going to do, Carrie? We have just two days left, and then the trek is over. And it *isn't* enough. I wish you could tell me what to do. When I say goodbye to him..." I broke off, unable to finish my sentence.

My heart will shatter into a thousand pieces.

"Please wake up, and tell me what to do," I whispered. I closed my eyes, listening for something—anything—that would indicate she'd heard me, that she was waking up.

But the only sound was the steady beeping of the monitors.

Chapter Forty

While Amelia made her phone call, I returned to the room and flopped down on the bed, staring blindly at the ceiling.

Two more days. That's all I had left before my time with Amelia would come to an end. Even if I could convince her to stay longer, that was only delaying the inevitable. She had to get back to Carrie, to her new job in a new city, where it was always summer.

To a life that didn't include me.

It was supposed to be a casual fling—just two consenting adults having some fun for a few days, and that was it.

And now? I almost wished we hadn't gone down that road. She'd made me feel again, made me think that I was worthy of some happiness. But in a few days she'd be gone, and I'd be alone again. I'd have a few amazing memories to hold onto after she was gone, but that was all they'd be—memories.

I had to start pulling back now, so it would be easier to say goodbye when we reached Broadford. When Amelia got back to the room, I'd tell her we needed to just be friends. That it had been great, and I'd miss being with her, but it had to be done before we became any more emotionally invested. Before I forgot myself and told her I loved her.

I'd ask the landlady for my own room, or if nothing was available, I'd sleep on the floor. And there'd be no more scenes like the one a few hours earlier in the shower. No more passionate kisses, no more touching her cheek, her hand, her hair. No more watching her bottomless brown eyes dilate with passion; no more feeling her body come apart around me.

I could do it. I'd endured far worse and survived. And so had she.

I heard her footsteps in the hallway. I got up from the bed, steeling myself for what I had to do.

And then she walked into the room, her eyes shining with tears, her shoulders slumped, and walked straight into my suddenly outstretched arms.

As I held her close and breathed in the scent of her hair, I knew that I would make the most of every minute we had left.

After Amelia assured me Carrie hadn't taken a turn for the worse, that she was just being emotional, I led her to the bed and just held her in my arms.

She fell asleep, and then I did, too, waking some time later as the sun was beginning to drop. I wanted that sunset picnic—another memory I'd be able to look back on after she was gone. I shook her shoulder. She opened her eyes and squinted up at me, clearly confused. "Is it morning already?"

I smiled. "No, but it's almost sunset. Did you still want to have that picnic by the loch?"

She sat up, suddenly wide awake. "Yes, I'd love that." She climbed out of the bed and pulled on her boots.

There was a perfect spot at the side of the loch with a direct view to Bla Bheinn, and we ate our dinner there, sitting on a plaid blanket the B&B's landlady had loaned us. The sun dropped behind the mountain, casting it in a fiery glow. As I gazed up at it, I imagined that Connor was up there smiling down at us. A hand closed over mine, and I glanced at Amelia. I could tell by the look in her eyes that she knew exactly what I was thinking.

I held her close as the evening sky turned yellowish in the wake of the sunset, then lavender and gray as the gloaming set in, then dark blue and finally black. We watched as the stars winked to life in a moonless sky. As night deepened, it grew colder, and we finally returned to the B&B around eleven and made love late into the night.

We set out late the next morning after a bracing swim in the loch and brunch at the café. The trail between Torrin and Broadford was generally easy, and we probably could have done all twelve miles or so in one day, but there was a spot about halfway that I wanted to camp at overnight, so we took our time and just enjoyed the slower pace. We wandered off the path here and there, exploring the coastline and doubling back.

The trail turned slightly inland, away from the coast. It wound gently uphill and then curved to the left, revealing a smattering of stone ruins.

"What is this place?" breathed Amelia.

"It was once the settlement of Suisnish."

"What happened to it?"

"The Highland Clearances. In the decades following the Jacobite defeat at Culloden in 1746, the English burned the villages in reprisal for the rebellion and then stripped the clans of their culture and their power. It became more profitable to the landowners to have the land free for sheep than to have people living here, so whole settlements were burned, their residents evicted. Suisnish is one of those, as is Boreraig, which is a few miles down. They were burned in the fall of 1853, the people forced out into the cold."

Amelia walked to the first pile of rubble and closed her eyes, running her hands reverently over the lichen-encrusted stones.

"I can picture them," she murmured suddenly, "the people who once lived here. Their children playing on the shore, the women gossiping and laughing as they hung the wash to dry, the men working the fields. It wouldn't have been an easy life, but it was the only one they knew, going back generations. And then to be suddenly forced out, to have your home burned to the ground as you ran into the freezing night with the few possessions you could grab, carrying your baby in your arms, helping your old grandmother walk with her arthritic knees…"

She moved to another crumbled wall. "Back home in the States, we have this romantic image of Scotland. We picture handsome, kilted warriors galloping their horses across heather-covered hills, rebelling against the evil English. We come here and drink whisky and listen to the bagpipes, explore castle ruins and walk the trails, and we forget that there were people who had to fight for their survival in this beautiful place. And many of them weren't successful. They died starving in the cold, with their homes smoldering behind them. It's so peaceful here now, but I can almost hear the screams and smell the smoke."

She turned to me, wiping her eyes. "Why are you staring at me like that?"

Because she could have pulled those words right from my brain.

"This part of the trail has always been difficult for me,"

I said. "Not physically, but emotionally. Scotland has a brutal and bloody history, and you're never far from a place that's believed to be haunted. There are plenty of sites more dramatic than this one, like the vaults in Edinburgh, or Culloden battlefield, or Glencoe.

"But here, in this quiet, remote section of coastline, the past has always seemed so much closer, the ghosts that much more real to me. I always get chills walking this part of the trail. Every now and then, one of the walkers in my group will sense it, too, but what you just said? It's exactly how I feel when I'm here."

Hand in hand, we walked slowly from one decimated croft to the next, paying our respects at each one. A light mist had rolled in off the water to wind its way through the stone ruins, making the dead settlement seem even more eerie, as if the spirits were closer than ever before.

We left Suisnish and continued on the path, which led through the heather and then down to the shoreline for a few miles, passing by a few waterfalls rushing from the high cliffs above, before reaching Boreraig, a settlement that had suffered the same fate as Suisnish. The buildings here were a little more intact, though no less atmospheric. And even though it was eerie, I'd always wanted to camp in this place, to feel close to the past.

"Will it bother you to stay here tonight?" I asked.

Her eyes grew wide. "Like, in one of the ruins?" she asked in a slightly panicked voice.

"No, we'll set up camp separately from the ruins. They obviously don't provide any real shelter, anyway."

"Okay, that's fine, then," she said, looking relieved. "I just, um, didn't want to trespass, you know?" She smiled sheepishly.

"I do know. Okay, I'll make camp."

It would be our last night on the trail.

Chapter Forty-One

AMELIA

While Rory set up the tent, I meandered through the ruins of Boreraig. The slower pace we'd set today had been relatively easy on my knee, and unlike the other days, when I'd basically collapsed after we'd finished the day's walk, I wanted to explore.

The buildings were mostly just walls—the roofs would have been made out of some kind of thatch that burned immediately when put to the torch.

I wandered into one of the larger structures that was more intact than some of the others. As I walked through what remained of the rooms, the mist swirled around me once more. A chill ran down my spine. It wasn't like the mist was a rare occurrence around here, but here, in this place, it felt like the ghosts of all the wrongly dispossessed people were watching me.

"Okay, I'm going," I whispered. I ducked back under the lintel and joined Rory at our campsite, grateful he'd set it up closer to the shore of the loch, a short distance away from the ruins.

We shared our final "dinner in a bag," passing back and forth Szechuan beef and Chicken Pad Thai. After we packed up the trash, we sat by the loch, sipping from Rory's flask, which the landlady at the B&B in Torrin had kindly filled for him from her stock of Talisker.

"When do you fly home to New York?" he asked as he passed me the flask.

"The morning of the sixteenth." *Too soon.*

"Today's the…thirteenth. So once we finish tomorrow, that gives us a day to get you down to Glasgow."

"Us?" He was going to come with me?

"I thought maybe I could drive you down, if that's okay with you? Unless you had a train ticket or something else lined up?"

"No, I have a hotel room near the airport for the night of the fifteenth, and I'd planned to take the train down, but I hadn't bought my ticket yet." Even if I *did* have a train ticket, I'd happily forfeit it to spend another day with him. "Do you have a car?"

"I do. Well, *Gav* has a car. Which I will borrow from him. If you can bear spending one extra day with me."

"I could be persuaded," I said, feeling a surge of happiness welling up inside me. One additional day—and night—with Rory.

He took the flask from me, capped it, and set it aside. "Will this persuade you?" he asked, kissing my forehead.

When he pulled back, I shook my head. "Sorry, I'm afraid it'll take more than that."

"This?" He cupped my chin in his hand and kissed my right cheek, then turned my head to kiss my left cheek.

"No," I whispered. "I need more."

He nodded. "I think I understand. How about this?" He

tipped my face to his, his lips capturing mine in a slow, tender kiss.

I'd fully intended to see how far he would take this little game, but the moment our lips met, I was lost. My hands came up around his neck, and I pulled him closer, opening my mouth to touch my tongue to his.

When he pulled back this time, the sun had dropped low, casting a fiery aura around him. "Have I finally persuaded you?"

"*Yes*," I replied, pulling his head down to mine once more.

• • •

I sat by the loch, staring up at the glittering black sky. It was so beautiful here, so peaceful.

There was a soft rustle and then someone sat down beside me. "Hey, lady."

Startled, I looked over. It wasn't who I expected it to be. "Carrie? Are you really here?"

She didn't answer, just tipped her head back to look up. "I've never seen a sky like this before," she mused. "It's magical. I can see why you don't want to leave. You have to travel really far to get a sky like this back home." She turned to look at me. "I think you'd also have to travel pretty far to find a guy like Rory back home."

"You saw him?"

She looked at the sky once more. "I didn't have to. I see you. Ever since we were kids, your every thought and every emotion have always been written all over your face. I heard it in the way you spoke of him to me, and I see it in your eyes now."

"What am I going to do, Carrie? I love him. I know it sounds crazy—I've only known him for a week. But it's true."

"I know it is."

"So what do I do? My life is three thousand miles away from here."

"You're going to have some difficult decisions ahead."

"Great, thanks. If you're going to appear mysteriously to me in my dreams, you could at least have something useful to say."

She grinned. "Sorry, dude. But I will say that if I had a man like that lying beside me, and just a couple more days to spend with him, I certainly wouldn't be sleeping. You should wake up."

"But if I wake up, you won't still be here. And I miss you so much, Carrie."

She pressed her lips to my forehead, then drew back. "I miss you, too. But you should wake up. Wake up!"

I came awake with a start. "Carrie?" I whispered. But there was no answer. It was only a dream. I was lying on my side in a dark tent with Rory's body wrapped around mine, his hand lightly cupping my breast, his breath gently stirring my hair.

I lifted his hand and pressed my lips to his fingers, then put it back where it was, covering it with my own. He murmured something in his sleep and snuggled closer.

I was about to close my eyes once more when I saw it—a flicker of green light outside the tent.

I blinked a few times to clear my eyes, but when I opened them again, the light was still there, green and unearthly.

Oh shit, why did we make camp near the creepy ruins?

"Rory, wake up!" I hissed, turning in his arms. "Rory!"

"Wha'ss wrong?" he murmured.

I shoved at his shoulder. "It's the ghosts!" The words sounded ridiculous even to my own ears, but we were a few yards from the ruins and there was a fucking green light outside.

He opened his eyes. "What? What are you talking about?"

"Look!"

He sat up and looked toward the door of the tent, where the green light was visible through an opening in the zipper.

He kicked free of the sleeping bag and got to his feet, reaching for his shorts. "Come on, let's go!" he said, a huge grin on his face.

I stared at him. "Go? Go where?"

"Out there. Quick, get dressed…and grab your phone."

My phone? "Are you out of your mind? I'm not going out there with the ghosts!"

His grin got bigger. "It's not ghosts, I promise. Trust me."

I pulled on the clothes I'd discarded earlier and shoved my feet into my flip-flops, then followed Rory. "There better not be freaking ghosts out here, or I'll—"

I broke off as I emerged from the tent and stared at the green swirls shimmering and dancing across the sky. "Oh my God," I breathed.

"It's the Aurora Borealis, the Northern Lights. It's extremely rare to see them so late in the spring."

We walked down to the loch. I pulled out my phone and set it to record video, then panned across the sky, as well as the loch, which was reflecting the swirling green light. "Oh Carrie, I wish you could see this. Although maybe somehow you did, and that's why you made me wake up."

I'd been hearing her voice in my head here and there throughout the trek. But this was the first time I'd really felt her there with me, as if she had been there all along, seeing every spectacular view through my eyes. And maybe, if there was any weird mystical chance that she *was* on this journey with me, maybe it meant I'd done the right thing by coming to Skye, by doing this trek. Maybe she'd be waiting for me when I got home.

At this moment, with this magical sight before me, I would believe anything. I recorded another few seconds, took some stills that I knew probably wouldn't come out, then put the phone in my pocket. I had enough pictures for Carrie. Now it was time for me to see it for myself.

Rory helped me sit on the ground, then dropped down beside me. I lay back and gazed at the unobstructed view.

I'd seen photos of the aurora, but no photo on a website could possibly compare to seeing it in person. The lights moved as if they were dancing to some kind of heavenly orchestra, and as I stared at the spectacular show before me, tears welled in my eyes.

"Are you all right?" Rory murmured, obviously hearing me sniffle.

"Yeah, I don't even know why I'm getting so emotional over this."

"The first time I saw the aurora was on an overnight trek I did with Tommy after Connor died. It was winter, and we were up in the Cairngorm mountains, which are in the East Highlands, not far from Inverness. There was snow up there, and the aurora went on for an hour, maybe, dancing across the sky and reflecting on the snow. I'd never seen anything like it before, and I was struck by this idea that Connor was up there, trying to communicate with me through the lights.

"I got all choked up, and being a fifteen-year-old lad, tried my damnedest to hide it, but then I looked over at Tommy, and he had tears in his eyes as well but made no effort to wipe them away. And I thought, if Tommy wasn't ashamed of his tears, I didn't need to be, either."

I could see it so clearly: Rory and Tommy, two boys brought together by tragedy, standing on that snow-covered peak, their shoulders hunched against the wind, tears falling unchecked down cheeks reddened from the cold, silently watching this incredible phenomenon.

"Most people I've spoken to who have seen the aurora have a similarly emotional response to it," he continued. "I mean, how could you not? I know there's a scientific explanation for it, but to me it will always be magical."

It *was* magical. "I love how it reflects on the loch," I said.

"And I love how it lights up your face," he whispered. He rose up on his elbow and kissed me, tenderly at first, then more passionately as I tangled my fingers in his hair and pulled him down to me, my body rising to meet his.

"Let's go back to the tent," he murmured against my mouth.

"No. Let's stay here."

He looked down at me, his eyebrows raised in surprise. I was a little surprised, too, to be honest. But there was no time left for being timid.

"I want you here. I…want this memory, of making love with you on this quiet beach, with the aurora dancing over our heads. Right here. Right now. Please." *Please don't deny me this one thing.*

"I'll be right back," he said, getting up and heading back toward the tent. He returned a moment later with our sleeping bags and mats, laying them out to make a pallet on the pebbly beach. He scooped me up in his arms and lay me down on the makeshift bed.

"I thought you were going to tell me no," I said, kicking off my flip-flops.

He joined me on the pallet. "Are you kidding me? I just figured we didn't need to lie directly on the pebbles. Now, where were we?"

Keeping my eyes locked on his, I took his hand and brought it up under the hem of my fleece to cover my breast, sucking in a breath at his touch. "I'm fast-forwarding a little."

"Works for me," he said, and straddled me, supporting his weight on his knees so he didn't squash me. His hands trailed along my ribs, dragging my shirt up and off. He folded it and placed it under my head for an additional pillow, then sat back, his eyes shining as he stared down at me.

"Look at you," he breathed. I raised up onto my elbows so I could see. "The aurora lights up your body like it's a gift, just for me. First here," he said, tracing a pattern on my skin with his fingertip, and then with his tongue. "And then here… and here," he said, tracing a new spot each time.

"It *is* just for you," I said, arching into him, shivering as his touch raised goose bumps on my flesh.

He scooted back to kneel at my feet. His hands moved to my waist, and he unsnapped the trekking pants I'd quickly thrown on, drawing them down my legs and baring my body to his hungry gaze.

He took my left foot in his hand and pressed his lips to the inside of my ankle, then my calf, then the inside of my knee, then did the same with my right, careful not to jostle it too much. He kissed the inside of my left thigh, then draped it over his shoulder, then did the same with the right. He cupped his hands under my butt and kissed my belly button, then looked up at me, his eyes glittering.

I watched as he lowered his head to press his mouth to where I ached for him. I gasped as his tongue touched my sensitized flesh, my head falling back to the makeshift pillow. I delved my fingers into his hair, holding him to me as he drove me wild.

My thighs began to quiver as he brought me higher and higher, and then I cried out his name as I was swept away.

When I opened my eyes a few moments later, he was sitting at my feet once more, just gazing at me. I sat up and held out my hand. He came closer, kneeling over me.

I skimmed my hands down his abdomen to unsnap his shorts, then reached for the zipper, my fingers grazing over his rigid flesh.

"Careful there," he hissed, setting my hands at his hips

while he eased down his zipper. I pushed his shorts over his butt, watching as his body was revealed to me, inch by inch. He kicked them off, and then stretched out beside me on his back.

I turned on my side so I could see him, illuminated by the shimmering green light overhead. I brushed a wayward curl behind his ear and then kissed him as my hand trailed down his body. He gasped into my mouth when my hand closed over him, and then gasped out loud when I dragged my open mouth down his belly…and lower.

His breath grew ragged, his hips arching up off the sleeping bag, his hands tunneling into my hair. He lifted me up and rolled me onto my back, then reached for his shorts. I heard the sound of foil tearing and then his fingers found me, making sure I was ready for him.

I was.

My breath caught as he brought my bad leg around his hip and slipped into me. He began to move, and I met him thrust for thrust, my hands roving up and down his back, feeling the ripple of his muscles. His hand came up to caress my breasts, and then moved down my belly to where we were joined.

All the while, our eyes were locked together, as if neither of us could bear to miss even one second of this. I loved him. I loved him so much, and I wanted to say it. I wanted to shout it to the aurora dancing overhead, to the ghosts at the ruins. To this amazing man, whose body was making my body soar, who'd gotten me through this trail, who'd shared his guilt, his sorrow, his beautiful country with me. To take the chance that he felt the same way.

But I couldn't. I could only cry out his name as my body shook, as the aurora continued to skip across the sky, as he pressed his mouth to my shoulder and joined me in sweet oblivion.

Chapter Forty-Two

RORY

I watched as the dark of night faded into the gray light of dawn. Before long, the sky was light enough for me to see Amelia, curled against me with her head resting on my shoulder, her hand splayed across my chest. The early morning mist sparkled like diamonds in her long hair. Her eyelashes fluttered against her cheeks; her lips curved in a slight smile.

I wondered what she was dreaming about.

After our wild lovemaking session under the aurora in the wee small hours of the night, Amelia had snuggled against me and fallen asleep. I'd thought to carry her into the tent, but she seemed so comfortable in my arms that I didn't want to disturb her. Instead, I'd pulled up the sleeping bag to cover us both and watched as Mother Nature continued her spectacular light show. When it was over, I tried to sleep, but my mind was spinning. So instead, I'd lain awake for the few hours remaining until dawn, staring at the glittering expanse of night sky above and thinking. I almost told her I loved her while the aurora danced overhead, when I'd stared into her eyes as her body shuddered around mine and my own body raced toward completion. But I caught myself, burying my face in her shoulder instead.

We'd be finished with the trek in a few hours. I'd have the long drive with her tomorrow, and a night in Glasgow, but then I'd have to let her go. She had a life to get back to across the sea. What if I told her I loved her, and she decided to stay here in Scotland? For me?

How could I let her do that? I was on the road week after week after week, on Skye, or on the West Highland Way, or up on the north coast, or crossing the Great Glen. When I wasn't doing that, I was taking kids and teens hiking and camping in every corner of the Highlands, or on Orkney, or in the Western Isles.

I couldn't ask her to give up her job and her life back home for that.

My life didn't lend itself to long-term relationships—I knew that well enough. But it was a good life. It was lonely sometimes, especially during the downtime of the winter months, when I had too much time on my hands and got tired of my own company. It was physically exhausting, more so if I strained a muscle or if the weather wreaked havoc on the trail, and it could be mentally exhausting when I worked with the teens, many of whom were troubled or had tough home lives that made me remember my own.

Every now and again, when I'd had a particularly trying group or a week of shit weather, I wondered what it would be like to sit at a desk in an office.

But I got to spend the majority of the year outside, exploring the wild beauty of my country and sharing it with others. No office job could ever compare to that.

Maybe Amelia would be okay with my crazy schedule,

and maybe it would work for a while. But it would only be a matter of time before she began to resent it, to resent *me*. Like Emma, she would start to wonder if a lass in one of my groups had caught my attention. Or I would start to wonder whether she'd found someone to keep her company on the long, lonely nights back home.

We both deserved better than that.

So, while my instincts had screamed at me to tell her I loved her last night, I'd held back.

It was for her own good. We'd finish the Skye Trail by midday, spend the next day making our way down to the city. One final night together, and then I'd say goodbye.

It would be the hardest thing I'd had to do since watching them bury Connor.

But there was no other way.

I tucked a strand of hair behind Amelia's ear, gently tracing her cheekbone with my thumb, then kissed her forehead. She blinked her eyes open and then peered up at me. I leaned down and kissed her lips.

Which took longer than I expected.

"Good morning," I said when we finally parted. "How'd you sleep?"

"Really well, actually," she said. "I think you wore me out. I can't believe I slept outside." She looked down and tugged up the top of the sleeping bag. "Naked, no less. Carrie will never believe this."

"Not much of an exhibitionist, are you?"

"Ha. No. Carrie was forever trying to get me to go skinny-dipping with her, and I could never do it."

"When she wakes up, you should both do it."

"Maybe," she said.

"Well if you do, take a picture and send it to me. Otherwise I'll never believe you did it."

"What? No! I'm not taking nude photos, and if I did, I

certainly wouldn't send them to anyone. That's how people get in trouble."

"Maybe I'll come to Miami, and you can take me skinny-dipping." The words fell out of my mouth before I realized what I was saying. And then I held my breath waiting for her reply.

"I'd like that," she finally whispered.

We both knew it wouldn't happen. We were heading into the busiest time of year for me, and it would be months before I could even consider asking Scarlet for time off. And by then, Amelia would be settled into her new job and her new life, and she would have moved on.

But we could hold on to the illusion for a little while longer.

After our last breakfast of porridge, cooked with the last bit of fuel, we broke camp. I took a final look around, my eyes landing on the place where we'd made love under the Northern Lights. I glanced at Amelia, whose gaze was fixed upon the same spot. Our eyes met, and she smiled sadly.

I took her hand, and we started up the trail.

Chapter Forty-Three

AMELIA

A few hours later, after a relatively easy stroll past the remains of an old marble quarry, we approached the outskirts of Broadford. The road dead-ended at the main street running through town.

It had been a quiet walk, for the most part, with both of us lost in our thoughts. But as we reached the main road, Rory laid his hand on my shoulder and turned me to face him. "We're almost done. It's just a bit farther to the officially unofficial endpoint of the trail."

"Okay. Let's do this."

"Is this a private group, or can anyone join in?" said a familiar male voice from behind me.

I turned to see laughing blue eyes under a shock of blond hair. "Tommy!" I exclaimed, a huge grin stretching my cheeks.

He pulled me into a crushing embrace. "What are you doing here?" I asked when I could breathe again.

"We were waiting for the rest of the group—meaning you two—to finally get here, so we could finish together."

We?

"Well done, Amelia," said Scarlet, stepping out from behind a pole with a huge smile on her face. She gave me a hug while Rory and Tommy man-hugged a few feet away. I guess Rory had texted them to let them know when we'd arrive.

A chorus of female shrieks had me whipping around to see Molly and Megan. On their heels were Pat and Linda, with two men who had to be their husbands. *They'd stayed to wait for me?*

Tears ran unchecked down my face as I was enfolded in one hug after another.

"I can't believe you're all still here. You finished three days ago!"

"We wanted to finish with you," said Molly.

"Besides, it wasn't exactly a hardship to spend a few extra days on Skye," added Linda. "The others had to catch flights back to the States, otherwise they'd have been here, too."

"Shall we?" asked Tommy.

Rory took my hand once more, and together with the whole gang, we turned right onto the main street and then left into a car park. The sea was right in front of us, shining in the sun.

Rory turned to me. "Welcome to the end of the Skye Trail!"

I burst into tears, my poles falling to the ground as I covered my face with shaking hands and sobbed.

I'd reached the end.

I'd hiked up mountains, slogged through bogs, picked my way along cliffs and crossed rushing rivers. I'd seen eagles and whales, sunrises and sunsets, starry skies and the Northern Lights. I'd been in the sea.

I'd walked tens of miles in bright sunshine and under

storm-swept skies, through driving rain and terrifying fog. I'd done it all with the unwavering, unselfish help of an incredible man, who'd been a stranger barely more than a week ago, but was now the man I loved.

It had taken ten days instead of seven, had caused me excruciating pain and emotional anguish. It had been the most amazing ten days of my life. And now it was over.

I wasn't ready for it to be over.

Rory pulled me into a crushing hug, pack and all. "Congratulations, sweetheart," he whispered in my ear.

When he pulled back, Scarlet pulled out a piece of paper and pen from her bag and handed it to him. He scrawled something on it, and then held it out to me, his eyes crinkling as he smiled.

It was a certificate of achievement from Scotland By Foot for completing the Skye Trail, signed by Rory Sutherland.

One by one, they all hugged me as if I'd just scored the winning goal in a playoff hockey game. Tommy gleefully showed me a photo he'd snapped of me bawling. "I got video, too," he added. "I'll email it to you." I punched him in the arm, but I was actually thrilled that he'd thought to capture the moment so I could share it with Carrie.

Then, while Rory conferred with Scarlet and Tommy, the ladies surrounded me.

"Don't think we didn't see Rory holding your hand, missy," said Pat.

"Yeah, we're going to need details," added Megan. "You and that braw lad, alone on the trail together. We're going to want to know everything."

I was too thrilled that they were all here to be embarrassed by their teasing. "I'm not going to tell you *everything*," I said. "A girl's got to have some secrets. But first, can you excuse me a second?"

I extricated myself from the group and pulled out my

phone. Helen picked up on the first ring. "Amelia, it's earlier than your usual time. Is everything okay?"

"I'm fine. I finished the trek, and I wanted to tell Carrie. Is there—there's no change, is there?"

"No change, but congratulations, honey, that's wonderful! Let me bring the phone to her."

A moment later, she told me Carrie was on. "Hey, Ree. I...I did it. I finished the Skye Trail. It was so much harder than I expected, and it was more beautiful than I could ever have imagined." I started to cry again, unable to help myself. "And it sucks so much that you're not here. I just...I just wish you were here. I'll be home in a few days, and I'm going to tell you everything, okay? I love you, and I'll see you soon."

The thought of leaving Rory made me cry even harder, and when I finally conveyed to Helen that I was done talking and ended the call, I was sobbing once more.

My phone was gently extracted from my hand, and I was folded into Rory's arms. He just held me, not saying anything, not trying to stop me from crying, just letting me get out all the emotion that had been building over the course of our journey.

When I'd finally cried myself out, I slowly raised my head from his chest, not wanting to face my friends. But when I opened my eyes, it was just Rory and me. "Where is everyone?" I asked hoarsely.

"They headed to the chippie to get a table," he said, referring to the fish-and-chips place by the waterfront. "I knew you needed some time alone, so I sent them ahead."

"Thank you. And thank you for—God, for everything, but specifically for the group meeting us here."

"That was a surprise for me as well. I had texted Tommy this morning with our ETA, and he told me to give him a heads-up when we were almost finished. I figured he'd be here—that buffoon has nothing better to do anyway—and I thought Scarlet might be here, too. But I didn't expect the lassies. That was really nice of them."

"It was the perfect way to finish the trek," I said. "And, by the way, the lassies, as you called them, all saw you holding my hand. They're expecting details. Lots of details."

"Oh, aye?" he drawled. "Well, don't be stingy with those details. Tell them how I brought you to heights of passion you'd never even dreamed were possible. Titillate them with details of my manly prowess, and feel free to embellish. My ego could use some stroking," he said with a wicked grin.

"I wouldn't need to embellish to have them fully titillated and green with envy." I leaned close to whisper in his ear. "And I'll save the stroking for later tonight."

We commandeered two waterfront tables and had a long, loud, boisterous lunch of fish and chips. Rory and I regaled the group with (some of) the anecdotes from our adventure. But I was starting to crash and trying to think of a polite way to excuse myself for a little while. I didn't want to be rude after they'd all stuck around for days waiting for me to arrive.

Scarlet must have seen the look in my eyes, because she made a show of gathering up her trash. "Amelia, you must be knackered and dying for a hot shower. Your room at the B&B should be ready."

"Oh God, yes. I could hug you right now," I said.

"Shall we do a ladies' dinner and drinks later?" asked Linda. "It's three now, so maybe at like five?" She named a pub up the street. "That should give you time for a shower and a lie-down."

"Perfect," I said. "Scarlet, will you come, too?"

"Thanks, but I have a ton of paperwork to do, and I need to sit down with Rory and Tommy for a while. Besides, I think you guys might like to catch up and chat about the trek without me keeping you from speaking freely," she added with a smile.

"Not true at all, but I get it," I said. "You know where we'll be, so if you change your mind, please come join us."

"Okay, thanks. Before I forget, when do you fly out?"

"The day after tomorrow," I said, hoping I sounded casual and not like I was dying inside.

"Are you taking the train down to Glasgow?" she asked.

"I, uh…" I wasn't sure if Scarlet knew that Rory and I were—whatever we were. And whether that was kosher.

"I'm driving her," Rory said. "Tommy's going to bring us to Sligachan first thing tomorrow, and then I'm borrowing Gav's car."

"Oh?" said Scarlet, casting a look at Rory. He met her gaze steadily, but there was definitely an undercurrent there. She turned to me, her usual smile in place. "It will be a nice drive. Just ignore Rory's road rage. It's a lot of driving on winding roads behind tourists, and our lad here isn't a fan."

Apparently, the subject of Rory and me would be brought up privately. "I remember that from when he picked us up at Fort William." *A hundred years ago.*

"Well, then. I'll say goodbye to you and get back to work." She gave me another hug. "Brilliant job, really. I hope you plan to see a doctor once you're home, get that knee checked out?"

"I will, and thanks for everything. I hope our paths will cross again," I said, swallowing back the lump in my throat, the first of several I anticipated over the next two days.

• • •

After a shower and a nap—and a phone call to my parents—I met the girls at the pub. Rory and Tommy had said they'd join us later on.

We grabbed a round table at the back of the bar, and Megan brought over a bottle of white wine and five glasses. "Honey, I hope that wasn't their last bottle," said Pat. "We're going to make short work of this one."

"Don't worry, that was the first thing I asked them. The bartender promised me they have a case of it. We should have enough to get *all* the details from the Yank."

"The *Yank* is sitting right here," I said, feigning offense.

"Brilliant! Then you can start talking," said Molly. "And remember, no detail is too small."

"Especially *that* one," Megan said, waggling her eyebrows suggestively.

"I'm not discussing *that* one," I said.

She shrugged. "We'll see. The night is young, and there is much wine to be had."

"First, we should toast, don't you think?" asked Linda.

Molly poured the wine, then held up her glass. "To Amelia, who finished the Skye Trail with a bum knee—a nearly impossible feat—and landed the complicated, mysterious, capable, and sexy-as-hell Rory Sutherland in the process, perhaps an even less possible feat. We're so proud of you." We drank, but although I plastered on a smile as big as theirs, all I could think was that I hadn't landed him. I'd caught and held him briefly, but would be throwing him back the day after tomorrow. (And it was really weird to think of Rory as if he were a salmon.)

"*Now* will you start talking?" asked Molly.

They all leaned forward at once, looking at me like a litter of puppies waiting for treats. This time, my smile was real.

Over the course of juicy burgers and several bottles of wine, amusingly replenished by the cute bartender, I gave them details. Not all, not even after consuming more wine than I'd ever had at one time, but enough.

After all, it *was* my womanly duty.

Chapter Forty-Four

RORY

While Amelia was meeting the girls for dinner and drinks, Tommy, Scarlet, and I ordered in takeaway and planned out the next few weeks of treks. The whole time, I was braced for her to say something about me getting together with Amelia. She hadn't seemed too upset when she asked if I was going to drive Amelia to the airport, but now that it was just us, she kept looking at me with an unreadable expression in her eyes.

When we were done with what we had to do, I told Tommy I'd meet him out front, and I turned to her. "Just say it, Scar."

She raised her eyebrows. "What should I be saying?"

"That I shouldn't have hooked up with Amelia, a client. I've known you a long time, and I can tell that you're not thrilled about it."

"You're right, we have known each other a long time. And I'm *not* thrilled about it, though not for the reason you think."

When I just stared at her, she sighed. "I could see from

the way the two of you were acting around each other that this isn't just some 'hookup,' to use your phrasing. The way you gazed at each other, the small touches, all of it. You looked happy. And for as long as I've known you, I've *never* seen you look happy, and God knows you deserve to be."

I didn't know what to say. She'd never spoken to me this way before—we were friends in the way of colleagues who've worked together for a long time, but she and I weren't confidantes like Tommy and I were. And now she was talking to me like a big sister might, and it totally left me speechless.

But *she* wasn't speechless. She laid her hand on mine. "But Rory, she's going back to the States. And *that's* why I'm not jumping for joy to see you guys together. She's going to break your heart—and you're going to break hers. How can I be happy about that?"

I swallowed hard. "I'm not sorry," I said hoarsely. "For a few minutes the other day, I *was* sorry. I regretted ever agreeing to a casual fling with Amelia, knowing it was going to kill me to say goodbye to her. But now? I can't regret even one minute I've spent with her. She brought me out of the darkness, Scar. And it is going to be awful to say goodbye to her, but it's *not* going to kill me. I've survived some pretty bad shit, and I'll survive this, too."

I got up to leave, not wanting to waste any more of these last few hours I'd have with Amelia.

Scarlet got up, too, looking almost as miserable as I felt. Impulsively, I wrapped my arms around her, and after a startled moment, she hugged me back.

"Thank you for caring. It means more to me than you can imagine."

She pulled back, a sad smile on her face. "You'd better go find Amelia before those troublemakers get her utterly pissed. They looked pretty determined earlier."

I grinned. "This could be amusing to see."

We said goodbye, and I met Tommy outside. "All good with Scar?" he asked.

"Aye, it's fine." Maybe I'd tell him about our conversation, but not tonight. We headed up the street to the pub.

We were not prepared for the scene that awaited us there.

The table was strewn with—was that *five*?—empty bottles of wine, wine glasses, and half-full water glasses. There was a mostly-empty basket of chips and some picked-clean dinner plates—at least they'd eaten—and the five of them were giggling like schoolgirls.

The door closed behind us, and as one, they turned to look, their eyes glassy, their cheeks red. There was a chorus of overly loud hellos.

"Holy shite, they're all sloshed!" exclaimed Tommy.

"Aye, they are," said Liam, the bartender, with a grin. "But I've seen worse. I kept their water glasses topped off and brought out the extra chips a little while ago."

"Cheers for that, mate," I said, grateful he'd kept an eye on them.

Pat's and Linda's husbands arrived a few minutes later, and then it was time for the goodbyes, which were soggier than they might otherwise have been.

Email addresses were confirmed. There were promises to share photos and stay in touch, with the possibility of a reunion trip somewhere down the line. There was another round of hugs and tears. And all of them told Amelia to "have fun tonight," accompanied by giggles and winks. *What was that about?*

Tommy insisted on walking Molly and Megan to their B&B, and the husbands were seeing to Pat and Linda. And then, finally, Amelia and I were alone. I handed her the trekking pole she was using as a cane, tucked her hand into my elbow, and we walked to the B&B.

"So, did you give them all the juicy details?" I asked.

She giggled. Again. "I mean, not *all*. I tried not to kiss and tell, but they were really persuasive."

"I'll bet they were." We headed up the stairs to the room. She squinted at the key as if she wasn't quite sure what to do with it, so I took it from her and unlocked the door.

She flopped across the foot of the bed. "The room is a little spinny. I think maybe I should have stopped like one glass of wine sooner. But it felt good to be silly for a little while, you know?"

I sat at the edge of the bed. "I do know. You've had a lot on your mind, and sometimes you need to set everything aside for a bit, give yourself a break. We do have to get an early start tomorrow, so I think we should head to bed soon, okay?"

She didn't answer, and when I looked down at her, she was sound asleep, which I should have predicted. I took off her shoes and jeans so she'd be comfortable and lifted her in my arms, laying her down properly with her head on the pillow. Without waking, she curled on her side, and I tucked the blanket around her.

I set a glass of water on the nightstand in case she woke up in the middle of the night, then climbed into bed and wrapped my arms around her, pulling her close.

The evening hadn't gone quite the way I'd anticipated. But when she murmured my name in her sleep and pulled my arm more tightly around her waist, I decided it was pretty perfect after all.

Chapter Forty-Five

AMELIA

My throbbing head woke me. I peeled one eye open, squinting in the bright sunlight. *Sunlight?* The last thing I remembered was flopping across the bed and closing my eyes so I wouldn't have to watch the room spin. What happened after that? Did Rory and I—?

"Good morning, sunshine."

I opened my other eye and turned to see Rory lying beside me, head propped on his hand, smiling down at me. "What time is it?"

"A little after six. How's your head?"

"Pounding," I whispered.

"I figured." He sat up and took something from his nightstand. When he turned back, he was holding a glass of water and two ibuprofen.

"You are a god," I said, sitting up and gratefully taking the pills. Okay, I was still in my shirt and bra, so if we had done anything, I hadn't gotten completely undressed.

"Aye, I keep telling people that, but so far no one's listening. Maybe you could spread the word."

"I'm going to tweet it. Hashtag Rory Sutherland is a god among men." I peeked under the blanket. No jeans, but I was still in my underwear and socks.

"Looking for something?" he asked, arching a brow.

"I just...I remember coming back to the room with you and lying across the bed. I closed my eyes, hoping the room would stop spinning, and that's it. Nothing after that. I do remember thinking of all the things I wanted to do with you last night—*shit*." I buried my face in my hands.

"Should I be worried?"

"I'm pretty sure I also told the girls about all the things I wanted to do with you last night. I am *so* sorry. I can't believe I did that."

He burst out laughing, the sound so unlike him I could only stare. He showed no sign of stopping, so I went into the bathroom to pee and brush my teeth. When I came out, he was wiping his eyes. He grinned at me. "That explains a lot."

I sat down on the bed. "What does?"

"Let's just say that there were some significant looks I got from the lassies last night, along with some giggly wishes for us to have fun, most accompanied by a nudge and a wink. Now I know why."

"Oh my God."

"Unfortunately, you'll have to make up some elaborate story if they ask, because the last thing you remember about last night *is* the last thing that happened. You were sound asleep about three seconds after you laid on the bed. I took off your jeans and shoes and tucked you in."

"I'm so sorry," I said again, disgusted with myself.

"For what?"

"For wasting a whole night with you. We only have one more day and night together, and—"

He kissed me, cutting off the rest of what I was about to say.

"You didn't waste anything," he said when he drew back. "You decompressed after a stressful, emotional week, and you had a good time with friends you won't see again for a while. And I got to sleep with you in my arms. But," he added, "if you really want to make it up to me, we have time for you to show me at least one of the things you told the lasses you planned to do with me before we hit the road."

"I can do that," I said.

. . .

A few hours later, it was my turn to watch Rory sleep. I studied his features, committing them to memory. His wild, dark red curls that shined copper in the sun, long enough to tangle my hands in. His handsome face, so stern and unsmiling when I'd first met him. Those features were a little softer now, his smile coming more easily, though a friendly and welcoming grin would not likely ever be his default setting. The strong jaw with its auburn stubble, softer now after days of not shaving.

And those stunning eyes, hidden from me now, but I knew their many colors. Clear gray-green, like the sea on a rainy day; liquid silver like the mercury in an old thermometer; bright green like the aurora that had danced across the night sky.

In a little over a week, I'd gone from thinking he was the biggest jerk ever to *knowing* he was the exact opposite. He'd been my nemesis, my helper, my friend, my lover. We'd shared laughter, tears, and the kind of passion I'd only ever read about.

And in just a few hours, I'd have to say goodbye to him.

Tell him you love him, said the voice inside me.

"I can't," I whispered. What purpose would it serve?

I had a life to get back to, thousands of miles away. And his life was here, striding over the hills and through the glens, climbing snow-covered peaks in winter and swimming in cold lochs in the summer. He might come for a visit, if he was even still thinking of me once we were thousands of miles apart, but that was it.

He didn't belong in a city like Miami. The heat would lay him out flat, the sheer number of people would stifle him.

What would he even do there? It wasn't like there was a market for long-distance trail guides in southern Florida, where the steepest terrain was walking up a few flights of stairs. And the thought of him staring at a computer screen in a tiny cubicle in an overly air-conditioned office, in khakis and dress shoes, wearing a button-down shirt and, heaven forbid, a tie?

He would wither away there. And he would come to hate me for making him leave his life of trails and open spaces and changing seasons and wild terrain.

No, I couldn't tell him. It was just a fling—an exciting, sexy fling between two people who were attracted to each other. Tomorrow we'd say goodbye, and we'd both be sad about it for a while. Eventually, we'd both move on. And maybe when Carrie was better, she and I would take our trip to Scotland, and maybe he'd meet us for a drink. Or maybe we'd do a trail with him as our guide.

And then we'd return to the States, and he'd stay here.

The thought of saying goodbye to him was unbearable, but I would do it.

There was no other option.

Rory's phone vibrated on the nightstand, making me jump

and waking him up. Muttering under his breath, he peered at it.

"Everything okay?"

He rolled his eyes. "Scarlet needs to see Tommy and me at nine thirty. It's what, nine now? We can run down for breakfast, and then I'll go meet them while you get ready. Shouldn't be more than an hour, and then we can get on the road. Okay?"

"Yeah, that sounds fine."

He swung out of bed and walked naked into the bathroom. A moment later, the shower came on.

I threw on the clothes I'd worn the night before—they were a bit wrinkled, but good enough to wear to the B&B's breakfast room. Five minutes later, he emerged from the bathroom and got dressed.

We had a lovely breakfast of eggs and grilled tomatoes, potato scones and toast, and then I walked him to the door. "See you in a little while."

"Aye, see you," he replied. He gave me a quick kiss and strode off down the street. I watched him go, finally heading inside after he disappeared from view.

I returned to the room. It was so strange to be alone after so many days in such intense close company with Rory. *He'll be back soon, and then you'll have the whole day and night together.* And then we'd say goodbye, possibly for good.

A wave of agony doubled me over. It felt as if my heart was literally breaking. Hugging myself, I sank down on the bed and sobbed.

Some time later, I got to my feet, my body raw and aching, and staggered into the shower, then got dressed and packed my bag.

When I was done, I sat on the bed and picked up my phone.

There was something I had to do.

Chapter Forty-Six

RORY

The meeting with Scarlet and Tommy took a little longer than I thought, as there were some logistics to work out for next week's West Highland Way trek. It was 10:45, later than I'd wanted to get on the road for the roughly two-hundred-mile drive to Glasgow, but Amelia's flight wasn't until tomorrow morning anyway. I was actually looking forward to the long car ride—anything to spend a few more hours with her.

"I'll get the van and meet you out front," said Tommy, who was driving us to Sligachan so I could borrow Gav's car.

"Aye, be right out."

I jogged up the stairs and unlocked the door. "Sorry, Amelia," I said as I entered the room. "Are you—"

The room was empty. Amelia wasn't there. Her rucksack wasn't there, though mine still sat on the floor by the chair. She was probably on the phone outside somewhere. I hit the loo, grabbed my pack, and headed downstairs.

I greeted the landlady, Mrs. Douglas, whom I'd known

for a few years. "Here's the second key for Number 2."

"Thanks, lovey," she said. "Your lass turned in hers already."

"Thanks—I guess she's waiting for me outside." I turned toward the door.

"Rory, wait. Amelia asked me to give this to you."

She held out a plain white envelope with my name written in cursive on the outside.

And I knew.

I took it from her as if it were a snake and stumbled to one of the chairs in the lobby.

That was where Tommy found me a few minutes later.

"Hey man, are we going or what? I got things to— What's wrong? Where's Amelia?"

Wordlessly, I handed him the single sheet of paper that had been inside the envelope. I watched him read the words I'd already read several times.

Dear Rory,

I know you told me that we shouldn't get involved, that you didn't think I was cut out for a short fling. And I know I told you I was, insisted I could handle it.

I lied. To you—and to myself.

This morning, it all came crashing down.

How would I sit beside you in the car for the whole day, making small talk? How would I have a nice dinner with you in Glasgow and not talk about what would happen after I went home? How would I spend another glorious night in your arms and pretend my heart wasn't breaking at the thought of leaving you? How would I say goodbye to you?

I was strong enough to complete the Skye Trail, but I'm not strong enough to say goodbye.

I changed my flight to this evening, and by the time you read this, I'll be on the bus to Glasgow.

I know it's for the best—for both of us.

There's no way I can ever thank you for what you did for me this week. But I'll say it anyway: Thank you. For helping me get through the trek. For making me feel. For everything.

Maybe we can email from time to time, and maybe our paths will cross again, but if not, that's okay. It'll have to be.

No regrets.
Amelia

Tommy lowered the letter. "Why are you still sitting there?" He held out his hand. "Let's go."

I looked up at him, my whole body numb. "Where? We can't chase the bus, Tommy. It left half an hour ago."

"We don't have to chase it. We know where she's going. If she changed her flight to tonight, it's probably leaving at what, like eight-something? We'll get there in plenty of time."

I threw up my hands. "In time for *what*? She's flying back to New York, to her new job, to her life. We could have had one more day—one more night—together, but she gave that up because she didn't want to drag this out."

"All of that may be true, but it'll eat you up inside if you don't get some kind of closure. So let's get in the goddamn car so you can say goodbye to her."

Resigned, I grabbed his hand and let him pull me to my feet.

Chapter Forty-Seven

Amelia

The bus ride was a blur. I ignored everyone and everything around me. I stared out the window, but didn't see the scenery. Instead I saw a series of scenes in my mind as I replayed the week with Rory: every conversation, every kiss, every caress. Over and over. Tears dripped from my eyes, and I brushed them away.

I knew I'd made the right decision—spending another day and night with him would have been agony—but that didn't make it any easier, didn't make me miss him any less.

What had he thought when he'd read the letter? Was he relieved to get out of the prolonged goodbye? Was he sad that I'd left without telling him? Was it both?

Had he been surprised by the extent of my feelings for him? Did he feel the same way? *Does it even matter now?*

After six hours, we finally pulled into the airport. I blew my nose, dried my eyes.

I turned off the video in my mind. Rory and I were a moment in time, an interlude. And now the moment was over—a memory, one of so many from this trip.

I'd given myself the long bus ride to grieve for what might have been. Now I needed to focus on what was. On getting home to Carrie, on preparing for Miami and my new job.

We pulled up to the curb. I shouldered my pack and stepped off the bus to begin my journey home.

I checked in, dropped off my bag, and limped through the terminal toward security. My knee was sore after the long bus ride, and it would be even worse after the long flight. I would just take it slow; I was in no rush. Besides, after hiking eighty miles on Skye, the airport was a piece of cake.

There was a Starbucks before the checkpoint. I hadn't eaten lunch, and it was a while until I'd get dinner on the plane, so I stopped to pick up a coffee and a pastry.

I turned from the counter—and nearly ran into someone. His hands came out to steady me, and I looked up into eyes the color of a stormy sea. My heart stopped, then began to pound.

"Rory?"

Was I hallucinating from lack of caffeine and food? No, his hands on my arms were warm and strong, and I could smell the citrusy soap he'd used that morning—*was that really just this morning?*

"Aye, it's me," he said with a slightly sardonic quirk of his lips.

"Wh-what are you doing here? I thought my note explained things." I didn't know whether to be angry or relieved or thrilled.

"It did. But I wanted to say goodbye to you the right way," he said.

He took the coffee and paper bag from my hands and put them—somewhere.

And then he kissed the hell out of me.

It was angry at first—on both sides. I'd wanted a clean break; he obviously hadn't. Then his arms came around me, and he crushed me to him, pulling me up on my tiptoes. I clutched his shoulders and just held on as our kisses went from angry to passionate to tender, as he lowered me so that my feet were on the floor, his hands cupping my face as mine twined in his hair.

Finally we drew apart, both of us breathless. "I—how did you get here?"

"I threw his ass into the car and drove him."

I dragged my eyes from Rory's face and turned to see Tommy standing a few feet away, holding my coffee and Starbucks bag. He raised the cup in salute.

I dropped into a chair, completely overwhelmed. Rory pulled over another one and sat facing me. "I couldn't let you leave without seeing you one last time." He took my hands in his. "Are you mad?"

I gazed into those luminous eyes, so full of emotion, and sighed. "How could I be mad?" And it was true. Even though I'd told myself I wanted a clean break, I was thrilled that he cared enough to come after me. "But it doesn't change anything, Rory."

He nodded. "I know it doesn't."

Tommy grabbed coffees for the two of them, and we sat for a few minutes. And then it was time. We got to our feet. Rory went to the men's room. I turned to Tommy, who pulled me into a hug.

"I'm really glad you made him come, Tommy. He's lucky to have you for a friend."

"And you were lucky to have him—there's no better man to be found."

"I know."

"He was lucky to have you, too, Amelia, however briefly. I wish you could stay. You make him happy. And if anyone deserves to be happy, it's him."

"He makes me happy, too," I whispered. "And I wish I could stay, believe me. But I can't. I need to get home to my friend, to the job I'm starting."

"Aye, I know." The smile left his face. "I hope our paths will cross again one day soon, Amelia Benson."

"Me, too."

He hugged me again, pulling back just as Rory returned. "I'm going to take a walk while you two say your goodbyes. Rory, I'll meet you back here."

Rory drew me into his arms. I laid my cheek against his heart and just held on. I didn't know what to say, and it seemed he didn't, either.

I couldn't let this drag out any longer. I mustered up a big smile. "Thank you, Rory. For agreeing to help me finish the trek. For facing your own demons so I didn't have to quit. For this past week, which has been the most amazing adventure." Tears flooded my eyes. "And...and for everything else," I whispered, my voice breaking.

He cupped my face in his hands, his thumbs brushing away my tears, and stared down at me with gray-green, shimmery eyes. "And thank *you* for helping me face those demons, for making me feel alive for the first time in so long. I..."

He started to say something else, then shook his head and kissed me instead, sweetly, tenderly, as if this was a first kiss and not a last one. I kissed him back the same way, but just when my fingers started to creep up into his hair, he pulled back and took my hand.

"Fly safe. And get your knee checked out as soon as you can." I nodded. "And will you let me know how Carrie's doing?"

"I will. Goodbye, Rory."

"Goodbye, Amelia. *Mar sin leat, a ghaoil.*"

He pressed his lips to my hand one last time, and then I turned and walked away, our fingers touching until they couldn't touch anymore.

Chapter Forty-Eight

RORY

I watched as Amelia's blurry form drew away from me and disappeared up the escalator, and then I sank down on the bench and dropped my head into my hands. Had I really just said goodbye to her?

Why hadn't I been strong enough to stay away from her? I could have gotten Amelia through the damned hike without getting involved with her, and then neither of us would be in agony now. But I'd let myself be selfish, let myself fall for her, so tired of being alone.

And now I was alone again. And it was so much worse than before.

A leg brushed mine as Tommy sat beside me on the bench. "You okay?"

He was unsmiling, his face grimly sympathetic. "I'm really not."

"Let's get the hell out of here. Unless you want to catch her before she gets through security? Last chance."

"I can't."

He nodded. "Come on, then." He pulled me to my feet, and we left the terminal.

Left Amelia.

When we reached the car, he went right for the driver's seat, not grumbling at all about having to turn right around and drive the two hundred miles back to Skye.

I let my head fall back against the headrest and closed my eyes. I could still smell her scent. Could still feel the touch of her body against mine when we were wrapped around each other that morning. Could still taste her kiss on my tongue, could still hear my name as a sigh from her lips. Could still see the sadness in her eyes when we parted.

"Did you tell her you love her?"

"No. Not so she'd understand it, anyway." *Mar sin leat, a ghaoil. Goodbye, my love.*

"Why the hell not?"

"How could I, Tommy? She had to leave. If I'd said the words, it would only have made things worse."

"But you didn't give her a chance. If she loves you, too—no, not 'if,' I *know* she loves you—but if she heard you say it, maybe she would have stayed."

"She has a friend lying in a coma back home. And a new job in a new city to look forward to."

"You should have tried."

Anger crawled up my spine. "What I *should have* done is stayed away from her, kept my hands off her. Then our goodbye would have consisted of a friendly hug and an exchange of email addresses, instead of this," I said bitterly.

"You don't mean that."

I sighed, the anger dropping away as fast as it had arrived. "No, I don't. What we had together, for the few short days we had it, was better than not having it. But now...now it just fucking hurts."

The rest of the drive back was mostly silent, other than the radio Tommy finally turned on. We stopped for a quick burger in Fort William, which I barely ate, and when we got back to Skye at nearly midnight, we went right to the Slig, where Tommy and Gav proceeded to get me drunk.

. . .

I woke up the next morning on Gav's ancient sofa, my head pounding, my mouth parched. I rolled to my feet, cursing at the pain in my back from the sofa, and staggered to the sink for some water.

I wondered what Amelia was doing, if she'd gone to see Carrie straightaway, or if she would go today. I wondered if she'd slept okay, alone in her bed. If she was going to the doctor to get her knee checked out. If she was missing me as much as I missed her.

I wondered how I was going to get through the day without her. Or the next few days, until my next group arrived for their West Highland Way trek, and I'd at least have some distraction during the day.

The door to Gav's flat opened, and he and Tommy walked in, bringing with them the smell of coffee and greasy food. Thank God.

Gav handed me a coffee. "How do you feel today?"

"Like I've been dragged through a hedge backwards."

"Not surprising, considering you drank half your body weight in beer last night," said Tommy.

After breakfast, I felt slightly more human. Tommy and I said goodbye to Gav and then headed out. As we approached the Sligachan Hotel, I gazed out the window at the Red Cuillins, clearly outlined against the brilliant blue sky. Glamaig, Marsco, and in the distance, Bla Bheinn.

Hard to believe that just a few days earlier, I'd walked

through the glen with Amelia, passing all those peaks, climbing Bla Bheinn. Would I ever have that opportunity again with her?

I glanced at Tommy, whose eyes were thankfully on the road ahead and not the view.

I didn't know what the future held for Amelia and me, and there was nothing I could do about that now. But in the meantime, there was something I *could* do—something that should have been done years ago.

"Tommy, we need to make a stop."

• • •

Two days later, I summited Bla Bheinn for the second time in two weeks. Unlike the last time, the sky was a cloudless blue the whole way. Unlike the last time, there was no Amelia, giving me the strength to face the monster that had haunted me for so long.

But I did have Tommy. We traveled light, each of us with only a rucksack instead of a heavy pack, and it didn't take much time to reach the top. I stood back while Tommy went to the wee cairn I'd built when I was with Amelia, bowed his head, and stood in silence for a long moment.

When he raised his head, I stepped forward. The purple-gray stone with the silver vein was right where I'd left it, shining in the sunlight. "I'm back, brother. Just as I promised. Tommy's with me. And I—we—have something for you."

Chapter Forty-Nine

My first week home from Scotland was awful, starting with the flight home.

I'd started going through my pictures, but seeing the beautiful scenery once more—and then the photos of Rory and me—was like a knife in my belly, so I gave up, not wanting to sob in front of the entire plane. I'd just stared out the window, occasionally falling into a fitful doze that left me feeling disoriented and even more heartsick when I woke.

Finally, the plane dipped, and I'd looked out the window to see the sprawl of Manhattan below. That sight always made my heart swell with pride that I lived just outside that iconic metropolis. Even though I'd never really loved the city, I always liked to look at it from the outside, whether I was above it in a plane or seeing it from a bridge.

Now it just looked discordant and gray and wrong. I should have been looking at castle ruins and mountains, not glass-encased skyscrapers and thousands of buildings packed in like sardines on the smallish island; lochs and glens, not hundreds of miles of traffic-jammed, potholed roads.

Carrie was here. My family was here. My life was here, if not in New York, then twelve hundred or so miles south in Florida.

But Rory wasn't here.

Three days after I left him in the Glasgow Airport terminal, I'd received an email with no text, just a few photo attachments. The first was a selfie of him and Tommy, their hair tousled by the wind, with a familiar view behind them. He'd gone back to Bla Bheinn, and had brought Tommy with him.

That photo had brought tears to my eyes. The second was harder to interpret—it was of a gray rock next to the cairn he'd built for Connor, shot from a few yards away to show the location and context. Okay, it was a rock...so? Then I'd opened the third photo. And I'd understood.

It was a close-up of that rock, and it wasn't just any rock, but one that had been placed there with as much care as the skipping stone. And it was engraved.

In memory of Connor Andrew Sutherland, 1994-2011.
Beloved son, brother, friend.
He will be remembered as long as this mountain stands.

I'd completely lost it, my tears at seeing the guys together on the mountain turning into outright sobs. God, I wished I had been there with them.

After that, there were no more emails. The clean break I'd wanted. The clean break I hated.

And Carrie still hadn't woken up. I grew more and more despondent each day that she never would. I wanted to share my fears with Rory, but I couldn't. He had his life, and I had no right to drag him into the pit of despair with me.

I spent hours at her bedside, giving her parents some

reprieve. I told her bits and pieces about the hike, but only the positive things, so as not to stress her out. No mention of my knee, or of Rory's trauma. Instead, I described the scenery, the wildlife, the group, Tommy, Rory. I discovered pretty quickly that it was really hard to have a completely one-sided conversation with someone, so then I just read to her from her favorite books or played her favorite movies on my computer. But not *The Lord of the Rings*, which she loved, too. I tried, but when I started crying five minutes in, I had to shut it off.

The only time I left her side was when the nursing staff chased me out at the end of the day and when I had my orthopedist appointments.

An MRI showed that I had sprained my ACL. The orthopedist was pretty surprised that I'd been able to complete the hike, and he clearly thought I was an idiot for doing so.

I probably was. I could have made it worse—could have torn the ligament completely, and that would have required surgery and months of rehab.

But I had no regrets. Not one. Some soreness in my knee that would go away with, you know, *not* hiking up a mountain, but it was worth every minute of the time I spent with Rory.

When I got the report from the doctor, I opened an email to tell Rory the news. But after a few false starts, I deleted the draft. It would only make things worse.

As the days went by following my return to New York, as Carrie's condition remained the same, as I missed Rory more and more, I fell deeper and deeper into despair. I went out with friends and gave them the highlights of the trek, but that only made it harder. My parents talked endlessly of my upcoming move to Miami, but I couldn't summon the enthusiasm they expected.

I thought about emailing Tommy. He would make me laugh, give me some strangely wise words of comfort and hope. But I knew if I did that, I wouldn't be able to stop myself from asking about Rory. And then if he told me that Rory was doing great, it would make me feel even worse.

• • •

It was the ninth day following my return to New York. I plunked down in the chair next to Carrie's bed and took her hand in mine. For the first time, I couldn't bring myself to be upbeat and cheerful.

"What am I going to do, Carrie? I tried to be bold like you, and just went for it. I knew it couldn't go anywhere, and I didn't care. I thought I could handle it, that a few days with him would be enough. I'd come home and be ready to go to Miami and move on to the next stage of my life, with a memory of this hot fling.

"But I was wrong, Carrie. It *wasn't* enough. I am so in love with him, and I'm so fucking miserable without him. Whenever I look at a clock, I imagine what he might be doing. In the afternoons, I picture him striding up a mountain with a group of tired but eager trekkers behind him on that last hill of the day—which is *never* the last hill of the day. If it's evening, I picture him swimming in a freezing bay, or having a pint with Tommy.

"And I want to be there with him, for all of it. But I can't." I buried my face in my hands, unable to stop the tears.

"Why...can't you?" came a husky whisper, *as if from someone who hadn't spoken in a month.*

I froze. Hope swelling inside me, I slowly lifted my face from my hands and turned toward the bed. Carrie's eyes were closed, but I swore I'd heard her voice. No, it was just a hallucination brought on by too little sleep. Still...

"Carrie?" I leaned over her, trying to see if she looked any more responsive than she had before. "Carrie, can you hear me?"

"'Course I can. You're...shouting in my ear." Her eyes fluttered—as they had so many times during the week I'd been by her bedside—only this time, they opened. Slowly, hesitantly, blinking against the sudden onslaught of light after so many days in the dark.

"Oh my God, Carrie! You're awake!" Through the haze of tears—of joy this time—I slapped at the call button. "Say something else...anything!"

"Your hair...is tickling my neck."

What? I looked down. Sure enough, my braid was dangling over her, the ends grazing her neck. I flung it over my shoulder. "I can't believe that you've been in a coma for a month, and that's the first thing you say?"

Just then, a nurse came in. "What's wrong—oh!" She turned and ran from the room.

Carrie licked her lips. I poured some water from the pitcher on the nightstand into a cup with a straw, then held it to her mouth. "Just a little. I don't want the nurses to yell at me if you're not supposed to have it."

She obediently took a few small sips, then nodded slightly to indicate she was done. I set down the cup and turned back to her.

"I've been...in a coma...for a month?"

"Do you remember what happened?"

She closed her eyes for a moment, her brow furrowing. Then they shot open again. "We were in the car...fighting... about a hike?"

I nodded miserably. Such a stupid thing to argue about, especially since the guy I'd wanted to hike with meant nothing, and I'd pulled the plug on that relationship the minute Carrie was stabilized in the hospital. "What else do you remember?"

"You didn't see...a stop sign. And then a truck—"

The door opened again, and I was banished from the

room as the doctors and nurses rushed in and started shouting commands.

I stepped into the hallway and dialed Helen. "Amelia? Is everything all right?"

"She's awake," was all I managed to get out before I broke down.

. . .

It was several hours before the flurry of activity died down enough for me to return to Carrie's bedside. The doctors had whisked her away for various tests, and now she was sleeping—but just normal sleep, I'd been assured. Her parents left to get some dinner—at a restaurant, this time, because she was out of the woods.

While she slept peacefully, I typed out a text to Rory. I knew he'd probably be at the end of the day's trek—if my memory of the mileage breakdown on the West Highland Way was correct, they were on their twenty-mile day—and I wasn't sure whether he'd even respond. But I needed him to know.

She's awake.

Within seconds, my phone vibrated in my hand. Not a text, a call.

I hurried into the hallway and answered. "Rory?"

"She's really awake?"

I smiled. "She's really awake."

"That's...fantastic news," he said after a moment.

It took a moment for me to realize that it wasn't the connection that was shaky—it was his voice. "Is everything okay? You sound a little off."

"I'm just so relieved for her—and for you." He cleared his throat. "How is she?"

Had he been choked up? Because of Carrie? I swallowed the lump in my own throat.

"She's resting now. The doctors ran a bunch of tests, and other than the broken bones, which are still healing, she's basically okay. She remembers the accident, and her short- and long-term memory both seem fine, which is amazing."

"I'm so happy to hear this. And your knee? Did you get it checked?"

"Yeah, it's a sprained ACL. No permanent damage, and I've been mostly sitting here with Carrie, so I've been staying off it."

"That's great. I'd say that you'll be scaling mountains before you know it, but you've already done that."

He went abruptly silent, as if the memory of us scaling those mountains affected him as much as it did me. I cleared my throat. "So, where are you now? I didn't think you'd be done yet for the day."

"I'm not. We're on the last bit of the twenty-mile day, coming down through Rannoch Moor. I wish you could see the sky—actually, hang on a sec."

A moment later, the phone buzzed with an incoming text. It was a photo of the iconic Buachaille Etive Mor, the often-photographed triangular mountain in Glencoe, under a gloomy sky.

"Wow, that's pretty epic," I said. "So, it's okay for you to talk on the phone right now?"

"We're on a straightaway, and Tommy's here, too. I can talk for a few minutes. So, when did she wake up?"

"A few hours ago. I was talking to her, and she just answered me. Out of the blue. We only had about two seconds before it was all doctors and nurses and tests, so I'm hoping she'll wake up again soon."

"That's amazing. What was it that finally got her to wake up?"

"I, um, was pouring my heart out to her about…things." *About you.* "Until then, I'd kept it pretty light, but stuff just kind of came out, and I was crying a little, and then I heard her voice in response to something I'd said. It was like she'd been listening all along, and me being sad was what finally got her to clear that final hurdle. I don't really understand."

"I do," he said. "She loves you just as much as you love her. And she couldn't bear to hear you cry."

And I couldn't bear to hear his voice anymore, knowing that I'd likely never see him again. "Anyway, I'd better go. I want to be there when she wakes up again. Thank you for calling. It means a lot."

"Amelia, I…" He hesitated, then said, "I'm glad she'll be okay."

I love you. I miss you. I wish I was there with you. "'Bye." I ended the call and dissolved into sobs.

Chapter Fifty

AMELIA

"I still can't believe you walked like forty miles—including over a goddamn mountain—with a sprained knee. For me. I...don't even know what to say to that."

It was a few days after Carrie woke up. I was sitting in the uncomfortable chair by her bed. My laptop was on a tray between us, and I was showing her the photos from the trek. Unlike most people looking at someone else's vacation photos, where they click through pretty quickly with an occasional comment or question, Carrie was looking at each one individually, as if she could absorb Skye through the screen.

The nurses had helped her bathe, and she had on pajamas with little sheep on them under a purple robe. Her blonde hair was in a long braid draped over her shoulder. Even with dark circles under her eyes and little lines of pain around her mouth, she looked beautiful.

And she would be okay.

I took her hand. "I couldn't let you down, Carrie. Not after… Can you forgive me?"

She tore her eyes from a photo of the sea stacks at Rubha Hunish. She cocked her head to the side. "For what?"

"For this!" I said, gesturing to the monitors, the bandages, the remains of the shitty hospital food on the cart. "For nearly getting you killed," I said, my voice breaking. "Over a stupid argument. Over a stupid boy who meant nothing." I clapped my hand over my mouth to stifle a sob.

She tugged my hand from my face and held it tight. "Look at me."

I looked at the beloved face that was as familiar to me as my own. She brushed away my tears with her other hand. "It was an accident, Mee. There's nothing to forgive. Besides," she added with a grin, "it got your ass out on the Skye Trail. And maybe that means you'll go hiking with me when this stupid leg gets better?"

"Not only that, we're going to do the goddamn Skye Trail, okay?"

"You'd go through it all again?"

"In a New York minute. Pinky swear."

"Pinky swear," she said, locking her pinky with mine. She turned back to the photos, meticulously scrolling through each one.

"Tell me about Skye," she said a little while later. "Your photos are fucking incredible, but as amazing as they are, I know it's not the same as being there."

She had no idea. "No, it isn't. Where should I start?"

"Tell me about this picture, this moment," she said, gesturing to the computer screen. "Close your eyes, and picture it. And then tell me what you see and how it made you feel."

I glanced at the photo. It was from the Trotternish Ridge, just after the rain. I closed my eyes. "It's the second day of the trek, and we're on the Trotternish Ridge—nearly eighteen miles of summit after summit. It's still morning, but everything already hurts. My shoulders and back are aching from my heavy pack, and my legs are just screaming—thighs, calves, everything. I'm wondering how the hell I'm going to get through the day.

"We just ascended our second peak, Beinn Edra, after a heavy downpour. I'd lost my balance in the mud and would have ended up on my face if Rory hadn't caught me."

I'm breathless, speechless. My hands are flat against his chest. His heart pounds beneath my palms, steady at first and then faster. I stare into his gray-green eyes, the color of the sea in the rain.

"Mee?"

I blinked, the vision dissolving. Carrie was looking at me, one eyebrow arched. "Sorry. Got lost for a minute there."

"You were on Beinn Edra."

"Right." I closed my eyes again. "I'm standing atop Beinn Edra. The rain has stopped, but the sky is still this threatening blue-gray color. The sunlight has found its way through the clouds, and everything has this strange glow. There are mountains to my left and my right, stretching as far as I can see. The sea lies before me, far below, and an eagle soars up from the ridge.

"I feel like I've stepped into another world, and I've left everything behind. My pain, my worry, my fear—they've all faded away. I take a deep breath, inhaling the scent of rain, of grass, of dirt. I feel the call of the land in my blood, in my soul. And I don't want to leave. Don't make me leave," I whispered.

I heard a sniffle, and opened my damp eyes to see Carrie wiping away tears. Oh no! I reached for her—not sure what I was going to do, exactly, but needing to do something. "Are you okay? Should I get a nurse?"

She waved away my hand. "No, dingbat, I'm fine. I'm just—I've never heard you speak like that before. About anything. I'm so glad you got to experience that."

I jumped up and looked down at her. "How can you be glad? It should have been you, walking up those mountains, feeling the rain on your face, breathing that air. But because of me, you were lying here, broken and in pain, while I was in that beautiful place, seeing those sights, falling in—" *Love.* I sank into the chair once more. "Because of me, you could have died."

"But I didn't! Look, it happened, it sucked, and it's over. Yes, I'm in some pain, and yes, I'm a little bit broken. But I'm going to be fine, and you're going to stop beating yourself up about it. Okay?"

"Okay."

"You're such a bad liar. I just thought of a way you can make it up to me, though."

The speculative gleam in her eyes gave me a moment's pause, but I would do anything to make things right. "Name it."

"I want to hear about the man you're in love with."

"What?"

"You've told me about the glorious scenery, and you've told me about the others in the group, including cute and charming Tommy, who I'd like to hear more about later. But you haven't said *anything* about Rory, only that he helped you finish the trek. Until just now, when you said he caught you when you would have fallen, and you got this faraway look in your eyes. I assume he's the guy you were talking about when I woke up, the one you spoke of while I was in the coma."

I gaped at her. "Wait, you heard that?"

She nodded. "Mostly just voices, but every now and then a few things came in clearer than others. That was one of them. So, how come you haven't told me about him yet?"

"I...there hasn't been time, between you needing to rest and your various tests and doctors and visits from people. Since you haven't said anything, I assumed you didn't remember from when you were just waking up."

She raised her eyebrows. "And in the days since then?"

I got to my feet again, unable to sit still. "I didn't know what to say! Hey Carrie, so I took your place on this trek because you were in a coma from the accident I caused. And not only was it a spectacular, life-changing experience, I *also* met this amazing, beautiful guy who taught me things about myself I never knew, who made my body sing, and who I'm completely in love with?"

"It's a start."

She awkwardly scooted over on the bed and patted the mattress beside her. I sat down, careful not to jostle her. "Now, talk. I want to know everything."

"I don't even know where to begin."

"How about with what he looks like."

"Oh, you'd love him, Ree. Longish, sorta curlyish, dark red hair, gray-green eyes. He reminds me of the guy who played Robb Stark on *Game of Thrones*."

"Holy crap." We'd spent many Sunday nights drooling over that actor, so I knew she'd appreciate the comparison.

"Yeah."

"I haven't seen a pic of him yet, have I?"

"I don't think we got far enough for there to be a good one." I clicked ahead in the photos to one of him standing on one of the peaks of the Trotternish Ridge, looking out into the distance. I'd taken it kind of sneakily. "And this one." It was the selfie we took on the bridge at Sligachan.

"Holy crap," she said again. "Tell me everything. No detail is too small."

I told her everything, from his condescending attitude at the beginning, to his freak-out on Sgùrr a' Mhadaidh Ruaidh, to his nightmare and the kiss, to his offer to help me complete the trek, and all our adventures since then.

When I finished, she stared at me. "Why the hell did you leave him?" she asked, almost angrily. "You love him, and he loves you. Why didn't you stay there?"

I shook my head. "How could I, Ree? You were in a goddamn coma from an accident that I caused! I needed to be back here, with you. And our jobs in Miami—I leave in two weeks to go look for an apartment for us. How could I have stayed there?" I looked down. "Besides, I don't know if he loves me."

"Of *course* he does."

"How can you be so sure?"

"I just sat here and listened to your play-by-play of that entire week. There's not even the slightest question in my mind that he loves you just as much as you love him."

"He never said he did."

"Did you ever say it to him?"

"No," I whispered. "I wanted to, so many times. But I couldn't. What would be the point? He's there, and I'm here."

"That's probably why he didn't say it, either. There has to be some way to make this work."

"My focus right now is on you. We need to get you back on your feet and get on with our move to Miami."

I said the words, and meant them. But while I was thrilled beyond anything that Carrie was awake and recovering, and didn't hate me, I still felt hollow inside. Because a piece of my soul was three thousand miles away, in the Western Highlands of Scotland.

• • •

Over the next few days, Carrie grew stronger. She was out of bed as much as possible. I would wheel her around the hospital or out into the garden for some fresh air, and she'd begun some light rehab on her arm.

I was doing some PT of my own, but walking on the treadmill in the noisy, smelly gym was no comparison to hiking a trail and breathing the fresh air, surrounded by mountains and lochs.

I was getting more and more depressed, in spite of Carrie's recovery, in spite of the upcoming move to Miami. I just missed Rory. And when I spoke about him to Carrie, I kept hearing her voice in my head: *"Why the hell did you leave a man like that behind? You love him and he loves you. Why didn't you stay there?"*

If not for her, I would never have met him. If not for her, I wouldn't have fallen for him. And if not for her, I would have stayed there—somehow.

And I felt awful for thinking that, which made everything worse.

Rory was about to take a new group out on the Skye Trail. He'd camp on the beach with them at Bearreraig Bay, where he'd kissed me that first time. He'd spend a night in Sligachan, having a few pints with Gav, in the hotel where we'd first shared a bed—platonic(ish) as it may have been. He'd possibly stay in the bothy at Camasunary, where we'd made love for the first time, and maybe even go over Bla Bheinn, if the cliff path to Elgol was still impassable. And maybe even if it wasn't.

He'd do all those things we'd done together—but not with me.

Chapter Fifty-One

RORY

I was fucking miserable.

I was doing the job I loved, leading a group of trekkers—all from the States—on the Skye Trail, with my best friend as co-guide. The weather was nearly perfect—not much wind on the Ridge, cloudless skies with brilliant sunshine. Everyone in the group was eager to be out there and having a good time.

But I felt no joy in traversing the Ridge, in seeing nothing but dramatic mountains and sapphire-blue lochs as far as the eye could see. I swam to the point of exhaustion in Bearreraig Bay that night, but still couldn't sleep. Tommy tried his best to cheer me up, but nothing helped.

Amelia wasn't there.

I lay awake in my tent, recalling how we'd gone from barely being civil to each other to so much more in a matter of days. Hours, really; the episode with Tommy on the edge of Sgùrr a' Mhadaidh Ruaidh leading to my nightmare, which led to that first kiss on this very same beach.

I winced, remembering how I'd grabbed him, shouted at him like he was a punk kid I'd caught stealing my wallet. God, that had been an epic fuckup that really could have cost me my job if the group complained.

But they hadn't complained. Instead, they'd praised me, especially Gordon, who'd actually told me he was impressed with me because of it.

I lurched upright, a glimmer of a thought popping into my brain. I turned on my torch and unearthed my journal from my pack. I flipped it open to the roster we got before each trek. There it was. Gordon Marshall, with his email address and phone number.

The next day, when we arrived in Portree, I tossed my pack into the room and told Tommy I was going for a walk. As soon as I was away from the B&B, I pulled out my phone and dialed. "Mr. Marshall?" I asked when the call was answered. "This is Rory Sutherland, from Scotland By Foot? I did part of the Skye Trail with you—"

"I remember you, son," he interrupted in his booming voice. "It was barely over two weeks ago, for goodness sake. And call me Gordon."

"Thanks, Gordon."

"How's Amelia? Did she finish the trail?"

"We finished about three days after you did. Turned out it was a sprained ACL."

"Good for her. She must be a hell of a young lady to finish with that injury."

"Aye, she is, sir." He had no idea.

"So, Rory, what can I do for you?"

I licked my suddenly dry lips. "I… Well, sir, you said on the trail that you'd hire me in a second. If that was true, then I'm calling about a job. Do you have any positions available in the States, specifically southern Florida?"

He was silent for a moment. "Why the hell would you want to leave Scotland for Florida? Aren't any mountains here, and it's hotter than hell for most of the year."

"I know, sir. But...the woman I love is there. Or she will be in a couple of months."

The woman I love. I thought it would be strange to say the words out loud to a stranger. But nothing had ever felt more right.

"Hmm, Amelia mentioned she was moving to Miami in a couple of months."

I smiled. "You have a good memory, Gordon."

"Strange coincidence."

"Not really."

"I see." And I knew he *did* see. "Well, why don't you tell me what you're looking for, then?"

When I returned to the room a little while later, Tommy was sprawled across his bed, his nose in a book. He looked up when I closed the door behind me, then did a double take, setting aside the book and sitting upright.

"You okay, Ror? You look...weird."

"Wanna grab a beer?"

Before I finished saying "beer," he was on his feet and stepping into his flip-flops.

We went to a pub on the other side of town, where we'd be unlikely to run into anyone from the group, and sat at a back booth, pints in hand.

"Okay, spill," he said after taking a long sip. "Everything okay with Amelia? With Carrie?"

"As far as I know. I haven't talked to her since last week when Carrie woke up."

"So what's that look for? It's almost like...part hope and

part dread, if that's even possible."

That about summed it up, actually. "Remember Gordon Marshall, from the last Skye Trail?"

"Of course. Didn't I just spend a week walking with him?"

"Anyway, he has a company in the States that books travel and tours for people."

"Right, I remember. He was doing the trek so he could recommend SBF to his clients."

"Oh. I don't think I knew that."

"Well, you were gone after what, day three? He may not have mentioned it by then. So, what about him?"

"Remember how he said he was so impressed with us he would hire us in a second?"

"Yeah…"

"I just called him."

Tommy's eyes widened. "Wait. What are you saying? You asked him for a job?"

"I mentioned that I might be interested in something in the States."

"Like in Florida, you mean?"

"Aye."

"And what did he say?"

"He has a Miami office, believe it or not. They do a lot of stuff with cruises and travel in South America and the Caribbean. And as he told you, he's been wanting to expand to booking adventure travel in the UK, so he was intrigued by my call. He said he'll get back to me in a few days."

Tommy sat back, his finger tracing patterns in the ring of condensation from his mug.

"What is it?" I asked. "I thought you'd be happy for me, that I might be able to be with her."

He looked up from the table, his eyes troubled. "I would be *thrilled* if you could be with her, man. It's just…you don't belong in an office, in business casual, staring at a goddamn computer screen and wearing a headset, offering people incentives if they book their trip with you. In Florida, where the nearest hill is probably four hundred miles away—or more."

"There may not be hills there, but there are other outdoor sports, like sailing, parasailing, scuba diving—I've always wanted to try that. Plus, it's warm and sunny all year. Might be a nice change from this place, especially in the winter when it's dark for sixteen hours a day."

He shook his head. "You'd be miserable."

I slammed my hand down on the table, rattling our bottles. "What do you want me to say, Tommy? Do I *want* to work in an office in Florida, staring at a computer screen and wearing a headset, four hundred miles from the nearest hill? No. I want to be out walking the Highlands. But if I was in an office in Florida, *she'd* be there. Her face would be the last thing I see before I go to sleep, the first thing I see when I wake up in the morning."

I took a long swallow of beer. "Since she left, I've been adrift. I looked out at the Ridge yesterday, and it was like looking at a stone wall. It doesn't feel like home anymore. And if putting on khakis and a button-down and sitting in that office means I can be with Amelia, then I'll do it happily."

Tommy nodded. "I get it, man. I'm just asking you not to do anything rash, okay? Just think about it before you make any decisions."

"I will. I promise."

But in my head, the decision was made. If Gordon offered me the job, and if Amelia wanted me, then I would take it.

I wouldn't let myself think about what would happen if she didn't want me.

Chapter Fifty-Two

RORY

Less than a week later, after an uneventful finish to an uneventful Skye Trail trek, I sat on a bench in Fort William, overlooking Loch Linnhe. I'd come out to my favorite spot in town for some peace and quiet, away from the loud party my housemates were having.

I brought the small flask to my lips and took a swig of whisky, settling in to watch the sunset. It had been a busy few days. I'd heard back from Gordon Marshall, who offered me a job in his Miami satellite office. He gave me a week to think about it. I hadn't yet said anything to Amelia, but my plan was to call her tonight.

Tommy had been uncharacteristically subdued since I'd told him about the call with Gordon. He'd kept his distance a bit, too, disappearing for long periods of time over the last few days, and even when he was around, he was often glued to his phone. He didn't tell me what was going on, and I didn't ask. Taking the job would mean leaving him—my best mate, the person who saved me from myself, who'd made me into the man I was today. I knew he was happy I might have an opportunity to be with Amelia, but it didn't make it easier.

He'd been gone all afternoon on some errand, but he'd texted to say he was back in town and would meet me shortly.

I took another sip, savoring the whisky's smoky taste before swallowing. I was nervous, more nervous than I'd been in a long time. Until Gordon officially made me his offer, it had just been a vague hope, but now it was real. What if she said no, she wanted a clean start in Miami, unencumbered by a guy she'd had a short fling with? *Better to know that now, than to take the job and move there and then find it out.*

I set down the flask and scrubbed my hands over my face. Where the hell was Tommy? Fort William wasn't that big.

"Is this seat taken?"

I froze. *It can't be.* Holding my breath, I raised my head and opened my eyes.

Amelia stood before me, as if I'd conjured her.

Chapter Fifty-Three

AMELIA

"Is this seat taken?" I asked nervously, hoping—praying—that Rory would be happy to see me.

He went still, then slowly raised his head and opened his eyes. They grew wide for a moment, and then he closed them and opened them again, blinking at me as if he'd just awakened from a ten-year slumber.

He stood, his fingers reaching out to touch my hair, running a lock of it through his fingers. His hands cupped my face as lightly as if I were made of crystal and then they slid over my cheekbones and down to my shoulders.

"Are you really here?" he breathed, as if he were afraid if he spoke too loudly, the dream would shatter.

I smiled. "I'm really here."

He opened his mouth as if he were going to say something, then crushed me to him and lifted me off my feet, kissing me as if his life depended on the air he would steal from my lips.

I twined my fingers in his hair and kissed him back with

all the longing I'd built up in the three weeks we'd been apart. His fingers caressed my back, as if he was still trying to prove to himself that I was real.

A lifetime later, he pulled back and gently set me on my feet. "I was going to call you tonight," he said. "I have a lot to talk to you about. I mean, this is better. Saves me the international charges," he added with a grin that quickly left his face. "But…what are you doing here?"

"I, um, have a lot to talk to you about, too. Let's sit."

Smoothing my skirt under my thighs, I sat on the bench. He dropped down beside me and took my hand, his fingers holding mine as if he couldn't bear *not* to touch me.

"So, I got an email from Tommy one night, almost a week ago," I began, staring at the sun as it started to drop. "It was the best news I'd received since Carrie woke up."

His fingers paused. "Did he…what did he tell you?"

I pressed my fingers to his mouth. "Let me talk without you interrupting, and you'll find out, okay?" He nodded, his lips curving slightly. "He told me that Scarlet's been feeling really swamped lately, that Scotland By Foot has grown pretty fast in the last year or two, and she's been having a hard time keeping up with the bookings and handling the inquiry emails, while still running support for one trek a week during the busy season. He said that even though she hadn't specifically mentioned anything to him about hiring someone, he knew I had a background in tourism and you'd told him that I wanted to get a job where I could arrange tours for people. He thought I should email her and send my resume."

His eyes widened. "Tommy did that?"

"Yeah. I got that email off to her within an hour so she'd see it first thing in the morning. And when I woke up, I had an email from her, asking me to let her know when we might talk on the phone. We spoke that day, and by the end of that conversation, I had a job offer to come work for Scotland By Foot."

Rory's whole face lit up. "You got a job with SBF?" he breathed, as if by saying it too loudly, it would all go away.

"At the start, she'd want me to do all the client bookings and handle the emails, and then branch out to visiting and vetting new B&Bs as she expands to adding more treks, which would give her the opportunity to actually guide. And maybe at some point, I could even start training to be a guide, once my knee is back to normal." I grinned. "I realized I kinda like hiking."

He smiled back. "I know you did. I could see it in your eyes on those last few days."

"I didn't know what to do. I mean, I'd sent that email and resume without even thinking twice, but when she actually made me the offer? I freaked out. I immediately went to see Carrie."

"What did she say?" he asked.

As the sun melted into the loch, I took his hand in mine and told him.

I walked into Carrie's hospital room like a defendant being told the jury was back with a decision. She started to smile, and then she saw the look on my face. "What's wrong?" she asked.

"I have to tell you something. I…got a job offer just now. And I don't know what to do."

"What do you mean? What kind of job?"

"Working for Scotland By Foot. The woman who runs it, Scarlet? She's been swamped lately as the company has grown, and she offered me a job handling the business end of things so she can be out in the field."

Carrie's eyes widened. "She just emailed you out of the blue to offer you a job?"

I swallowed. "Um, not exactly." I told her about Tommy's email. "I just reached out to her, without even thinking about it," I confessed. "And now I don't know what to do."

"Girl, what are you even talking about? You're going to say yes. Obviously."

I stared at her in disbelief. "Carrie, don't you understand what it means? The job is in Scotland. *I can work from home there, because it's mostly just computer and phone work. But I need to be in the same time zone. And I need to be there when it's time to check out the new B&Bs and stuff."*

She rolled her eyes. "Well, duh. What would be the point of taking a job with a Scottish company if you weren't going to be working in Scotland? *That'd be like working for Hershey and never being able to sample the goods."*

"But what about Miami? We're supposed to start there—"

She stared at me. "Are you out of your mind? You're going to say 'thanks, but no thanks' to the Miami job. Why in hell would you want to go to Miami when you can be in Scotland?"

I didn't understand why she wasn't mad. "But we had plans!"

I turned to Rory. "She handed me her phone, which was open to an email." I took the printed version out of my purse and handed it to him. "Go ahead, read it."

He unfolded the paper, and I watched him read the words I knew almost verbatim from reading them so many times in the past few days.

To: *Tommy@scotlandbyfoot.co.uk*
From: *Carrie Peterson*
Sent: *Friday, June 2, 2017, 10:15 a.m.*
Subject: *Amelia and Rory*

Dear Tommy,

You don't know me, but I'm Amelia Benson's friend, Carrie—you know, the reason Amelia did the Skye Trail? She told me a lot about you, mostly what a helpful, friendly, funny, and all-around great guy you are. (And that you're really cute, which I was skeptical about until I saw photographic evidence. ;))

She also told me how you were the captain of Team "Arory" (or is it "Ramelia"?), and that's why I'm emailing you.

We need to get that ship back on course, Tommy. Amelia is miserable. She talks a good game, about how stoked she is to go to Miami and whatnot, but it's because it's what she thinks I want to hear. She feels so guilty about the car accident, about going to Skye in my place, that she'll set aside her own happiness to make me happy.

But how can I be happy when my best friend is so unhappy?

She misses Scotland, and no hotel job in Miami is going to fix that. More importantly, she misses Rory. So much that it hurts me to see how she lights up when she mentions his name while telling me about the trip, and then to watch that light go out of her when she browses Miami apartments online and tries to sound enthusiastic about it.

I'm obviously speculating, but given how she spoke of Rory, I am pretty confident that he's just as lost without her.

So, what are we gonna do about it, Tommy? Will you help me?

Write back when you can, or feel free to give me a call at +1-516-555-1784. I do love a Scottish accent...

My best,
Carrie Peterson

To: *Carrie Peterson*
From: *Tommy MacDonald*
Sent: *Friday, June 2, 1017, 11:30 a.m.*
Subject: *RE: Amelia and Rory*

Hey Carrie,

Nice to e-meet you! I heard a lot about you from Amelia. She didn't tell me that you were cute, but she did show me your photo, so I came to my own conclusions about that. ;)

With regard to our wayward friends, your timing is LITERALLY perfect. I should be finished with the day's walk in another hour or so, and will call you after. We have much to discuss.

Looking forward to chatting!

Cheers,
Tommy

Rory read it once, and then read it again. He lowered the paper to his lap and looked up at me incredulously.

"Seriously?"

"That's what I said, after I read it like three times. She said I was her best friend—her sister—and she loved me, but I was being an idiot. Actually, I think she used the word 'numpty.' Didn't I want to work for a cool company in Scotland and be close to the man I love?"

Rory's hand tightened around mine, his gray-green eyes shining. "And what did you say?" he asked, his voice husky.

"I said yes, I did want to work for a cool company in Scotland and be near the man I love."

"And what did she say?"

"She said, 'Then why are we even discussing this? You're going to take the job, and then I'll have someone to stay with when I finally get to Scotland. Win-win.'"

I told him the rest.

I opened my mouth to reply, but she held up her free hand. "I'm not done yet. I think we can agree that life is unpredictable, that shit happens when you least expect it, and your life can end in a crunch of metal and glass, or in any number of horrible ways. Right?"

I nodded.

"When you're offered an opportunity to be with the person you love, you take it," she continued. "And you live the hell out of your life. Don't worry about me. It'll be a while before I'm up and around enough to go anywhere, let alone start a new job. It may be both of us telling Miami thanks, but no thanks. Who knows, maybe they'll have an opening here in New York. Or maybe Scotland. Or some other cool place. And if not, I'll find something else when I'm ready."

I met Rory's gaze once more, my heart quickening at the hope I saw there. "'But what if he doesn't love me, doesn't want to be with me?' I asked Carrie. She said, 'Well, there's only one way to find out.' And so here I am."

"So here you are," Rory whispered.

The look in his eyes made me bold. "And do you? Love me?"

"So much," he breathed. "So much that I've been empty since you've been gone. So much that Scotland hasn't felt like home without you here. So much that I was going to tell you tonight that I have a job offer as well. In Miami. Working for Gordon Marshall from your trekking group."

I clutched his hand, my heart pounding. He loved me. He was ready to give up the job he loved, leading hikes all over Scotland, to work in an office in Miami. For me.

"You weren't really considering it, were you? That job would be the death of you."

"Not if I could see you every day."

"What did you tell him?"

"Nothing yet. I wanted to make sure you loved me."

My heart soaring like the eagles we'd seen on the Ridge, I took his face in my hands and gazed into those luminous eyes. "I do. More than anything," I said. "And I don't want you to work in Miami."

His lips curved in a smile that made my breath catch in my throat. I pressed my lips to both corners of that smile, then twined my fingers in his hair and kissed him, letting all my love shine through.

He pulled me onto his lap and kissed me back just as tenderly, holding me like he'd never let me go.

After a few minutes, we drew apart, both of us breathing hard. He tucked a strand of hair behind my ear and gazed at me. "I wanted to tell you I loved you so many times, but I knew you had to leave, and I didn't want to make it harder than it already was."

"And I wanted to tell you, too, so many times. But I knew I couldn't stay, and your life was here." I grinned. "Good thing we had our fairy godmothers looking out for us, huh?"

"Aye, it is." He glanced down at the paper he'd set on

the bench. "In fact, looking at the dates on these emails, I'm pretty sure that Carrie's email to Tommy came the morning after I told him about the job with Gordon, which goes with what he says about the timing."

"And the next night is when he emailed me about SBF," I added.

"It explains a lot."

"What do you mean?"

"He's been cagey the last few days—wandering out to take phone calls, preoccupied with his phone. I figured he was just unhappy about my job offer in the States. But I guess he was conspiring with Carrie."

I nodded. "He was nervous on the drive up from Glasgow today, too. When I asked him why, he told me he'd been meddling quite a bit this past week, and he was afraid you'd be furious with him."

"I think I'll forgive him," he said, kissing me again. When he drew back, he was grinning. "I think I owe him a beer, too, huh?"

"At least one. So do I. But maybe after?"

"After what?"

"After you give me a proper welcome home."

"So tomorrow, then?"

"Aye, tomorrow," I said, and pulled him to me once more.

Epilogue

AMELIA

Almost A Year Later

"Welcome to the beginning of the Skye Trail!" I announced from the car park near Duntulm Castle. "I'm Amelia Benson, and I'm training to be a guide. Today's walk should take about six hours, but remember, it's not a race. We are a group, and we will do this trek as a group. If you wander off ahead, you are no longer our problem, as we won't be leaving the group behind to go look for you."

I looked at the people standing before me. "How am I doing?"

"So far, so good," Rory said with a grin.

"Not bad, but if you're trying to channel Sutherland, you need to curl your lip a little more. And your scathing glare needs work. Ow!" Tommy said, rubbing his arm.

I pointed at the two troublemakers—and narrowed my eyes. "You two. There's no horsing around on the trail."

"Much better," said Tommy.

"Getting there," said Rory.

Carrie put her arm around me. "I'm so proud of you, Mee. You look and sound like a pro!"

I hugged her tight. "I'm just so glad you're finally here!"

Carrie had taken the job at the hotel in Miami. They'd been kind enough to delay her start date until she was able to get around, and had been super-accommodating after that, as well, while she rehabbed her leg. She'd ultimately made a full recovery, though it had taken her leg a little longer than expected to be up to the strain of the Skye Trail.

Rory and I lived in a flat in Fort William, where Scotland By Foot's office was, and we were starting to talk more seriously about the future. He still had occasional nightmares about his brother, but those were rare. He went up Bla Bheinn once a month, and I'd gone with him on Connor's birthday. The mountain was no longer Rory's enemy, but a place where he could feel close to the brother he loved and lost.

My job with SBF was awesome. Scarlet was a fantastic boss, who'd given me more and more responsibility as the year went by. And she was letting us all take this week off to do the trail together.

Carrie had told me when she arrived in Scotland a week ago that there was a good chance the hotel was transferring her to their new Edinburgh location, so I'd have my best friend close by once again.

And she and Tommy had been flirting since she'd arrived—apparently they'd been emailing quite a bit over the last year—so maybe her transfer to Edinburgh wasn't only to be closer to *me*.

Today was the one-year anniversary of when I began the Skye Trail—when Carrie was supposed to have begun it—and now, finally, we were going to do it together.

It was a special group. Rory and Tommy were the official

guides. I was training to become one, though it would be a long time before I was certified. Carrie was there, and so was Gav. Though he'd done the portions of the trail closest to the Slig, this was his first time doing the whole thing.

Rounding out our little group were Rory's friend Tristan MacDougall, son of the beloved Mrs. Mac, who was the first mate on a schooner that did semester-at-sea programs in the States. His girlfriend Ari was with us, too, a sweet redhead who had just graduated from the University of Miami with a marine science degree. They were taking the summer off to explore Scotland before she started her new job in the fall. I'd met them last year, and was looking forward to spending more time with them.

The Skye Trail had brought me so much joy, and I was so thrilled that this group of people that had become so dear to me were here to share it. Rory took my hand and smiled down at me, his gray-green eyes the color of the sea on a rainy day. "Ready?"

"Ready."

"Lead on, then."

"Okay, gang, let's move out."

I led the group out of the car park and onto the path. A year ago, I'd taken that first step full of fear, trepidation, worry, and doubt about walking eighty miles across the imposing, rugged, remote, and intimidating Isle of Skye for the friend I loved.

Today, I took that first step full of excitement and joy, this time eager to walk for eighty miles across the mountainous, wild, and utterly spectacular Isle of Skye with the people I loved.

Author's Note

The Isle of Skye is one of the most stunning places I've ever seen, with its dramatic mountains, spectacular sea views, and alien-looking formations like the Quiraing. I tried to stay as faithful to the Skye Trail wherever I could, but I did take a liberty or two here and there. I can only hope I did justice to this magnificent place, and that I've inspired you to put it on your bucket list of places to visit. And if you do get there, you should make a point of taking a wee ramble up Glen Sligachan, from the hotel toward Marsco, or walking the path through the Quiraing (but watch out for that wind!), even if the rest of it is too intimidating. But don't try to hike without the proper gear and safety precautions!

If you decide to do the Skye Trail—or want to experience other parts of Scotland on foot—check out Thistle Trekking, the company that inspired the fictional Scotland By Foot. When I got it into my head a few years ago that I wanted to walk Scotland's ninety-six-mile West Highland Way, I knew I had to do it with a guide. My search led me to Thistle Trekking, which offers guided walks and scrambles all over

Scotland, as well as in England and Wales. The director, Scarlet Trevett, is fabulous. She patiently answered the many questions I had prior to my booking, and advised me on which trail I should attempt next, given the difficulties I'd had on the WHW.

Thistle Trekking attends to every detail (including baggage schlepping) so that you can just show up and walk. You have a highly-qualified Mountain Leader as your guide, and you'll have a small group of people to walk with. I went by myself, and the people in my group, whether they were married couples, singles, or family groups, were wonderful and welcoming, and I made friends that I reunited with on the East Highland Way trail the following year, and with whom I hope to walk again next year as well.

If you're looking for an amazing experience walking over Scotland's hills (big and small), through her glens and bogs, and along her sparkling lochs, you can do no better than Thistle Trekking: www.thistletrekking.co.uk.

And if Wales is on your bucket list, Alex Kendall, the guide and Mountain Leader who helped me get through the West Highland Way (including lingering at the back with me as I struggled up the damn hills), has written a guidebook to walking the Snowdonia Way, a long-distance trail in Wales's Snowdonia National Park. You can check it out here: https://www.cicerone.co.uk/the-snowdonia-way.

Pronunciation Guide

Bealach Uige: BEE-lach (with the -ch as in *loch*) OO-ig
Beinn Edra: Bayn Edra
Ben Tianavaig: Bayn CHEE-a-na-vaig
Biodha Buidhe: Beeta BOO-yeh
Bla Bheinn: BLA-ven
Boreraig: BAH-re-raig
Buachaille Etive Mor: BOOK-all ET-iv More
Eilean Donan: EE-lin Do-nan
Rubha Hunish: Roo-ah Hunish
Sgurr a'Mhadaidh Ruaidh: Skurr a VAT-ee RU-ay
Slàinte mhath: SLAN-jeh vah
Sligachan: Sli-GA-chan
Suisnish: SEESH-nish
Mar sin leat, a ghaoil: Mahr shin layt, a geyl
Soraidh leat, mo bhràthar: SO-rai layt, mo BRA-her

Acknowledgments

To my parents, Lois & Sam Miller, for...well, everything, really, but specifically for instilling the travel bug in me from an early age.

To my brother, Rob Miller, for making me cry on the train when I got my final paperwork for the West Highland Way and saw what you did. You're my favorite brother.

To my editors Stacy Cantor Abrams and Alexa May for their excellent edits and insights.

To Eden Plantz for her wonderful copyedits, Greta Gunselman for proofreading, and to Fiona Jayde, Heather Howland, and Liz Pelletier for the beautiful cover.

To Curtis Svehlak, Holly Bryant-Simpson, Riki Cleveland, and the rest of the Entangled Team for the wonderful work they do.

To my agent Josh Getzler for his support and enthusiasm.

The following people were instrumental in helping me write a book set on the Skye Trail. Any mistakes are mine.

To Scarlet Trevett, director and founder of Thistle Trekking, for all her advice, suggestions, and input; for answering my many questions on logistics and pronunciation, for her support and enthusiasm, and for letting me use her name in the book!

To Alex Kendall, my guide on the West Highland Way, for patiently answering all my many and varied questions about the Skye Trail and being a guide, and for keeping me going on the West Highland Way when I thought Conic Hill would kill me, and then when I thought the Devil's Staircase would kill me. There's always another damn hill.

To Ed Terry, my guide on the East Highland Way, for answering my questions about being a guide, and to Ollie Mentz and Chris Withers for their input regarding the Bla Beinn section.

To the Skye Trail Map, by Harvey Maps, *The Skye Trail* guide book, by Helen and Paul Webster, and Walkhighlands. co.uk: all excellent resources regarding the geography and logistics of the Skye Trail.

To Juliet Chadwin at Harvey Maps, Lesley Flood and Linda Prentice at Ordnance Survey, and Laura at Cicerone Press, for their help with the maps and appropriate credits and licenses for their use.

To Greg MacThomais for his Gaelic translations. Any mistakes are mine.

To Dr. Lisa Bartoli for her medical advice on knee injuries. Any mistakes are mine.

To Alec Shane, Heather Evans, and Mike Evans, for their input regarding knee injuries. "So, exactly how much *did* that hurt?"

To Jen "Jescott" Wills, for her advice and input and support and enthusiasm.

To Meredith Giordan, for being my books buddy, TV buddy, and movie buddy, and for the daily conversations and Gchats, as well as the late-night grammar help.

To Monica McCarty, for the fabulous endorsement.

To Megan Westfield, for reading the first draft and providing excellent editorial suggestions (I even took some of them!), and for your friendship and the wonderful endorsement.

To Kelly Siskind, for the lovely endorsement, support, and friendship.

To Joe Volpe and Al Araneo for their legal advice regarding the use of Tolkien quotes in the book, i.e. "Don't."

To Jacquie Holland, for help with Scottish slang and for hanging out with me for two awesome days on Skye (and for doing all the driving!). I still have nightmares about that ridiculous wind out on Neist Point.

To Jamesie Johnston, for help with Scottish slang and suggesting the walk through Glen Sligachan to Marsco. We didn't get as far as I'd wanted, but it was a stunning walk that I'll just have to go back and do again one day.

To Ali Newman, for brainstorming this book with me, and for your love and support my whole life.

To Jill Jazwinski, Robin Mendez, Robin Ruinsky, Raakhee Shirsat, Genevieve Gagne-Hawes, Robin Rue, Michael Mejias, Stacy Testa, Samantha Wekstein, Katie Stuart, Abby Barce, Addison Fox, Joanna Volpe, Helen Lowe, and Jamie Snider for your support and friendship.

To Iris Beiss, Rob & Alison Tollafield, Christine Palin, and Vikki Grimes, for being fabulous hiking companions on two Scottish treks—here's looking ahead to the Pembrokeshire Coastal Path in 2019!

The Skye Mountain Rescue Team, for the invaluable work they do for people getting lost and injured on the Isle of Skye.

About the Author

Beth Anne Miller has a fascination for all things Scottish (including, but not limited to, men in kilts), which has influenced all her writing to date. Her first novel is a time travel called *Into the Scottish Mist*; her second, *A Star to Steer Her By*, has a Scottish hero; and her newest book, *Under a Storm-Swept Sky*, is set on the Isle of Skye, and was inspired by her own long-distance treks in Scotland. A native New Yorker, Beth Anne lives on Long Island and works in the publishing industry. She's looking forward to her next trip to Scotland.

Also by Beth Anne Miller...

A STAR TO STEER HER BY

Discover more New Adult titles from Entangled Embrace…

CINDERELLA AND THE GEEK
a *British Bad Boys* novel by Christina Phillips

I'm not looking for love or a Happily-Ever-After because I know how that ends. I just need to concentrate on my degree and look after myself. But there's something about my boss, Harry, I can't resist. It's crazy since he's so hot and smart it should be illegal. But I'm off to pursue my dreams, and he's taking his business to the next level. There's no way this fairytale has a happy ending, but that doesn't keep me from wishing for it.

LEAVING EVEREST
a novel by Megan Westfield

Emily Winslowe has had an adventurous upbringing, climbing the world's highest peaks with her father. But there's something important her best friend, Luke Norgay, doesn't know. It's the reason she ended up in the Himalayas in the first place…and the reason she must summit Everest this year. It's also the reason she can't risk her heart to follow him back to Washington. But none of that matters if they can't survive the mountain.

Maybe Someone Like You
a novel by Stacy Wise

Their paths never should have crossed. The bright, accomplished new attorney and the tattooed and laid-back kickboxing trainer. But when Katie opens the door to the gym instead of the yoga studio next door, everything she ever imagined was about to change. Everything.

Too Hard to Resist
a *Wherever You Go* novel by Robin Bielman

One rookie assistant + one demanding executive = flirting that is too hot to handle. My new boss is the gorgeous and clever Elliot Sax, but workplace hookups are against the rules. When our attraction flames hotter, our best efforts are put to the test. I never imagined having to fight my feelings for him on a daily basis and keeping my hands to myself is absolutely killing me. Until I can't. Until we can't. And what's at stake becomes more than our jobs. What's at risk is our hearts.

78976776R00227

Made in the USA
Middletown, DE
06 July 2018